# De Vane.

# DE VANE:

## A Story of

# PLEBEIANS AND PATRICIANS.

BY

HON. HENRY W. HILLIARD,

EX-MEMBER OF UNITED STATES HOUSE OF REPRESENTATIVES FROM ALABAMA.

"The rank is but the guinea's stamp,
The man 's the gowd for a' that."
BURNS.

*TWO VOLUMES IN ONE.—VOL. I.*

New-York:
BLELOCK & COMPANY, 19 BEEKMAN STREET.
1865.

JOHN A. GRAY & GREEN,
Printers,
16 & 18 Jacob Street, New-York.

When every worldly thought is utterly forsaken,
Comes the starry midnight felt by life's gifted few,
Then will the spirit from its earthly sleep awaken
To a being more intense, more spiritual and true.
So doth the soul awaken,
Like that youth to night's fair queen.

*The Awakening of Endymion.*

# DE VANE.

## A Story of

# PLEBEIANS AND PATRICIANS.

---

## CHAPTER I.

And ne'er did Grecian chisel trace
A nymph, a naiad, or a grace
Of finer form or lovelier face!
—Lady of the Lake.

An October sun was shedding his dying splendors upon earth and sky. The level rays bathed the valley through which the river poured its swift current in warm light, and gilded the spires of the little capital seated on the eastern bank of the stream with a richer lustre than gold could give. A purple haze rested upon the landscape, and the tints which the sky wore were of that soft and delicate kind, peculiar to a southern climate in autumn.

Two young gentlemen were walking arm in arm on the river-bank, observing the effect of the light as the waters rushed over the adjacent falls and flowed at their feet, the spray touched by the glowing hues of departing day. A ferry-boat, or flat, as it was called in the dialect of the country, had just reached the opposite bank, and a travelling-carriage drove into it, followed by a gentleman and two ladies, who walked after it. The current being rapid and deep, the boat was drawn from the one bank to the other by means of a rope stretched across the stream and fastened at both sides securely; but it required some time to make the passage, and the two gentlemen reached the steep road which led up from the river in their walk, and stood there observing the objects about them as they would have studied a picture.

One of them appeared to be about twenty-four years of age, and there was an air almost of sadness about him as he surveyed the wide-spread landscape. The other was younger, certainly not more than twenty, and his manner was animated.

"Waring," said he, "this picture almost equals our Virginia scenery; but you want the mountains, and the Germans say you must have them, or a landscape is nothing."

"I do not suffer the Germans to decide questions of taste for me," replied the other, "nor do I feel any more respect for their opinions in such matters than I do for their theological views. For tranquil beauty, nothing can surpass this scene."

"Ah! you have not forgiven me for my transcendentalism, as you style it, because I express some admiration for German speculations. Yet I am sure that they hold almost supreme dominion in that realm, that is, if you accept Jean Paul Richter for authority, for he says: 'The land belongs to the French, the sea to the English, and the air to the Germans.'"

"Certainly," said Waring, "and Jean Paul Richter confirms my opinion; for he means, that the German mind has nothing practical about it, and is simply speculative, and I think generally misty."

"Still, Waring," answered the other, "you must admit

that a sunset in the mountains does excel this; here you have quiet beauty, I agree, but standing in the midst of our Virginia mountains, you realize what Beattie means, in those fine lines of his Minstrel:

"The pomp of groves, and garniture of fields;
All that the genial ray of morning gilds,
And all that echoes to the song of even,
All that the mountain's sheltering bosom shields,
And all the dread magnificence of heaven."

At this moment, the boat having reached the bank, the carriage drove up the steep ascent, and the party in the boat followed it on foot, coming up to that part of the road where the gentlemen were standing; when the elder of the two suddenly started, and then advancing toward the travellers, exclaimed: "Why, Mr. Springfield! have you returned? I am delighted to see you."

"Ah! Mr. Waring, you are here to welcome us!" the gentleman to whom he addressed himself replied, grasping his hand: "We begin to feel now that we are already at home."

Waring then spoke with the ladies, who received him warmly, and expressed their gratification at reaching home once more.

So sudden had been the recognition of the travellers by Waring, that he had no time for explanations to his friend, who remained standing on the roadside, apparently interested and pleased with the scene; but now Waring, turning to him, said: "Mr. De Vane, let me present you to Mr. Springfield." And the young gentleman, advancing, was also introduced to the ladies. One of these was Mrs. Springfield, and the other her niece, Miss Wordsworth.

There was in the manner of De Vane a blended self-possession and embarrassment, which did not escape the observation of Mrs. Springfield, and which interested her; she saw that his bearing had in it something of stateliness, and yet perfect good breeding. As the party entered their carriage and drove off, the two young gentlemen turned their steps in the same direction, and resumed their conversation.

"Waring!" exclaimed De Vane, "are those people friends of yours? *Mehercule!* I never saw so lovely a person as that young girl. I give it up! With that addition to your picture, I never saw any thing, even in Virginia, to rival it."

"What!" said Waring, "does she compensate for the absence of mountains?"

"Mountains! she would shed a glory over Siberia. She is absolutely radiant. Who are they?"

"The gentleman," replied Waring somewhat gravely, "is a man of fortune, cultivation, and taste; yet a Methodist, and what it may perhaps surprise you still more to learn, is a lay preacher. Learned, accomplished, and thoroughly acquainted with the world, he is a Christian, and while he is unwilling to assume the responsibilities of a clergyman proper, yet he preaches habitually, and with an earnestness and power rarely equalled."

De Vane's face expressed astonishment and yet interest, but he was too well bred to say all that he felt. To see such a man, and to hear him thus described, was so unlike any thing coming under his own observation, that he was surprised, and he could not repress some remark of that kind; but knowing his friend Waring to be a Christian, he restrained himself.

"And the ladies," said De Vane, "what of them?"

"The ladies," replied Waring, "are Mrs. Springfield, the wife of the gentleman to whom I have just introduced you, and a woman of the highest order. The younger lady is Miss Esther Wordsworth, a niece of Mrs. Springfield."

"A Methodist, too?" exclaimed De Vane.

"A Methodist, too," replied his friend.

"*Mehercule!*" said De Vane, using his habitual classical exclamation when he was excited, and added: "I must really know more of them; for that young girl might be an angel just arrived, to show us what the inhabitants of heaven look like."

They walked on for a few moments in silence, and then having reached the College grounds, each one sought his own room.

John Waring was a native of Georgia. He had grown up in that State; and after struggling with adverse fortunes for years, had acquired sufficient means to enable him to take a collegiate course. His parents died when he was quite young, leaving a very slender property for their two children, the son, of whom we have already spoken, and a sister still younger than himself.

John, then about sixteen years of age, at once decided to give his sister the whole advantages of the estate; and began even at that early age to teach a school. He persevered in this, until he acquired what he felt would enable him to complete his own education; and in his twenty-second year had entered the celebrated College in which he was now a student. He was in his senior year, and expected to graduate in December, at the approaching Commencement. He was deeply pious; and had been trained in that religious denomination which had acquired such influence in Georgia, as to number among its members the poor and the rich, the humble and the aristocratic. He was a Methodist.

George De Vane was a young Virginian. He had been for more than two years a student in the College, and in the same class with Waring. He, too, looked to a speedy graduation. Younger by several years than his friend, yet he had become intimate with him, shared his love of nature, his passion for books, and his disposition to seek recreation out of the common ways of life. Seeing his matured and well-knit form, no one would have supposed that his health was not perfect; yet his friends fearing that a disease not unknown to his family, might develop itself in him, advised him to pass some years in a milder climate than that of the mountain district of his native State. He was the only son of General Charles De Vane, a gentleman of large fortune, who had seen actual service in the army, and had acquired distinction in the late war with England. His property was so large, as to make it important for him to reside on his estate; and as his tastes were aristocratic, he saw little of general society. He belonged to that class of gentlemen, now almost extinct in Virginia, who were as exclusive in their social intercourse as the English nobility. He never travelled but with a coach and four horses; kept his servants in livery; and all the appointments of his large establishment were as formal and elaborate as if the world had undergone no change; just as if the law of primogeniture had not been destroyed, and suffrage made universal. His wife had died when George was but five years of age, and a widowed sister came to reside with him, who took charge of his household.

Mrs. Hester De Vane, who had married her cousin of the same name, to whom she was ardently attached, and whose death she still mourned, shared her brother's aristocratic tastes, but she was in almost every other respect widely different from him. Several years younger than her brother, she still retained traces of personal beauty; and having been plunged into deep grief by the loss of her husband, who died just four years after their marriage, she had sought that consolation which a stricken heart finds nowhere but at the feet of Him who invites the weary and heavy-laden to come to him—and she had found rest. Cultivated, refined, elegant, she was a Christian; preferring her own church, the Protestant Episcopal, she yet often attended religious services elsewhere. Her brother never accompanied her when she attended "chapels," as he styled them. She was childless; and she bestowed on George De Vane all the exuberance of her fine nature. She instructed him in those things which only a woman can teach: taught him to love music, for which she had a passion; to draw, encouraging him to sketch from nature; and she opened to his young mind the hidden treasures of that noble library which had been accumulating in his ancestral home for more than half a century. She saw the grand nature of the boy: grand, yet with faults that might shed disastrous eclipse over all the heaven of his future. Generous, brave, impetuous, full of truth and ardor, sympathizing with every thing great and noble, yet with strong aristocratic tastes, and not resolute where his tastes were offended; full, too, of sensibility, and impatient of restraint; a genius that almost disdained labor—such were the outlines that characterized the young nature which stood upon the threshold of manhood. No one of his age was better informed; his teachers had fitted him for college at an early age, delighting in his proficiency; and his aunt had instructed him in elegant learning to such a degree, that few of any age could surpass him in acquaintance with English literature.

In the society of gentlemen—such gentlemen as were entertained at General De Vane's table — George was full of sympathy, entered freely into conversation with them, and unostentatiously, indeed unconsciously exhibited those rare acquirements which attracted to him the attentions of persons much older than himself. When, too, he accompanied his father in his visits to the capital of his State, he found much to stimulate his ambition. Often he rambled in the great forests which stretched out almost illimitably about his home, taking his gun with him; lifting his voice in reciting the lines of favorite poets; and sometimes, like the great Athenian, addressing an imaginary audience, in his loudest tones, until the wild woods echoed with his vehement harangues. Oh! what a training for genius, ambition, and sensibility such a youth gives—a youth alternating between society and solitude! How the intellect grows and the soul expands, like nature in that zone lying between the extremes of northern ice and tropical fervors, when Spring breathes upon it!

## CHAPTER II.

> "LADY that in the prime of earliest youth
> Wisely hast shunn'd the broad way and the green,
> And with those few art eminently seen,
> That labor up the hill of heavenly truth."
>
> MILTON: *Ode to a Virtuous Young Lady.*

DE VANE, closely engaged in his studies, did not quit the college grounds again before the following Saturday. His closing examination was about to take place, and he was roused to unusual exertion. The youngest member of a large and strong class, he wished to distinguish himself; and as he had not bestowed that attention upon his Mathematical course, which the importance attached to it in the College required, he now redoubled his diligence.

In Metaphysics and Belles-Lettres, he was without a rival; and few equalled him as a classical scholar. As an orator, he was transcendent, and his Society had already chosen him to deliver the Valedictory Oration at the approaching commencement. But in Mathematics, his tastes had not been met, and he was respectable, without being distinguished in that department. In the Faculty he had friends; but the Professor of Belles-Lettres and Oratory was especially attached to him, and that gentleman had advised De Vane to devote the remainder of his time mainly to the neglected branch of study. Professor Niles was a man of large acquirements; had attained eminence at the bar, and then, while yet young, had given up his profession, and had passed some years in European travel. Before his return, he was elected by the Trustees to the

Chair which he now filled, and from the first recitation made by De Vane, in his department, he had formed a high estimate of the young student, which soon ripened into a friendship. He had married in France a young, beautiful, and accomplished woman, and De Vane often passed his evenings at their house, where his tastes were cultivated—music, books, conversation, every thing contributing to the encouragement of his favorite pursuits.

Walking in the College campus, De Vane saw his friend Waring descending the steps of the chapel, and he immediately joined him.

"Waring, what are you to do with yourself this fine day? Are you disposed for a walk?"

"Yes," replied Waring; "where shall we go?"

"Into the town; we may perhaps meet your fair friends once more. Have you seen them since our meeting on the river-bank?"

"Yes," said Waring; "I called the next evening, and Mrs. Springfield asked after you with interest."

"Indeed!" said De Vane. "I am grateful. I hardly supposed she would think of me again. I owe it to you, Waring."

"Not at all; she was really pleased with you, and made me give a full account of you."

"I trust you were generous, Waring, and did not make her believe that I am a free-thinker."

"No; I told her that you wanted discipline; that you were somewhat spoiled, and inclined to be transcendental."

"Did the young lady ask after me, Waring?"

"No; she sat by, and heard my description of you."

"And did not ask a single question about me?"

"Not one," said Waring.

"That is not flattering; she must be as cold as a Greek

statue—she is certainly as beautiful as one. If the Venus de Medici can excel her, I shall pronounce it faultless."

"She would consider it no compliment to be compared with Venus, even in marble," said Waring; "if you must go to the fine arts, why not say Raphael's Virgin?"

"Because," replied the other, "she does not in the least resemble her. Nor does she remind me of her, except by her near relation to something divine. I am willing to say Iphigenia, or, if you prefer, Ruth, or Eve; but she is Eve yet in Eden."

"As you will," replied his friend.

By this time the young gentlemen had entered the principal street of the town; and, walking leisurely, they enjoyed the animated scene. The morning was fine, handsome equipages dashed past, and the sidewalks were thronged with pedestrians. Quite a number of young people were walking; the students from the College, and the young ladies from the academy and the schools, were enjoying the bright, bracing air.

"Waring," said De Vane, "let us look into this book-store; I love book-stores—they are the most agreeable of all places on earth to me."

They entered the book-store. It was an unusually fine one; its shelves were enriched with the handsomest editions of the best works in the language; rare old volumes too might be found here; and De Vane had passed many an hour in looking through them. He was soon absorbed by a splendid copy of the Paradise Lost, bound in two large volumes. Raising his head at length, while a smile broke over his fine face, like a sun-beam, "Waring," said he, "come here; I will give you the portrait of your young friend, and even you will not object to a single feature in it." Waring walked up to his side, and De Vane read in his finest style—a style unsurpassed by any one of any age—the lines in which Milton describes Eve:

> "For softness she, and sweet attractive grace;
>
> . . . . . . .
>
> She, as a veil, down to the slender waist,
> Her unadorned golden tresses wore
> Dishevel'd, but in wanton ringlets waved,
> As the vine curls her tendrils."

At this moment Miss Wordsworth entered the store; and Waring and De Vane both colored. She led by the hand a little girl, plainly dressed, but with perfect neatness, and whose young face glowed with animation. Esther Wordsworth was, as De Vane had said, radiant; her complexion was perfect, and her rich, heavy, golden curls fell about her face "waving," in the language of Milton; her large dark-blue eyes had in them a fathomless depth, which reminded one of a lake; the face was oval; and the mouth and chin, perfect in themselves, gave an indescribable charm to her expression. The profile was classical; the outlines, as clear as if the chisel of an artist had traced them, were what we call Grecian; and when she smiled, her teeth revealed their perfect beauty. Slightly above the medium height, her form possessed that roundness which suggests health and activity, with grace; and her walk was elastic and rapid; her dress, made of some dark, rich material, fitted her shape exquisitely. As she entered, both the gentlemen advanced to meet her, and she frankly extended her hand to Waring; her manner showing that she recognized him as an established friend. She bowed to De Vane, who stood by his side.

"We are fortunate, this morning, Miss Wordsworth," said Waring; "we came to look at books, and did not know that we should have the pleasure of meeting you."

She rewarded him with a gracious smile.

"We often find in books," said De Vane, "unexpected pleasures; and in book-stores we may always look for something agreeable."

Esther turned her eyes full upon the speaker; there was in his manner something that impressed her—a grace and dignity rarely seen; and his language might be construed into a compliment to herself, or it might mean nothing more than he had literally said. She replied:

"I am often here; there are few places more agreeable to me; and if I could consult my tastes, I should pass many hours here. But I came this morning to select a book for my little friend here, who is to be rewarded for her diligence and good conduct."

The child looked up into the face of De Vane earnestly, for a moment, and then smiled. He gave her his hand.

"And how has your little friend earned her reward?" he asked.

"By learning well, and by doing well," said Esther; "I always make my gifts depend on good conduct as well as proficiency."

De Vane was surprised; it seemed that Miss Wordsworth was a teacher, and yet it could hardly be so. Her position in society, her circumstances, made it improbable. Esther read his embarrassment perfectly, but said nothing.

"To whom do you go to school?" said he to the child, still holding her hand.

"Miss Esther teaches me, sir," said she, half timidly and half proudly.

"I see, Mr. De Vane, that you do not comprehend it," said Esther, smiling. "This little girl, Mary Sinclair, is one of my pupils. I have ten."

De Vane could not conceal his astonishment; but his good breeding prevented his expressing it in words. There was in Esther's manner something so lady-like, so aristocratic, as De Vané thought, that he could not comprehend how she could be a schoolmistress. She did not explain it, but remarked that having examined her pupils since her return from her summer excursion to Virginia, she had found the little girl, whom she had brought to the book-store, entitled to a reward, and she had come to purchase it. De Vane bowed low, and Waring, observing the scene, smiled.

Esther, turning to the counter which stood in the middle of the store, began to look over the new bright books, which were temptingly ranged upon it, and presently selected one.

"Did you pass the summer in Virginia, Miss Wordsworth?" De Vane asked.

"The greater part of it," she replied; "we passed a few weeks in Philadelphia, and at Cape May. But Mr. Springfield yielded to the wishes of my aunt and myself, and we entered the heart of the Virginia mountains, and lingered there until the frosts admonished us that we must leave."

"And do you admire mountain scenery? And prefer it to cities and watering-places?"

"I love the mountains," she replied. "They are glorious."

De Vane was delighted, and he turned his face, lighted up with a smile of triumph, upon Waring.

"But," said that gentleman, "it is only in their summer garb that you have seen them; you would not reside in such a region?"

"I have never seen them in winter, it is true, but I can imagine that they only exchange their summer verdure for higher glories in winter."

"Still," insisted Waring, "you love this dear Southern clime."

"Oh! yes, dearly. I love my home, but I should be very sorry to think that I should never see the mountains again."

"Miss Wordsworth," said De Vane with emotion, "you do not know how much I owe you. You speak of my home when you speak of the Virginia mountains; and my heart answers to your language in sympathy which I will not attempt to express in words."

Other persons entered the store, and Miss Wordsworth and the two gentlemen turned into one of the alcoves, and began to examine the books which looked to them as friends.

Esther had taken down Madame De Staël's L'Allemagne, and was turning its pages. De Vane asked if she had bestowed much attention on German literature. She said: "I have not explored it, but have looked into it, as a traveller passes through a strange country."

"And did you admire it?"

"The question is not easily answered," replied Esther, "there is much that is beautiful—indeed, fascinating; but I suppose I must admit that I share that prejudice which Madame De Staël says exists in England, against the philosophy and the literature of Germany."

"But you observe how she accounts for that, do you not?" said De Vane, taking the book from Esther's hands and reading the paragraph: "*Le goût de la société, le plaisir et l'intérêt de la conversation ne sont point ce qui forme les esprits en Angleterre; les affaires, le parlement, l'administration, remplissent toutes les têtes, et les intérêts politiques sont le principal objet des méditations. Les Anglais veulent à tout des resultants immediatement applicables, et de là naissent leurs préventions contre une philosophie qui a pour objet le beau plutôt que l'utile.*"

"Yes," said Esther, "Madame De Staël is ingenious; but she was too thoroughly continental in her tastes to comprehend the English. I think she gives us the true reason for what she calls the prejudice of the English people against the philosophy of Germany, when she states, as she does in another part of the volume in your hands, that the chief subject of intellectual pursuit in Germany is Metaphysics, and that their system aspires to solve the mystery of creation, and to explore the infinite."

"And do you object to that, Miss Wordsworth? Do you not agree with her that the enigma of the universe has always engaged the attention of the noblest minds, and that although they continue to revolve about the abyss of fathomless thoughts, from age to age, we must still strive to scale the heavens?"

He spoke with great animation. Esther hesitated a moment before she replied; a glow flushed her face, and her eyes almost swam with tears. She sympathized with the enthusiasm of the young, ardent nature, seeking to find the true and the infinite, and yet without a guide.

"Mr. De Vane," she said, gently looking into the glowing face of the young student; "we shall strive forever in vain to scale the heavens, unless we follow the steps of Him who has gone before, to prepare a place for us."

De Vane started. There was so much of gentleness, and yet so much of courage in this young girl, who made the appeal to him, in behalf of her religion, with such a total absence of affectation, that he was deeply moved. He bowed, and then added: "I think you will agree, Miss Wordsworth, that Schiller sought the divine way. Do you remember what Madame De Staël says of him in his last moments? Allow me to render it in English. 'Stricken while yet young, with a hopeless malady, his children, his wife—who merited by a thousand touching qualities the attachment which he had for her—had soothed his last moments. Madame De Wollzogen, a friend capable of comprehending him, asked him, some hours before his death, how he did: "Still more tranquil," he answered. Indeed had he not reason to confide in the Divinity, whose reign upon earth he had favored? Was he not approaching the sojourn of the just? Was he not at this moment near his peers, and about to rejoin the friends who awaited him?'"

"Beautiful!" exclaimed Esther. "Beautiful! Madame De Staël could appreciate the good when it was associated with genius and refinement. I thank her for vindicating the superiority of sacred over classical poetry. Will you lend me the book for a moment?" De Vane placed it in her hands, and she turned to the notice of poetry, and read: "Groves, flowers, and brooks sufficed for the poets of paganism. The solitude of forests; the ocean without limits; the starry heavens, could hardly express the eternal and the infinite, with which the soul of Christians is filled."

De Vane looked into her face, as if it had been the face of an angel. She replaced the book; and taking the little girl by the hand, bowed to the gentlemen, and left the store. Waring had stood leaning against one of the bookshelves, and had silently observed and heard all that passed between De Vane and Esther. His face wore an expression of sadness, and yet the flush of something like triumph overspread it.

"Waring," said De Vane, "who *is* Miss Wordsworth?"

Waring smiled. "She is, as I have already informed you, a niece of Mrs. Springfield."

"Oh! yes; but give me her history."

"Her history," said Waring, "is a brief one, for she is very young—scarcely seventeen. But let us walk, and I will make you acquainted with it, so far at least as I know it myself."

They turned their steps toward a fine garden in the eastern part of the town, which was open to visitors.

"Miss Wordsworth," said Waring, "is an orphan, and resides with her aunt. Her father was a young Methodist minister, an only brother of Mrs. Springfield, and younger than herself. Thoroughly educated, with cultivated tastes and ample means, he felt it to be his duty to preach the Gospel; and he entered the self-denying, heroic company of men, who are known to the world as Methodist preachers. He was a native of Georgia, and he married in the neighborhood of Athens, in that State, a young, accomplished, and beautiful woman, who loved the cause of Christ as well as he did.

"In the fifth year of his ministry he was sent to Savannah, and in September an epidemic appeared, which swept hundreds into eternity. Mr. Wordsworth sent his wife and their child Esther—then four years old—into the country, and devoted himself to the care of the sick and the dying. The eye that saw him bare witness to him, and the ear that heard him drank in the tones of his cheerful voice, and dying lips whispered thanks and blessings. Worn down with fatigue, he contracted the disease, and sank under it. Mrs. Wordsworth, hearing of his illness, hastened to his bedside, and reached him in time to cheer his dying hours. She, too, fell a victim, and in the course of a few days was laid by his side. One of the most beautiful spots in the cemetery in that city, is that where Edward Wordsworth, and Ellen his wife, sleep side by side; a spot which many feet visit, and upon which many hands yet drop flowers. Esther was taken into the arms and into the heart of Mrs. Springfield, who was childless, and she has resided with her ever since. Masters have been called in to instruct her, and a governess was for four years in the family, but she has never been in a public school. And now you know the history of Miss Wordsworth," said Waring, as they entered one of the broad walks of the garden.

"But does she teach?" asked De Vane. "I suppose that she inherits her father's estate, of course. Why should she teach?"

Waring smiled. "I see, De Vane, that your aristocratic tastes are offended. Yes, she teaches! Some day we will visit her school. It is not very far from here, and lies hidden away in a garden almost as large as this."

Gay groups were seen in the wide grounds, and a fashionable party promenaded in the walk just before them. Fruits, flowers, and birds yet rejoiced in the lingering autumn, and the sun shed almost summer splendors over the scene. The two friends took one or two turns through the ground, and then departed for the College.

2

## CHAPTER III.

"STILL in the soul sounds the deep underchime
Of some immeasurable, boundless time.

. . . . . . .

For otherwise, why thus should man deplore
To part with his short being? Why thus sigh
O'er things which fade around, and are no more;
While, heedless of their doom, they live and die,
And yield up their sweet breaths, nor reason why,
But that within us, while so fast we flee,
The image dwells of God's eternity?" WILLIAMS.

THE next day was Sunday. The morning rose upon the earth in cloudless splendor. The serene heavens seemed to bend nearer to a redeemed world, as if they would embrace and purify it. The mocking-bird poured its joyous song upon the air; and the robin uttered its quick cheerful notes, as it sprang from branch to branch of the China-trees, with which the town abounded.

De Vane looked out upon nature, but he turned away and plunged into his books.

Waring went to church, as he did habitually. No studies could tempt him from attending the morning and the evening service.

Upon his return he entered the apartments of De Vane, and found him deep in his studies.

"Where have you been, Waring?"

"Where you should have been," replied the other. "I have been engaged in worshipping that God who made the heavens and the earth—both so bright to-day."

"Ah! Waring, you are a Christian."

"And what are you?" he asked.

"Come, come, sit down," said De Vane, "and then you may read me a lecture."

"De Vane, will you go with me this evening, if I call for you?"

"To go where?" asked De Vane.

"To the Methodist Church. Mr. Springfield is to preach: it was announced this morning."

"Most willingly," replied De Vane; "but to tell you the truth, I never was in a Methodist chapel in my life. To hear Mr. Springfield, however, I will go. I feel quite an interest in him."

"Very well," said Waring; "I will call for you at seven o'clock. We must go early to find a seat; they are all free, you understand; and Mr. Springfield attracts large congregations."

Punctually at seven Waring called, and they walked to the church, or meeting-house, as it was most frequently called. It was a large framed building, destitute of ornaments, and seated with benches, a rail running down the middle of each row of seats, dividing them; the two sexes being rigidly separated during public worship. The building was already crowded; but Waring being a well-known member of the church, found a seat for De Vane and himself quite near the pulpit.

As De Vane took his seat, he surveyed the scene; it was new to him. A gallery ran along the end and two sides of the building, for the accommodation of the blacks; and it was filled with them. The pulpit was high above the seats of the building, as if its construction was designed to impress the hearers with the authority of the preacher. Clusters of candles, hung against the walls, and the pillars which supported the gallery, lighted the house. De Vane was impressed with the air of quiet earnestness, which pervaded the audience, composed mainly of well-dressed people, apparently in the middle walks of life; but he observed many who were evidently of the higher and wealthier class, and some gentlemen whom he knew to be persons of distinction, among them Mr. Hallam, a man of the very highest intellect, and Dr. Dahlgreen, who seldom attended any religious service, and who was suspected of entertaining the sceptical opinions attributed quite generally to Dr. Hume, the President of the College. At this moment two ladies entered the opposite aisle, and took their seats upon the very bench where De Vane and Waring were seated; the former separated from them only by a slight strip. They were Mrs. Springfield and Esther; and De Vane found himself by the very side of the latter. His heart beat quick; for his eyes met Esther's as she entered, and she recognized him instantly. The ladies knelt, and engaged for a few moments in silent prayer. Mr. Springfield entered by a door in the rear of the building, and ascended the pulpit. He rose, and there was deep silence throughout the crowded assemblage; he opened the services by reading the sixty-seventh Psalm—that grand appeal to God—to cause his face to shine upon the people; and teaching that, when the people acknowledged God, even temporal blessings would abound.

Then followed the hymn:

"Thou God of glorious majesty,
To thee, against myself, to thee
A worm of earth I cry!
A half-awakened child of man,
An heir of endless bliss or pain,
A sinner born to die.

"Lo on a narrow neck of land,
'Twixt two unbounded seas I stand,
Secure, insensible!
A point of time, a moment's space,
Removes me to that heavenly place,
Or shuts me up in hell.

"O God! mine inmost soul convert,
And deeply on my thoughtful heart
Eternal things impress;
Give me to feel their solemn weight,
And tremble on the brink of fate,
And wake to righteousness."

The whole congregation rose to their feet, and united their voices in singing the lines; the blacks in the gallery joined in the song, and swelled the mighty stream of sound, which rolled upward, and away to the throne of God. Esther's voice rose rich and clear, every word distinctly uttered; and such was the ravishing sweetness of her tones, that De Vane felt as if an angel stood by his side, to lead him to the gates of heaven. Such music he had never heard before. The tones of Esther were not lost in the volume of the swelling sound about her; but with a clear tender cadence they penetrated the very depths of the soul, and De Vane felt the tears starting to his eyes. After the first stanza had been sung, Esther, observing that De Vane did not join in the music, handed him her own book; and standing nearer to Mrs. Springfield, used hers. The prayer followed the hymn, the congregation kneeling, in which act of devotion De Vane's good breeding made him take part. A second hymn succeeded the prayer, and the text was announced, without the least preface. It was from the Acts of the Apostles, seventeenth chapter, thirtieth and thirty-first verses: "And the times of this ignorance God winked at; but now commandeth all men everywhere to repent: because he hath appointed a day, in the which he will judge the world in righteousness, by that man whom he hath ordained; whereof he hath given assurance to all men, in that he hath raised him from the dead."

The sermon was of the highest order. It brought Athens to view, and portrayed the scene where the first great public conflict took place between Christianity and enlightened Paganism. It represented St. Paul, standing on the Areopagus, surrounded by temples and statues, by all that was majestic or graceful in architecture, and elevated and refined in art; the spot where the intellect of Greece displayed its highest forms, and achieved its noblest triumphs. It depicted the Apostle with his learning, his courage, and his ardor, rebuking the vain attempts of man to embody the Deity in visible forms; and announcing the sublime truth that, since the coming of Jesus Christ, the Son of God, incarnate, suffering, dying, triumphing, the world was under a higher responsibility than before; and that God would bring all men before the dread tribunal of that august Being who, shrouding for a time the splendors of his divinity in the human form, had actually submitted to death for us; but who had risen again, refulgent with the glory of an all-conquering Prince.

De Vane was borne away by the rich, massive current of thought, which was wholly new to him, and he for the first time saw the glory of classical learning pale before the higher glory of Christianity. The temples of antiquity, and the whole gorgeous world of mythology, perished before him, and the cross stood the symbol of the world's hope, bathed in the serene light of heaven.

At the close of the sermon, the whole audience seemed released from some invisible influence which had held them in moveless subjection; and a stir—an indescribable moving of feet and change of posture—evinced how earnest had been the attention of the whole living mass during its delivery.

A young minister rose, offered a prayer, another hymn was sung, and then the congregation dispersed. De Vane instantly extended his hand to Esther, and she saw that he was deeply moved. Mrs. Springfield, too, came forward, and gave him her hand warmly, inviting both Waring and himself to visit them. De Vane gladly promised to join his friend in his future visits to the family, and, taking h leave of the ladies, he put his arm in that of Waring, a they turned their steps toward the College.

"Well, De Vane," said Waring, "what do you think of a Methodist meeting?"

"I must say," he answered, "that I am amazed. I never witnessed any thing so impressive. The music, or rather the singing, was glorious, and the sermon was the finest to which I ever listened. I am almost ready to say that I never heard true eloquence before. How the whole pagan world shrunk, dwarfed before the majesty of the Redeemder, sublimer in his death than all the gods in their triumphs!"

"I rejoice to hear you speak thus, De Vane. It proves what I have long believed, that you are capable of appreciating goodness and truth, wherever you find them."

"I deserve no credit," said De Vane. "Any one would have been impressed by what we have witnessed this evening. Oh! that my aunt, Mrs. De Vane, could have been present. I must write her such a description of it as I am able to give. Waring, Miss Wordsworth is almost——"

"An angel?" interrupted Waring. "I do not think she has wings."

"I trust not," said De Vane, "for she might spread them and quit this world, to seek her native home above those stars."

The heavens were brilliant; countless numbers of stars burned in the deep blue. The cool October air was pure, and the angelic hosts seemed to look out from the sky, to light the pilgrims of earth to the realms of the happy and the immortal.

## CHAPTER IV.

HER voice is hovering o'er my soul. It lingers,
O'ershadowing it with soft and lulling wings;
The blood and life within those snowy fingers
Teach witchcraft to the instrumental strings.
PERCY BYSCHE SHELLEY.

As the students were leaving the College chapel, after evening prayer, Waring put his arm in that of De Vane, and walked out with him. "De Vane, I have a note from Mrs. Springfield. She wishes me to ask you to join me to-morrow evening at her house. They receive visitors every Thursday evening, and I think you will be pleased, if you can spare an hour or two from study, to meet some persons who will probably be there."

"I shall go, with great pleasure," said De Vane.

Little did Waring comprehend the thrill of joy that warmed the soul of his friend at the thought of meeting Esther once more. De Vane was ardent, but he was sensitive and proud; and while he did not hesitate to express his admiration for Miss Wordsworth in glowing terms, yet Waring supposed it was only the language of a natural homage to a person of such resplendent beauty. But De Vane was conscious of a far intenser sentiment than that which we call admiration. He had often admired women, but now he felt his whole nature moved. The first warm ray of real love beamed upon his soul, and it responded, like the statue of Memnon, to the rising sun—if not in vocal tones, in thrilling consciousness of the new power which controlled him. He was himself amazed at the strength of his own passion; for he felt that already the ascendency of the young, bright girl whom he had so lately met was complete. Her beauty at once attracted him, and her manners, her intellect, her cultivation, so far transcending what he had seen in others, asserted their domain over him triumphantly.

Thursday evening came, and when De Vane entered the parlor with Waring, he found the room pretty well filled with persons, engaged in animated conversation. Mrs. Springfield welcomed them warmly, and presented them to two gentlemen who were conversing with her as they entered. One of these was Mr. Hallam, whose fine face, full of kindness and intelligence, De Vane remembered to have seen on more than one occasion; but as he had not gone into society generally, he had not met him before. There was an awkwardness in his lounging attitudes that gave him the appearance of rusticity, and his modesty was such that he was easily embarrassed; but his fine mind shone out everywhere. He engaged De Vane at once in conversation, and soon interested the young student so deeply, that he was startled when Waring, coming up to him some little time after, laid his hand on his shoulder, and asked leave to interrupt him, that he might present him to some other persons.

They walked into the next room—the library—into which the parlor opened by two doors, with a pier between; and De Vane observed that it was furnished with exquisite taste. The walls on three sides were hung with pictures, and the third wall was fitted with shelves for books, and entirely filled with them. Large, handsome *fauteuils*, sofas covered with bright stuff, and a few light, tasteful chairs, were placed in the room so as to afford seats for those who wished to examine a book or print in any part of the room. A rosewood cabinet-table stood near the centre of the floor, and rich crimson silk curtains draped the windows. On the white marble mantel stood a splendid French clock, ornamented with the figure of Petrarch seated, his arm resting on a tablet, inscribed with the name of Laura. Against the pier was placed a pianoforte, a splendid instrument, open, and some sheets of new music laid on it. Over the instrument hung a portrait of Esther, in the highest style of art. It was a bust, the head turned and looking away, so as to show the profile in part, while yet the expression of the whole face was preserved. It was in an oval frame, of a rich, massive style. De Vane saw all this at a glance, accustomed as he was at home to such surroundings. Several gentlemen were standing with Mr. Springfield as De Vane and Waring entered the room, in conversation with him, but when he saw the students he advanced to meet them.

"Mr. De Vane," said Mr. Springfield, "I am happy to see you in my house. Your friend, Mr. Waring, has made me feel as if I had long known you."

De Vane bowed low, and he was presented to the other gentlemen. Up to this time, De Vane had not seen Esther; but, turning away from the gentlemen, who now resumed their conversation, he saw her seated in the midst of a group of ladies, over whose chairs two or three young men were bending, listening to a narrative which some one was giving, of a distressing accident which had occurred that day. De Vane drew near, and Esther rose to meet him, extending her hand to him with frank cordiality. He joined the group, and the conversation became general.

"Ah! Miss Wordsworth, you are, as usual, surrounded in such a way that one with less courage than I possess would hardly venture to attempt to reach you."

De Vane quickly turned to observe the new-comer. He was a large, well-formed man, who appeared to be but little more than thirty years of age. His ruddy complexion, blue eyes, and light hair gave him somewhat the appearance of an English gentleman. His face beamed with animation, and there was unusual grace in his attitude. His voice and his enunciation at once attracted and charmed De Vane, and as he approached Esther he bowed very low, and taking her hand, touched it with his lips.

"O Mr. Clarendon!" she exclaimed, "I am delighted to see you. Is Mrs. Clarendon with you?"

"Alas! no," he replied, "she charged me with kind messages to you, but dared not take the night-air."

Esther, turning to De Vane, said: "I wish to present you to Mr. Clarendon; he too is a Virginian, and loves the mountains of his native State."

Mr. Clarendon shook his hand warmly, and expressed his pleasure at meeting him.

"I wonder," said he, "that I have not met you before; you must have hid yourself."

"I have not gone out much," replied De Vane, "and when not engaged in College duties, I have found in the library so much to interest me, that I pass most of my hours there. I did not know until now how much I was losing."

Esther was standing by the side of Mr. Clarendon, and De Vane's glance was for an instant turned on her as he said this. Still the remark might have been intended to take in Mr. Clarendon too; and while she colored—she was conscious that she did so—she replied that she was happy to have the good fortune to introduce him to her friend, to whom she felt herself indebted for so many bright hours.

Mr. Clarendon bowed, and said: "Mr. De Vane, I trust you are acquainted with the art of self-defense; if not, I suggest that you begin presently to study it."

They all laughed, and the conversation took a general range, embracing books, the fine arts, and religion—a subject which Esther introduced by remarking to Mr. Clarendon, that during the past summer she had heard the venerable Bishop McKendree preach, and added:

"I am happy to say that he is to be here sometime this winter."

Mr. Clarendon replied: "I am happy to hear it. I have been taught by a good aunt of mine to venerate him, for she ranks him next to her friend Bishop Asbury."

De Vane took part in the conversation, spoke with animation upon the several subjects, and disclosed a degree of cultivation which surprised Mr. Clarendon; while he, on his part, felt his admiration of that gentleman rising into enthusiasm. Speaking of him to Esther afterward, he said:

"Your friend, Mr. Clarendon, charms me; he has

'The large utterance of the early gods.'"

"Did you ever hear Bishop McKendree?" Esther inquired of De Vane.

"I ashamed to say," he answered, "that I never heard any preacher of that denomination until last Sunday evening, and you may imagine my surprise—and gratification."

"I always go to hear my friend Springfield, Mr. De Vane," said Mr. Clarendon, "and I will go anywhere to hear a true man who can interest and instruct me. We are too much governed in our good old commonwealth—which I love as well as you do—by aristocratic habits; and the same thing may be said of this State. It is giving way, however, to some extent; for intellectual power has a certain majesty about it which compels reluctant homage where it is not freely yielded; and the Methodist Church numbers in its ministry some men of the highest order."

Waring came up at this moment.

"My friend," said De Vane, turning to him, "has said so to me, and I shall hereafter put myself under his guidance—at least, in spiritual matters."

"Better seek a better guide," said Waring gravely. "There is One always ready to lead us into all truth."

"I think, Waring, you follow Him closely," said De Vane, "and if I keep by your side, I shall not be far out of the way."

Esther gave him a smile, which showed how she valued this frank tribute to the worth of Waring.

Mr. Clarendon said: "Miss Wordsworth, will you give us some music?"

She took his arm, and he seated her at the piano.

"What shall I give you, Mr. Clarendon?"

"There is a song that has just been written by a friend of mine, a Georgian, an eminent lawyer, and I believe it has been set to music," he replied. "It is very sad though—perhaps too much so for you:

'My life is like the summer rose.'"

"I have it here," said Esther; "it was sent to me to-day by the author of the lines, who was a friend of my mother." Her voice almost trembled.

She took up one of the sheets of music lying near her, spread it before her, and running her fingers over the keys of the instrument, drew from it such notes that it seemed to have a soul. Her golden hair fell in rich ringlets about her face, except the heavy braid which was held by a clasp of Etruscan gold on the back of the head, and the blue of heaven shone in the lustre of her eyes. She seemed to De Vane a youthful priestess, transcending in her loveliness, the highest impersonations of classical beauty; warm, and yet pure, as if an angel had come for a season to sojourn on earth and bring human passion under the dominion of Christian sentiment.

She sang the lines with indescribable tenderness, and it seemed as if the very spirit of sadness dwelt under the keys which she touched.

"My life is like the summer rose
That opens to the morning sky,
But ere the shades of evening close
Is scattered on the ground—to die!
Yet on the rose's humble bed
The sweetest dews of night are shed,
As if she wept the waste to see—
But none shall weep a tear for me!

"My life is like the autumn leaf
That trembles to the moon's pale ray;
Its hold is frail—its date is brief,
Restless, and soon to pass away!
Yet, ere that leaf shall fall and fade,
The parent tree will mourn its shade,
The winds bewail the leafless tree—
But none shall weep a tear for me!

"My life is like the prints which feet
Have left on Tampa's desert strand;
Soon as the rising tide shall beat,
All trace will vanish from the sand.
Yet, as if grieving to efface
All vestige of the human race,
On that lone shore loud moans the sea—
But none, alas! shall mourn for me!"

"The lines are very beautiful," said Mr. Clarendon, "but, oh! how sad."

"And do you not love sad music?" she asked, looking up.

"Not at all times—I am capricious; but I love your music, whether it be joyous, or steeped in sorrow."

De Vane had not uttered a word—he could not. Esther turned to him, and asked if there were any piece of music which he especially admired. He roused himself, and breathed deeply, as if just restored to consciousness.

"Do you sing Jephthah's Daughter, Byron's Hebrew melody?" he inquired.

"Yes," she answered, "but that, too, is sad."

"I can scarcely feel that any thing deserves the name of music that is not sad," said De Vane.

"I quite agree with you," she answered with animation, "except in sacred music. There I love the joyous, the exultant, the triumphant, as well as the tender."

"You should hear the *Miserere*, Miss Wordsworth, as I have heard it in Rome, if you would comprehend the depths of sadness in music," said Mr. Clarendon.

Quite a number of persons had now gathered about the piano. Esther touched the keys and sang, with unrivalled pathos, the song for which De Vane had asked; and as she uttered the prolonged cadence of the closing line—

"And forget not I smiled as I died!"

tears were in the eyes of many who heard her. De Vane could not conceal his emotion, and he observed that Mr. Clarendon was moved; but that gentleman said:

"Miss Wordsworth, I did not come here this evening to have the fountain of my tears unsealed, and I shall insist upon something brighter than all this."

"Yet," said Esther, "what a glory breaks over the dirge—what a wild, passionate, exultant triumph bursts forth from the dying Jewish maiden, as she remembers that she had won the great battle for her sire, and that her country was free! How grandly she says:

'Though the virgins of Salem lament,
Be the judge and the hero unbent!'"

"Thanks, Miss Wordsworth—thanks," exclaimed De Vane, "for your vindication of my taste."

"The wonder with me is," said Waring, "that Lord Byron could write such a song."

"Men are often much misunderstood," said De Vane. "Lord Byron had in his nature the elements of religion; if he sinned, he was sorely sinned against."

"His religious elements must have been sadly perverted, to permit him to live as he lived, and to write as he wrote," rejoined Waring.

"Yet," said Mr. Clarendon, "if he was a fallen angel, he was like Milton's—his form had not lost all the original brightness."

Esther looked at him as if grateful that he had said a word somewhat favorable to De Vane's estimate of the noble poet.

"Esther," said Mr. Springfield, "will you give us one of your sacred songs?"

"Gladly," she replied; and she sang that beautiful hymn,

"Rock of ages, cleft for me;"

while Waring accompanied her, his voice sustaining hers admirably. Again De Vane was subdued, and could only bow, as the song ceased and she rose from her seat.

"That," said Mr. Clarendon, "excels the *Miserere*," and then added: "Is that line of the first song which you gave us, Miss Wordsworth—where the prints which feet leave on Tampa's desert strand are introduced—correct? Does not the writer mean Tempe?"

"I should refer that critical difficulty to you for solution," she replied.

"Well, I am a little puzzled about it," said he.

"I think," said De Vane, "that the author of the lines means what he has written. The vale of Tempe in Thessaly, can hardly be called desert, for its charms are well known, and the banks of the Peneus, which flows through it, could not, by even poetical license, be described as a strand.

"What, then, can he mean? Where is Tampa?" said Mr. Clarendon.

"It is on the coast of Florida," said De Vane. "It so happened that I made a visit to that coast just before I entered college; and hearing the temperature of Tampa spoken of as favorable to invalids, I passed some weeks there. A more sad and even desert strand I do not know anywhere; and the wail of the sea on the lone shore is the most mournful of earthly sounds."

"You have solved the problem," said Mr. Clarendon. "I thought Wilde had been using his prerogative as a poet somewhat freely; for I remember how the valley of Tempe impressed me with its wild beauty—Ossa on the one side, and Olympus, rich with its woods and herbage, on the other. It was not a desert."

De Vane had made a life-long friend of Mr. Clarendon. Before taking leave of Mrs. Springfield, he said to her:

"Madam, I commend that young Virginian to you. He is my countryman, and I am proud of him. If I read him rightly, Virginia will be still prouder of him."

The evening closed. The guests departed, and De Vane felt as if his real life had just begun. Light had spread over his soul as over the young world, when it was said: "The evening and the morning were the first day."

## CHAPTER V.

MOTHER, mother, up in heaven,
Stand up on the jasper sea,
And be witness I have given
All the gifts required of me.
ELIZABETH BARRETT BROWNING.

WHEN Saturday came—the college exercises being suspended, that the students might seek recreation outside of the grounds—Waring and De Vane walked together into the town.

When we first love, a new glory seems to overspread the face of nature. The soul invests every object with its own hue; the heavens above and the earth beneath, yield us their sympathy; and hope sheds a glow, surpassing the splendor of tropical sunlight, over all the future. De Vane thought he had never beheld a season so lovely. The autumnal glories which met his view; the leaves just changing their hues under the early frost; the lingering roses which breathed their fragrance upon the pure air; the songs of birds that never deserted the spot where they uttered their first notes in spring for a milder climate, even in winter—all made the little world about him seem a far brighter region than the happy valley of Rasselas.

"Waring," said he, "you were to take me to see Miss Wordsworth's school; shall we go there now?"

Waring smiled. "Why, De Vane," said he, "this is a holiday, and we shall not find Miss Wordsworth there."

"Still," said De Vane, "I should like to see the place

where she spends her days. How is it that she can bring herself to submit to such drudgery?"

"I shall answer you as Philip did, when Nathanael asked him if any good thing could come out of Nazareth: 'Come and see.'"

In the eastern part of the town, not very far from the public garden, which De Vane had already visited in company with Waring, there was another, covering some two acres of ground, inclosed with a neat fence, inside of which was a hedge of wild orange-trees, that shut in the grounds from observation. The two students entered the gate, and found themselves in the midst of evergreens, so rich and profuse, that De Vane felt as if he had been suddenly transported to the tropics. Hardy flowers—such as required little cultivation—bloomed still, and a few rare ones were seen protected by the vigorous shrubbery near them. Winding walks led through the grounds, neatly kept, and they converged upon a central spot, where a small edifice, in the cottage style, stood. The main building was a framed structure of two stories, with a wing on either end, and with light piazzas connecting with the porch of the principal house. Creepers covered it almost completely, the ivy climbing to the very top of the chimneys, and waving its branches like little banners. A broad gravelled walk passed quite around the house, cutting it off like an island from the surrounding garden. As the students approached the house, they met an old, respectable-looking black man, with a rake in his hand, who at once recognized Waring, and evidently regarded him as a friend.

"How are you this morning, Uncle Jacob?" exclaimed Waring.

"Thank the Lord, Master Waring," said the old man, taking off his hat, "I'm well; and I hope I sees you well, too."

"Yes, thank you," said Waring; "and I have brought my young friend here to see the school. He's from Virginia."

"Mighty glad to see him," said the old man; "I'm from Virginny, too."

"Are you, indeed, Uncle Jacob?" said De Vane heartily; "then I'm your countryman, and we must get to be good friends."

Old Jacob was highly gratified, and he bowed very humbly to the young gentleman, scraping his foot under him as he bent his head low.

"Is Mrs. Greene at home?" asked Waring.

"Oh! yes, master, and my Missis, too," said Jacob.

"What! is Miss Wordsworth here? Why, Uncle Jacob, it's Saturday—don't she give holiday?"

"Yes, master; but she comes sometimes Saturday, too; and she fetched a little girl with her to-day, that an't been here before."

Bidding the old man good morning, the gentlemen walked directly to the house.

"That old negro," said De Vane, "is thoroughly well-bred."

"Yes," replied Waring, "I have often observed it; he belongs to Miss Wordsworth—was one of her father's slaves—and is now a sort of patriarch. She keeps him employed here in looking after the grounds; and he is as happy as the days are long."

"His language is good," said De Vane; "and he seems to be as humble as if he had never been indulged."

"Yes, he loves his young mistress—thinks himself too happy in being permitted to serve her; and he is a Christian."

By this time they had reached the house. Waring knocked at the door, and it was opened by the little girl who had accompanied Esther to the book-store. She looked up into Waring's face with a bright smile, and asked him to walk in.

"How are you this morning, Mary?" said Waring, stooping to kiss the child. "Do you not remember this gentleman?"

"Oh! yes, sir; I saw him with you at the book-store."

De Vane took her hand, and thanked her for not having forgotten him.

They entered the little hall of the cottage; and Mary, throwing open the door of the room on the right, invited them to follow her. As they entered, they found Esther seated on a low chair, two or three little girls standing by her, and a still smaller child seated on a cushion at her feet; a bright fire blazed on the hearth, neat, simple furniture was arranged in the room tastefully, and chintz curtains hung from the windows; a middle-aged, respectable-looking woman stood near the group. It was a picture which De Vane never ceased to remember; a picture hung forever in the chamber of his memory, and which he would not have exchanged for Raphael's master-piece, or Claude Lorraine's *chef d'œuvres.*

Esther turned her face quickly toward the gentlemen as she heard their tread on the floor, and a glow overspread her face, rising to her very temples; her attitude was one of perfect grace; and De Vane felt that nothing in the whole range of classical mythology, neither nymph nor goddess, could rival her as she sat startled, and for a moment moveless; the profuse curls falling from her uplifted face, the lips parted, and the eyes flashing with an earnest glance.

"We owe you an humble acknowledgment of our rudeness in trespassing upon you, Miss Wordsworth," said Waring; "but we did not know until we entered your grounds that we should find you here."

De Vane said nothing, but bowed very low. Esther

rose and shook hands with them, and expressed her gratification at their visit.

"I am pleased, Mr. Waring, to see that you and your friend feel any interest whatever in my little retreat. I am not usually here on Saturday, but came to-day to bring a new pupil."

She then introduced the gentlemen to Mrs. Green—"my assistant," as she said graciously, "in the task of taking care of these little people."

She turned to the girl, who still kept her seat on the cushion, and taking her hand, raised her to her feet. She was a child of great beauty, apparently some six years of age, whose dark eyes and glossy black curls presented a perfect contrast to those of the friend who had just brought her from her desolate home to this "retreat," as she named it.

"You remember, Mr. De Vane, do you not, that you heard at Mrs. Springfield's—a very painful narrative of a sudden death, and of a little girl left without parents, or a near relative in all the world? Well, this is the child. Her mother died about six weeks since, and last Thursday her father, a young man of excellent character, while standing upon a scaffold, fell backward and was instantly killed. This was the only child, and I have brought her here, that she may be cared for. I was just taking leave of her as you entered, having brought about her some two or three little girls, who will try to make her happy."

She added not a word, but invited the gentlemen to walk through the grounds with her. De Vane's astonishment could not be expressed. That one so young, so bright, so accomplished, so full of sympathy with all that was beautiful in nature, in books, in the living world, could pass so many hours in the task of instructing little girls how to read, to write, to sing—he could not comprehend. He could imagine a lady of fortune bestowing her ample means in charity—in founding a hospital—or in establishing a school, and in employing others to take the drudgery of the benevolent scheme; but that the brightness of one's own youth should be surrendered to this repulsive labor, was a scale of self-sacrifice he had not contemplated. His love deepened almost into reverence; and he followed her steps silently as she walked with Waring in advance of him. Reaching a spot somewhat lower than the level upon which the house stood, they came to a spring of water which bubbled out of the gravelly slope, and emptied into a small marble basin. Trees of larger growth than those in other parts of the grounds sheltered the spot, and broke the fiery splendors of even a Southern mid-day sun. To-day, the clear sunshine glancing through the trees, imparted to them variegated lights and shadows; and the view of the higher grounds was as if an artist of surpassing skill had spread the rich tapestry of the looms of France over them. Seats were ranged around the spring, and the party resting upon them surveyed the limited but exquisite landscape.

"I wonder, Miss Wordsworth," said De Vane, "that I never discovered this enchanted spot before; its loveliness would have tempted me to visit it often."

"Do you love nature?" asked Esther.

"Earnestly, passionately," said De Vane. "In the primeval forests of Virginia I have learned almost to worship her."

"It is a taste in which I fully sympathize; and I have striven here to shut out the sights and sounds which disturb the perfect repose of nature."

"Feeling, I suppose, with Cowper that

'God made the country, but man made the town.'

You wish to spread here, at the very base of this gay capital, the triumphs of nature."

"Yes," said Esther, "I have an intenser consciousness of the presence of God in the midst of trees and flowers than I can have here in the streets, or even in the houses about us. Do you recall Thomson's lines?

> 'The love of nature works,
> And warms the bosom, till, at last, sublimed
> To rapture and enthusiastic heat,
> We feel the present Deity, and taste
> The joy of God to see a happy world!'"

"When very young," replied De Vane, "I learned to love Thomson; for my youth was passed in the country, and I observed the seasons, as we study the human face; and the descriptions which he gives might, many of them, have been written in the presence of our own landscapes. Albemarle, Miss Wordsworth, is unrivalled for its scenery."

"So I must believe from what I have heard of it from others, but I have not yet seen that part of Virginia. Passing over the Piedmont road, and entering the mountain range of Southern Virginia, I have been deeply impressed with the grandeur of the scenery."

"You must not concede, Miss Wordsworth," said Waring, "that Virginia has all the fine scenery in the country. The State pride of my friend is already too great, and we must bring that down, if we can not level his boasted mountains."

De Vane smiled, and asked: "Where, short of Niagara, is there any such scenery?"

"On the French-Broad," replied Waring, "to say nothing of Upper Georgia, with its waterfalls second only to Niagara."

"The French-Broad!" exclaimed De Vane. "I never saw it, but surely its scenery can not rival ours."

"The scenery along the banks of the French-Broad is wonderfully fine. Set out in the morning from the warm springs of North-Carolina, and make the day's travel to Ashville, and you will be amazed and bewildered. The river cuts its way through mountains. They rise in steep precipices hundreds of feet above it on both sides, fringed with laurel and variegated shrubbery to the very summit. Much of the road is made by cutting away the solid rock, and the wheels of your carriage actually dip in the stream on the one side, while they scrape the mountain-rock on the other side."

"I must at some time see it," said Esther. "I did not suppose that any thing so wild could be found in our southern country."

"Such scenery in Europe," replied Waring, "would attract thousands of travelers from remote parts, and would be world-renowned."

The gentlemen, after some further conversation, rose to take leave of Esther, who invited them to visit her grounds, as often as it might be agreeable to them to do so. De Vane assured her of the pleasure it would afford him to avail himself of her gracious invitation; and, bowing low to her, followed Waring, who had already preceded him in the walk.

When they were once more in the streets, De Vane put his arm in that of Waring, and said: "I *must* understand all this. What *does* it mean, Waring?"

"What?" replied the other. "What is there that you do not understand?"

"When I first met Miss Wordsworth, you told me she was a Methodist. Afterward I learned she was a teacher. To-day I find that she has established a home for friendless little girls, and that she passes the greater part of her time there. Why should one so young, so bright, so qualified to adorn society, give so much of her time to such tasks?"

Waring walked on for some minutes before he spoke; he then said: "De Vane, I respect you. Allow me to say, I know your high qualities, and am sincerely your friend. But I am a friend also to truth. You admire Miss Wordsworth, that is plain; but you can not appreciate her. Your aristocratic tastes and habits unfit you for it; you are incapable of self-denying labors, except such as ambition prompts; and you are unable to comprehend how a young, bright, joyous nature can unostentatiously seek to do good, following the humble, the poor, and the outcast into their revolting abodes, that she may rescue and save them. The whole philosophy of Miss Wordsworth's life is to be found in the simple obedience of child-like faith: 'If any man will be my disciple, let him take up his cross daily, and follow me.'"

De Vane was touched. He felt that Waring's rebuke was not unjust, and he knew it was not intended to be harsh. He had almost shrunk from Esther, when he learned that she was a Methodist. He was shocked when he supposed that she was a teacher; and but for the casual meeting at the book-store, where he discovered the extraordinary wealth of her mind, he might not have sought to know more of her. And even now, when he had discovered that she did not teach from any reference to pecuniary reward, but solely under the influence of a high sentiment, he felt that he could not sympathize with that sentiment, however much he respected it, and he feared that her virtues were of too severe a cast. He scarcely knew how to answer Waring, but he said frankly:

"I may not be able to feel the dominion of a great religious principle, or the ascendency of a purely religious sentiment, as Miss Wordsworth does, or as you do, Waring; but still I must revere the principle, and admire the sentiment, as I do whatever is really noble."

"Miss Wordsworth," said Waring, "is a very uncommon person. You, of course, see her beauty, and are impressed with her extraordinary intellectual qualities; her training has been such as to give her a range of thought and of sentiment quite out of the line which you have been accustomed to observe. Her parents, as you already know, are both dead, her mother surviving her husband but a short time. When she felt the approach of death—still conscious and resolute—she called for writing materials, and addressed a letter to her child. She impressed on her young mind, even then—and the impression deepened with every year as she grew, and read, and re-read the dying message—the importance of living for others. And she enjoined it upon her not to squander the ample fortune which she would inherit upon false objects, but to devote much of it to the training of orphan little girls, without father or mother, like herself, in the way to heaven. That as her father had died young, giving his life a sacrifice for those whom Christ had bought with his own blood; and as she, her mother, was about to follow him to a world of bliss, it was her duty to carry out their wishes in consecrating herself in some good measure while yet young, to active ministrations, for the good of those who, like herself in orphanage, were not like her in fortune. She has faithfully followed the counsels of her saintly mother. She will not consent yet to commit to others the entire care of these young beings; and while she has established this home, which you have seen to-day, out of her abounding means, and employed a trustworthy person, Mrs. Green, to take charge of them, she will teach them herself. Otherwise she would be but giving of her abundance, but it would be no consecration of herself."

"It is glorious," exclaimed De Vane. "I begin to comprehend how the woman that brought the alabaster box of precious ointment to anoint the head of the Saviour, not content with that costly sacrifice, poured the richer tribute of her tears upon his feet, and wiped them with the hairs of her head."

Waring turned upon him a face beaming with satisfaction, but said not a word.

## CHAPTER VI.

> "The vague but manly wish to tread the maze
> Of life, to noble ends."
>
> Aubrey De Vere.

November came; the closing examination of the Senior Class was very near, and De Vane plunged into his studies deeper than ever. He would not indulge himself in a single visit to Esther. He loved, and loved profoundly, but ambition swayed him in these closing weeks of his college career, and love stood by, waiting for the day of his deliverance.

The day at length came. The examination was passed, and De Vane was awarded a diploma, and an honor; not so high an honor as he had hoped for. But he felt that his course had been irregular; that he had given to some branches of study greater attention than he had bestowed on others, and that there were those in the class who, taking the whole course, excelled him. In some of his studies he was peerless; and as these were his favorite studies, he was satisfied. Then, too, he had the Valedictory of his Society to deliver, and this soothed him—cheered him indeed—for it was a great distinction, being conferred by the students themselves, who were his peers. The highest honor was given to Waring, and at this De Vane rejoiced. Congratulating his friend, De Vane sought Professor Niles, and urged him to prevail on the Faculty to excuse him from preparing an oration for Commencement-day, as he had to appear in the evening to deliver his Valedictory. His request was granted.

Relieved now from the pressure of College duties, the whole tide of his nature flowed with impetuous current toward Esther.

He sat down and wrote to Mrs. De Vane, giving her a full account of his course as a student, and requesting his aunt to obtain his father's consent for him to remain where he was, that he might enter the office of Mr. Clarendon, and study the law. In his letter he could not omit some mention of Esther, and of Mr. and Mrs. Springfield, describing them in language sufficiently glowing to interest his aunt, while he made no revelation of his love. He wrote also to his father, limiting himself to an expression of his wish to read law in the office of Mr. Clarendon, and describing him as a Virginian, a rising man, a brilliant orator, and an accomplished gentleman.

The Legislature assembled; eminent men from all parts of the State coming to the capital, to sojourn during the brief but brilliant session, which did not usually transcend four weeks.

The Governor was elected—a gentleman of wealth and great worth, residing at the capital—and a day was fixed for his inauguration. Waring was too much engrossed in preparing his speech for Commencement to attend, interesting as the event always was, and much as he respected the Governor-elect; so that De Vane went to the State-House alone. It was thronged; floor and galleries were densely packed. De Vane made his way into the lobby of the Representative Hall, and was standing near the door, when Mr. Clarendon saw him, and bowed to him. He was standing at the end of a sofa, upon which three ladies were seated, and De Vane recognized Esther as one of them. He observed Mr. Clarendon speak to her; she turned her face, saw De Vane, and bowed. He felt the blood rush through his veins wildly, and his frame almost shook with emotion. They had not met since the hour they had passed in her garden; and he did not, until this moment, when he saw her once more, comprehend her absolute power over him when he was in her presence. It was as if he approached the shrine of some celestial being, who spread around the sacred spot an enchantment too potent to be resisted. Yielding to an impulse which he could not resist, he made his way through the crowded lobby to the sofa where she was seated. Mr. Clarendon extended his hand to him, in welcome.

"Gallantly done, sir," said he. "I applaud your spirit, and think you have won your spurs."

De Vane smiled, and bowing very low to Esther, said:

"It has been so long, Miss Wordsworth, since I met you, that I could not deny myself the pleasure of coming to you, even through such obstructions."

"I am very much pleased to see you, Mr. De Vane," she replied, raising her sincere, soul-lit eyes, while a glow overspread her face. "You have been so engrossed with your studies, I learn, that you denied us the gratification of seeing you. So Mr. Waring informed us."

"Ah! Waring is a generous friend, and he has been studying to some purpose," he said; "he bears away the great prize."

"Yes; but he says that he is not sure you were not entitled to it; he speaks of you with enthusiasm."

"I suspect, Mr. De Vane," said Mr. Clarendon, "that you resemble me somewhat—if you will allow me to say so. You yielded to your tastes, and pursued such studies with ardor as gratified them."

"You are quite right, sir; nor do I regret it. Waring's thorough scholarship, however, fairly entitled him to the distinction which he obtained, against all possible competition."

"My friend, Professor Niles," said Mr. Clarendon, "was strongly disposed to place you at the head of the class, as I happen to know."

The two ladies seated by Esther listened eagerly to the conversation. One of them was Mrs. Clarendon, a splendid woman, of marvelous beauty. Her hair was very dark chestnut, and her eyes so deeply blue, that they might in shadow be mistaken for black. Above the medium height, her person was disposed to fullness, and yet her form was rounded and graceful. The traces of declining health could be seen in her fine face, slightly touched with sadness.

The other was the wife of a Senator from the sea-board. She was a blonde; her blue eyes, and light hair, which floated about her face in soft curls, gave her the appearance of extreme youth. She was almost fragile, and yet animated, and very lovely. Still De Vane felt that Esther was peerless, and he yielded her from the depths of his soul, a homage more intense than that which Eastern idolatry pays to its divinity.

A gun was heard, announcing the arrival of the Governor, and the ladies started, as the windows shook with the reverberation. A burst of music followed; and presently the Governor, with his attendants, entered, and the Speaker, in his blue silk gown, met him, conducted him to the platform, and the usual forms of the inauguration followed.

When they were ended, De Vane accompanied Esther, following Mr. Clarendon, who escorted the two ladies. The carriage was drawn up near the entrance to the grounds, and the three ladies entered it and drove away.

"Mr. De Vane," said Mr. Clarendon, "you must not leave us. What do you propose to do with yourself?"

"It is my wish, sir," said he, "to remain here and read law. I have written to Virginia, asking my father's permission to do so."

"I am very glad to hear it," replied Mr. Clarendon. "Why not come into my office?"

"It is just what I propose to do, Mr. Clarendon, if my father should approve my plans."

"This is the place for you," said the other, taking out of his pocket a very handsome snuff-box, and offering the fragrant tobacco to De Vane; "this is the very place for you. With your tastes, and, I shall add, your talents, you will find here an ample field." De Vane bowed.

"I prefer it to Virginia, taking all things into the account, and so will you."

He fixed his eyes upon De Vane's face, looked at him steadily for a minute, and then, lifting his hat, took leave of the young student with a bow of stately grace.

De Vane was fascinated. Attentions from eminent men are very grateful to the young, the ardent, the ambitious. It is delightful to be appreciated, especially by great souls; and the young student, full of noble and generous qualities himself, yielded to the grand nature of the man who had just turned away from him, the tribute of boundless admiration.

"*Mehercule!* Waring," said he, rushing into his apartment upon reaching the College, "what a magnificent man Clarendon is!"

"The whole world will soon acknowledge that," said Waring; "but what has happened to make you so enthusiastic about him just now?"

De Vane gave his friend a description of what had transpired at the capitol—the inauguration, his seeing Miss Wordsworth, his presentation to the ladies who were with her, and his interview with Mr. Clarendon.

"And after all that, you feel it necessary to invoke the aid of your friend Hercules, to help you sustain the burden of accumulating honors—do you?"

De Vane laughed. "Ah!" said he, "you know, Waring, I never swear."

## CHAPTER VII.

EACH one of us, perchance, may here,
On some blue morn hereafter,
Return to view the gaudy year,
But not with boyish laughter:
We shall then be wrinkled men,
Our brows with silver laden,
And thou this glen may'st seek again,
But never more a maiden.

THOMAS WILLIAM PARSONS.

THE College chapel began early in the day to show signs of a great occasion. Many seats were already filled. Carriages dashed through the Campus, bringing new-comers, and crowds of pedestrians made their way across it. Certain reserved seats were guarded by a committee composed of students, wearing badges. The stage was carpeted; chairs were placed thickly upon it, and the President's black servant, Scipio, (the students added Africanus to his name,) bustled about with an air as important as if the weight of the whole establishment rested on his sable shoulders. The younger students usually greeted his appearance with a shrill whistle; but he was much too grave to-day to pay the least attention to any such liberties. In the middle of the Campus, in striking contrast to all the surrounding activity and excitement, Dr. Hume's white mare, Blanche, grazed peacefully, enjoying the lingering herbage which survived the mild approach of winter. She was well known to the students, who sometimes exercised their skill shaping her mane and tail to suit their own taste, of which the Doctor never complained and Blanche seemed unconscious.

Then came the long procession of official persons. It had formed at the State House, and was now entering the wide western gate of the grounds. The Governor and Trustees, the Senators, the Representatives—all came, the dignitaries wearing their robes of office. As they entered the chapel, the whole audience rose to their feet. The Governor and Trustees ascended the platform and took their seats with the Faculty. The scene was a brilliant one. Official persons of the highest dignity laid aside their occupations to be present; for it was the policy of the State to cheer, by its countenance, as well as foster by its means, the noble institution, which already was a glory in the midst of it, crowning its brow like a diadem flashing with precious stones. Its graduates, some of them, were even now men of renown.

Ladies, too, in their rich and showy attire, made the place radiant; and Mrs. Springfield and Esther were seen by De Vane about midway in the chapel, seated by Mrs. Clarendon. Near them were two ladies, one of them, who seemed to be about forty years of age, with a complexion of extraordinary whiteness, and large, dark eyes. The other was a much younger person, scarcely above twenty, and her beauty was imperial. Classical in her whole aspect and form, her dark eyes full of lambent fire, and her rich, black hair, thrown back from the face, worn in a style quite unlike that of other ladies, she reminded De Vane of Aspasia in the full glory of her charms. The elder of the two ladies was dressed in rich mourning costume; the younger wore a dress of black velvet trimmed with lace, and her hat, which was singularly becoming to her, was of the same material; a diamond buckle, fastening the dark plume on the hat, flashed with every movement of her head. Seated by Waring on the platform, De Vane turned to him, and called his attention to the party of ladies, and asked who the persons were, seated on the right of Mrs. Clarendon. He replied that they were unknown to him.

A burst of music from the band opened the programme. Then came the orations, Waring leading the way with the salutatory in Latin, which he uttered so as to give full effect to the majesty of the language. After the several orations were ended, the President rose, and walked to the middle of the platform. He was very short, with a large, finely formed head and intellectual face ; the expression was that of great benevolence. His hair, now gray, had fallen off from the front of the head, leaving the temples bare, and the large zigzag veins on either side of the forehead were visible, through which the blood coursed like lightning. His waddling gait, short stature, and bent form, together with his strikingly intellectual head and face, presented a grotesque blending of different elements, and suggested the grave and ludicrous. The graduating class formed about him. He delivered a brief address to them, marked with practical sense and tinged with politics, handed to each his diploma; and then, the band playing a national air, the audience dispersed.

Mrs. Springfield and Esther waited to speak with Waring, who, with De Vane by his side, advanced to the ladies, and received their warm congratulations.

"Mr. Springfield," said Mrs. Springfield, "was called to the country yesterday, and expected to be here this morning. I know how deeply he will regret the loss of your oration to-day. And, Mr. De Vane, we shall all come to hear you this evening." He bowed very low.

"Mr. De Vane well knows," said Esther, "the interest which my uncle feels in him, and he will certainly join us."

"To be appreciated by Mr. Springfield," he replied, is very flattering to me; if I could only approach his standard, I should be most fortunate."

The ladies were evidently gratified at this tribute to one so much admired and beloved by them, for their faces beamed upon the young student.

The evening came. The chapel was again filled to its utmost capacity, and brilliantly lighted. The students had evidently exerted themselves to make the evening eclipse the splendor of the morning.

Again Mrs. Springfield and Esther were present, attended by Mr. Springfield and Waring, and seated nearer to the stage than in the morning. There, too, was Mr. Clarendon, this time in attendance on the ladies who had attracted De Vane's attention in the morning.

The Faculty were out in force, Professor Niles seated nearest the spot where his young friend was to stand, and his young, beautiful wife, full of animation, sat by his side.

The orator was announced. He came forward full of dignity and grace, blending the self-possession of manhood with the sensibility of extreme youth. A burst of applause greeted him, (he was a great favorite in the College,) and he bowed very low in recognition of the tribute. Every eye was fixed on him; and Esther felt her heart beat quicker than usual. De Vane had never breathed a word of love to her, but it would have been impossible not to see the admiration which his manner toward her always revealed when in her presence. She had not analyzed her heart; she was really unconscious of the depth of the interest which she felt in the young student; and she was ready now to chide herself for the emotion which she experienced. She had never loved; her soul was as fresh as Paradise before a cloud flitted over it, and from those pure lips no sigh had ever been breathed laden with any earthly passion. She became very pale, and feared that her aunt might observe how deeply she was moved.

"Esther," said Mrs. Springfield, turning to her as the applause died away, "this is enough to spoil our young Virginian."

She did not reply.

The subject of De Vane's oration was Classical Learning. It was a magnificent argument in defence of a generous education. The enriching influence of an acquaintance with the works of antiquity was exhibited; and Milton's example and authority were adduced in support of the proposition, that such learning best fitted a man for a high performance of the great tasks of life. The value of common-schools was not underrated; but it was insisted that an exalted training of even a few minds did more toward advancing the progress of our race, than the widest diffusion of the mere elements of knowledge. One illustration was received with rapturous applause. "The rising sun," said the orator, "first gilds the summit of the Alps, and afterward pours his splendors upon the mountain slopes, until, reaching the highest heavens, he bathes the valleys with his broad and fertilizing beams. So, in the world of letters, the leading minds catch the first glories of humanizing light, and reflect them from their elevated stand-points upon the surrounding world."

The leave-taking, in the closing part of the speech, was in fine taste, characterized by manliness, and yet imbued with sensibility. Deafening applause greeted De Vane as he took his seat; and Professor Niles, rising, was the first to grasp his hand. The other members of the Faculty offered their congratulations, and the leading students rushed forward eagerly, to pay their enthusiastic tribute to their splendid representative. It was a complete success—a triumph.

"Mr. Waring," said Mr. Springfield, "your young friend must be looked after. Such a mind must be made acquainted with something higher than classical learning; he must be brought under the influence of that power invoked by Milton, whom he seems so much to admire:

> 'And chiefly thou, O spirit! that dost prefer
> Before all temples the upright heart and pure,
> Instruct me.'

He will then learn how much sublimer are inspired themes than even the most heroic of heathen exploits; for his own great poet is described by Barrow as singing in worthy lines—the war in heaven:

> '*Stat dubius cui se parti concedat Olympus,*
> *Et metuit pugnæ ne superesse suæ,*
> *At simul in cœlis Messiæ insignia fulgent,*
> *Et currus animes, armaque digna Deo.*'"

"Oh!" exclaimed Mrs. Springfield, "it is so fine."

Esther said not a word; but the color had returned to her face; for it now glowed—she was radiant.

"Yes," said Waring, "I have long known what De Vane can do. His future involves a degree of responsibility nothing short of fearful."

"Mr. Clarendon was seen to quit the ladies under his charge, for a moment; and advancing toward De Vane, who had now descended from the stage, and was coming to where Mr. Springfield and his party stood, he grasped the young student's hand in both his, and said:

"I *thank* you, sir! Every man who loves the classics is indebted to you."

De Vane bowed with quiet dignity, but did not attempt to reply. His eyes sought Esther. She had seen and heard all; and as he reached the group where she stood, she greeted him with an uncontrollable flash of joyous sympathy, which sent its radiance into the depths of the young student's soul, with as bright a glory as a cloudless summer morning sheds over a landscape.

## CHAPTER VIII.

"Forgive me, if I can not turn away
From those sweet eyes that are my earthly heaven;
For they are guiding stars, benignly given
To tempt my footsteps to the upward way;
And if I dwell too fondly in thy sight,
I live and love in God's peculiar light."

Coleridge: *Michael Angelo.*

De Vane's College course was now ended, and the great world opened before him. There comes in life but one such season. The spring, with its all-vivifying fervor, comes upon nature with each recurring year; but it warms the human heart once, never to revisit it. When its promise deepens into the summer verdure, we look for the matured fruits, and then the autumnal glories, closing with the long, long winter.

Letters came to De Vane from home. His father approved his plans, and expressed his satisfaction at his course. Mr. Clarendon's family were known to him; but he had never met that gentleman—his reputation he was acquainted with—and General De Vane was gratified that his son was to enjoy the advantages, which an intimate association with such a man was sure to yield. He gave him his views, at some length, of public affairs, and looked forward to a complete triumph throughout the country, of his party, at the approaching election for the Presidency. "You will, of course, have read," he continued, "the late speech of Mr. Randolph. He denounces the Administration in just terms, and characterizes its abuses in language so severe, that it is thought the leading Cabinet Minister will call him out. I should regret this, for I admire the splendid abilities of that gentleman, nor do I give credence for a moment to the injurious suggestions which are made as to the terms of his obtaining office. His public services and his statesmanship entitled him to the position preëminently; and I know him too well to believe that he would sully his honor by a corrupt, or even humiliating agreement, in regard to any office. But I do agree with the strong classical figure which Mr. Randolph employs to describe the state of affairs at Washington. The Augean stable needs cleansing, and I think we have the Hercules who will accomplish the task."

The letter from his aunt was very long. It gave him the details of home affairs, in which he felt a deep interest, and which Mrs. De Vane recounted with charming fidelity. His home rose before him: his books, his servants, his horses—all came to view vividly; and he breathed once more the native mountain air, which had exhilarated his early youth. Passing to other matters, she wrote:

"I observe, my dear George, that you have found new friends lately, and found them, too, where I should hardly have looked for them—in the family of a Methodist minister. It seems he is not a clergyman, but one of Mr. Wesley's lay preachers. Do not understand me to mean that I disapprove you seeing such people; but I wish to guard you against an intimate acquaintance with them, or an intercourse so frequent as to bring you under their influence. I do not doubt that very good people are found among the Methodists. I have known such myself, and some of their preachers are men of great oratorical power. But a few days since I attended the chapel in our neighborhood, and heard Bishop McKendree, really a venerable man, and a most eloquent preacher. I was charmed with him, and under his sermon my tears fell like rain. He was stopping for two or three days with our friends, the Hamiltons, who are Methodists, you know, and as refined and cultivated as any persons of my acquaintance; but they are exceptions, you understand, to a rule so general, that I should hardly expect to find another family like them. Your description of Miss Wordsworth, I confess, interests me. Such beauty, such culture, such refinement, and such a self-sacrificing spirit, one rarely meets in any circle. But, dear George, have you not a little *élevé la vertu de votre sainte?* According to your description, she is quite a Saint Cecilia; and Malibran can not rival her. *Prenez garde!* My George, the illusion which love sheds around youth and beauty often misleads us.

"The Guilfords have just returned from Europe. Clara is wonderfully improved; and she remembers you vividly. I did not venture to inform her of your enthusiastic admiration of the young *Methodist;* it would have been cruel.

"Have you read the last book of Sir Walter Scott's, which has just been published, The Fair Maid of Perth? Remember that 'eagles must not pair with linnets.' Do not neglect your French. I like your sketch of the river-bank, the ferry-boats, and the soft landscape. What is Mr. Waring to do with himself—your first-honor man? He ought to shine. God bless you, my dear George.

"Yours, with true affection, HESTER DE VANE.

"P. S.—The Guilfords have this moment called. I forgot to say that Mr. Randolph spent yesterday with us, and asked after you with interest. He is charmed with your course as a student, and says that he knew you promised well; for you learned, when young, the three great accomplishments—'to ride, to shoot, and to speak the truth.'

"H. DE V."

The lights and shadows that flitted over De Vane's face as he read his aunt's letter were like those which we see on a summer landscape, when light clouds fly through the sky. He loved Mrs. De Vane dearly, and respected her judgment and taste, and the light way in which she spoke of Esther and her friends disturbed him. The strong feeling of *caste*, which was deep in his nature, was roused, and he felt his patrician tastes powerfully revived by the description of the Guilfords, a family of great wealth and of high ancestral pride. Their estate was the largest in Virginia, and the lands had descended from father to son through every generation since John Guilford—a younger brother of an English nobleman—first settled in the country. Clara he well remembered as a brilliant and attractive girl, dashing fearlessly on her spirited horse over the mountain-roads; for he had often accompanied her, when she had tasked his horsemanship in leaping ravines, and sometimes rail fences. She had now been in England on a visit to her relatives, for the families still kept up a frequent intercourse. How resplendent she must be, how superbly she would grace the mansion of a gentleman—sympathizing with all his tastes, and adorning his whole career!

He had walked to the public garden to read his letters, and he now paced through the broad walks, plunged in thoughts which made him insensible to every thing about him. Turning into one of the less frequented walks, he found little Mary Sinclair, seated on one of the benches, with a book in her hand, and the beautiful child whom De Vane remembered that he had seen seated at the feet of Esther upon his first visit to her school. They were enjoying the warm sunshine which, even on a December day, bathed the spot where they sat with the temperature of May in less favored climes. Mary knew him instantly, and her face beamed with pleasure as he approached. Rising from her seat, she gave him her hand with the sweet confidence of innocent childhood, unheeding aristocratic distinctions or the world's cold rules. De Vane was touched, and stooping down, he kissed the bright little cheek before him. She had come at this moment when the great world of state and fashion was spreading its attractions before the eyes of De Vane and shaking its gleaming gifts in his view, like a bird from some dear retreat which he knew and loved, to make its mute appeal to his better nature. Who has not, by a sight or a sound, been recalled from the dreams of ambition or the schemes of worldliness? The tones of music recall our fresh youth, our early love, our dear loyal friends long since parted and gone, and a glance of loving eyes melts in an instant the frost-work which had been forming about our hearts. Let the Switzer wander where he may, the *Ranz des Vaches* brings to his view the loved valleys of his childhood, and nature asserting her supremacy, he gives the tribute of his tears to the home of his happiest and most innocent hours.

"So you are out to-day, Mary," said De Vane. "Is it a holiday?"

"No, sir," replied the little girl; "Miss Esther sent me with Susan to the book-store to get a book which she had promised her, and we were just returning. We stopped here to rest a little while, as Susan can not walk so fast as I do, without becoming tired."

"And where is Miss Wordsworth?"

"At the cottage," she replied. "Mrs. Green is not very well to-day, and Miss Esther would not leave her till her headache got better. And," she added, "we must now go on, for she will be uneasy if we stay out too long."

"Well," said De Vane, "I will go with you." And taking the hand of little Susan, he walked by the side of the child. . A few minutes' walk brought them to Esther's inclosure, and opening the gate, De Vane walked with the children to the house.

Mary Sinclair darted forward, threw open the door, and

announced the approach of Mr. De Vane. Esther sprang to her feet and came forward, "blushing like the morn," and saw De Vane leading little Susan, whose steps could not keep up with Mary Sinclair's, and she felt that never had she seen him when he appeared to such advantage—not in the hour of his triumph before the assembled College, nor when walking amidst his peers, the object of universal admiration. A true man never does attract the higher qualities of a woman of noble nature so powerfully as when he descends from the sterner ways of life to use his strength in succoring or guiding or protecting the weak; and the picture which Esther saw as De Vane approached, tenderly helping the little child whom he held by the hand to walk as briskly as she desired, was never effaced from her heart. She smiled brightly, and running to meet them, her long fair hair catching the sunbeams as they fell, and encircling her like a glory, she exclaimed:

"Ah! Mr. De Vane, this is very good; you are achieving your highest triumph now, for you are guiding heedless little feet in the right path—the path that leads homeward." Tears were in her eyes—those glorious eyes, full of quenchless tenderness, and as De Vane saw her standing thus for a moment as she reached the spot where he stood, he felt that in her surpassing beauty and goodness she transcended even the visions which his imagination sometimes painted.

He entered the house with Esther, and found the little girls, the objects of her care, seated at their desks, neat and light desks, each one having exclusive jurisdiction over her own, and rivaling each other in the tidiness with which they were kept. The whole aspect of the place was cheerful. A small organ stood on one side of the room, used at the morning and evening devotions, in which the children took part, singing by note, for Esther made music a part of her system. Engravings—landscapes and cattle pieces—adorned the walls, and a light *étagère* held a collection of entertaining books, selected by Esther with care.

"Miss Wordsworth," said De Vane, "I begin to comprehend how you are able to lead this life. You have succeeded in blending the graceful with the good and useful in such a way that, an angel, straying from his native home, might pass the days here cheerfully."

Esther laughed heartily, and said: "Your tribute to my little cottage, Mr. De Vane, is so beautiful that I must ask you sometimes to visit it. Possibly, if you suffer from *ennui*, you may find relief here in talking to these little girls, and telling them of the world of knowledge they have yet to explore."

"Much better would it be for me," he replied, half gayly, half tenderly, "to sit at your feet and learn."

"You do me too much honor," said Esther, blushing. "Would you wish to see what your sable friend Jacob has been doing in my grounds within a few weeks? He is an extravagant admirer of you, and while I do not mean to detract in the least from your merits, I suspect that you owe something of his good opinion to your nativity. He thinks that every thing good and great must have some connection with Virginia. My grandfather was from that State, and therefore Jacob extends to me his good opinion, supposing that I possess inherited virtues."

De Vane had never known Esther so gay. Excusing herself for a moment, she went out of the room, and presently returned with her hat and shawl, accompanied by Mrs. Green, who had recovered from the morning's headache, and who greeted De Vane deferentially.

"Mrs. Green," said Esther, "I shall not return before to-morrow morning. Good-by."

The little girls rose, and stood until Esther quitted the room. Turning into a walk which De Vane had not yet explored, she conducted him to a part of the garden where the highest skill had been bestowed. Rare plants stood in tropical glory, sheltered by shrubbery, which protected without overshadowing them; the brilliant pomegranate displayed its beauties, and the luxuriant Cape jessamine shed its fragrance, safe from frosts; roses grew in profusion; birds, lingering where the reign of winter seemed unknown, made the air vocal.

"Miss Wordsworth," said De Vane, "has your place yet been named?"

"Oh! no," she replied; "it is too simple for such an ambitious distinction as a name. Parks and country-seats must aspire to such an honor."

"I will name it, if you will permit me. Shall I?"

Esther bowed.

"Let it be called 'LEASOWES,' then—the name of Shenstone's seat."

"Thank you, Mr. De Vane, for your appreciation of *my* little seat."

And from that day it always bore the name of LEASOWES.

"I should have called it Paradise," said De Vane, "but for the temptation, and the sin, and the expulsion, which are ever associated in my mind with the Eastern garden."

Esther looked at him earnestly. A shade of sadness rested for a moment on his features, and he added:

"Is it not too sad that since that hour of primeval bliss the world offers no retreat where the circling seasons may be passed, unconscious of the doom that awaits us—the inevitable grave?"

"But," said she, "there *is* a paradise where no shade of sorrow can come, where every joy is immortal, and where we need fear neither sin, nor temptation, nor expulsion."

She spoke with trembling earnestness, and they walked side by side silently.

"But, Miss Wordsworth," at length said De Vane, "what is to be done to make this world a happy seat? It is so conventional, so imperious in its exactions, so heartless in its estimate of the good and the beautiful, that I sometimes wish for some happy valley, like that which shut in the Abyssinian Prince. The shrine of the world is a cruel one, more so than that of the Mexican Indians, who tore the palpitating heart from the living breast, and offered it to their god as a sacrifice: its throbs soon ceased upon the broad rock where it was placed; but society leaves the heart still to throb on, in the long course of lapsing years, and yet tortures the victim by resisting every true impulse and every natural emotion. In its dread imperiousness, it listens neither to the appeals of youth nor the voice of nature. The Greeks would have sacrificed Iphigenia, in her innocence and beauty, regardless of her tears and entreaties, had not the relenting goddess at whose shrine she stood, rescued and saved her; but it was their love of glory that impelled them to the deed. Society brings to its shrine victims that are to be sacrificed to the advancement of pride and selfishness."

He spoke with bitterness, and Esther, turning a quick glance upon his face, saw that it was very stern. She did not comprehend him. She saw that he was in some extraordinary mood, that he was unhappy; but she could not read the mysterious depth of the shadow which had darkened his young and bright spirit. She did not know that Mrs. De Vane had thrown such temptations in his way, that she had called upon his ardent nature to tear itself away from the sweet and purifying influences which had of late been attracting him. De Vane had been educated to respect the opinions of the world, to value its conventionalisms, and to seek its high places—not at the sacrifice of truth or self-respect; but the broad social distinctions of life were made to appear very important; and his relatives would doubtless be as much shocked at his taking for a wife a person not strictly of their own *caste*, as the royal household are when a king contracts a *morganatic* marriage. He felt this; and once more in the presence of Esther, his spirits rose with indignation against a system which would rank such a being below its scale, merely because she adopted a religious creed more evangelical than it recognized, and cast in her lot with a people too fervent in their faith, and too exact in their lives, to please the taste of the votaries of fashion, or the circle which thought, because it was exclusive, it was refined.

Esther was silent, and De Vane continued:

"Is all this life to be sacrificed to the future? Is the glory of this our earthly being to be ignored, that we may attain that Paradise of which you speak, and where we shall be happy and sinless?"

"Oh! no, Mr. De Vane," she replied. "The highest glory of this life is in perfect harmony with that future glory which awaits the faithful. But we must not follow false lights; we must not suffer our own hearts to betray us; we must learn what true glory is."

"Would you condemn fame, and wealth, and power, Miss Wordsworth?"

"I would condemn nothing really noble; but I would not make the attainment of fame, or wealth, or power, the guiding-star of my course through life. May I remind you of the words of the Great Exemplar of humanity, 'Seek ye first the kingdom of God and his righteousness, and all these things shall be added unto you'?"

There was a thrilling tenderness in the tones of her voice, which reached the depths of De Vane's soul. He was deeply affected, and he did not immediately reply. When he did speak, he said:

"Miss Wordsworth, you will pardon me for saying that I feel as Adam must have felt in the paradise which Milton describes, when the angel discoursed to him of the world that lay before him:

> 'The angel ended,
> And in Adam's ear so charming left his voice.'"

Esther blushed deeply.

"Mr. De Vane, when do you return to Virginia?" she asked, after walking a few steps in silence.

"It may be never," he replied; "I am to enter Mr. Clarendon's office, and I can not read my future."

Her embarrassment deepened; she trembled. At this moment they reached the gate, and she said:

"Mr. De Vane, I am about to return to Mr. Springfield's; I am expected there at this hour. Having made a longer stay here than I anticipated, I must beg you to excuse me."

"Let me accompany you," said De Vane; "having detained you, I must atone for it by seeing you safely home."

Esther smiled, and they walked together to the residence of Mr. Springfield. De Vane took leave of her, and sought his lodgings.

The patrician felt that there was a higher glory than any that the world could give, and he felt too in that hour that he would gladly renounce all the splendor of the realm where society sat supreme, the Sphinx of the modern world, its cold eyes looking to the future, and its dread form the impersonation of heartlessness and power, to follow through the world's vain mask such a guide as had just now turned from him her soul-lit face.

## CHAPTER IX.

> "She's dangerous:
> Her eyes have power beyond Thessalian charms,
> To draw the moon from heaven. For eloquence,
> The sea-green sirens taught her voice their flattery;
> And, while she speaks, night steals upon the day
> Unmarked of those that hear."
>
> Dryden's *Cleopatra.*

De Vane had entered the office of Mr. Clarendon, and taken up his course of study. Waring was about to visit his friends in Georgia, but it was his intention to return, and study for the ministry, availing himself of the use of Mr. Springfield's extensive library, and enjoying that gentleman's instructions. Sincerely attached to De Vane, he wished to be near him; and it was his hope that he might contribute somewhat toward bringing the noble nature of his friend under the controlling power of evangelical religion. He was well acquainted with his generous qualities, and he ardently desired to see his imperial intellect submit itself to the teachings of Him who spake as never man spake. Somewhat bewildered with German speculations, and thoroughly aristocratic in his tastes, there was much to hinder his coming to the feet of One who invited the weary and heavy-laden to seek him, because he was meek and lowly. Yet the love of truth within him was strong, his scorn of the meaner ways of life was intense, and he had the courage to avow his sentiments in regard to any thing. His nature was too grand to suffer him to sacrifice himself to false gods, if they could be stripped of the illusion which invested them.

The two gentlemen were walking in the main street near the State House, when a very handsome English coach, drawn by a pair of splendid horses, dark bays, with black manes and tails, two black servants in livery seated on the box, came dashing by. In the carriage the two ladies were seated, who had attracted De Vane's attention on Commencement day; and as they passed the gentlemen, the younger of the two looked quickly out, as if she desired to observe them. It was but for a moment, and presently the carriage drew up, and the ladies, alighting from it, entered the State House.

"Waring," said De Vane, "do you know those ladies?"

"I do not," he replied; "they must be strangers. The person who leaned from the carriage is very beautiful. I never saw a finer face."

"Brilliant," said the other; "and their equipage is perfect in its appointments. Those are English horses."

"Indeed! I share your taste for fine horses, De Vane," said Waring.

"And for fine women, too?"

"*Cela depend*," answered Waring. "I am not easily dazzled. I should not choose a woman as I would a horse—for a glossy coat, fine form, and fine action only."

"Yet, Waring, you would demand beauty?"

"I do not underrate it, but I should require the intellect and the soul to harmonize with the outward form."

"As in the case of Cleopatra—*par exemple*."

"Never," replied Waring, "never. A merely voluptuous, accomplished woman could never ensnare me."

"What! not such a woman as enslaved Julius Cæsar, and held Mark Antony captive in her gilded saloons, until he lost a world?"

"No; for in the society of such a woman I might lose what is worth more than the world," said Waring gravely.

They met Mr. Clarendon. "Ah! young gentlemen!" he

exclaimed gayly. "*Vous allez ensemble*, eh! I am fortunate in meeting you, for I was seeking you. The Duke of Saxe-Weimar is here, and we are to entertain him to-morrow evening. The time for preparation is so short that I must press you both into the service. Mrs. Clarendon has just taken up Miss Wordsworth, and they are now driving to distribute verbal invitations, there being no time to prepare cards. You must be good enough to do the same thing for the gentlemen. Here is a list of chosen names."

Waring and De Vane expressed their readiness to serve him, and took their leave. Mr. Clarendon proceeded to the State House.

"The Duke of Saxe-Weimar!" exclaimed De Vane. "I am delighted."

"Yes," said Waring, "it will be a rare treat for you—you are half German. By the way, too, we shall meet eminent political men there. Senator Caldwell is in town, and he will of course be present."

"Indeed," replied De Vane. "I shall be gratified to meet him. I am assured that he is brilliant in conversation."

"So I learn," said Waring.

They called a carriage, and drove to such places as their instructions required.

Thursday evening came. It was propitious, cloudless, and mild. The moon was too young to afford much light, but the stars were out in countless hosts.

As Waring and De Vane approached the residence of Mr. Clarendon, they observed that it was brilliantly lighted. In the extensive garden which surrounded the house, lamps were hung from the trees, and the scene was one of surpassing beauty. They entered, and were ushered into the splendid rooms: the walls adorned with pictures, the works of masters, which had been collected by Mr. Clarendon in Europe; old armor, busts, elegantly bound books, musical instruments, and the nameless objects which give such a charm to houses where taste and genius guide the decorations.

Mrs. Clarendon, with Esther by her side, stood to receive the guests, and as the two gentlemen entered, the latter colored a little for an instant, but soon recovered her self-possession, and welcomed them gracefully. Her dress was in perfect harmony with her style of beauty; simple, rich, and fitted to her shape, so as to show the form to advantage, without being in the extreme of fashion. She wore no jewelry, except a diamond ring, of extraordinary brilliancy, but in her hair natural flowers were braided. The rooms were rapidly filling, and De Vane, after exchanging a few words with Esther, passed on to where Mr. Clarendon stood, surrounded by some half-dozen gentlemen. One of these was a striking-looking person, short, stoutly built, with a grand head. His features were large, the lips somewhat sensuous, the *tout ensemble* pleasing. He was a member of the House of Representatives from the largest city in the State, and a man of mark. Both as a speaker and writer, he was distinguished for the richness and power of his style. He had travelled with Mr. Clarendon in Europe, and they admired each other. De Vane was presented to him, and he expressed his gratification at meeting the young gentleman, saying that he heard his speech in the College chapel, and was so much pleased that he had been wishing for the opportunity to tender his congratulations.

"Your vindication, sir, of classical learning," said he, "does you great credit."

De Vane thanked him warmly, saying that commendation from such a source was most gratifying to him.

At this moment the Duke of Saxe-Weimar entered, and came directly to where Mr. Clarendon was standing. He was gigantic in stature, broad-shouldered, with enormous hands and feet, a beaming, intellectual face, and a certain grace in his movements. He wore glasses, and looked altogether like a man of culture.

He was presented to the gentlemen grouped about him, and he entered into animated conversation with them, in which the leading part was borne by the eminent man who had just addressed himself to De Vane.

Waring came up, and touching De Vane's shoulder, invited him to accompany him to the front drawing-room. As they entered it, they saw the two ladies who had attracted their attention the day before in their carriage, standing in the centre of the room, in conversation with Mrs. Clarendon. The younger lady was of such resplendent beauty, that she was dazzling. Her rich, dark hair, turned back from the face, was gathered in heavy braids, through which pearls were intertwisted; and her large, lustrous eyes, shaded by the long lashes, were full of sentiment—a sentiment too pure for passion, and not sad enough for sorrow—fascinated those on whom they rested. Her finely-moulded arms were as perfect as if chiseled from marble, and her attitude was the impersonation of grace. Her costume was brilliant. The dress, of purple velvet, trimmed with black Brussels lace, fell in rich folds about her person, which was scarcely taller than that of Esther, but more matured. She wore diamond bracelets, set in enamel; a diamond necklace to match, and a single ring, in which a diamond of large size flashed.

"De Vane," said Waring, "Mrs. Clarendon wished you to be presented to the ladies with whom she is conversing."

"*Mehercule!* Waring," replied De Vane, "what a superb woman!"

"She is very brilliant," replied the other.

De Vane advanced, and was presented by Mrs. Clarendon to the two ladies, Mrs. Habersham and Miss Godolphin. Waring had already enjoyed that honor, and entered into conversation with Mrs. Habersham, a stately but agreeable lady.

"You must have come to us but recently, Miss Godolphin," said De Vane, "or I should have met you, surely."

"I came only last week," she replied, "but I have not been ignorant of you, Mr. De Vane. I met in Switzerland, a few months since, the Guilfords, of Virginia, who spoke of you, and told me that you were here at college, and I had the pleasure of hearing your valedictory."

De Vane acknowledged the compliment with a low bow. "You are, then, quite lately from Europe," he said. "I had learned that the family of which you speak had returned, through my aunt, Mrs. De Vane."

"They corresponded with her while abroad, and I felt, upon coming home—for this is my home—that I almost knew you personally."

De Vane felt gratified at her gracious interest in him. So brilliant, so attractive, so commanding, that she should honor him with her regards was indeed a distinction. When on the threshold of manhood, attentions from a woman of our own age, or somewhat above it, if she be lovely and accomplished, have a peculiar charm for us. They please, while they flatter our *amour propre.*

"I am most fortunate," said De Vane, "in having been favorably reported to you, before meeting you."

"Yes," she answered, "and you must allow me to say that, having heard your speech, I feel myself indebted to the friends who prepared me for such a performance. I love the classics, Mr. De Vane, nor do I think there is any thing in modern literature which can rival them."

"And which of the works which have come down to us from the golden ages do you prefer?"

"Oh! Homer, of course."

"Indeed, do you find him more agreeable than Virgil?"

"A thousand times more so," she replied. "He is heroic, and he does justice to woman."

"How?" said De Vane, smiling. "In making the charms of Helen inflame the world with war, and bring destruction upon Troy?"

"Not at all," she answered. "Helen was not worthy of such deeds, wrought in her behalf. It was to Menelaus a calamity that he succeeded in winning her. But in Andromache and Penelope he vindicates our sex."

"And how does Virgil offend you?" inquired De Vane.

"By representing Dido as dying of grief, because forsaken by Æneas—a most unworthy passion; for he was not a hero. Had he been, I might have pardoned her."

"Then, too, she had loved before," said Waring, who had for some minutes been standing, with Esther on his arm, in silence.

Miss Godolphin flushed to the temples, turning to the speaker with a glance which seemed to seek to read his soul. She did not reply.

"Do you think it possible," said De Vane, "that Æneas really loved the Carthaginian queen?"

"No," said Miss Godolphin. "If he had loved, how could he forsake her?"

There was the deepest sadness in her tone, and a shadow came over her face.

"The love of glory," said De Vane, "impelled him to spread his sails, and she could no longer detain him."

"How was it, then," she replied, "that Cleopatra held Antony? What do you say, Miss Wordsworth?"

Esther started. "I think," she said, "that Antony was true to neither Octavia nor Cleopatra. If he had loved either, he would have been loyal, and his ambition would have yielded to his better nature."

De Vane was astonished. Here stood a young girl, scarcely seventeen, and yet she had solved a problem which the world was discussing, with so true a judgment that all who heard her yielded to it.

"You are right," said Miss Godolphin. "Antony was incapable of love. The ruling passion was the love of glory, and no tender sentiment can live in its fierce blaze. Hector was a hero, but he would never have deserted Andromache, save to defend her against the invading Greek! See with what tenderness he takes leave of her and embraces his boy."

There was a wild, passionate sadness in her tones which touched the hearts of the group about her. She might herself have been some queen, standing in her superb beauty, sad at desertion, and yet conquering it by pride. What a contrast Esther presented! Her glorious beauty was that of youth unsaddened by a shade of infelicity. Her brilliant complexion, her auburn hair, her deep-blue eyes, with heaven mirrored in their clear depths, her sylph-like form, and her perfectly-chiseled features, over which no cloud of earthly sorrow had ever darkened, constituted a combination of charms at once pure and glowing. As they stood near each other, they seemed the impersonation of Night and Morning, both gloriously beautiful: the one adorned with the stars of evening for a diadem; the other decked with dewy flowers, which the burning rays of the sun had not yet kissed. The one brilliant, like Ariadne, her crown flashing from her brows after the desertion of Theseus; the other like Iphigenia in her innocence, pure enough to minister in the temple of Diana.

"I quite agree with you," said Waring, "that the love of glory must be subdued before we see any of the objects of life in their true proportions. There is something in our nature grander than ambition—the love of truth, for the sake of truth. It is ignoble to live for human applause. It is glorious to seek, amidst the illusions of life, the path which leads to a realm whose shadows are lost in all-revealing light.

Miss Godolphin looked at him earnestly. "And how," said she, "are we to find that path in the bewildering mazes about us?"

"It is marked by foot-prints," replied Waring, "that lead us unerringly."

At this moment Mr. Clarendon entered the room with the Duke of Saxe-Weimar, and the gentleman who had been in conversation with him. They all came to where Miss Godolphin was standing, and the gentlemen were introduced to the party.

"You have just returned from Europe, I learn," said the Duke. "Were you in Germany?"

"Yes," replied Miss Godolphin, "and in Weimar."

"Ah! and were you pleased?"

"I could not be otherwise," she answered. "It well deserves its name, the ATHENS of Germany."

The Duke bowed low.

Miss Godolphin continued: "The tone of society is charming. Nature and genius conspire to make the place attractive. Such gardens I never saw. The theatre is classical, and the scholars entertaining. What more can one want on earth?"

The conversation now became general. The Duke asked Esther if she admired the works of his countrymen, and she replied:

"Such of them as are known to me possess a certain charm, but I can not judge them critically."

"Mendelssohn, for instance?"

"Do you speak of the younger," said she.

"Oh! no—Moses, the author of Phædon."

"I admire his fine spirit," said Esther, "but I must lament his blindness in refusing to acknowledge the Redeemer."

The Duke bowed.

"Then," said the gentleman who stood by his side,

whose fine head Esther had observed with admiration, "you may like Wieland?"

"I admire him," she answered, "but fear that his ideal of moral beauty was not that of the Christian believer."

"I am not by any means sure of that," said the gentleman. "His father was a Lutheran divine, and his tutor deeply imbued with the spirit of religion; and in his Dialogues of the Gods, it would seem that he intended in the words of the Unknown to pay a tribute to Christianity as the only system which can remodel men."

Waring was delighted.

"I must now thank you," said De Vane, "for your vindication of one of the most agreeable of all writers."

"I must confess my admiration for Lessing," said Miss Godolphin. "His love of the beautiful was intense; he was not misled by the French taste, but made his countrymen acquainted with the creations of the ancients and the moderns—of the Greeks and of Shakespeare."

Mr. Clarendon's face beamed. "Allow me, Miss Godolphin," he said, "to thank you;" and with his hand upon his breast, he made her a stately bow.

The conversation continued. The merits of Goethe, of Schiller, of Herder, and of Jean Paul Richter were discussed.

"Upon my soul," exclaimed the Duke, "I can fancy myself at Weimar. Nowhere in this country have I found any thing like this before."

De Vane had fascinated him by his enthusiasm, and the acquaintance of the others with the literature of his country had been unexpected.

A party of gentlemen who had been dining together now entered, and among them Senator Caldwell, accompanied by Professor Locke and Professor Niles. The Senator's appearance was striking. Tall, almost slender, erect, with features distinctly chiseled, and eyes that blazed, he was the impersonation of intellectual power. Soon after his entrance, the conversation turned upon metaphysics, and the Senator engaged in it with ardor, finding in Professor Locke an antagonist who drew out all his power. His whole faculties were engaged, and his profound analytical power displayed itself in the most captivating way.

"What do you say to that, Le Grande?" he at length said, addressing himself to the gentleman whose short stature and intellectual appearance had already attracted the attention of De Vane; and from that time he, together with Mrs. Clarendon, took part in the discussion, which was only interrupted by the notes of the piano: some hand of surpassing skill was touching its keys, and the gentlemen all gathered about the performer.

Miss Godolphin was seated at the instrument, and was playing a piece of German music which had just appeared. Her execution was brilliant. After the piece was ended, Professor Niles asked her to sing. A shade of sadness touched her features, but after a moment's hesitation, she sang Moore's beautiful lines:

"I saw from the beach, when the morning was shining,
A bark o'er the waters move gloriously on;
I came to that beach when the sun was declining—
The bark was still there, but the waters were gone!"

She sang the entire lines, in tones of wild, passionate, almost wailing sadness, until she uttered the words,

"Give me back, give me back the wild freshness of morning!"

when she threw an energy into them which was startling.

An irrepressible burst of applause followed. Her glove had fallen, and as De Vane stooped to hand it to her, he observed that tears were in her eyes. She rose, and turned away.

Mrs. Niles was prevailed on to sing. She took her seat, touched the keys with the skill of an *artiste*, and sang a song which had just been set to music by a royal hand—

"Partant pour la Syrie."

The Duke was charmed. He had heard it in Europe, and he exclaimed: "You know that the composer is in exile. Sad that the enemies of the peace of Europe should bring misfortunes upon such a spirit!"

Mr. Clarendon turned to Esther, and taking her hand, seated her at the instrument. She was pale, but she offered no remonstrance. She felt how very trying the ordeal was through which she was about to pass, for her own knowledge of music disclosed the faultless performance of those who had preceded her. She ran her fingers over the keys lightly, and then played a selection from Felix Mendelssohn Bartholdy's "Walpurgisnacht," and sang a translation of the words of Goethe. The effect was magical, the power of the music rose into sublimity. Miss Godolphin seemed breathless with emotion, and the Duke was enthusiastic in his applause; his great hands, hid in white kid gloves, made the room echo, while his *Bravo! Bravo!* rang like a trumpet. De Vane could not utter a word, but his excitement was so visible, that Mr. Clarendon smiled as he saw his earnest face and compressed lips. Esther's form had seemed to be swept by the power of the music; her face wore a glory that was caught from the inspiration of the moment, and when the keys were silent, her faultless hands were clasped unconsciously before her. Never had De Vane witnessed such enthusiasm in her before; she was like a sibyl absorbed by the revelation of her own faculties. Waring spoke to her, and asked her to add a single song more.

"What shall it be?" said Esther.

"Any thing which you may select," he replied.

She sang those lines in which the genius of Moore seemed under the influence of heavenly inspiration—

"O Thou who driest the mourner's tear!"

Her voice almost trembled with sensibility, and as the dying cadence was lost in the air, the sympathy of the company was so deep and their taste so appreciative, that not a word was uttered.

She rose from the instrument, and Miss Godolphin, advancing, took her hand in both her own, and said:

"Miss Wordsworth, I thank you for interpreting music to me in a way which makes me feel its glory."

"Such a tribute from you, Miss Godolphin," said Mr. Clarendon, "my young friend may well prize."

"I prize it very highly, Mr. Clarendon," said Esther.

Some one proposed that they should visit the lighted garden. De Vane gave his arm to Esther, and they walked out, followed by Waring and Miss Godolphin and others of the party. The scene was one of rare beauty. The walks led through evergreens lighted with lamps of various colors.

"Miss Wordsworth," said De Vane, "you must have thought me misanthropic when we last met, but you cannot comprehend, of course, my social philosophy; you have seen nothing of the heartlessness of society."

"No, Mr. De Vane," she replied, "I have found nothing but kindness. I see that there is unhappiness in the great world about me, but I seem to walk in a charmed circle."

"Yes, you remind me of what Coleridge says:

'O lady! we receive but what we give,
And in our life alone does nature live.

. . . . .

Ah! from the soul itself must issue forth
A light, a glory, a fair luminous cloud
Enveloping the earth.'

All within you is so bright that you see the world about you under the light which your own spirit sheds over it."

"You judge me quite too favorably, Mr. De Vane," said Esther.

"My observation has taught me," he said, "that the world surrenders the beautiful and the good for the ad vancement of its own system. It worships false gods, and the sacrifices which it brings to their altars are the most costly of all that are laid upon any shrine—living hearts. It reproduces in modern times the cruel worship of that people denounced in the Scriptures, who made their sons and their daughters pass through the fire in the wildness of their cruel idolatry."

"I do not know that I understand you, Mr. De Vane," said Esther, surprised at his earnestness.

"I trust," he replied bitterly, "that you never may."

"Perhaps," she said, "you are taking your estimate of society from Coleridge. But you would not abandon it, as he proposed at one time to do, nor reconstruct it upon his ideal system—would you?"

"I'm not sure that I would not," said De Vane. "I value the conventionalisms of the world less every day that I live."

"Better contend with what is bad in the world, and strive to make it happier," said Esther. "I do not think that we should withdraw from the world, because it is distasteful to us."

"But," said De Vane, "it offends me. I love its better aspects, but I scorn its meaner ones; and so perverse am I, that I am repelled on the other side by goodness itself, if it has not the graces which certainly do belong to good society. I sympathize intensely with the Greeks in their love of the beautiful, the *τό καλον*. I could not worship the good, if stripped of its loveliness."

"Undine," replied Esther, "might have felt thus before she received a soul, but surely not afterward."

"De Vane," called out Waring, "do you intend that Miss Wordsworth shall lose her supper?"

"Ah!" said De Vane, "it seems that we must not forget our bodies. We were just speaking about the soul, Waring."

"Indeed!" he replied. "I am glad to learn that your thoughts are so well directed."

"We, too, were looking heavenward," said Miss Godolphin; "for I was just saying that these lamps could not obscure those stars that burn so far above us, though they seem so brilliant."

"They looked upward, and the quenchless stars could be seen in the pure heavens, burning calmly far above; lights which would still endure, when the glaring lamps were all extinguished, and the scene about them lost its illusions. They entered the house, and a gay conversation followed at the supper-table.

When the guests were dispersing, De Vane sought Esther, adjusted her wrappings, and conducted her to the carriage, where Mr. and Mrs. Springfield were already seated. Before reaching it, he said:

"We did not conclude our conversation, Miss Wordsworth. I am in a labyrinth, and you must extricate me."

She smiled, but made no reply. The carriage dashed away; and De Vane really felt as if he had lost a GUIDE.

## CHAPTER X.

"THE highest honors that the world can boast
Are subjects far too low for my desire;
The brightest beams of glory are at most
But dying sparkles of Thy living fire."

FRANCIS QUARLES.

ON Saturday, at noon, a small traveling-carriage, drawn by a pair of well-matched dark bay horses, drove up to Mr. Springfield's residence. Two gentlemen alighted from it, one of them a venerable man, of most impressive appearance, the other much younger. Mrs. Springfield came to the door to meet them, and her face flushed with pleasure.

"Bishop McKendree!" she exclaimed, "I am delighted to see you. We were looking for you;" and she conducted the gentlemen into the house.

Bishop McKendree and his traveling companion, a young minister of the Tennessee Conference, were welcomed with a warmth that gratified them, and made them feel that they had reached a *home*. Some such homes there were throughout the wide extent of country embraced within the Bishop's diocese, where it was felt to be an honor to receive such a guest; but it was with very great satisfaction that he entered this house. Its well-known hospitality, its refinement, its abounding comforts, and the ties of personal friendship—all endeared it to him. Esther came in soon after the Bishop's arrival, and she was warmly greeted by him. He had known her father. Laying his hand solemnly upon her head, bright with its rich golden hair, he said:

"May the Lord bless thee, with the blessings of heaven above and of earth beneath!"

As she raised her head, Mrs. Springfield saw that tears trembled upon her eyelids; and Esther felt that she bore away with her, as she left the room, a treasure of priceless value in the blessing of an apostolic man, whose hands had been laid upon the head of her father, consecrating him to the self-sacrificing ministry in which he had laid down his life. Mr. Springfield, who had been out on horseback, arrived, and hastened to renew the welcome which had already been extended to the venerable guest. In those days the visit of a Bishop of the Methodist Episcopal Church was an event as marked and as highly appreciated as a royal visit to some nobleman, when his palatial residence is graced by the presence of his sovereign. In the evening several of the leading Methodists of the town came in, and some hours were passed in delightful conversation. Waring was present, and gave great interest to the conversation, his fine mind being fully roused, and his spirits exhilarated by the presence of a man so much venerated by him. The social qualities of the Bishop were such as to make him an agreeable companion for both young and old. There was dignity, but nothing of coldness in his manner; and his benevolence was so shining, that children and servants felt they could approach him. The hour of nine came—the Bishop's hour for retiring; the Bible and the hymn-book were placed on a table by his side, and he proceeded to conduct the evening service. After reading one of the Psalms, he rose and gave out the lines of a hymn, which all joined in singing; and then, all kneeling, he offered a simple, earnest prayer. Upon resuming their seats, every one felt calmed—spiritualized—as if an angel, in passing had shaken his wings, and left a heavenly atmosphere, which filled the place. The Bishop rose, and taking leave of the company, was conducted to his chamber. Most of the persons present left at the same time; but Waring remained, and continued for some time in conversation with the family.

Mrs. Springfield expressed her gratification at having the Bishop with them; saying that they were entertaining "an angel," but not "unawares."

"Yes," replied Waring, "no purer man, nor kindlier one, breathes the breath of life. He blends the courage of Peter with the gentleness of John. What stay is he to make with you, Mrs. Springfield?"

"He will not leave us before Thursday. He is about to preside, as you know, over the Conference, which is to meet in Augusta."

"Yes, and he can reach there easily by Saturday in the forenoon, taking an early departure on Thursday. I must bring De Vane to see him. He is a Virginian, you know; so is the Bishop; and he has heard favorably of him, through an aunt of his in that State."

Mrs. Springfield said: "We shall be happy to see Mr. De Vane. I think highly of him. Do you know his religious sentiments, Mr. Waring?"

"He has no well-defined religious opinions," replied Waring. "He was brought up in the Protestant Episcopal Church, and yields a general assent to its creed, I believe; but for two or three years he has been looking into German literature, and I fear lives somewhat in cloud-land."

"Yes," said Mr. Springfield, "I remember your saying something of that kind to us when we first made his acquaintance. We must bring him into the clear light."

"I should rejoice to see him reach it," said Waring. "His nature is a noble one, and if converted, he would not hesitate to profess his faith anywhere, though the whole country rang with the cry: 'Is Saul also among the prophets?'"

"I hope the cry may soon be heard," said Mr. Springfield.

"It's a little strange," said Waring, "that De Vane has never heard more than one sermon by a Methodist minister in all his life. He heard you, you remember, and he was delighted; but he insists that such a discourse in a Methodist Chapel is to be heard only on rare occasions."

They all smiled, and Mr. Springfield remarked that he was very much obliged to him for his appreciation.

"You will bring him to hear the Bishop to-morrow morning, Mr. Waring, will you not?" said Esther.

"Oh! yes, he will feel an interest in him from what his aunt has written. She describes him as a most eloquent preacher."

"How is it," asked Mrs. Springfield, "that he is so exclusive? His nature seems to be a generous one."

"Why," replied Waring, "his family is one of the most aristocratic in Virginia. He is a PATRICIAN, so by descent, by alliance, by education, by taste—in short, by every thing. The great wealth of General De Vane puts it in his power to give his son—and George is an only son—every advantage. He would not permit him even to attend a common-school, but employed masters for him at home; and he would not have consented that he should enter any other college in the Southern country than this. The great wonder is, that he is not spoiled; but he is not in the least so. He loves rank, glory, fame, but he loves truth better than either; and while he feels the value of *caste*, he will never sacrifice himself for any ignoble object. Many would call his ideal of the good and the true romantic, but his sterling sense is not under any illusion; and he would sacrifice every thing before he would abandon what he felt that he ought to adhere to and vindicate."

"You speak of your friend with enthusiasm, Mr. Waring," said Mrs. Springfield.

"He rouses my nature," replied Waring. "He is my friend. I am strongly attached to him; he rises so far above the ordinary standard of young men whom I meet, that I honor him as much as I love him."

"We shall expect you to bring him to see us, Mr. Waring," said Mrs. Springfield. "I am sure that he will be charmed with the Bishop, who has himself the appearance of a patrician."

Esther had listened to the conversation with interest, but she remained silent.

Waring rose and took his leave.

Sunday came, and overspread the world with its tranquil beauty. The arrival of Bishop McKendree being widely known, the Methodist church was filled to overflowing at an early hour. The citizens generally, of all denominations and of every class, pressed into the humble meeting-house. The aristocratic, the great, and the humble, were all eager to hear a man so eminent for his virtues, his heroic services in the cause of Christ, and his eloquence as a preacher. Waring was in his accustomed seat, De Vane by his side; and as the former glanced over the congregation, he was pleased to see Mr. Clarendon, Mr. Hallam, and other eminent men; and among the ladies, Mrs. Clarendon, with Mrs. Habersham and Miss Godolphin. The Governor of the State entered with his family, and seats were found for them quite near the pulpit.

Precisely at half-past ten o'clock, Bishop McKendree entered the church, attended by Mr. Springfield and Mr. Kennedy, the pastor, and walked up the aisle to the pulpit. The appearance of the Bishop was very impressive. Nearly six feet in height, and well-formed, he was the impersonation of manly vigor and activity, yielding somewhat to the advance of age. His face exhibited intellectual power, blended with benevolence and firmness. His hair fell away from the forehead in heavy locks, and rested on his collar. He wore a long-waisted, single-breasted black cloth coat, with a standing collar, black vest, and breeches of the same material terminating at the knee, where they were fastened with silver buckles, long black stockings, and polished shoes, with silver buckles—the style of dress which one sees in the portrait of Washington by Stuart. After kneeling for a few moments in silent prayer, the Bishop rose, and opened the services by reading from the Scriptures of the Old and the New Testaments. He then read the hymn deliberately and impressively, and afterward recited the lines, two by two, while the congregation, rising to their feet, sang them with a good spirit, the Bishop pausing occasionally to invite attention to the sentiments which they were uttering in song. The prayer which followed was comprehensive, earnest, spiritual, and deeply reverential, as if the glories of the eternal world were in view. No taste, however critical, could be offended; no heart, however worldly, could be untouched; and many felt that angels' wings rustled in their midst, as the fine, pleading voice of the Bishop ascended to the celestial courts. After the prayer, another hymn was sung—the volume of sound swelling beyond the tones of an organ, and rising heavenward.

The text was from the First Epistle to the Corinthians, chapter thirteenth and verse thirteenth: "And now abideth faith, hope, and charity, these three; but the greatest of these is charity."

The sermon was one of extraordinary interest and power, blending grandeur and tenderness; and tears fell from many eyes unused to weep. The graphic power of the Bishop was great, and his illustrations brought the living scenes to view. In describing faith as a principle, he insisted that one of the tests was obedience—simple, thorough obedience; and he showed how Saul, the stately king of Israel, erred, in departing from the instructions given him as to the destruction of the Amalekites. "Thus saith the Lord of hosts: I remember that which Amalek did to Israel—how he laid wait for him in the way, when he came up from Egypt. Now go and smite Amalek, and utterly destroy all that they have, and spare them not, but slay both man and woman, infant and suckling, ox and sheep, camel and ass." The battle was fought; Saul was victorious. The next morning, Samuel, the prophet, goes to visit the conquering king, encamped at Carmel, who comes forth to meet him, saying: "Blessed be thou of the Lord: I have performed the commandment of the Lord. The prophet replied: What meaneth, then, this bleating of sheep in mine ears, and the lowing of the oxen which I hear? And Saul said: They have brought them from the Amalekites; for the people spared the best of the sheep and of the oxen, to sacrifice unto the Lord thy God; and the rest we have utterly destroyed. Then Samuel said unto Saul, Stay, and I will tell thee what the Lord hath said to me this night. And he said unto him, Say on. And Samuel said, When thou wast little in thine own sight, wast thou not made the head of the tribes of Israel, and the Lord anointed thee king over Israel? And the Lord sent thee on a journey, and said, Go and utterly destroy the sinners the Amalekites, and fight against them until they be consumed. Wherefore, then, didst thou not obey the voice of the Lord, but didst fly upon the spoil, and didst evil in the sight of the Lord? And Saul said unto Samuel, Yea, I have obeyed the voice of the Lord, and have gone the way which the Lord sent me, and have brought Agag, the king of Amalek, and have utterly destroyed the Amalekites. But the people took of the spoils, sheep and oxen, the chief things of which should have been utterly destroyed, to sacrifice unto the Lord thy God, in Gilgal. And Samuel said, Hath the Lord as great delight in burnt-offerings and sacrifices as in obeying the voice of the Lord? Behold, to obey is better than sacrifice, and to hearken, than the fat of rams. For rebellion is as the sin of witchcraft, and stubbornness is as iniquity and idolatry,

Because thou hast rejected the word of the Lord, he hath also rejected thee from being king."

All this was recited in a manner so life-like, that a panoramic view of the scene could not have brought it more distinctly before the audience; and he proceeded to describe the confession of the king, his being overawed by the people and yielding to them, which was the result of want of faith in God; the eagerness of Saul still to reign; his grasping the mantle of Samuel to detain him; its rending in his hand; and the prophet's prediction of the king's overthrow. Every one felt impressed with the dread majesty of God—awed in his presence—and trembled before the unswerving rectitude of his administration.

Then, when the Bishop had shown what faith is, he described hope—its exulting, far-reaching view of the world which lies beyond the boundaries of time; its revealing splendors, filling the soul with joy unutterable and full of glory; its power to hold the soul steadily amidst the storms of life. Then came his beautiful description of charity, greater than faith or hope—a mighty principle, dwelling on earth and in heaven; the same love warming the heart of an archangel and filling the soul of the Christian. The power to work miracles; the gift of tongues; the most boundless munificence in ministering to the wants of others—all, all paled before the surpassing glory of love, which would give us the victory over all things, and enable even an expiring martyr to exclaim:

"Sink down, ye separating hills!
Let sin and death remove!
'Tis love that drives my chariot-wheels,
And death must yield to love."

The effect of the discourse was visible throughout the congregation, and Waring looking about him at its close, saw tears coursing down the cheeks of Mr. Hallam. Miss Godolphin's face was buried in her handkerchief, and Mr. Clarendon's countenance exhibited deep emotion.

Another hymn was sung,

"O glorious hope of perfect love!"

and the volume of song which swelled loud and strong, could scarcely drown the sobs and exclamations which would break forth from some hearts. De Vane was impressed. He felt the immeasurable superiority which the glorious views spread before him possessed over all the pageantry of human life in its most imposing aspects. The sublime outlines of the Redeemer's kingdom, embracing the universe, were seen by him, and the pomp and splendor of the world paled before its transcendent excellence. Ambition, power, empire—all appeared, in that moment, trifling and insignificant; and the largest interests of time shrank into nothingness before the eternity which stretched illimitably around him. Then, too, the earnestness of this religion touched his heart; no mere routine of duties, no cold outline of forms, but a living, fervent, spiritual worship was all around him. Even his tastes were not offended; for the very presence of the Bishop—a man of culture and refinement, as well as of earnestness and power—impressed the whole service, and guided and elevated it. After another prayer, the Bishop pronounced the benediction, and all felt the calm and spiritual influence of his apostolic face, his outspread hands, and his words, beneficent as heaven itself.

Long lingered the influence of the morning's service in the hearts of the great congregation; and the unpretending chapel seemed, to the view of many, like the glorious temple which crowned Mount Moriah, the singers lifting up the voice in praise and thanksgiving, with the trumpets and cymbals and instruments of music, saying: "For He is good; for his mercy endureth forever." Then the house was filled with a cloud, so that the priests could not stand to minister, by reason of the cloud, for the glory of the Lord had filled the house of God.

## CHAPTER XI.

"As pilot well expert in perilous wave,
That to a steadfast star his course hath bent,
When foggy mists or cloudy tempests have
The faithful light of that fair lamp yblent,
And covered heaven with hideous detriment;
Upon his card and compass firmes his eye,
The maystery of his long experiment,
And to them does the steddy helm apply,
Bidding his winged vessell fairly forward fly."

SPENSER'S *Faerie Queene.*

MONDAY evening came, and Waring, accompanied by De Vane, walked to the house of Mr. Springfield at an early hour. They were warmly welcomed by Mr. Springfield, who conducted them to the library, where they found several persons, who had called to pay their respects to the Bishop. Others called in the course of the evening, and among them Mr. Clarendon and Mr. Hallam.

Mr. Hallam's father had been a Methodist minister, had known Bishop McKendree, and had died, leaving a spotless memory.

Mr. Clarendon had learned to venerate the Bishop from the teachings of an aunt, who had long been a member of the Methodist Church in Virginia. The conversation became general, and the Bishop was so genial that he charmed every one. His manners stately and yet gentle; his fine sense, his thorough knowledge of public affairs; and his broad views of questions which came up for discussion, made him a most agreeable companion; and De Vane felt that he would grace even the most aristocratic circles of the land.

Without ostentation, he succeeded in bringing every thing in subordination to Christianity, treated every topic in its relations to it, and impressed every one with the idea that the true solution of all questions must be found in the philosophy of God's government of the world. All statesmanship, he argued, must be guided by the divine law, if it would advance the true glory and prosperity of the country.

"But, Bishop," said Mr. Clarendon, "you would not bring about an alliance between the Church and the State?"

"No," replied the Bishop. "But I would recognize Christianity distinctly. I would conduct the affairs of the government in direct reference to the teachings of Jesus Christ. There need be no political arrangement such as exists in England; but the principles of Christianity should be acknowledged as the only basis of the government."

"Would not that involve the necessity of providing for some particular mode of worship?" asked Mr. Clarendon.

"Not at all," said the Bishop. "It would be unwise to erect an establishment, but the institutions of Christianity should be recognized by the organic law of the state. We ought not to content ourselves with a general reference to the government of God in our state papers; but Christianity—the system of truth revealed in the New Testament—should be accepted and honored, if we would perpetuate our free institutions."

"I think, Bishop, that is already done to some extent," said Mr. Hallam. "We observe the Christian Sabbath, and protect it by law."

"Quite true," replied the Bishop. "But I fear that the tendency is to conduct the government of this country upon principles of human wisdom; and I believe that no political system can stand that does not clearly and broadly recognize the law of God as the all-impelling power which guides the fortunes of our race."

"Certainly," said Mr. Hallam, "there is much in history to confirm your view."

"Yes," said Mr. Clarendon, "both in ancient and modern history; and I must say that I admire the British government, however much I condemn its ambitious and aggressive policy. The stability of that government is wonderful. Its people are free, and yet the empire stands amidst the convulsions of the world with the repose of majestic strength. What do you say to it, Mr. Waring? Am I conceding too much?"

"I think not," replied Waring. "The very subject which we are now discussing has attracted my attention much of late, and the philosophy of history seems to me to be unmistakable. Nations have perished because they knew not God."

"The British government," said Mr. Hallam, "has been much misunderstood in this country. Having been at war with it, we have accustomed ourselves to denounce it; but it is really, if we except our own, the finest government on earth."

"I think, Mr. De Vane," said Mr. Clarendon, "you will agree heartily with that opinion; for it seemed to me that you favored, in your oration, which we all heard with so much pleasure, the distinctions in society which are so broadly marked in England."

De Vane colored slightly, but instantly recovered his self-possession, and said: "It was my object, Mr. Clarendon, to show that the education of English gentlemen surpassed that of any other class in any country, and I attributed that to the advantages which they enjoyed under the aristocratic system of that country. I must say, too, that I admire the British government."

"I think," said the Bishop, "that I observe that tendency in the Virginia gentlemen, and I believe, Mr. De Vane, that you are a native of that State."

"I am, sir," said De Vane, "and I am happy to know that some of my relatives heard you, upon your late visit to Virginia."

"Which of them?" asked the Bishop.

"Mrs. De Vane, an aunt of mine," said De Vane.

"I remember," said the Bishop, "to have met her at the house of my friend, Mr. Hamilton; and if you will allow me to say so, I was much pleased with the interest which she manifested in evangelical religion. She impressed me with her earnestness as a Christian."

De Vane was highly gratified. Without analyzing it, he felt as if something had occurred to lessen the distance which separated his family from Esther. He said:

"Mrs. De Vane wrote me in such terms as satisfied me that she fully sympathized with your sentiments."

The Bishop bowed. "Well," said he, "you think well of the British government. I trust that if we do not rival their aristocratic establishment, we shall not suffer them to outstrip us in reverence for the institutions of Christianity. Do you not think it remarkable that the free states of antiquity could not perpetuate their liberty?"

"It is, sir," replied De Vane, "an impressive lesson which we learn from ancient history."

"And yet," said Waring, "unstable as political institutions have proved themselves, how striking is the fact that Christianity, springing up at the very feet of the colossal power of the Roman Empire, has come down to our times without the protection of governments, and is to-day statelier and stronger than it ever was before!"

"Yes," said the Bishop, "and that might teach us that a system so self-sustaining will infuse its own conservative influence into any government with which it is incorporated."

"Your philosophy, Bishop," said Mr. Clarendon, "is sustained by modern history, too. Look at England and France, with only that narrow strip of sea dividing them which lies between Dover and Calais."

"Something must be attributed to the difference of races," said Mr. Hallam. "The French people have their religion too, and the reigning family seems to be quite devout."

"Still," said Waring, "it seems too much to claim, for a difference between races, to attribute to that the well-ordered political system of England, as contrasted with the instability of government in France. I think that Protestant Christianity has much to do with it."

"You are quite right, I think, Mr. Waring," said Mr. Clarendon. "The popular mind of England, emancipated by the Reformation, is fitted for the reception of free principles. The wide diffusion of Christianity among the masses is so conservative, that liberty of thought and speech may be allowed. The same latitude permitted in France, would inaugurate anarchy, and make it impossible to uphold any government."

"Then," said the Bishop, "it becomes very important to spread the Gospel as widely as possible through these lands."

"Indeed, it is so," said Waring; "and, therefore, I should oppose any thing like a Church establishment in this country. Let the people be free to choose their own form of worship; and let the Gospel be preached to them with as little restraint as possible."

"Free seats, too, Waring?" asked Mr. Clarendon playfully.

"Oh! by all means," said Waring; "free seats and free grace."

All smiled, and the Bishop seemed pleased.

"Does not that strike you, De Vane, as somewhat too democratic?" asked Mr. Clarendon.

"I am not very well qualified to judge," De Vane replied, smiling. "I am too little accustomed to that form of worship to decide upon its merits. But I must say, that I am disposed to favor free seats, if the system works as well everywhere as it does in this place; for I did not witness the slightest confusion in the very large congregations assembled in the Methodist church, on both occasions when I was present."

"Ah!" said the Bishop, "I am sorry to say that we sometimes are troubled. I have witnessed a good deal of disorder; but, after all, I do prefer free seats, that the Gospel may be preached to the poor."

"Can you not provide for that, Bishop, by leaving some free pews?" said Mr. Clarendon.

"No," said he. "The poor are sensitive; they do not like to be set apart as a class, to be looked at, especially when they assemble in the Lord's house."

"The rich and the poor meet together," said Mrs. Springfield, taking part in the conversation, "and the LORD is the Maker of them all."

"Madam," said Mr. Clarendon, "I think that settles the question. I shall hereafter favor free seats."

"Yes," said De Vane, "however broad we may think proper to make the social distinctions of life, there ought to be one place in the universe where these distinctions vanish, and that is, where all meet before God, conscious of the wants and the aspirations of a common humanity."

He spoke with ardor. The Bishop fixed his eyes on him earnestly and kindly, and every one seemed impressed with the elevation and beauty of the sentiment uttered by one so young, reared so proudly, and making no profession of the Christian faith.

A sunbeam passed over Esther's face.

"What stay do you propose to make in this place, Mr. De Vane?" asked the Bishop.

"It is not at all certain, sir," he replied. "I am at this time in the office of Mr. Clarendon, and it is my wish to pursue my studies there for some time to come."

"Your father is in Virginia, I believe?"

"Yes. He remains much at home, and I shall visit him in the course of the next summer; but it is by no means settled that I shall ever return to Virginia to fix my residence there."

"No," said Mr. Clarendon, "we do not intend to permit Virginia to reclaim Mr. De Vane. We shall keep him among us, Bishop. We can continue to love our mother, even when we go forth into the wide world."

"Yes," said the Bishop, "that I know to be true. A Virginian myself, I cherish a sincere love for my native State; but I do not expect even to visit her again. My pilgrimage is nearly ended, and I shall probably lay down my staff in Tennessee, where I have passed much of my time of late years. No matter where, if, in my last moments, I shall be able to say: ALL'S WELL!"

The gentlemen here rose to take their leave of the Bishop, and as he took the hand of De Vane, he said to him:

"Farewell, sir. You are young. The great world is before you. Let me urge you to take the Word of God for your guide; it will be a lamp unto your feet, and a light unto your path."

De Vane bowed low, and all who saw the picture long remembered it: the venerable form of the Bishop; his gray locks resting upon his collar; his face full of apostolic earnestness, and the tall stately form of the young patrician bending before him; his dark massive hair; his noble face; his features beaming with emotion, as he heard the parting counsel of the man of God. All who stood grouped around this picture, felt that they had never witnessed a more impressive scene—age and youth confronting each other—a pilgrim who was approaching the silent river which separates TIME from ETERNITY, and a young man just entering upon his course, full of strength, and ardor, and hope.

Waring and De Vane retraced their steps toward their

lodgings. As they walked under the star-lit heavens, neither spoke for some minutes. At length De Vane said:

"Waring, we have sometimes talked of impressive objects in nature; but for moral sublimity, I have never seen any thing to rival the spectacle which that venerable man presents."

"I agree with you," replied his friend; "one quits his presence feeling that he has been enjoying a privilege almost equal to that of him who witnessed the departure of the prophet. It is true we do not see the fiery chariot, but we can not doubt that the man of God, upon whose face we have just now looked, will soon enter the courts of celestial glory. His whole life has had but a single object—the glory of God. He has looked to that as the mariner of early times did to the polar star; and one can well imagine that angels even now attend his steps."

"O Waring!" said De Vane, "I wish that I had a fixed religious faith like yours! I am far out at sea; and while I admire and venerate such a man as Bishop McKendree, my sentiments are rather a tribute to the grand career and heroic character of the man, than to the faith which he professes. I should admire a statesman, a philosopher, or a great military leader just in the same way. The death of Socrates, of which Plato gives us an account in his PHÆDON, filled me with admiration. The calm dignity, the tenderness to his friends, the gentleness toward his enemies, the steady resistance to the entreaties of those about him, that he would delay a little longer to drink the poison, after the cup had been brought to him, his taking it while the sun yet lingered upon the mountains, all this impresses me unspeakably."

"It is a fine picture," replied Waring, "and Plato has sketched it exquisitely; but really the spectacle of this venerable man, so heroic, so full of deep sympathy with life, so self-sacrificing in his whole career, standing, as he does, near the invisible boundary of the future world, so calmly surveying that future, so cheerfully walking upon the

> 'silent solemn shore,
> Of that vast ocean he must sail so soon,'

transcends, in my view, the scene which is brought before us by the eloquent philosopher of the Academy in describing the closing hours of the illustrious Athenian moralist. Socrates exclaimed: 'I go to die, you to live: but which is best, the Divinity alone can know.' But this disciple of Christ feels that, while it is his duty still to live and toil for his Master, to die will be gain. The clouds of doubt hung about the horizon of the one, the splendors of supernal glory light the way of the other; and while both fill us with admiration, excited by the heroism exhibited by each, our highest homage is due to the system of truth which enables the disciple of Christ to see the immortal light which overspreads the scenery of the future world."

"Waring," said De Vane, "I have never yet found a solution for the tremendous questions which addressed themselves to me while I was yet young: the PAST—the FUTURE. How thick the clouds which cover both! See those stars in countless numbers above us. When were they formed and marshaled in their mighty hosts? Was there ever an hour when the universe was a solitude? And if the Being who created these shining orbs, which you and I know to be worlds, fills the throne of the universe, in the midst of such an empire, how can it be that he will fix his regards upon us? These dread questions filled my thoughts when, yet a boy, I wandered at night in the unbroken solitude of the forest which surrounds my home, looking at the stars as they seemed to climb the mountain side; and often have I watched their course deep into the night. Like Manfred:

> 'My joy was in the wilderness, to breathe
> The difficult air of the iced mountains' tops,
> Where the birds dare not build, nor insect's wing
> Flits o'er the herbless granite; or to plunge
> Into the torrent, and to roll along
> On the swift whirl of the new-breaking wave
> Of river-stream.' . . .

Or—

> 'To follow through the night the moving moon,
> The stars, and their development; or catch
> The dazzling lightnings, till my eyes grew dim;
> Or to look listening on the scattered leaves,
> While autumn winds were at their evening song.
> . . . . . . . and then I dived,
> In my lone wanderings, to the caves of death,
> Searching its cause in its effect.'

Since I came here, I have sought in books to find some revealing light; but so far, I have searched in vain."

"De Vane," said his friend, "I have long feared this. You are following false lights, blind guides, wandering stars. I have observed your course of reading. Neither German philosophers, nor English essayists, nor French ontologists can do any thing for you. I sympathize with the scorn—yes, the scorn—with which an Apostle—himself a scholar of the highest order, and of imperial intellect—treated such speculative teachers in his day—a day when Roman literature was striving to rival the glory of the intellectual triumphs of Greece. 'Where is the wise? where is the scribe? where is the disputer of this world? Hath not God made foolish the wisdom of this world?' We can make no discoveries in the region of morals. Every thing which comes to us from the invisible world is a pure disclosure, and God alone can break the silence that reigns over the space which separates time from eternity. If we would learn, we must open the volume of his revelation."

"It does not solve the mysteries which fill the chambers

of my soul," said De Vane. "It is too arbitrary. I am urged to believe, as if believing were an act of volition, and I am instructed that my state for eternity depends upon my acceptance of a creed which I can not comprehend. I recall the past—Egypt, the Eastern nations, the states of Greece, the Roman Empire; all the wonders of science which marked their career; all the splendid achievements which light their chronicles; all the literature and the arts which adorned their annals: and I ask myself, can it be possible that the Ruler of the universe overlooked these peoples, and concentrated his regards on a race escaping from bondage on the banks of the Nile, and making their home afterward in that narrow region which skirts the Mediterranean Sea, where, even according to their own records, they rebelled constantly against the very God whom they professed to worship! Then, too, the appeal made to me to accept as DIVINE a young Galileean, dwelling nearly his whole life in the provincial region of a mere dependency upon the Roman Empire, and put to death at last by his own countrymen! So that the mysteries of nature baffle me, and the teachings of the very Revelation to which you refer me bewilder me. Dread arcana meet me at every glance; these outspread heavens, this mother earth: fathomless depths open before me in my own nature; and the system of Christianity, so full, as I see it to be, of what is good and beautiful, stands before me like a cunningly-devised fable, intended to soothe the agonizing doubts of a being longing to explore the future, and to read the mysteries of another state. Who can solve the two great questions of life—the Whence? and the Whither?"

"Ah! De Vane," said Waring, "you are indeed at sea—a sea tossed with tempests; and being shaken by tumultuous waves, you are losing sight of the friendly lights which mark the shore, and of the guiding-stars of heaven. You are in great danger of shipwreck. Acquainted, as you are, with the philosophy of the Greeks, you ought to know that you can find no guide there. Splendid speculations dazzle you, and you must sympathize with the earnest, hopeful minds which sought to explore the universe without the guiding lights of revelation. God's system for the recovery of a revolted world is a gradual one, for it is a moral one; but it has been steadily expanding, until, at length, it has attained the noon-day splendor which overspreads the Christian states of the nineteenth century. Not to enter upon the wide sea where you are drifting just now, let me ask you, is it not wonderful that one man—MOSES—should, in the midst of the debasing idolatry of Egypt, its polytheism, with all its boasted learning, comprehend the existence of the one true and living God? Is it not also wonderful that a people—the Israelites—dwelling upon the shores of the Mediterranean Sea, which washed the shores of Greece, of Italy, and of Carthage, should alone possess a knowledge of the one God? and that one of their kings should have written such sacred poems in praise of him that, coming down through centuries to our own times, a believer can read them in the very blaze of our modern civilization, and feel them to be the noblest tributes to the Divine Majesty ever offered? Where did they make their discoveries? And is it not wonderful, too, that a young Galileean, as you style him, should come forth from a provincial home, and utter such words as eclipsed the learning of all the world before his time, and construct a code which stands to-day confessedly the purest, the sublimest system of morals which the world ever knew? From whence did he derive his learning? Where did he find a teacher, so far in advance of those who walked on the banks of the Ilyssus, or instructed their disciples in the groves of Academus? And does this not satisfy you that he was divine? Leaving out of view now his miracles wrought in attestation of the divinity of his mission, does not the very fact of his transcendent and peerless utterances, emerging, as he did, from a small, uncultivated, immoral village—Nazareth—satisfy you that his illumination was from the uncreated splendors of the ETERNAL HIMSELF?"

De Vane looked with wonder upon the glowing face of his friend, as he stood under the brilliant sky. They had stopped in their walk, both absorbed by the great questions which they were discussing. His own features were lit with intellectual power, and he could not withhold his admiration from Waring, now roused to an enthusiasm which he had never witnessed in him before.

"We must talk further of all this, Waring," he remarked. "I am indeed tossed upon the waves. There are views, still more bewildering, of a later philosophy, which I must compare with yours."

"Philosophy falsely so called," said Waring.

"When do you leave for Georgia?"

"On Thursday morning, with the Bishop. Good-night!"

"Good-night!" said De Vane.

## CHAPTER XII.

"If to spurn at noble praise
Be the passport to thy heaven,
Follow thou those gloomy ways—
No such law to me was given."
MARK AKENSIDE.

WARING was absent for several weeks. After his departure, De Vane entered upon his studies with increased ardor. He rarely went into society; and after passing the day at Mr. Clarendon's office, closely engaged in reading, he would turn at night to other studies; and often his light was seen burning, by those who passed his lodgings, long after midnight. His taste for German literature was decided; and he found in the book-store of Mr. Muller the finest collection of works in that language which this country afforded. The Reviews, too, interested him; besides the British Quarterlies, he had ordered two from Paris, and was supplied with periodicals from Berlin. Just at that time, quite an impulse was given to the German view of Roman History, by Niebuhr's great work, *Römische Geschichte*, which had been translated by one of the librarians of the British Museum, and he found his ambition fired by turning the pages that recorded the deeds of those

"sons of ancient fame,
Those starry lights of virtue that diffuse
Through the dark depth of time their vivid flame."

His enthusiasm was roused, and all that was heroic in his nature acquired new vigor. There was every thing to encourage him; and as he traced the principles that gave such expansion to the power of Rome, and sent its victorious eagles at the head of conquering legions to so many distant provinces, he felt that his own country afforded a broad field for the display of the qualities which had made the men who had constructed that imperial republic immortal.

He communed, too, with scholars—the dead and the living—and learned to disregard society. He corresponded with Mr. Le Grande, and his tastes were directed by the cultivated mind of that fine scholar. He was eager to illustrate the statesmanship of his country, to make its annals glorious; not by military exploits only, but by the higher triumphs of the arts of peace. Patrician as he was by birth, fortune, and association, yet he believed firmly in a popular government; and it was his wish to see the institutions of the country developed upon the principles so clearly set forth in the Constitution. Impressed with the wisdom of the British Government, he aspired to still higher statesmanship than the nature of that government permitted to be exhibited. It was his wish to guide the complex political system of this country to still nobler triumphs. Aristocratic in his tastes, yet he desired the widest expansion for popular sentiment, and he felt that it was a far higher position to stand before the world called to the great places of trust by the people, than to accept a portfolio from a monarch. Then, too, this great continent, so widely separated from the empires of the old world, afforded, in his view, a field for the cultivation of the highest powers of statesmanship. Free States, united by a common government, would rival each other in the glorious task of advancing human liberty; and he looked forward to the day when a great people, enjoying the freest political institutions under the heavens—inheriting the laws, the language, and the religion of England—would spread the highest civilization the world ever saw, between the two great oceans, the Atlantic and the Pacific; realizing the glowing tribute to our country which had just then been paid to it by a noble poet who laid down his life in Greece, a martyr to his heroic love of that classic land:

> "Still one great clime,
> Whose vigorous offspring by dividing ocean
> Are kept apart, and nursed in the devotion
> Of freedom, which their fathers fought for and
> Bequeathed—a heritage of heart and hand,
> And proud distinction from each other land—
> Still ONE GREAT CLIME, in full and free defiance,
> Yet rears her crest, unconquered and sublime,
> Above the far Atlantic."

Mr. Clarendon observed him with great interest, and encouraged him in his generous studies, and a strong friendship grew up between them. De Vane sometimes called in at Mr. Clarendon's and passed the evening; rarely, however, for his books engrossed him; and he met occasionally, at Mr. Clarendon's dinners, the leading men of the State. Chancellor De Lolme, too, a man of culture, and whose elegant hospitality was well known, distinguished as his house was for refinement, induced him sometimes to accept his invitations, and honored him by marks of attention, which he always bestowed gracefully. The fine manners of De Vane, his splendid talents, his acquirements, his dignity and purity, made him already a man of rank; and a high career was predicted for him by the eminent men in whose society he appeared.

Calling one evening at Mr. Clarendon's, he met Mrs. Habersham and Miss Godolphin, who, preferring that hour to visit Mrs. Clarendon, were in the library. De Vane would have retired, but Mr. Clarendon would take no excuse.

"Come, De Vane," said he, rising, "this is just what you

ought to do every evening. These ladies you know, and I intend to try to bring them to my aid, in inducing you to quit your books in the evening, and give some of your hours to your friends."

De Vane advanced and took his seat with the ladies, saying: "Really, Mr. Clarendon, you know how happy I am to meet friends, as you do me the honor to style them, when I can do so."

"When you can do so, indeed!" said Mr. Clarendon. "I assure you, ladies, he is killing himself. Not content with the light which day gives him, he robs the night, and may be fairly classed among the sleepless."

The ladies smiled, and Mr. Clarendon said: "It is too true, Mr. De Vane, you will seriously injure your health. Dr. Dahlgreen was saying only yesterday, that you must be looked after. He was driving past your lodgings on his return from a visit to a patient in the sand-hills as late as two o'clock in the morning, and he says he saw your two sperm-candles burning in the window. Shocking! and there can be no mistake about it. Your two lights betrayed you; for you must know, ladies, that this gentleman, classical as he is, disdains the lamp, and insists that two candles make the only light fit for a student."

"We must bribe your good landlady, Mrs. Bowen," said Mrs. Clarendon, "to deprive you of that luxury."

"That would be very hard to do," said Mr. Clarendon, "for I called there last week to see De Vane. He had walked out; and upon my saying to Mrs. Bowen that she must not permit her young boarder to sit up so late, she said that it was a great pity, but that she had never known him do any thing but what was right—that he was absolutely perfect, and that she had not the heart to interfere with any of his wishes. So I very meekly bowed my way out, glad to escape some mark of displeasure for my impertinence."

The ladies laughed heartily, and De Vane said: "Mrs. Bowen is really very kind to me, and I fear that I give her more trouble than I ought."

"She has not prevailed on you to attend church yet?" asked Mr. Clarendon.

"No," said De Vane, "and that really seems to grieve her."

Turning to Miss Godolphin, he said:

"Speaking of attending church, Miss Godolphin, reminds me that I saw you at the Methodist church, when Bishop McKendree preached there. Did you like him?"

"I never heard a sermon that affected me so much," she replied. "If he were residing here, I should attend his church constantly. His very appearance impresses me strangely."

"It is very striking," said De Vane; "and his conversation has for me a perfect charm."

"I never met him in society," she said; "I should be delighted to do so. My aunt and myself were both so much captivated by him, that if he had remained longer we should have called on him."

"Yes," said Mrs. Habersham, "I said to Miss Wordsworth that she should have sent for us; and that if we had known of his being in town so long, we should not have waited for an invitation to call."

"Have you met Miss Wordsworth very lately, Mrs. Habersham?" asked Mrs. Clarendon.

"Not within the past fortnight," she replied.

"Nor have we. She must be out of town, for we have the pleasure of seeing her here every week when at home."

"Do you know her well, Mrs. Clarendon?" asked Miss Godolphin.

"Oh! yes," she replied; "no one better. And she is such a favorite of Mr. Clarendon, that I do not know how he has suffered two weeks to pass without seeing her."

"Yes," said Mr. Clarendon, "it's hard to say which of us loves her most."

"And you permit him to say that, Mrs. Clarendon!" said Miss Godolphin, smiling.

"Oh! yes," she answered, "he loves Miss Wordsworth, extravagantly, I should say, if I did not know her so well."

"She is angelic," said Mr. Clarendon.

"She is very beautiful," said Miss Godolphin. "I never was more captivated by the appearance of any one. I met her first in this very house, and I at once felt that neither in the living circles of Europe, nor in the picture-galleries which adorn its palaces, had I seen so lovely a person. Then, too, her accomplishments seem to equal her beauty."

"Yes," said Mr. Clarendon, "she is very accomplished; her music is nothing short of wonderful. Of that you need not be informed, however. I heard your tribute to her, and I saw how she prized it. She is perfectly enthusiastic about you, and thinks she never heard any thing to equal your performance. She says that your singing is unrivaled."

"Ah!" said Miss Godolphin, "the dear, generous creature! She ought to know that she herself is peerless in song. Did you, Mr. De Vane, ever hear any thing to rival her 'Walpurgisnacht'?"

"It was glorious," he replied.

"Is she a German scholar?" asked Miss Godolphin.

"Yes," said Mr. Clarendon, "a thorough one. The Duke of Saxe-Weimar conversed with her for a half-hour in that language, and he told me that her pronunciation was remarkable for its accuracy and purity."

"It is wonderful," said Miss Godolphin, "how she could have acquired it! She has never been abroad, I suppose?"

"Never," said Mr. Clarendon; "but she has had the best masters. No expense has been spared in her education. Her own fortune is large, and her uncle, Mr. Springfield, is wealthy and without children; so that every thing has been done, that could be accomplished, to educate her in the highest sense."

"I learn," said Mrs. Habersham, "that her tastes are peculiar. It is said that she has founded a retreat for young orphan girls, and that she actually passes much of her time in teaching them."

"Yes," said Mr. Clarendon, "it is so. A finer instance of true womanly benevolence I have never witnessed. I have visited the 'Retreat'—by the way, it is called 'Leasowes' now, after Shenstone's seat—and a more beautiful and attractive place I do not know on earth. Miss Wordsworth does not reside there; but she has employed a respectable person, admirably fitted for the place, to take charge of it; and she lives in Mr. Springfield's family. De Vane, did you ever see the place, in your rambles about the town?"

"Yes," replied De Vane, coloring; "my friend Waring was good enough to take me there."

"Well," said Mr. Clarendon, "you young gentlemen were entering a very dangerous place, if Miss Wordsworth happened to be present. I should say that Calypso's famous retreat was nothing to it. You must have found Waring very useful, in the way of a Mentor, to help you break away."

"She was there," said De Vane, smiling; "but we did not expect to find her at home. It was Saturday. It was an extraordinary scene. Her extreme youth, the little girls grouped about her, and the surpassing beauty of the place—all made a rare picture."

"The effect very much heightened," said Mr. Clarendon, "by two young gentlemen looking on."

"Really, Mr. Clarendon," said Miss Godolphin, "you must take me there."

"That I will," said he, heartily. "By the way, De Vane, when do you look for Waring?"

"Next week," he replied. "I had a letter from him this morning. He has been making a visit to his sister."

"He is a noble fellow," said Mr. Clarendon; "a true man. With great parts, he has a heart as generous as ever beat in a man's bosom; and his religion absolutely rises into grandeur."

"I am delighted, Mr. Clarendon," said De Vane, "to hear you speak of him in such terms. I wish all the world knew him as you and I do."

"The world will know him," said Mr. Clarendon. "He is destined to be a burning and a shining light."

"We met him here," said Miss Godolphin. "I very well remember him. He was the first-honor man."

"Yes," said De Vane, "and richly deserved to be."

"It seems to me," said Mrs. Habersham, "that I heard some one say he was quite devoted to Miss Wordsworth. Is it so, Mr. Clarendon?"

"He admires her beyond measure," said Mr. Clarendon; "but I do not know that there is any thing beyond that."

"I am quite sure," said Mrs. Clarendon, "that Miss Wordsworth is free. She is, you know, very young, just seventeen, and she has never loved."

Miss Godolphin fixed her large dark eyes on Mrs. Clarendon's face, and seemed to be about to speak, but she checked herself, and said nothing. De Vane observed her emotion; he could not comprehend it.

"Are you very sure?" said Mrs. Habersham. "Very young persons sometimes feel the fatal passion."

"I am very sure," said Mrs. Clarendon. "Esther Wordsworth has never loved. When she does love, if that should ever happen, it will be for always."

"Is she ardent?" asked Mrs. Habersham.

"Her nature is one of great depth," said Mrs. Clarendon; "and she adheres with tenacity to any purpose which she forms."

"Miss Godolphin, are you ill?" exclaimed Mr. Clarendon.

She was deadly pale, and seemed about to fall from her chair, but she rallied instantly, and the rich warm blood, returning from her heart, rushed to her temples.

"No," she replied, in a voice whose mournful depth startled De Vane.

A servant entered the room with refreshments; and Mr. Clarendon, filling a glass with wine, handed it to Miss Godolphin, and said:

"Let us, Miss Hortensia, take some Madeira together; it is a generous wine, and will strengthen you." He bowed to her, and as she replaced the glass, she said:

"I must see more of your friend Miss Wordsworth, Mr. Clarendon. I must know her."

"She will, I am sure, be happy to make you her friend, Miss Hortensia," he said.

"As to Waring, the fellow has been so busy with books, that I don't think he has ever thought about loving any one. He has known Miss Wordsworth for some years, certainly ever since he entered college; for he has been intimate with Mr. Springfield from the time of his first coming to pursue his studies here. You must permit me to show him the way to your house, Mrs. Habersham."

"We shall be most happy to see him," she replied.

"And what do you say, Miss Hortensia? Will you be merciful to my young friend?"

"Oh! yes," she said, smiling, half sadly; "he will have nothing to fear from me."

"Nothing to fear from you!" said Mr. Clarendon; "Pray, why not? A more dangerous person it would be hard to find."

"Ah! Mr. Clarendon," she said, "I am very, very far from being dangerous. I have no faith in the grand passion. Your sex are swayed by ambition; and as for ours, I shall not undertake to interpret their souls. Did you see the Sphinx when you were traveling?"

"No," said he, "but I saw woman in marble, everywhere, and in every form I read the soul, beneath the cold outlines. Depend upon it, Miss Godolphin, a woman's heart never dies; and as to a young and beautiful woman, talking of *impassibilité*, it is quite as rational as to suppose the harp is voiceless, which only waits for some hand to sweep its chords, that is skilled in music."

Miss Godolphin's eyes were fathomless in their dark depths. She said:

"May not the strings of the harp be broken?"

"They are often hung upon the willows, from sadness," he replied; "but when love informs the soul, then they are swiftly snatched from the melancholy boughs, and made to discourse most eloquent music."

"Love, Mr. Clarendon! it is a myth."

"You are all the more dangerous," he said, "for teaching that doctrine. You beguile your victims. Unconscious of danger, they are helplessly ensnared before they see the fetters."

"You know nothing about it," she replied, "and shall not persuade me to accept your philosophy."

She spoke playfully; but De Vane, who observed her, felt that some indefinable sadness reigned within her. He could not comprehend it. Young, splendidly beautiful, accomplished, full of intellect and soul, she was as sad as Jephthah's daughter upon the mountains of Israel.

"At all events," said Mr. Clarendon, "I shall leave Waring to take care of himself. I shall observe the process with interest. It will be a study full of instruction, even for a married man."

All laughed heartily, except Miss Godolphin, who smiled, but said nothing.

"You know, Miss Hortensia," said Mrs. Clarendon, "that

before you left us for your travels in Europe, Mr. Clarendon admired you, and you are still a great favourite. He will not spare his friends."

Mr. Clarendon assumed an air of great surprise, and said:

"How have I offended? Does it occur to you, Mr. De Vane, that I have said any thing out of the way, in pronouncing young ladies—captivating?"

"I am afraid," said De Vane, "to hazard an opinion upon so grave a question, without bestowing some reflection upon it."

"Ah! non-committal. Well, that has become so much the fashion in politics, that the young gentlemen are all falling into it."

The ladies rose to take their leave, and the gentlemen handed them to the carriage. The spirited horses dashed off. De Vane bowed, and walked away to his lodgings. He could not withdraw his thoughts from Miss Godolphin her glorious beauty, her sadness, her emotion when allusion was made to an all-engrossing passion, and a life-long attachment—all this interested him in her. He had met her but rarely, and this evening she had impressed him deeply. The interest which he felt in her was indefinable. She was very unlike Esther. Both were lovely—both accomplished; the one was as pure as an angel which had never passed the bounds of Paradise, the other might be an angel just returning from some ministering office, which had touched her celestial spirit with sadness.

6

## CHAPTER XIII.

"He has been dreaming of old heroic stories,
And the poet's world has entered in his soul;
He has grown conscious of life's ancestral glories,
When sages and when kings first upheld the mind's control.
When will he awaken?
Asks the midnight's stately queen."

*Awakening of Endymion.*

UNHEEDING the remonstrances of friends, De Vane still pursued his studies. Still his light burned in his room until long past midnight; and passers-by remarked it. History, politics, metaphysics, engrossed him. The pictured pages of Livy fired his ambition; and he reviewed with delight the early history of that wonderful people whose empire, beginning upon the Tiber, grew until it overspread the world. The politics of the world, too, interested him, and he sought, in history, to discern the great principles which might enable him better to comprehend the merits of the great struggle going on throughout the country. What constituted the real wealth of a nation, or contributed to its true glory, he searched for; and, rising above the small considerations which swayed so many about him, he investigated the philosophy of statesmanship. Metaphysics he delighted in. He had gone over the whole field of the modern school in his senior year, but he now explored the wider range of speculative philosophy, and was deep in the Serbonian bog of fathomless disputation. The brilliant papers of Heine fascinated him; the sombre, cheerless philosophy of Leibnitz involved him in the toils of fatalism; and the subtle disquisitions of Bolingbroke captivated him. The cold unbelief of the first of these writers troubled him; for, with an ardent nature, he desired to believe and trust. He could not look out upon the universe and pronounce it unmeaning; nor could he tolerate the thought that humanity was in a state of orphanage. He looked upon the world in its glorious beauty of hill and dale, and mountain and valley, and ocean and plain, smiling with summer verdure, or grand with the splendors of winter; or to the heavens in their immensity, through which the countless orbs rushed with so much velocity, and yet so much order; and he could not consent to yield up his early belief that upon the throne of the universe there was seated a God of boundless benevolence. Still he was troubled. He comprehended the deep yearning of the spirit for the right way. He felt, with Plato, "that every soul is unwillingly deprived of truth." Deprived of truth he would not be, if he could succeed in exploring the wilderness about him, and find the way lighted by the Divinity. His consciousness assured him of the existence of his soul. Was that soul immortal? The dread question which troubled Job haunted him: "Is there not an appointed time to man upon earth? Are not his days also like the days of an hireling?"

And then came the response of the patriarch to his own question: "If a man die, shall he live again?" Here was the great cry of the soul which had been heard on the plains of the east so long ago, uttered once more.

"Mr. De Vane," said Mrs. Bowen, "you are not looking well. I think you study too hard." De Vane was at the breakfast-table. He had been up very late the night before, and his long course of study began to tell upon his health. Young, vigorous, and active as he was, he was becoming thin, and his face had lost its color. His large dark eyes seemed to increase in depth and splendor, and his appetite was gone.

Mrs. Bowen had forborne as long as her kind nature would permit her to forbear. She loved the young student as if he had been her son; and her eyes filled with tears as she saw him this morning, seated at the table, languid and thoughtful.

De Vane smiled, and said: "Why, Mrs. Bowen, would you have me indulge myself—you who are so active and so busy?"

"No, Mr. De Vane," she replied, "there is no danger of that. You will never indulge yourself; but you must spare yourself. Young people ought not to break themselves down. When they get older and stronger, then they can bear more."

"But I am not working very hard. There is so much to learn, that I am trying to do something while I am young."

"Yes, sir; but you see Solomon says that much study is a weariness to the flesh; and he knew all about it. There, you have eaten scarcely any thing at all—one egg, but one biscuit, and half a cup of coffee. Why, that would not do for a child."

De Vane smiled and said: "Never mind, Mrs. Bowen. I will make up for it yet. I must take a little more exercise, and then I shall eat like a mountaineer, as I am."

"It was only last week," said Mrs. Bowen, "that Mr. Clarendon scolded me for letting you sit up so late, and yesterday I was at Mr. Springfield's, and Mrs. Springfield asked about you, and said she was afraid you were not well, and that she understood from Dr. Dahlgreen that you were killing yourself with books."

"Indeed!" said De Vane. "Was Mrs. Springfield kind enough to ask after me?"

"Certainly she did," said Mrs. Bowen. "And she said that Miss Wordsworth was going on in the same way; for, after passing nearly the whole day at her little school, she would sit up half the night, studying."

De Vane felt the blood rising to his face. He had not seen Esther since Waring left the town, and this sudden mention of her name in connection with his own by Mrs. Bowen, in her kindness of heart, bringing the strictures of Mrs. Springfield to her support, recalled her so vividly, that he was conscious of a very indefinable sensation."

"I hope Miss Wordsworth's health has not suffered," he said, looking earnestly at Mrs. Bowen.

"She says not; for she was sitting by when Mrs. Springfield spoke to me, and she was looking as beautiful as I ever saw her. She is as good, too, as she is pretty."

"Why, Mrs. Bowen, you are actually becoming poetical in your descriptions. One of the very finest tributes ever paid to a lady has that very thought in it:

'Yes; she is good as she is fair.'"

"Well, Miss Wordsworth deserves it," said Mrs. Bowen. "If I did not know that no human being can be perfect, I should say she is. If she has a fault, it has never been discovered. Yet her whole life is spent in doing good. Taking care of little orphan girls, most people would think was enough; but she visits the sick, and helps the poor besides. For about two weeks she has been nursing Mrs. Gildersleeve's daughter, who is dying of consumption."

"But could no one be found to take her place?"

"No; no one can take her place, Mr. De Vane. Little Eva Gildersleeve was one of her Sunday-school scholars, and now about twelve years old; but she is dying, and she clings to Miss Wordsworth as if she was the only person in all the world that could do her any good. And to hear her talk to that child about Jesus, and about heaven, as I did, day before yesterday, is better than a sermon. I thought I could almost hear the rustling of angels' wings in the room."

Mrs. Bowen's eyes filled with tears, and De Vane was impressed with the fine expression of her matronly face, as she uttered the beautiful tribute to Miss Wordsworth, unconscious of the exquisite picture she had painted—a picture worthy of the pencil of Raphael—this young, bright, accomplished woman, ministering to a dying girl, in a way so comforting and tender, as to make the spectator feel that angels must press forward to witness the scene.

This, then, accounted for her absence from society; this explained why Mrs. Clarendon had not seen her for the two weeks past. He said nothing. He rose from the table, and walked out into the streets; but through every hour of that day, and for many days afterward, did he recall the scene which Mrs. Bowen had described.

The next day Waring returned. He came in the evening coach; and, very soon after his arrival, he walked to Mrs. Bowen's, and inquired for De Vane.

Mrs. Bowen welcomed him warmly. Waring was a great favorite, and she really venerated him, young as he was.

"Well, Mr. Waring," she said, "I'm glad you've come. We've all missed you; and as for Mr. De Vane, since you left, he has hardly gone out at all. He does nothing but study from morning till night; till night indeed—I might say till the next morning."

"Ah!" said Waring, "I must look after him; is he in?"

"No," she replied; "this is the only time in the day when he takes a walk. But he'll be in very soon; it's nearly supper-time, and he never keeps me waiting. Come in, and stay to supper."

"Thank you," said Waring, "I will do so," frankly accepting the hearty invitation. "And I must beg you too," said he, "to consent to take me as a boarder. You can spare me a room, and I shall try to help you take care of De Vane."

Mrs. Bowen's face brightened.

"You know," she replied, "I have hardly ever taken any one to board. Sometimes two or three little girls, who come here to go to school, and whose parents will make me take them; but when Mr. De Vane came and told me how he hated to stay at a hotel, and how he wished to be quiet, I took him. Opposite to his room there is one just as large, and if that will suit you, you know that there is no one in the world I would rather have than yourself. And as to Mr. De Vane, he will be delighted, I know. He told me when he came to keep it, and said he would pay for it just as if some one was in it; but he preferred to have it vacant, until some friend of his came to take it. He did not say who it was. I told him he ought not to do that, but he said I must let him have the room, and that it would do him a great favor."

"Very well," said Waring; "that's all right. I'll settle that matter with De Vane. I'll take the room for my own, and I am very much obliged to you, Mrs. Bowen, for your kindness in consenting to be troubled with me."

"Troubled indeed!" said she. "If people in this world gave no more trouble than you and Mr. De Vane do, I would think the millennium had come."

Waring laughed, and the good old lady busied herself in preparation for tea.

Soon after, De Vane's step was heard in the hall; and, opening the door, he walked into the room.

"*Mehercule!* Waring," said he; "where did you drop from, old fellow? I'm delighted to see you."

"Not from the clouds," said Waring, "like another classical friend of yours, or I should, like him, have broken my leg. As it is, I am only very much bruised by beating about in a stage-coach from Augusta."

"You have been gone an age," said De Vane, "and deserve to be bruised for staying so long."

"But, see here, De Vane," said Waring, "what is the matter with you? You are thin and pale. What have you been doing with yourself?"

"Nothing," said De Vane. "I suppose I have not walked as much as I was accustomed to do, when we took our strolls together. Now that you are here, I shall do better."

"Yes," said Waring, "I intend to see to that. My good friend, Mrs. Bowen, here, says that I may have that room opposite yours, which, I take it for granted, you intended I should have from the beginning."

"Why, in all candor, Waring, I am heartily glad that you take it, but I acted upon the plan of Englishmen upon the Continent. I'm told that to make sure of their comfort, when they find a pleasant hotel, they engage all the rooms on the same floor, so as to exclude all comers, except some people who may happen to be agreeable to them. The room is yours, of course. When will you take possession?"

"To-morrow; if Mrs. Bowen will suffer me to do so?"

"Oh! yes, sir," said Mrs. Bowen; "it can be put in order to-morrow morning. It is already pretty well furnished, and any thing else that you want I will get for you."

"I think, Waring," said De Vane, "I shall transfer, if you will permit, sundry articles from my own room. I have been indulging my taste in selecting articles from time to time, until I can hardly turn around in my room; and, with other things, I selected, the other day, a melodeon, which has not yet been sent home. You must take charge of that, and I shall charge you for the use of it by making you instruct me, as you did during our summer vacation."

"You see, Mrs. Bowen," said Waring, "that he intends to make me a music-teacher forthwith."

"You must take away some of his books," said Mrs. Bowen. "Mr. Clarendon told me to do it, but I was afraid to trouble him."

"I'll attend to his case," said Waring. They sat down to supper, and two little girls, from ten to twelve years of age, took their seats with them. It was a round, cheerful table, loaded with luxuries, for Mrs. Bowen was a famous housekeeper.

Waring asked a blessing.

It had been many months since Mrs. Bowen was so happy; and in her heart she sent up a thanksgiving to the Lord, for spreading sunshine through her house. She had a competency, and was childless. A woman of good sense and good breeding, she was highly respected, and saw the best society in the town. She was a fervent Christian, too, abounding in good works; and the young and the old loved her for her gentleness and kindness. She was especially a favorite with Mr. Clarendon, who often declared, that when he felt at all depressed, he would walk to Mrs. Bowen's to get her to cheer him.

Her house was always cheerful. If there was a single ray of sunshine breaking through the clouds, it somehow fell on her. She loved Esther as she loved no one else on earth; and often accompanied her on her visits to the sick and the poor.

It was at the special request of Mr. Clarendon that she took De Vane as a boarder; and the young student had already become strongly attached to her. His ample fortune enabled him to gratify his tastes, and with great delicacy he often supplied luxuries which he persuaded her no one could find so well as himself.

More than once, he had enabled her to relieve cases of suffering by supplying means just at the moment when they were needed. Now that Waring had come, she felt that her happiness was complete, for she loved him next to Esther.

"How is my friend Mr. Springfield, Mrs. Bowen?" asked Waring.

"Very well, sir. He was speaking of you a few days since, and said that you staid longer than he supposed you would; but that he hoped to see you soon."

"I'm very much obliged to him. I found that my affairs in Georgia required my attention. The Conference was in session a week."

"So I heard, from Mr. Arthur."

"Ah! yes. How do you like that appointment?"

"Oh! we are all pleased," said Mrs. Bowen. "You know that he is a great favorite here, and his congregations are very large. The old church will hardly hold them."

"I supposed it would be so—he is really a very fine preacher. He has a way of reaching the heart, that gives him access to it before you know it."

"Mr. Springfield is very much pleased with the appointment," said Mrs. Bowen; "you know they are good friends."

"Yes," said Waring; "intimate as brothers."

"And Miss Wordsworth," said Mrs. Bowen, "she says that he writes as well as he preaches. He has written for our new paper, and she is very much pleased with his letters. You know that she is a judge of such things."

"Indeed she is," said Waring, "and I agree with her. The truth is, he has one of the best libraries that I know; in fact, the very best that I know belonging to a traveling preacher. Have you heard him, De Vane, since he came?"

"No," said De Vane. "I have not been in a church since you left me."

"Really, Mrs. Bowen," said Waring, "we must look after this young Virginian. He is far from home, and we must try to induce him to return to his early habits."

"I like to hear good preaching," said De Vane, "and will go with you sometimes with pleasure, to hear this gentleman who is so highly esteemed by you. If you and

Mrs. Bowen and Mr. Springfield think so well of him, I am sure that he must be worth hearing."

"He began to preach at eighteen," said Waring, "and has been a hard student ever since. He is sometimes as eloquent as Jeremy Taylor, and yet is perfectly unaffected."

Some time after, Waring rose, and saying to Mrs. Bowen that he would come back in the morning, proposed to return to his hotel.

De Vane accompanied him, and they entered into a conversation about their plans for the future. It was Waring's purpose now to enter upon his theological studies; and his plan embraced a two years' course. The large library of Mr. Springfield was open to him, and he should enjoy the instructions of that gentleman, and of Mr. Arthur, the minister just appointed to the station. Licensed already to exhort, it was his purpose to engage, as extensively as possible, in the duties of that office, while pursuing his regular course of study. There was not the slightest cant about him, but he spoke seriously, and even earnestly, about his work—its duties, responsibilities, and encouragements.

"Have you seen Mr. Springfield within a few days, De Vane?"

"No," said he. "I have scarcely made any visits since you left me."

"He expressed a strong interest in you," said Waring, "and you ought to see as much of him as possible. He is a thorough scholar—a man of extraordinary breadth of view, and one of the most delightful men in conversation that I have ever met."

"I am very strongly disposed to like him," said De Vane, "and I have the greatest respect for him; but the truth is, I hardly know how I have spent the time that has elapsed since you took your departure. How long has it been?"

"Six weeks, to a day," said Waring.

"Is it possible?" exclaimed De Vane. "It seemed an age when I thought of you; but I did not know that the winter was so nearly gone."

"Yes," said Waring; "spring is almost here. How swiftly the winter has gone by! It will soon belong to the past. Do you remember, De Vane, the address of Apollo to Mnemosyne?

'I can read
A wondrous lesson in thy silent face.'"

"Yes," replied De Vane, "memory is silent, but a powerful teacher."

"Do you hear any thing of Miss Wordsworth these days?" asked Waring.

"Only through Mrs. Bowen," he said. "She was describing to me yesterday a scene which was so exquisitely touching and beautiful, that it has been before me ever since. It seems, that for some two weeks past, she has been watching by the side of a little girl dying of consumption."

"Did you hear the name of the child?" asked Waring.

"Eva Gildersleeve. I was struck with its beauty.

"Ah!" said Waring, "I have been looking for that through the winter, but she must have declined very rapidly, to be in a dying state. She is one of the brightest little creatures on earth. I know her well. I must call and see her before it is too late. De Vane, you will excuse me?"

"Certainly; but you will not go to-night?"

"Without a moment's delay," said Waring, and De Vane, taking leave of him, returned to his lodgings.

Waring walked rapidly to the house where the little girl was waiting for death. It was a small, neat house, with a garden in front, and through the closed blinds Waring saw a light shining cheerfully. He knocked at the door, and it was opened by Mrs. Gildersleeve, who instantly recognized him and invited him in.

He entered the room where Eva's little bed was placed, and in which a cheerful fire was burning. No one was present but an old colored servant belonging to Mr. Springfield. Aunt Hester—as she was called—was seated near the bed. She was an excellent nurse, and her qualities were invaluable. She knew Waring well, and often declared that he was "a saint on earth." She was of that class of servants so rarely met with now; faithful, strongly attached to the family of her master, humble, cheerful, and feeling as deep an interest in the welfare of the family as if every thing belonged to her.

She rose when the young gentleman entered the room, and her face showed the pleasure which his coming gave her.

"How are you, Aunt Hester?" said Waring, frankly extending his hand to her.

"Thank the Lord! Master Waring, I'm well," she said, with a low courtesy.

Waring walked to the bedside. The little girl was sleeping. Her fair hair fell in natural ringlets about her face; the delicate features were as clear as if cut from marble, and the lips, slightly parted, disclosed the fine regular teeth. Even in sleep the face was full of expression, and it was luminous, as if some unseen being whispered in her ear words which thrilled her. Waring looked down silently into her face, and the tears, trembling for a moment on his eyelids, stole down his cheeks.

"So He giveth his beloved sleep," he said, almost unconsciously.

Turning away from the bed, he took a seat near Mrs. Gildersleeve, and inquired if there were any one to sit up with the child through the night.

"Yes, sir," she replied, "Miss Wordsworth will be here

presently. She comes every night, for Eva will ask for her if she does not find her by her side. I do not know how she keeps up, sir, for she has been here every night for two weeks, except one, and she scarcely sleeps at all."

"Could I not relieve her?" asked Waring.

"I fear not, sir," she said. "I wish some one could, for it distresses me to see that young lady wearing herself out. She is an angel on earth, Mr. Waring."

He made no reply, but sat quietly watching the face of the sleeper. How impressive is such sleep! In all the wide realm of nature, there is nothing so touching as the face of a child in sleep! The unconsciousness, the helplessness, the coming future, with its trials, its temptations, its sufferings, its perils! Who that has bent over the forms of his own sleeping children has not experienced unutterable emotions? Who has not felt an indefinable sadness as he thinks of the wide, hard, dreadful road which those little feet must tread till they stop at the grave, where the weary head is to be laid down in the long, long sleep?

And who can look down upon such a sight without a silent prayer to the FATHER, that he would guide the feet aright and cover the defenseless head?

A carriage drove up to the gate, and Esther came in silently but quickly. She saw Waring, and her face brightened; a smile broke over it, and as he rose to meet her, she grasped his hand warmly, saying: "I am very glad to see you."

"And I am happy to see you, Miss Esther," he said, "very happy. I see that our little friend is passing away from us. I feared it, but is it not a rapid decline?"

"Very," she said; "she took cold on New-Year's day, and has been sinking rapidly since then. When did you return?"

"Only this evening, and hearing that little Eva was in

a dying state, I hastened to see her. Will you not suffer me to relieve you to-night? You must need rest."

"No," she said, "she would miss me, and she can stay but a night or two longer with us. I can not leave her."

"Then," said Waring, "I will come to-morrow night, and if you will not consent to be relieved, I will watch with you."

She smiled, and laying aside her wrappings, gave some instructions to Aunt Hester, and seated herself by the bedside.

Waring stood for a moment, looked once more at the little sleeper, took leave, and walked out of the house,

## CHAPTER XIV.

"DEATH is upon me, yet I fear not now.
Open my chamber-window; let me look
Upon the silent vales—the sunny glow
That fills each alley, close, and copsewood nook."
ROBERT NICOLL.

THE next morning, Waring took possession of his room, and was for some hours industriously at work, arranging his books and furniture. De Vane assisted him, and they felt as if their college days had returned. Their rooms were divided by a hall, and both opened upon the street, so that they wore a cheerful aspect. Their books, which were numerous, were arranged upon small movable cases, so that they could be reached without inconvenience; and quite a number of engravings adorned their walls. There was a home feeling about their lodgings which gave them a great charm; and as De Vane surveyed his friend's room, he looked brighter than Mrs. Bowen had seen him appear for weeks.

"Well, Waring," he exclaimed, "now we shall be able to work like Trojans. We may venture to accept Sir Walter Scott's challenge. You know, when he adjusted himself to his labors—about to enter upon a new field—he said that he took for his motto, 'Time and I against any two.' I think there are two here that will give him something to do, if he beats us at hard work."

"You know I am a Methodist," said Waring, "and that name was applied to us at first because we were exact and methodical in all things. Now, we must adopt system in our work. None of your sitting up all night. We will study by rule."

"That's right," said Mrs. Bowen, who stood by, cheerfully surveying the room. "See to that, Mr. Waring, and we shall all thank you. Mr. Clarendon says that he sits up most unreasonably late."

De Vane laughed, and said: "Well, Mrs. Bowen, you will not send me to bed before twelve o'clock, will you?"

"I think ten o'clock is late enough," she said; "but if you will really be in bed by twelve, that will be doing so much better than you have been doing, that we must not quarrel with you."

"We consider that a treaty, formally agreed on, then, Mrs. Bowen," said Waring, "and I will undertake to see that it is carried out in good faith. There is another thing, too, that I shall insist on, De Vane, and that is, that you and I walk two miles every evening at sunset, and we will begin to-day."

"Very well," said De Vane; "you may make it five miles if you like; and I am with you, through storm and sunshine."

"Two miles will do," said Waring; "and as this is a bright day, we shall make an auspicious commencement."

Punctually at five o'clock, Waring rapped at De Vane's door, and reminded him that the hour appointed for their walk had arrived; and they set out with rapid strides. They turned their steps toward that part of the town where Mrs. Gildersleeve resided; and as they were passing the house, Mr. Springfield's carriage dashed up to the door, and Mrs. Springfield and Miss Wordsworth alighted from it. The gentlemen instantly stopped, and advancing to the ladies, spoke with them.

"O Mr. Waring!" exclaimed Esther, "I have just been sent for. Little Eva is sinking so rapidly, that it is feared she will die in the course of a few hours." Her eyes glistened with tears, and in her eagerness, she laid her hand on Waring's arm, and looked up into his face, as if he could help her in this hour of suffering.

"I will go in with you, to see her," he replied. "Mr. De Vane, will you come with us? This is the little girl that I spoke of last night."

Mrs. Springfield had already entered the house. Esther turned her face full upon De Vane, and *looked* an entreaty that he would join them. He was touched. He might possibly be wanted; he might render some service in this house, when the angel of death had crossed the threshold, and was about to lay his dark wings about a helpless child. He bowed, and entered the house with them. They found the little girl lying on a sofa that was drawn up in front of the fire. Her fair curls were brushed away from the face, and her large blue eyes beamed with expression. As Esther entered the room with Waring, Eva's face lighted up with almost celestial radiance, and she turned her eyes on Waring, and said:

"I am so glad to see you, sir. Mother told me you had come."

Waring seated himself in a chair by her side, and taking her hand, said:

"Yes, my dear little Eva, I came to see you last night, but you were sleeping, and I would not disturb you."

Esther was kneeling by the sofa, and bending over, she kissed Eva's forehead. The little girl smiled, and gave her a look of unutterable love. De Vane stood leaning against the mantel-piece, while Mrs. Springfield and Mrs. Gildersleeve were seated at the feet of the little girl.

"Mr. Waring, I am so glad to see you. I was not willing to die till I saw you again. I have heard you so often speak of Jesus, that I felt anxious to have you here, that I might tell you how much I love him now."

"Dear, dear child!" said Waring, "I have long known that you loved him; and I have often told you that Jesus loved you."

"Yes," she said, "and I feel it now. It seems to me that I can almost hear the tones of his voice; and last night, while I slept, it seemed to me that angels filled the room."

Esther's eyes rained tears, and the large drops rolled down Waring's face. De Vane was very pale, and his lips were compressed firmly, as if he braced himself against emotion.

"Miss Esther," the child said, "has been so kind. I am sure that the angels in heaven can not be kinder to me than she has been; and she has talked to me so sweetly about Jesus, that I felt I loved him more and more."

"My precious little Eva," said Esther, "you may be sure that Jesus loves you, and that good angels are all about you."

"Yes, Miss Esther, I know it now. I am going to see the Lord in his bright abode. Oh! how bright it is! I am not afraid to go. I was, for a long time, afraid to die; but not now; no, not now. I am sorry to leave my mother, and you, Mr. Waring, and Miss Esther, and my friends; but heaven is so bright, and Jesus is there, and you will all be coming before long."

Mrs. Gildersleeve's frame shook with emotion, but she could not disturb the calm heaven which filled the heart of her dying child.

"Miss Esther," said the little girl, "is not the sun shining bright?"

"Yes," said Esther, "it is almost sunset; but the evening is very beautiful, dear Eva."

"Well, then," said she, "open the blinds, if you please, and let me see the sky and the trees once more. I shall never see them again."

De Vane raised the sash and threw open the blinds.

The rich, warm rays of the sun streamed in, and the trees and tall shrubbery about the house were touched with colors such as painter never yet spread on canvas.

"It is a beautiful world," said Eva, "very beautiful; but I shall soon see a brighter one. Miss Esther, did you not tell me last night, that Jesus said he would go to prepare a place for us?"

"Yes, my dear Eva," said Esther, "he said so; and it is a lovely place. So many good people have already gone there; and the angels are there, and our Lord himself is there."

The little girl's face was radiant. Upon her features, over which an unearthly beauty lingered, the glory of the upper world was shining.

"Miss Esther," said she, "will you sing for me?"

"My dear, dear Eva, what shall I sing?"

"Oh! the lines that you sang for me when I was so weary, last week; they are so beautiful!"

Esther calmed herself; and having regained her composure as far as was possible in such a scene, she sang some lines which the Methodists had introduced into their social meetings—

"Oh! sing to me of heaven;"

and as her voice, almost trembling with the strong emotion which she could scarcely repress, uttered the words,

"Let music cheer me last on earth,
And greet me first in heaven,"

the lips of the dying child parted, and a smile of more than earthly brightness illuminated her face. Esther felt the little hand which she held grasp hers more closely, and then, with an earnest look upward, she said faintly, "Heaven!" and the light faded out of her eyes.

"Let us pray," said Waring. All kneeling, Waring

breathed a fervent prayer, thanking God for having guided the little feet of this child in the way to heaven; entreating him to enable them all, by his grace, to follow in the same way, observing the footprints of our ascended Lord; and imploring the divine blessing upon the mother, now left a lonely pilgrim on earth.

Waring and De Vane withdrew from the room, and left the house.

"What a scene," said De Vane; "what a scene! How nearly weakness and strength touch each other, and the sublime and the gentle are sometimes brought together!"

"Yes," said Waring, "there indeed weakness and strength were brought together: a little girl dying in her weakness, and the strong angel leading her by the hand, and shining away all her fears."

"It is very wonderful," said De Vane.

"Out of the mouth of babes He can ordain strength," replied Waring.

"A sublimer scene I never witnessed," said De Vane; "a hero perishing in battle can not eclipse that."

"That is just such a tribute as Rousseau paid to Him who died for that little girl. You of course remember his comparing the last hours of Socrates, taking the cup of poison in the midst of cheerful conversation with his friends, with the dying hour of our Lord, expiring in the midst of enemies, and his body torn with anguish, yet praying for his murderers. The tribute wrung even from that man was the highest he could yield. 'Socrates died like a philosopher; Jesus Christ like a God.' I tell you, De Vane, that since the triumph of Jesus Christ, all who trust him may conquer death."

"That was indeed a victory which we just now witnessed. Of what priceless value that faith must be which can enable a child even to triumph over such an enemy!"

"Yes," said Waring; "and I hope, De Vane, that you will soon find it."

"Ah! Waring," he replied, "I am in mists; sometimes I fancy that I see the rifts which let in the sunlight, but the clouds roll once more over the heavens, and the very stars are blotted out."

Waring did not think it best to press his view of the great question just now. He knew that De Vane, like a strong swimmer, would buffet the billows, disdaining help, until his natural strength was exhausted. He comprehended the structure of his character—his pride, his candor, his love of truth, his veneration for all that was really noble and good; and he inwardly hoped that he would yet exclaim with Nathanael, when the true light reached his soul: "Thou art the Son of God: thou art the King of Israel."

The next day was Sunday. De Vane asked Waring at the breakfast-table when the funeral of the little girl would take place.

"This evening, I learn," said Waring, "from her mother's residence."

"It is proper," said De Vane, "that some grown persons should act as pall-bearers; and, if it be agreeable to her friends, I will join you in performing that office. I suppose that you will assist in that way."

"Thank you," said Waring warmly. "It is very kind of you, and it will gratify us all."

Mrs. Bowen's eyes swam in tears.

At five o'clock, quite a large number of persons assembled at Mrs. Gildersleeve's residence; and among them, persons of the highest respectability. Mr. Springfield conducted the services. He took no text, but made some remarks, sketched with fine taste the beautiful character of the little girl, and described her last hours. "Over such a death," said he, "there can be no bitter tears; the hour for grief has gone by, the suffering is ended, and the spirit has found in its native heaven perfect bliss in the smile of Him who, when on earth, took little children in his arms, and blessed them. Let us bear this beautiful, lifeless form to the grave, where flowers will soon spring over it, and the night-dews will water it. She is not dead, but sleepeth."

Waring and De Vane, with two of the larger boys of the Sunday-school, walked on either side of the hearse.

Esther saw De Vane with indefinable emotions. She knew his aristocratic tastes; and yet here he was, walking by the side of the remains of a little girl of humble family to the grave. Mrs. Springfield could not repress her astonishment.

"Esther," said she, "do you observe Mr. De Vane? The patrician must have something very gentle in his nature."

Dr. Dahlgreen, a warm friend to Mrs. Gildersleeve, coming up to the carriage, said:

"Bless my soul! Mrs. Springfield, this is the most aristocratic funeral that I have attended in an age. There is Waring, the first-honor man. I can account for him on the score of his Methodism; but what on earth can have induced that young Virginian, who is as proud as Lucifer, to take his place there?"

Without waiting for an answer, he walked off to his gig, and followed the procession.

The burial-service was read at the grave, and as the mound was raised above it, the whole party of Sunday-school children threw flowers upon it. The level rays of the setting sun streamed over it, and Esther felt as if the smile of God warmed the lowly couch of the little sleeper.

That night, when Waring had returned from church, De Vane entered his room, and said:

"Waring, what are Mrs. Gildersleeve's means of living?"

"Very moderate," replied Waring. "She is industrious, and lives mainly by her own labor."

"She will of necessity incur some unusual expenses now. Will you be good enough to hand her this?"

He put into Waring's hand a purse of dark silk, containing one hundred dollars in gold.

"I do not know her personally," he added, "and I do not wish that she should know that it comes from me. She might feel hurt at accepting any thing from a stranger."

"It is very kind of you," said Waring, "and I will see that she receives it."

"Thank you," said De Vane.

"Sit down," said Waring. "I took tea at Mr. Springfield's this evening, and he and Mrs. Springfield both enjoined it upon me to urge you to visit them. You must do so; it will be good for you in every way."

"I go nowhere," said De Vane; "there is absolutely so much to do, that by the time I get through with a day's work, I am not fit for any thing."

"You will get on better with our systematic way of doing things. Remember the wholesome motto, '*Festina lente.*' An occasional visit to such a family as Mr. Springfield's will do you good in every way."

"Well, I will go with you, and if you find me becoming idle, you must admonish me. By the way, I heard Mr. Clarendon promise Mrs. Habersham that he would take you to see her. What do you say to that?"

"I am very much obliged to him, I'm sure," said Waring. "I should think her house a very attractive one."

"Yes, and filled with works of art, I'm told. I met her at Mr. Clarendon's, some short time since. Miss Godolphin was with her, and was as splendidly beautiful as ever. But it is very strange that she seems to be so sad. I do not understand it."

"Did she appear so when you last met her?"

"Oh! yes; more unmistakably than before."

"I can not comprehend it. She must have suffered. She is certainly an extraordinary person."

"Very," said De Vane. "She is brilliant. We must solve the mystery."

"Take care!" said Waring; "she may be dangerous."

"Just what Mr. Clarendon said; but she disclaimed it, in terms of sadness which absolutely impressed me with their earnestness. But I am trespassing upon you. Good night!"

"Good night!" said Waring. "You're going to bed?"

"Oh! yes. I am somewhat fatigued to-night."

He entered his room; but he did not retire immediately. He sat before his fire in deep thought. The scenes of the day were before him—the grave of little Eva strewn with flowers, and the form of Esther bending over it, and bedewing it with her tears. Even when he slept, the form of Esther floated before him, and seemed to rise heavenward, her face turned toward him, and smiling in the midst of her tears.

## CHAPTER XV.

"Winter is worn that was the flowers' bale.
And thus I see among these pleasant things
Each care decay, and yet my sorrow springs."
Lord Surrey.

Spring opened gloriously. Every vestige of winter was gone. Leaves, flowers, birds, all appeared. The air was balmy; the trees were vocal; windows were raised, and doors thrown open. The town—remarkable for its fine gardens, its shrubbery and trees—was full of sweet odors and cheerful sounds. Leasowes was beautiful; its shrubbery and flowers were never finer. The graveled walks and grassy slopes were delightful. The clear water filled the marble basin to overflowing, and the birds filled its shady recesses with joyous notes. The walks of the public garden were thronged; and nurses drew in Lilliputian carriages, their little charges over its smooth walks.

There is something in the smile of nature to awaken the soul. It cheers the rich and the poor alike; and unlike the luxuries of the artificial world, the flowers, the trees, the balmy air, and the music of birds, may be had without money and without price. The benevolence of God scatters, without stint, flowers in the wilderness; and the laborer in the fields may smell the sweet breath of the earth, and survey the wide expanse of woods and sky. Thank God for the deep-blue heavens, for the great trees, for the wild flowers, for the birds of the air, for little bright streams, for majestic rivers, for the wide sea, for hills and valleys and the great mountains, for solitudes in the wilderness, and for great water-falls which utter his praise in reverberating tones of thunder! Thank God for the green grass, for meadows where cattle graze, for the glory of ripening grain and fruits, for the splendor of summer verdure, for the yellow autumnal harvests, for the stern magnificence of winter!

All nature utters her deep hymn of praise, and breathes her incense. Let the thanksgiving from human hearts mingle with the pure adoration of our MOTHER EARTH!

De Vane had become a regular visitor at Mr. Springfield's, where he was sure to find a warm welcome. Mr. Springfield felt a high respect for him, and enjoyed his conversation, which took a wide range. He saw that the young Virginian was ambitious; but he saw, too, that he was generous. His aspirations were not for distinction merely, but for usefulness. Not for the applause of mankind only, but for the richer applause of his own consciousness of deserving honors. Too proud to stoop, the warmth of his nature made him enter, with ready sympathy, into the condition even of the poor and humble. Some of his warmest friends were among laboring men. There was a stone-cutter employed upon one of the public buildings, a man of intelligence, with whom De Vane contracted a sort of intimacy. He was cutting a Corinthian cap, one day, as De Vane was passing, and the young student stopped to speak with him; examined the pattern by which the man was working, and explained to him the origin of that order of architecture, suggesting, at the same time, that the pattern was too stiff, and that it would be in better taste, if the leaves were somewhat more curved. The man, being one of the head workmen, acted upon the suggestion, and finding his work greatly improved by it, was pleased. He became a fast friend of De Vane, and was in the habit of saying that the young student knew more about stone-cutting than he did. The blacksmith, who shod the horse which De Vane often rode, was very deferential, and did not hesitate to say that the young Virginian could beat him at his own trade.

Mr. Springfield found his range of reading so wide, that he declared himself always refreshed after an hour's conversation with De Vane. They often spoke of Moral Science, and the depth of De Vane's views surprised him. He carefully avoided controversy with him; but suggested lines of thought which he knew would help to conduct the noble, ardent, truthful nature of his young friend, to the spot from which he could look out upon the harmonies of the realm of truth. Mrs. Springfield became much interested in him. She learned from Waring his kindness to Mrs. Gildersleeve, and it deepened her respect for him. Highly cultivated herself, De Vane enjoyed her conversation, and spoke with less reserve to her, perhaps, than to any one else, except Waring. He learned to venerate her true piety, and never, in her presence, uttered a word which could give her pain.

His intercourse with Esther was delightful to him. She grew in his esteem, and her acquirements and accomplishments filled him with admiration. He learned one fact, which he had not discovered in their early acquaintance, that there was a deep enthusiasm pervading her character. He had thought her somewhat too grave, and possibly cold, when he first met her. He saw her passion for music, but even that awakened the thought that she might love that too well to be able to love any thing else with ardor. But he now observed, as he was oftener with her, that her nature was full of ardor—ardor perfectly well regulated, and under the dominion of reason and principle; but there was ardor. Like the soil which produces the finest grapes, there was a warmth which could not be felt on the surface, but which made its presence known by the fruit which it yielded, and diffused itself in the generous wine which exhilarated without intoxicating. He needed no urging now from Waring to induce him to visit Mr. Springfield's; and his friend smiled as he saw the change, but did not remark upon it to him, further than to say, that he was pleased to see him learning to prize good society.

"Haven't I always done that, Waring?" he replied, when his friend made the remark to him.

"Why, some time ago," said Waring, "there was no inducing you to go anywhere, and you seemed to waste your sweetness either on your books, or in conversation with your friend Stiles the stone-cutter, or Hobbs the blacksmith, or Swan the public gardener."

"Now, Waring," he answered, "you know that I always would inflict myself upon you, and that I did visit Mr. Clarendon's, from the first. You are not growing aristocratic, are you?"

"Oh! no, not at all, but I thought you a little inclined that way; and I did not exactly comprehend your liking for the blacksmith, who does swear outrageously."

De Vane laughed, and said: "Yes, I'm trying to break him of that habit. I tell him that it is not gentlemanlike, but he doesn't seem to feel the force of the appeal; for I heard him yesterday calling my horse some very hard names, because he did not choose to have one of his hind-feet held up in the air for thirty minutes."

"You'll have to give him up, unless you reform him. But what do you say to our calling this evening at Mrs. Habersham's?"

"Quite at your service," said De Vane. "You have been there, I believe, once or twice?"

"Yes," said Waring. "Mr. Clarendon invited me to an evening drive with him soon after my return from Georgia, you remember, and we called on the ladies. They were good enough to invite me to visit them, and I have been there once or twice since."

"And how do you find Miss Godolphin? Is she still the queen of night?"

"I do not comprehend her," said Waring; "but she is a very interesting person, and, if I do not mistake, she is a noble woman—full of character."

"As to character," said De Vane, "she has enough of that; and there is a fascination about her. Her beauty, her genius, her accomplishments, her sadness, invest her with a wonderful charm."

"So they do," said Waring. "She is a person, too, of great generosity; her appreciation of others is fine. She speaks of Miss Wordsworth in a way that is very pleasing."

"She could not do less," said De Vane. "Miss Wordsworth's qualities would awaken admiration anywhere; and her purity is such, that even her own sex must admire her."

"Yes," said Waring; "and do you know that though very unlike in person, both being impersonations of the highest but different styles of beauty, I think their organization strikingly similar?"

"Indeed!" said De Vane. "I think Miss Wordsworth the most cheerful—I may say, the happiest person I ever knew, grave as she generally is, while Miss Godolphin seems to be the very impersonation of sadness."

"That does not prove a difference in organization so much as in circumstances. They are both cultivated, thoroughly accomplished, full of enthusiasm, passionately fond of music, of great depth of character; but Miss Wordsworth is a Christian—has never felt in her nature the awakening of human passion, and has never known disappointment. Miss Godolphin has suffered in some way, in what way I do not know. Her pride must have been wounded, and she may have been deceived in some object of her regard. Her history during her stay in Europe is not known to me. But she is a splendid woman of very noble nature. Of that I am sure."

De Vane smiled, but said only: "I shall be pleased to know her better. You have interested me in her."

"I learned to-day," said Waring, "that, hearing of the affliction of Mrs. Gildersleeve, the day after the funeral she drove to the desolate home, and passed an hour in conversation with the bereaved mother, and with great delicacy supplied her with articles of mourning. Esther's gifts and Miss Godolphin's have relieved every want of that kind, and your generous donation has made her altogether comfortable."

After early tea, the two gentlemen called at Mrs. Habersham's. It was a large brick mansion, built in the English style, the offices being in a range with the main building; and it was furnished in the most costly way. English carpets covered the floors; the furniture, also imported, was massive and rich, and the walls were adorned with paintings—copies chiefly of the great masters.

Miss Godolphin's father had married a younger sister of Mrs. Habersham. Both parents were dead, and Mr. Habersham also; and the two ladies, soon after the death of those who were so dear to them, had gone to Europe, where they resided for several years. Mrs. Habersham was wealthy, and Miss Godolphin's fortune was ample.

The gentlemen were received at the door by a footman in livery, and shown into a drawing-room exquisitely fitted up. A grand piano-forte stood near the middle of the room, and a harp was not far from it, by which a chair was placed, as if it had been just occupied. Light chairs of different patterns were distributed over the floor, and two sofas, of graceful form, and covered with chintz, were on either side of the fire-place. On the mantle-piece, a French clock, representing Sappho leaping into the sea, was placed, and over it hung a portrait of Miss Godolphin, in the highest style of art. It was a half-length. The attitude was that of contemplation. The head, slightly drooped, rested on one of the hands; the hair, parted simply in front, was gathered in a full band at the back of the head; the other hand held a Tuscan bonnet, wreathed with wild flowers, as if it had been just covered with these natural adornments; and the back-ground afforded a view of the sea. The picture was exquisite, of great merit as a work of art, and the likeness was striking.

Waring had never seen it, this being his first introduction to this room; and he and De Vane were standing observing the picture, when the door was opened, and Miss Godolphin entered.

She received the gentlemen with warmth, and expressed her gratification at their visit, saying that Mrs. Habersham would soon join them.

"We were observing your picture, Miss Godolphin," said Waring, "and we thought it every way a triumph of art."

"It is thought to be so by all who have seen it," she replied. "It is the work, too, of an American artist."

"That enhances its value," said Waring.

"Yes," she said. "I am intensely American. We found, in Naples, a countryman of ours who has been in Italy for years. He passed two years in Paris, and then went to Florence, afterward to Rome, and when we met him he had taken a villa near Naples, and was attracting large numbers of English and American travelers. He painted that picture."

"He will return to this country, I suppose?" said De Vane.

"That is by no means certain," she said. "His world is that of art. He paints but few portraits; but his favorite subject is, nevertheless, the human face. He has a picture of extraordinary power, representing Jephthah's daughter going out to meet her victorious father. The contrast between her glorious, exultant face, full of pride and joy, and the anguish which speaks from every feature of the hero, is wonderful."

As De Vane looked at the portrait before him, he fancied that it might resemble the Jewish maiden after she learned her fate; but he did not venture to say so.

"There is another of his pictures," she said, rising and walking across the room. It represented the daughter of Herodias bearing the head of John the Baptist to her mother. The conception was original: the maiden bore the grand head upon a silver dish, and her averted face showed her horror of the act which she was performing under the injunction of her imperious mother. The form and face were superb, and the whole picture a great success. Departing from the usual ideal, the artist had given the maiden auburn hair and blue eyes. The rich, heavy ringlets fell about the face, and the hair, gathered in a braid on the back of the head, was clasped by a golden serpent. Tears stood in the lustrous eyes, and tenderness touched the features, giving to the face a blended expression of anguish and compassion. The form was stately for so young a person, and a matchless grace was in the attitude. De Vane was startled at observing, in the whole form and features, a close resemblance to Esther. She might have stood for the picture; and gazing upon it for some minutes in silence, he found his eyes moisten. There is wonderful power in a picture, and as De Vane stood before this, he really was conscious of an intenser interest in Esther than he was aware of before. He had never analyzed his sentiments; he had formed no purposes; and he was startled to find himself so moved by a representation which associated her with a scene of horror and suffering. The real state of the heart is often disclosed to us suddenly. It is especially so in great and generous natures. A dream, a leave-taking, a song, the presence of danger, or the hand of suffering laid upon the object, wakes up within us the consciousness of the depth of a sentiment whose existence we had not suspected before. Startled, alarmed, we wake to the real, where before we had been reposing in dreamy listlessness; and we realize what Comus experienced when he heard the music which arrested his steps, and filled him with wonder.

"De Vane," said Waring, "do you find any resemblance between that form, and any of our friends?"

"It is wonderful!" exclaimed De Vane.

"Of course," said Miss Godolphin, "I know that you see in it a strong resemblance to Miss Wordsworth. Do you know that it is so faithful, I am myself amazed at it? The first time that I met her, her face was perfectly familiar to me. I could not recall it. She was so very young when I left for Europe, that I did not know her; but yet, upon seeing her upon my return, I found myself startled. I could not say why, but the thought that I had known her elsewhere haunted me; nor could I account for it until some two weeks since, when our pictures were brought home and unboxed. Then, when this was hung, I saw in an instant what had so long bewildered me."

"It is very remarkable," said Waring.

"It is positively wonderful," said Miss Godolphin. "If it were only that some features resembled, it might be accounted for by supposing it to be the meeting of the ideal and the actual in some accidental way, which I think often occurs; but here is every thing—hair, eyes, mouth, the bust, the very form; and, I repeat, it is nothing short of marvelous. The artist valued the picture highly, was reluctant to part with it, and would not sell it to me; but as we had purchased several large and costly pictures from him, he presented that to me, saying that it would go to the very place where he desired to be known and appreciated by his works.

"It is very strange," said De Vane. "A more perfect likeness I never saw. Can it be possible that the artist has seen Miss Wordsworth?"

"Oh! no," she said. "He went abroad when she was a child."

"Do you remember, Miss Godolphin," said De Vane, "to have seen it stated that a man of science, having observed the effect of the dome of St. Peter's upon the beholder, and thinking it perfect in its proportions, he resolved to measure it? He did so. He tested the strength of the curve, and he found that the arch of the dome was the curve of greatest strength; thus making the discovery that the lines of beauty and strength were identical. Michael Angelo sought for artistic effect in its construction, and that conducted him to strength; so that the dome is matchless."

"The incident is charming," said Miss Godolphin; "and do you know, Mr. De Vane, that you have paid a very striking tribute to the beauty of Miss Wordsworth, by accounting for the resemblance which we all see, upon the principle that the artist pursuing his line of ideal loveliness, we find it verified by the real?"

De Vane colored, and bowed.

"But you need not be ashamed, Mr. De Vane, at the thought of having committed high treason against a lady in her own realm, by laying down the proposition that the perfection of beauty is to be found in a style wholly different from her own; for I quite agree with you, that Miss Wordsworth is perfect."

"Pardon me, Miss Godolphin," he said. "In the human face, widely different styles may yet be perfect."

"Thanks, Mr. De Vane," said she. "It is so gracefully atoned for, that you need not regret the treason."

Waring and De Vane were both surprised. They had never seen her so bright.

Mrs. Habersham came in, and renewed the welcome to the gentlemen.

The conversation turned upon foreign travel, and Mrs. Habersham expressed her gratification at being once more at home, declaring that nothing could induce her to go abroad again.

"It is a pleasure that I promise myself," said De Vane, "and I should not willingly relinquish it."

"Of course," said Mrs. Habersham, "you should go; nor do I regret having gone, but I would not tempt the ocean again."

"To me," said Waring, "it would be very agreeable to visit Europe; but if I ever cross the Atlantic, I shall go to the East. It must be deeply interesting to trace the rise and progress of civilization, and to explore the countries where the most important events have occurred. The Nile and the Holy Land would be irresistible to me, if there were no barriers between us."

"I felt just as you do, Mr. Waring," said Miss Godolphin; "but my aunt and myself had no one upon whom we were willing to impose ourselves for such a journey. My uncle, who was with us, is an old gentleman, of confirmed habits, and loves his ease. He declared that the very idea of being subjected to the tender mercies of the outlandish people who hold those countries, once the seats of civilization, made him shiver. 'Then, too,' said he, 'where would one find *café au lait* for breakfast, and *truffles* for dinner?'"

"Yes," said Mrs. Habersham. "Yet Godolphin has lived so much in Paris and London, that he will never reside even in this country permanently."

"Very bad taste it is, I think," said Miss Godolphin. "England is to me intolerable, though most of my relatives are there. I love the vigorous, active, boundless life which opens before me in this young country."

"I rejoice to hear you say so, Miss Godolphin," said Waring.

"Yes," said Mrs. Habersham, "Hortensia is thoroughly American, quite as much so as I am."

"Still," said De Vane, "there must be much to admire in England; and social life is in perfection there."

"Very far from it," said Miss Godolphin. "Of course there is refinement and cultivation; but there is a great deal of heartlessness too, and there must be where the social organization is so artificial and frigid."

"I had not supposed so," said De Vane. "Some of our Virginia families find their chief delight in visiting England, and passing months with their relatives in that country."

"Yes," said Miss Godolphin, "I know it. The Guilfords, for instance. But, Mr. De Vane, I do not sympathize with them. I am an American woman, and I rejoice in being able to claim such a country for my own. How I exulted in undeceiving them when on the Continent! I was mistaken for an Englishwoman; and how they opened their eyes with amazement when I told them I was an American!"

All laughed, and Waring said:

"You do not know, Miss Godolphin, how much pleasure it gives me to hear you speak in this way."

"Oh!" said she, "I have no patience with women who come home from their travels, only to look with disdain upon every thing here, and to sigh for luxuries which they have left behind them."

"You rouse my patriotism, Miss Godolphin," said De Vane. "I shall hope to return home, if I ever make my tour, as loyal as you are."

"I do not doubt it, Mr. De Vane," she said. "You are too earnest to be captivated by any thing artificial, however brilliant it may be."

"Thank you," said De Vane. "I shall hope to deserve your confidence."

"There is one thing we ought to do, however," said she; "we ought to exert ourselves to cultivate the taste of our people, and to import every thing good that we can from abroad. I love my country, and I wish to see society here what it ought to be, exhibiting the only aristocracy worth calling by the name; a system that admits the true, the good, the cultivated, the men of soul and intellect, and the women of worth and culture, into its highest circle, no matter how humble their birth, or how poor their fortunes. An aristocracy of birth is simply ridiculous; for I have seen people of the very best families, as they are called, as vulgar and stupid as possible."

Waring and De Vane both looked at her with admiration; she was so noble, so full of courage, so disinterested. She could afford to utter such sentiments without the fear of misconstruction, for her own family was really aristocratic.

"Yes," she continued, "to see some of these specimens of noble blood, inferior in form, in mind, in manners, assuming airs and treated with deference, has roused me so that I could scarcely be civil."

"You are right, Hortensia," said Mrs. Habersham. "I have seen you at times when you were scarcely civil to some of the people we met abroad. Your uncle was distressed."

"Very sorry," she said; "but my American blood was up, and I could have defied the whole House of Lords."

They all laughed heartily. Waring asked for music. Her whole aspect changed, and the habitual sadness returned upon her.

"And do you love music, Mr. De Vane?" she asked.

"Passionately," he replied; "yes, passionately."

She rose, and took her seat by the harp.

"I will not venture to touch the piano this evening," she said. "If I had Miss Wordsworth here to accompany me, I should gladly do so. What a voice she has! I assure you that I have never heard it rivaled in so young a person. In four years more, if she cultivates herself, she will surpass any one that I know, on the stage or off it."

She touched the strings; they breathed the sweetest harmony. The low tender notes were almost human in their utterance; and she sang:

"When 'midst the gay I meet
That gentle smile of thine,
Though still on me it turns most sweet,
I scarce can call it mine;
But when to me alone
Your secret tears you show,
Oh! then I feel those tears my own,
And claim them whilst they flow."

She sang the entire song, and then, rising from the instrument, seated herself near De Vane.

He thanked her for the song, and spoke of the exquisite beauty of the figure—of the frozen snow on Jura's steep melting under a glance of fire.

"Yes," she replied, "it is very beautiful. Mr. De Vane, you are young; you are ambitious, too, I know. Do not suffer your tastes to mislead you. You will go to Europe. I heard the Guilfords speak of you. Do be loyal to your country."

"That I shall be," said he. "I am as thoroughly republican as you are. My tastes in social life might lead me far; but as to my political principles, they are perfectly well established."

"I am rejoiced to hear you say so. It is a grand thing to be a true man."

After some general conversation, the gentlemen rose to

leave. Mrs. Habersham expressed the wish that they would often visit her house; and with thanks for the invitation, they bade the ladies good-night.

On their way to their lodgings, both expressed their admiration for Miss Godolphin.

"*Mehercule!* Waring," said De Vane, "she is magnificent."

"Very fine," said Waring. "Really, a noble woman. How animated she was this evening!"

"Yes," said De Vane. "I should like to see the Alpine snow fairly melted."

"What a republican she is!" said Waring. "I had no idea of it."

"Nor I," said De Vane. "I supposed she was as aristocratic in her ideas as she is in her appearance. I like her intense patriotism. We must see her often."

Waring was by this time in deep thought, and De Vane walked by his side in silence.

As they entered the house, Waring said: "De Vane, Miss Godolphin is the most extraordinary person I have ever known. We must see her often."

"May she not be dangerous?" said De Vane, opening the door of his room.

"Ah! you are quoting Mr. Clarendon," said Waring. "Good night!"

## CHAPTER XVI.

"Now, thanks to Heaven, that of its grace
Hath led me to this lovely place!
Joy have I had."

WORDSWORTH.

DE VANE had ordered, from the stone-cutter, Mr. Stiles, a monument for the grave of Eva Gildersleeve, and as he had not yet seen it since it was erected, he walked alone to the cemetery, that he might examine it. It was a little earlier than the hour when he usually took his evening walk with Waring, and it was some few days after they had made their visit to Mrs. Habersham's. He had not met Esther since; but she had been with him, in that spiritual way which we have all experienced. In his day-dreams and night-dreams her form was before him. His interest in her had deepened strangely. Still he did not enter into an analytical examination of his sentiments toward her, nor had he formed any purpose in regard to her. Ambitious yet ardent, he had formed large plans for his future, and he had no thought of entangling himself just now in any way that might hinder their grandest development; yet he was conscious of the pleasure which he enjoyed in the society of Esther. She grew constantly in his esteem; and so completely had he come within the sphere of her attraction, that he found himself seeking her presence oftener than he had ever before sought the society of any one. He selected books for her, and her library grew under his contributions. He sketched for her, and in her chamber there hung several views of the Virginia mountains, which his own hand had produced.

The cemetery was in the midst of a small forest of natural trees, chiefly pines, and was on a gentle eminence that afforded a view of the soft Southern landscape that spread through the valley of the river and took in the hills beyond it. It was a place of resort for those who had relatives or friends there; and strangers at times visited it, to observe the tasteful decorations which affection had bestowed upon the graves of the loved and departed who slept there. There were a few very handsome monuments, and quite a number of smaller ones.

De Vane walked through the grounds, silent but for the songs of birds. They made the place vocal with their joyous notes, as if they would cheer the watchers over those who slept there; and sometimes, soaring heavenward, seemed to invite them to look there for consolation.

He found the grave of Eva. It was a grassy mound, and on the centre of it, a square, white marble block was placed, upon which stood a vase of the purest Italian marble, encircled with the name of EVA GILDERSLEEVE. Through the letters a running vine was carved, bearing leaves and half-opened flowers. Mr. Stiles had shown great skill in carrying out the design which De Vane had handed to him. The vase was an open one, intended to receive earth, that it might bear natural flowers.

De Vane stood looking at the work, and his mind reverted to the evening when the little child who slept under the turf expired. Her sweetness, her faith, her tranquil leave-taking of the world—all came to view vividly. He saw, too, the group about the dying child—Esther clasping the wasted little hand while she sang of heaven; and involuntarily he asked himself if it could be possible, that the spirit then beaming through the features, luminous even in death, could have ceased to live. He was lost in thought, and stood leaning against a tree. Suddenly he was roused by a step just at his side, and turning, he saw Esther. He started. Her presence was so unexpected, that she seemed to have come from the world of spirits to solve the doubts which were gathering about his soul. She was dressed in white, and her graceful form appeared almost unearthly in its loveliness.

"I did not know that I should find you here, Mr. De Vane," she said, "or I should not have ventured to disturb your visit to our little friend's grave."

He instantly advanced, and gave her his hand.

"Nothing could be more agreeable to me, Miss Wordsworth," he said, "than your coming. I had not yet seen the monument placed over Eva, and I came to examine it."

"It is very beautiful. I have seen it. I came last Sunday evening with my aunt, and we both admired it greatly. Nothing could be more appropriate—flowers interwoven with the name. The design is, of course, yours?"

"Yes; I was so impressed by the scene which I witnessed when she died, that I would not deny myself the happiness of paying this little tribute to her memory."

"We are all deeply indebted to you. She was an extraordinary little girl, as you saw, and her triumph was glorious. It was so serene; and I think, Mr. De Vane, that the serene is most to be desired in our last moments."

"Oh! yes; a calm death is always beautiful."

"It realizes what is spoken so beautifully of the Christian's death—'falling asleep in Jesus.'"

De Vane was silent.

"I have come, Mr. De Vane, to fill the vase with flowers—such flowers as will grow and bloom perpetually."

She called a servant who stood near the gate, and he came forward with an earthen vase filled with earth and flowers, and taking it from his hands, she was about to transplant them into the marble vase.

"Allow me," said De Vane; "this must be a joint labor with us."

She yielded to him. He took the earthen pot, and care fully transferred the contents to the marble vase. Esther directing the servant to bring some water from the little stream which ran near the spot, she watered the flowers which De Vane had planted. Pausing for a few moments to look at their work, they turned away silently, and walked through the graveyard. The conversation naturally turned upon the scene about them.

"To me, Mr. De Vane," said Esther, "this is a cheerful place. I look upon these hillocks as beds, where weary pilgrims are resting. But they will awake out of their sleep."

"Do you know that you have almost literally quoted a line from the Swedish poet Tegner?—

'Where his fathers sleep in their hillocks green.'"

"No, I did not know the line. But what is it but another rendering of our Lord's words, and of those of the apostles? After all, the Bible is the source of all beauty, as it is of all wisdom."

"It is a wonderful book, and I read it with increasing admiration. I can scarcely comprehend how such a book as that called Job could have been produced in so early an age. Older than the poetry of Greece, it surpasses in sublimity any thing in Homer."

"I am much pleased to hear you say so, for I know your admiration for the classics."

"Oh! yes. I do not modify to any extent my settled estimate of classical literature, but I have been astonished of late, in reading the book of Job, to find it so full of the sublime as well as the beautiful. 'Hast thou entered into the springs of the sea? Have the gates of death been opened unto thee? Or hast thou seen the doors of the shadow of death?' As if death were a dread monarch, whose lofty gates, yet invisible to mortals, threw their appalling shadow over the world. Then the glorious marshaling of the constellations in their nightly circuits. 'Canst thou bind the sweet influence of Pleiades? or loose the bands of Orion? Canst thou bring forth Mazzaroth in his season? or canst thou guide Arcturus with his sons? Knowest thou the ordinances of heaven? Canst thou set the dominion thereof in the earth?' The description of the war-horse is the noblest picture of the kind in the writings of any age or people."

Esther looked at him as he spoke with great animation, uttering the sentences which he quoted in a way to give them their greatest effect, with admiration.

"And do you not find," she asked, "in the New Testament much to interest you? Is it possible to read the Evangelists without feeling their inspiration? Or to listen to the teachings of our Lord, with their gentleness, their purity, their spiritual power, without being thrilled and awed as if the Divinity stood in our midst? O Mr. De Vane! you must see that in the life and the death of our Lord, there is a higher sublimity than in all else that has been made known to us. How immeasurably his teachings transcend those of men! What is there in the words of Socrates to rival them? He did not venture to teach positive truth. All he aimed at was an approximation to the true, the real, the immortal. And the fine speculations of Plato charm us by their beauty, but after all they are but speculations. In this wide world we need a sure guide, and when we approach the boundaries of the invisible world, we look for some strong arm to bear us up, and steady our tottering steps."

Her face was radiant, as she stood for a moment and looked up to De Vane.

"The aspirations of humanity," he said, "are such as you represent them to be, Miss Wordsworth. A traveler upon a wide plain, far from home at night, does not turn his eyes more anxiously to the heavens to see if he can find a guiding-star, or pause and listen with suppressed breath for some human voice, more earnestly than does man in his pilgrimage for some sure guidance. Life is full of dread mysteries. The future is the unknown."

"Oh! not unknown. It is true we see dimly through the mists which surround us, but it is not best for us, while in this state of discipline, to have revealed to us too clearly the objects of a future world. But the future is not covered with impenetrable clouds. Through the rifts golden rays come, and upon this sea of life, tossed as it is sometimes with tempests, there is heard a voice which says: 'Be not afraid.'"

"You are happy in your faith, Miss Wordsworth. Would that I could share it! But while I would not, if I could, disturb to the slightest extent the beautiful repose of your nature upon a base that seems to you so solid, I should be uncandid if I did not say to you how hard I find the task of submitting my reason to the dominion of any system which I do not comprehend. I see the beauty of Christianity, but I do not understand its great mysteries."

"And do you not intend to seek to explore what is so awful in its relations to us? Surely you will not live so as to have it said of you, with all your rich endowment of mind, in the language of my namesake, William Wordsworth:

'The intellectual power through words and things
Went sounding on a dim and perilous way."

"I should be too happy," he said, "to be able to make my escape from a path which the Poet of the Lakes has so powerfully described; but how shall it be done? I stand upon a sea of doubt, and if I would borrow wings to bear me across it, I fear that, like those of Icarus, they would fail me, and leave me to perish in the waves."

"You will perish, if you trust to any of the inventions of man. There is one book that teaches us the way to the invisible world, where the good of all ages will be assembled. The teachings of man will mislead us. The world is full of illusions; it deceives and flatters: but the Bible does neither. It teaches that even the best must suffer. It invites us to tread a narrow path, but it is a path which the true, the good, the heroic have trod. Suffering and tears have stained it; but the feet of Him who came to seek and to save that which was lost have consecrated it."

They walked on in silence. The western heaven was resplendent. The clouds which floated through it seemed to be phantom ships, their sails illumined. The delicate opal spread wide above the deep orange that rested on the horizon. A single star glittered in the pure depths of boundless ether. A shoreless sea of glory appeared to stretch beyond the visible objects. Esther stood gazing upon the glowing heavens. She seemed to forget the presence of De Vane. The lingering light played upon her features, and kindled a glory about her brow, such as the old painters love to trace upon the head of the Virgin; and she uttered, in tones scarcely audible, those words, so full of consolation to a stricken world: "God is love."

De Vane never forgot the picture. It entered his soul, and spread through it the light of immortal beauty. Upon the wide sea and in far distant lands, he often recalled it; and the words uttered by those pure lips, over which no earthly passion had ever breathed, sounded in his ears as if a celestial being spoke to him.

Neither moved for some minutes. Esther then turned to De Vane, and said:

"It is time we should return."

They retraced their steps to the gate of the graveyard, where Mr. Springfield's crariage was drawn up, awaiting Esther. She invited De Vane to take a seat with her, and he, handing her into the carriage, entered it also; and they drove away. When they reached Mr. Springfield's residence, that gentleman came to the carriage to receive Esther, and seeing De Vane, invited him to go in with them and pass the evening. The invitation was accepted. It was the first time that he had taken tea in this way with the family. His evenings had frequently been passed there, but he had called at a later hour, and somewhat in a formal way; and as he took his seat at the table, he felt that he was now really welcomed into the unrestrained confidence of the house, as a friend. There is a charm about the ease and unrestraint of sitting down to a tea-table in the evening with friends. It dissolves the little frost-work of ceremony instantly; familiar topics spring up, and we discuss in a genial way whatever interests us.

The table was spread with luxuries; early fruits, strawberries abounded, and rich cream, and snowy curds. Flowers were on the table, and they lent a refreshing air of refinement to it. Mrs. Springfield did not disdain housekeeping, and the tastefulness of her establishment and the elegance of her entertainments were universally known. What a charm there is about such a home! How the picture comes up to us now of one in the far South, where purity and goodness, and unwearying kindness, and the patient ministry of self-sacrificing love, abounded! The presiding form is gone; the true, steady blue eyes are closed, and the busy hands gently laid across each other in the still sleep which will not last always!

Esther sat opposite to De Vane, and never appeared more attractive. Her pure white dress was becoming to her, and in her rich hair she wore wild flowers, the long crimson drops mingling with her curls.

"Is it your first visit to our graveyard, Mr. De Vane?" asked Mr. Springfield.

"Yes, my first."

"We often go there, and find it any thing but a gloomy place. There should be more care bestowed upon it, and then I think it would be really attractive."

"Yes, I think so. I was surprised to find so much taste displayed in the tombs; for often one is offended by the neglected graves which he sees, or by the bad taste shown in their decoration."

"I have often observed it," said Mr. Springfield; "for I make it a rule, in my travels, always to visit the burial-places of the cities, and even villages, where I stop for a day or two. To read the epitaphs is to me a source of endless interest."

"And how strange some of them are!" said De Vane. "It is a department of literature which brings the ludicrous into sad juxtaposition with grief."

"Yes; it is too true."

"I was much pleased," said Esther, "with Washington Irving's description of Westminster Abbey. How impressive it must be to walk through it, to look down upon the marble forms of old heroes, stretched at full length; their faces upturned, their hands meekly closed, as if in prayer—in full armor, but the sword laid aside forever!"

"It is the most beautiful of all his sketches, I think," said De Vane.

"One epitaph which he mentions," said Mr. Springfield, "is singularly affecting. It is an inscription on a family tomb: 'All the brothers were brave, and all the sisters virtuous.'"

"Very fine," said De Vane.

"Far the most beautiful cemetery that I have visited," said Esther, "is Laurel Hill, near Philadelphia. At the entrance, carved in brown stone, stands a group which arrests you at once: Sir Walter Scott—Old Mortality—and his pony. It is very appropriate, and gives an air of cheerfulness to the grounds. The tombs, too, are pretty, some of them fine; and the Schuylkill winds silently by the grounds, as if unwilling to disturb the repose of the place."

"It made the same impression on me," said Mrs. Springfield.

"I have never seen it, but I must do so," said De Vane. "Your description is a charming one."

"What do you think, Mr. De Vane," asked Mr. Springfield, "of the manner of disposing of the dead by some of the ancients—burning the bodies?"

"It has something to recommend it. It takes away the dreadful idea of slow decay, and enables the surviving friends to preserve the precious ashes in an urn, which may at all times be visited with satisfaction. But it must be appalling to see the remains of one dear to us suddenly and utterly consumed."

"Oh! yes," said Esther; "dust to dust, as in our Christian mode of interment, is the most consolatory mode, after all, of putting out of sight those we love."

"Do you remember," said De Vane, addressing himself to her, "the scene described in regard to the remains of Shelley? He was drowned in the Bay of Spezzia, having set sail in his boat from Leghorn, where he had been to make a visit: a storm came on, and all on board perished. When the remains were found, it was decided to burn them; and the act was performed in accordance with what it may be supposed would have been the poet's wishes. Frankincense and wine, and other classical materials for burning, were used; and the flame arising from the pile was observed to be of extraordinary beauty. Lord Byron was present."

"Poor Shelley!" said Esther, "his life, death, and every thing seemed to be in harmony with nothing but the ideal. But his friends were sensible enough to take his ashes, and deposit them in the Protestant burial-ground at Rome."

"What a thrilling description," said De Vane, "Virgil gives of the death of Dido! She mounts the pile, made of objects dear to her by association, and yet filling her with anguish, and stabs herself before the flames are kindled, which are to mingle the ashes of the cherished memorials with her own. Æneas, looking back from the sea, beheld the walls glowing with the flame from the funeral pile of the unhappy queen, whom his desertion had filled with despair."

"What a picture!" said Esther. "She acted under the impulse of womanly passion, without the principles of a pure faith to guide her, or its consoling truths to sustain her."

"To me," said Mr. Springfield, "nothing in connection with burying the dead is more impressive and touching than the conduct of Abraham in purchasing the cave of Machpelah, for the last resting-place of Sarah."

"It is," said Mrs. Springfield, "exquisitely beautiful. The noble bearing of the patriarch, grand even in his grief, and with too profound a respect for the memory of his wife, to accept a burial-place for her as a gift."

"Wonderfully fine!" said De Vane, "and it is to be observed how much importance the Hebrews, from the earliest time, attached to the spots where their remains should rest. I was impressed with this, in reading, some time since, the account of the death of Joseph. So deep was his sentiment in regard to it, that he took an oath of his brethren, that they would take his bones with them, when they went up to the land of promise."

"All the early nations," said Mr. Springfield, "had that sentiment, so far as we are able to learn any thing respecting them. The pyramids are tombs, undoubtedly."

"Speaking of the Egyptians," said De Vane, "reminds me of their mode of preserving the bodies of their dead, which I must say is to me hideous."

"I entirely agree with you," said Esther, "and I like vaults as little. The earth—the fresh, dear, mother earth—is the true place where the weary should lie down to rest."

"But you do not object to tombs?" said Mr. Springfield.

"No; but they must be light and graceful to please me. At least, the green grass and the wild flowers must spring and encircle the marble, and mark the outlines of the grave."

"Except in the cases of great men," said De Vane; "then I think that grandeur should be the prevailing effect in the tomb."

"I should make no exceptions," said Esther. "Death parts us from the great world, with its pomp and grandeur; and while I should, of course, mark the spot where an eminent man sleeps, by some appropriate monument, I would surround it too with those simple things, such as flowers, which appeal to the common sentiment of humanity, a love of the beautiful, and a clinging to nature."

"But would you not break the impression, and mar the effect, in that way? The lofty column is to express the grand, the heroic; and if you associate with it objects of simple beauty, you lessen the veneration which the structure is intended to raise in the breast. For instance, the tomb of Themistocles, at Athens, overlooking the sea, where his genius achieved its noblest triumphs, would be less impressive if the grass encircled it, or flowers entwined it."

"The artistic effect might be less," said Esther, "though I am not sure of that. A contrast might be produced which would serve to heighten the aspect of grandeur; but

I would sacrifice something of that to a still higher effect: the teaching that in death the purest sentiments of humanity are shared by the great and the lowly—the fondness for nature, and the love of the beautiful."

"Then you prefer rural graveyards to the finest cemeteries?"

"Yes; but I would intermingle the objects of nature with the works of art. This is done at Laurel Hill, and will, I think, be carried out more perfectly as our country grows older."

"I certainly hope," said Mr. Springfield, "that every thing will be done, that can be, to cultivate the taste of our people for the beautiful. We are in great danger of becoming too practical, and I confess my horror of the utilitarian philosophy. It is pleasing to see the dead cared for; and it must be a generous sentiment which strives to perpetuate the memory of the departed, who can no longer serve us. And even if the display which we sometimes witness in elaborate tombs be intended as an atonement for neglect to the person while living, still it ought to be encouraged."

"Speaking of country churchyards," said Mrs. Springfield, "I think that some of the most touching testimonials of affection for the departed, are to be found in them. The green sod, carefully kept, and the ever-springing flowers, are simple but beautiful tributes."

"And the impression which such a spot makes upon a person of refinement and sensibility," said Esther, "is shown in Gray's Elegy. That poem alone has made him immortal."

"And ought to do so," said De Vane. "The sentiments are as noble as they are exquisitely expressed."

"I am very impatient myself," said Mr. Springfield, "of any thing which perpetuates the aristocratic distinctions of life beyond the grave, and I share Mrs. Springfield's preference for rural burying-places."

"It is a sentiment," said De Vane, "which every generous nature must sympathize with; and the poetry of all ages shows this. Shakespeare comprehended the superiority of natural adornments for the resting-places of the beautiful, the good, and the innocent. Laertes says of Ophelia:

'Lay her i' the earth;
And from her fair and unpolluted flesh
May violets spring!' "

"I well remember it," said Esther; "and the queen says, as she scatters flowers in the grave:

"'Sweets to the sweet: Farewell!' "

"Poor Hamlet!" said De Vane, "he could only exclaim:

'I loved Ophelia: forty thousand brothers
Could not, with all their quantity of love,
Make up my sum.'

His love was too intense even for the tribute of flowers!"

"It is often so in deep grief," said Mrs. Springfield. "But when the grief is somewhat softened, then we come with our offerings. Then we plant the sweetest flowers, and re-visit the spot from time to time, to train them."

"One of the most perfect odes in the language," said De Vane, "is, by some law of association which I do not exactly comprehend, recalled to my memory by your remark; it is by Collins. He pays a tribute to the brave, sinking to rest amidst the blessings of their country—they sleep—and he says:

'When Spring, with dewy fingers cold,
Returns to deck their hallowed mould,
She there shall dress a sweeter sod
Than Fancy's feet have ever trod.' "

"It is perfect," said Esther, with enthusiasm. "Nothing of the kind can be finer. The dewy fingers of Spring—cold—returning as if her sole mission were to dress the sod under which the brave sleep. Ah! Mr. De Vane, after all, my aunt's country churchyards do seem very sweet resting-places."

"Yes," said De Vane, "nature triumphs over art; and however we may be attracted by the artificial in health and prosperity, our tastes must become purer as we feel the hand of the destroyer upon us, or experience any great calamity."

"And yet," said Mr. Springfield, "Lord Nelson exclaimed, upon going into his last battle, I believe: 'Victory or Westminster Abbey!' "

"Yes," said De Vane, "he was in health, and felt the excitement that a brave man feels when going into battle. His ambition blazed with all its intenseness. But when he received his wound, which he felt to be mortal, his tender sensibilities triumphed, his affections asserted their sway, and he spent his last hours in making some provision for the woman whom he loved."

Esther's face glowed with interest. The extreme beauty and felicity of the criticism which De Vane uttered, she saw clearly, and, turning to Mr. Springfield, she said:

"I think Mr. De Vane is right."

"If you both take part against me," said he playfully, "I must consider myself vanquished; but instead of surrendering to either of you young people, I shall lay my arms down at the feet of my wife, for I believe she first suggested the superiority of country churchyards, while you were both disposed to have them a good deal embellished by art."

"Very gallantly done," said Esther. "My aunt deserves the trophies."

"I shall use my authority, then," said Mrs. Springfield,

"if a triumph is decreed me, to invite you all into the library, where we shall find it more agreeable, perhaps, than here."

She rose from the table, and they all followed her.

There was an indescribable charm about this house. A refined taste presided over all its arrangements, and De Vane never visited it without feeling refreshed, as one does upon quitting the dusty plain to walk in the midst of gardens.

He sat for an hour longer, conversing with Mr. Springfield upon subjects of public interest—for both were observers of the actual, living world, much as they loved books; while Mrs. Springfield and Esther employed themselves with some light embroidery-work, of a pattern just introduced from Germany, and occasionally took part in the conversation.

Happy hours! Time glides by without reminding us of his flight. Happy homes! where the duties of life are not overlooked, and where the heart and the intellect are both improved; where taste presides, and all that is good in our nature is cheered and invigorated; where books, and music, and cheerful conversation close the day, and give to each passing evening the tribute of genial natures.

## CHAPTER XVII.

"Thanks, thanks to thee, my worthy friend,
  For the lesson thou hast taught!
Thus at the flaming forge of life
  Our fortunes must be wrought—
Thus on its sounding anvil shaped
  Each burning deed and thought!"
LONGFELLOW.

THE summer vacation of the College was drawing near. The annual examination of the classes was about to commence, and the unusual increase in the number of the students induced the Trustees to think of adding another member to the Faculty. Hitherto no very marked attention had been bestowed upon studies which had a theological tendency. It is true moral philosophy had been taught, and well taught, and natural theology had not been overlooked; but no decided training was given to those inquiries after revealed truth which every one who comprehends the claims of Christianity to any extent must feel to be so transcendently important. The religious sentiment of the State began to look into this subject, and to inquire into the reasonableness of bestowing more attention upon studies which should in all Christian states be recognized as of the highest importance. And while it was not desired that a strictly theological school should be opened in the College, such as would fit young men for the ministry, yet it was insisted that every young man who came to that seat of learning, now so renowned for its scholarship, should be instructed in that department of knowledge which it became every gentleman to understand as a part even of polite education. The great argument, so long urged, that it was best not to make religious instruction a part of education, because it might give a bias to the mind of the student in favor of some particular creed, had been exploded; and it was said, in reply, that the soul was like the earth—if no cultivation were bestowed upon it, no seed planted which might yield good fruit, it would surely send up noxious weeds and poisonous berries. In support of this view, the great name of Lord Brougham was quoted. That nobleman, statesman, and scholar had written powerfully in support of strengthening the bonds of society by a wider diffusion of knowledge, and he argued in favor of spreading along with the elements of science the elements of moral truth, as eminently conservative. Happily for England, the argument prevailed there, and the prosperity of the empire is largely indebted to this system. The mind of England is instructed in divine truth, and the heart of England is filled with Christian sentiment. Her cross of St. George not only is emblazoned on her victorious standards, but her rulers learn to respect the authority of the Supreme Ruler. She proclaims her trust in God everywhere—it is the national sentiment. Walking in the streets of London, in the very midst of the busiest mart of commerce on the globe, one reads, with a glow of admiration, upon the façade of the new Exchange the words:

"The Earth is the Lord's,
And the fullness thereof."

This is a part of public education, and the lesson is not lost upon the people. Proud Empire! wherever thy flag floats, Protestant Christianity goes with it.

Happily for this country, the same sentiment is in the hearts of many of the people; and in those States where simple and evangelical truth is best known, there the principles of free government are best understood and the organization of society is least disturbed. We do not desire to see in this country an Established Church, but we do wish to see CHRISTIANITY recognized as the basis of our institutions. Happy is that people whose God is the Lord!

Appreciating this sentiment, the Trustees, at their next session, provided a chair for a Professor of Sacred Literature, whose duty it should be to teach Biblical learning and the Evidences of Christianity.

Waring was young, but he was well known to the Faculty and the Trustees, and he was unanimously elected to the new chair. He conferred with De Vane in regard to it.

"It was my wish," said he, "to pursue my studies without interruption, and to fit myself for the work of the ministry as rapidly as possible—I mean the regular itinerant work; but I confess the offer of this place does draw me powerfully. It will enable me to carry out some of my plans sooner than I could otherwise do it—that is, to travel in Europe and the East."

"Do not hesitate a moment," said De Vane; "it is the very place for you. Of course I have too much respect for the sacred office, and too much regard for you, to venture to obtrude any counsel upon you in reference to such a question; but if you will allow me to say what I really do think, without attributing to me presumption, I will do so."

"My dear De Vane, you are at liberty to speak to me freely upon any subject, and I shall be glad to hear your views."

"Then, Waring, I think that the new Chair is the place for you. I am not prepared to judge of the field of usefulness which the traveling ministry opens; but with my knowledge of you, I do not hesitate to say that the College will afford you a theatre for the exercise of your highest qualities. There are many who can instruct the people, but fitness for such a place as the Trustees have just now originated is rare indeed. And if anywhere the great principles of truth ought to be taught well, it is certainly in those places where young men are trained for life."

"The traveling ministry requires very high qualifications," said Waring, "far higher than I can lay claim to. A preacher in that wide field meets persons of all classes—the high and the low, the rich and the poor, the learned and the unlearned—and he ought to be able to meet the wants of all. You, of course, remember Mr. Springfield's description of St. Paul, his discourse on Mars' Hill, at Athens? That will give you some idea of what an itinerant preacher has sometimes to encounter. Such a work demands a Wesley, a Whitefield, an Asbury, when its largest requirements are met."

"You must not understand me to underrate the work of a traveling minister—far from it; but the ordeal of a life in a college is a very severe one. The learning, the winning manners, the dignity, the firmness, the nameless qualities which constitute a gentleman, and which no mere scholarship can confer—these I know you to possess, Waring, and you must not withhold them from our College."

"I'm very much obliged to you," said Waring, smiling; "and I am, of course, gratified to witness your interest in the success of the new chair."

"Oh!" said De Vane, laughing, "you know my taste for such studies; and if I do take a wider range in my researches than you think exactly safe, still I wish to see the place well filled, and I love the College."

"I must think of it," said Waring, "and confer with Mr. Springfield about it."

"I'm sure that he will agree with me," said De Vane.

"Then, Waring, we shall have you here *en permanence*, and that, I think, would settle the question as to my making it my home."

"That would be very agreeable to me. We both like the place, and I do not know that we could find one in all the world that has more attractions."

"It is full of them. Cultivated people abound here; the society is remarked for its refinement; and every winter brings us the first men of the State, who come here either as members of the Legislature, or to attend its session."

"Well, let us take our walk," said Waring.

They walked in the direction of the river, and in their way passed the shop of the blacksmith, whose ringing blows upon the anvil saluted the young gentlemen as they drew near.

"There is your friend hard at work, De Vane. He is an industrious fellow."

"Yes, and something of a philosopher in his way."

"How are you, Mr. Hobbs?" said De Vane, stopping in front of his door. The sparks flew as the blacksmith brought down his heavy hammer upon a piece of glowing iron which he had just taken from the forge.

"Pretty well, thank you, sir," said he. "How d'ye do yourself?"

"Always hard at work, it seems to me. You never rest, do you?"

"Of nights, and Sundays," said the blacksmith, shaping his iron with quick strokes. "Life's short, you know, sir, and there's a heap of work to do."

"Yes, but what time do you take to read?" asked De Vane.

"Why, you see, sir," the blows falling thick and heavy upon the piece of iron, which now began to take the shape of a horse-shoe, "these days are pretty long, and that nigger-boy who works with me ought to have a chance to rest in the middle of the day; so I bring a book with me, and my dinner, too, and so I get about an hour. Then, at home, about another hour after supper, and of Sundays, all day."

"What are you reading now?" asked De Vane.

He gave a few more sharp, quick strokes with his hammer, cut off the shoe from the bar of iron, and plunging it into the furnace again, wiped his face with a towel that hung near, and, stepping to a shelf, took down a book and brought it to De Vane. It was an illustrated copy of Bunyan's Pilgrim's Progress.

"There," said he, "there's a book that my wife's been reading, and she asked me to read it. I've got nearly half through, and it's an uncommon book."

Waring smiled, and said: "Do you find it interesting?"

"Oh! yes, sir—interesting enough. It's as good as a book of travels."

"The journey that the Pilgrim is making," said Waring, "is a very important one."

"Yes," said the blacksmith, "and he's a brave fellow. I think he'll get through. He's not afraid of the devil himself."

De Vane was a little uneasy. He feared the blacksmith might become too animated in his descriptions. Waring managed him very well.

"You observe, however," said Waring, "that he wore good armor, and had a good sword."

"Oh! yes," said the blacksmith, "he had that all right. That was a desperate fight he had with that fellow Apollyon. I thought, when he straddled out over the whole road, that Christian was in a bad way; and so he would have been, if he had backed at all. But when I saw him draw his sword, I knew he had pluck in him, and I felt sure that he'd do to depend on; and, sure enough, he gave the fellow thunder."

Waring smiled, and De Vane laughed heartily; but the blacksmith was too deeply interested to observe the effect produced by his remark.

"You observe," said Waring, "that Christian was a man of courage. That's very true, but do you know what gave him courage?"

"I suppose he was naturally a man of grit," said the blacksmith.

"Not only so," said Waring, "but he believed that there was One much greater than himself, who was able to protect him if he kept on his way; and you know, too, that he was going to the city where his great Friend dwelt."

"Oh! yes," said the blacksmith, "it helps a man mightily to know that he's on the right road and well backed; but the man must have the real stuff in him to fight against heavy odds."

"When you have finished the book, Mr. Hobbs," said Waring, "I should like to talk with you further about it."

"Very well, sir; I'd like to see you. My wife asked me to read the book. Miss Wordsworth gave it to my little girl last Christmas; and my wife is a member of the same church with that young lady. She says the book's interesting, and I think so too. She'll read any thing that Mrs. Springfield or Miss Wordsworth asks her to read; for she believes in 'em."

"Well, Mr. Hobbs," said De Vane, "I shall send my horse round to have that right shoe behind rasped. He cuts his ankle."

"Yes, sir, do. The infernal rascal won't stand still long enough to let me fit his shoes; but I'll put it right. He's a fine horse, but he's got the spirit of ——"

"Well, never mind," said De Vane, quickly. "You'll

rasp the shoe a little on the inside. Don't take the trouble to change it. Good evening."

"Good by, gentlemen," said the blacksmith, walking up to his furnace, and grasping his iron bar.

The young gentlemen, as they walked on, soon heard his ringing strokes once more.

"The blacksmith is a character," said Waring. "His industry sets an example worth following."

"Yes," said De Vane, "there is to me a charm in such a scene—a stalwart fellow, shaping iron with lusty strokes, and full of independence and cheerfulness. I sometimes call at his shop to talk with him."

"I see that he is a friend of yours. His running remarks upon the Pilgrim interested me. They are pert and natural. The idea that Christian would have been overcome if he had backed, was capital; and his opinion that it helped a man to feel that he was well backed had pith in it."

"I should like to hear him review the whole book when he has finished it," said De Vane; "it would be far more entertaining than many lectures that we hear."

"I feel a strong sympathy with such men," said Waring. "What a respect the man has for his wife! She is a genuine Christian, and Hobbs knows it; and it is beautiful to see the ascendency which a pious woman acquires over such a man; strong, courageous, manly, honest, and yielding meekly to the admonitions of a mild woman. O De Vane! I wish the Christian world saw this more clearly. There would be far more toleration for unconverted men of high qualities than we witness now. With all the faults of that sturdy smith, and with his proneness to swear, yet I feel a respect for him. He is respectful to his wife, tender to his children, and would fight for any cause that he thought good."

"Yes, there is nothing of meanness in him. His heart is

large, and he is fond of books, which gives me a fellow-feeling for him, rough as he is."

"Such men almost certainly come under religious influence. Their very frankness disposes them to receive great truths with favor."

"I find myself benefited," said De Vane, "by my visits to his shop. The energy with which he brings down his hammer is positively exhilarating, and the perseverance with which he takes up a rough piece of iron, and shapes it into some implement for agriculture, or a shoe for the foot of a horse, never fails to teach me a lesson. I go from him with firmer resolve to shape the affairs of life with vigor, and I find myself roused to new ardor and activity. The truth is, I have a sincere respect for a laboring man: he is the pioneer of civilization; his strong arm and honest heart are powerful in forming society, and building up a state."

"Yes," said Waring, "a thousand times greater respect than for idlers and drones, who, because they have the means of living without labor, fancy that the exemption from toil constitutes them gentlemen."

"Gentlemen," said De Vane, "must possess the quality that Cicero says is essential to an orator. You, of course, remember his remark, that no one but a good man could be an eloquent one, upon the principle that he must rouse the higher qualities of our nature, if he would move us by his oratory; and while I regard the social distinctions ot life as of very great importance, yet I am quite ready to admit that you may find gentlemen in all classes. It would be a great calamity if it were not so. One who is honest, has self-respect, and is considerate of the feelings of others, is a gentleman, no matter where you find him."

"I never heard a better definition anywhere, De Vane. I approve it heartily. Cicero's definition is not so felicitous, though he may have intended to embrace something more than to live honestly, or rather honorably, by his phrase."

"As to what the world calls honor, it is wholly unreliable; it is artificial and heartless. The code is frigid, and some of the worst men on earth profess the greatest regard for it."

"I thoroughly agree with you," said Waring. "I could point to one or two such instances. A gentleman is a gentleman always, with the code or without it. The code of honor restrains some men undoubtedly, who would act much more mischievously without it than they are allowed to do in view of its penalties; but a gentleman is a true man, whose real refinement and nobleness no code can express."

"Yes, the quality that makes a gentleman belongs to the inner man," said De Vane. "A gentleman always yields the best room to a lady at an inn; gives her the most comfortable chair; sees that she has access to the fire; considers her feelings, by saying and doing nothing which can offend her sensibility; spares a poor man every mortification, and treats a little child with kindness. A gentleman spares the weak and confronts the strong. He governs his life by the proud maxim of the great empire:

'*Parcere subjectis, et debellare superbos.*' "

"In short," said Waring, "he has very thoroughly studied the thirteenth chapter of the First Epistle to the Corinthians."

"Waring," said De Vane, "here we are upon the river-bank. Just here we met Mr. Springfield first, you remember."

"I very well remember it," said Waring. "It seems but a short time, and yet it has been months. Let us make them a visit this evening; the sooner I advise with Mr

Springfield in regard to my affairs, the better; for I must decide promptly."

"I am quite at your service," said De Vane.

They retraced their steps to Mrs. Bowen's, and after tea they made their visit to Mr. Springfield's.

The moment they entered the house, Mrs. Springfield came forward, and said with animation:

"Mr. Waring, I congratulate you. We are all very happy to learn that you are to take the new chair in the College."

"I came to talk over that matter. Is it already settled?"

"Definitively and irreversibly. Mr. Springfield, Esther, and I, all say so. Are we not right, Mr. De Vane?"

"Perfectly so, madam," said De Vane. "I do not see that Mr. Waring can hesitate about it. We have gone over the ground together already, but he reserved his decision until he could hear Mr. Springfield's views."

"He will join us in a few moments; he accompanied Esther to make a call, at the hotel, on some friends of ours from Georgia, who are on their way to the North, to pass the summer at some of the watering-places. They will soon be in."

"And you think, Mrs. Springfield, that I ought to accept the professorship?"

"I have not the shadow of a doubt about it. If I had been called on to arrange a plan of life for you, I could not have more satisfactorily accomplished it. There is every thing to recommend it. You will make your influence felt in the best way, and your tastes will be gratified without any sacrifice of your sense of duty."

"That is just the point," said Waring, "where I am not clear. The place would be so agreeable to my tastes, that I can hardly feel, in deciding to accept it, that I am not yielding to my inclinations, and shrinking from the rougher path of duty."

"Mr. Waring, you know my interest in the great work. I wish to see it prosper; but I assure you that the want of our Church at this time is men who can influence sentiment in the higher circles of life."

Waring was silent for a minute or two. The view just presented had not been overlooked by him, but he feared that, in entertaining it, he was encouraging his own wishes. Now that it was brought before him so directly, and by one so much esteemed by him as Mrs. Springfield, he felt it in all its force. Who has not found himself guided aright by some woman of sense and character, in a moment of doubt or hesitation? There is an unspeakable satisfaction in the counsels of a true woman. The heart is loyal, the perceptions clear, the mode of presenting truth captivating; and he who has for a friend such a woman, may safely trust her when the strength of men would fail, and the wisdom of men would be at fault. O woman! loyal, noble, courageous, generous woman! may we never want thy words of sympathy to cheer, nor thy counsels, unselfish and true, to guide us!

At this moment Mr. Springfield and Esther came in, and they both tendered their congratulations to Waring. Esther seated herself without removing her hat, and was very animated.

"So, then," said Waring, "you all say that I must accept?"

"There ought not to be the slightest hesitation," said Mr. Springfield. "The subject is not new to me; I have long considered it. In my judgment, the traveling ministry is very important; the beneficent results of the system can not be overrated: but there are other departments of the service, where certain qualifications are demanded, that can not be readily supplied. To suppose that no one can labor properly or effectively but in the itinerant work, is so extravagant, that it is not worth our while to consider the question in that light. To say so, would at once ignore the usefulness of the ministry of every Church but our own; and neither you nor I can consent to do that."

"Of course not," said Waring.

"Besides this," continued Mr. Springfield, "the Methodists of this country ought not to limit their aims to a mere control of the popular mind. Our doctrines are incontestably sound. We must bring the higher classes under their influence: the cultivated, the learned—these we must deal with. We already number in our ranks such persons, as you very well know; but it is not to be denied, that our access to that class is difficult. Our influence over persons of taste and refinement must be increased, otherwise our children will depart from us; and as society becomes matured, other churches will take the control of the learned and cultivated classes, leaving us to perform the task of pioneers."

"Certainly," said Waring; "the Methodists of England are acting upon your views, and their influence is spreading over the higher classes."

"You are quite right, and it ought to be so. Methodism was born in the first university in the world—Oxford. It was patronized then by Lady Betty Hastings; and her sister, Lady Margaret, married one of the Methodists who accompanied Mr. Wesley to Georgia. Her sister-in-law, the Countess of Huntingdon, after experiencing the power of the doctrine taught by them, became the friend of Whitefield, and coöperated with the Methodists, throughout her long life, in the most marked and energetic way. In her Chelsea mansion, near London, where the most aristocratic and fashionable circles were habitually met, she established a place for preaching; and it is a remarkable fact, that when Whitefield preached there, the first people of the realm assembled to hear him. Chesterfield heard him there, and invited him to his chapel at Bratby Hall.

His wife, and her sister, the Countess Delitz, both accepted the faith as taught by him, and died in it. Horace Walpole, Hume, Bolingbroke, and others, heard with admiration the eloquent evangelist; and Lord St. John, a brother of Lord Bolingbroke, became a convert to the doctrine which he preached, and died in the hope of the Gospel. A prayer-meeting was established in London by ladies of the highest rank. The Marchioness of Lothian, in declining health, the Countess of Leven, Lady Balgown, Lady Francis Gardiner, Lady Jane Mindard, and Lady Mary Hamilton, formed a part of the company, the meetings being held alternately at their houses; and they were continued for years.

"Subsequently, in the most aristocratic quarter of London, the meeting was conducted by the Countess of North cote and Hopetown, the daughters of Lord Leven, the Countess of Buchan, Lady Maxwell, Lady Glenachy, Wilhelmina, Countess of Leven, with her sisters, Lady Ruthven and Lady Bauff, Lady Henrietta Hope, and Sophia, Countess of Haddington. It was but a day or two since, in looking into some strictures upon Methodism, in the Edinburgh Review, I was induced to take up the Life and Times of Lady Huntingdon, by a member of the House of Shirley and Hastings, where I find the account given at length. By the way, it is a book which will interest you greatly. It was sent to me from Philadelphia, and is at your service."

"I shall read it with great interest," said Waring. "The notices which I have seen of it have interested me. It is believed that if political troubles had not driven Lord Bolingbroke to the Continent, he would have yielded to the power of evangelical religion. It is unquestionably important that our seats of learning should be made acquainted with it, and I did not at all underrate the importance of the place which is offered me; but really, it was so tempting, that I felt some distrust of my own judgment."

"But now," said Esther, "you will accept it?"

"I do not see," said he, "how I can do otherwise. It is only too pleasing to me to do so; that makes me doubt its being my duty."

"The path of duty," said Mr. Springfield, "is not always rugged."

De Vane had been an attentive listener to the conversation, and his respect for Mr. Springfield and for Waring was heightened by all that he heard. Both were earnest, both took the largest view of the question, both divested it of its personal relations, both decided in reference to considerations which even the great Task-Master might see without disapproval. The question was now settled. Waring was to take the new Chair in the College.

## CHAPTER XVIII.

"SOME woes are hard to bear.
Who knows the past? and who can judge us right?"
ROBERT BULWER LYTTON.

SOME days after Waring's interview with Mr. Springfield, having fully made up his mind to accept the Professorship to which he had been elected by the Trustees of the College, he called on Mr. Clarendon to thank him for his kindness in having brought about that result; for that gentleman, being a member of the Board, and knowing the preëminent qualifications of his young friend for the task, had brought him forward in such a way as to concentrate the entire vote upon him.

"You owe me nothing, Mr. Waring," said Mr. Clarendon. "I love the College. I came to it, from Virginia, a young, ardent man. My heart expanded in the College, my mind grew and strengthened there, and I am zealous for its honor and success. I was not willing to see our new Chair filled by a mere professional teacher of religious doctrine. I wished something higher. I knew well your qualifications, your sincerity as a Christian, your thorough scholarship, and your character as a gentleman. I beg you to consider me your friend, sir, and, at the same time, a friend to the College."

Waring was deeply impressed with the frankness and generosity of this speech. He said:

"I can only assure you, Mr. Clarendon, of my wish to serve the College faithfully, so that I may do my duty, and continue to enjoy your friendship and confidence, which I have long prized."

Mr. Clarendon gave him his hand, made him a stately bow, and asked him to take a seat—they were standing in the library. It was early evening, and the windows being thrown open, the western sky was in full view. The horizon was yet glowing, and the western breeze came freshly through the shrubbery, which had not yet lost its sweetness. Pedestrians were enjoying the fine, fresh air, and carriages rolled through the handsome streets, filled with ladies without their hats. The capital wore its brightest summer aspect. The two gentlemen were in conversation, when Mrs. Habersham and Miss Godolphin drove up in a light, open carriage, and without alighting from it, sent the footman to ask if Mrs. Clarendon would join them in their drive. Mr. Clarendon walked to the carriage to answer the invitation, stating that Mrs. Clarendon had gone, but a little while before, to drive with her sister, Mrs. Hallam.

"Will you not, ladies," said he, "come in, and await her return?"

"Oh! no," said Miss Godolphin, "we must continue our drive; and I think, Mr. Clarendon, that you had better join us."

"With all my heart," said he gayly, "provided you will permit me to bring a young gentleman with me. A proper man, I assure you."

"It will only increase our pleasure," she said.

"Then we shall join you in a moment." And returning to the house for Waring, they advanced to the carriage.

"Allow me, ladies," said Mr. Clarendon, "to present to you Professor Waring, of the College which you see just over the way there. You have known him as a gay young gentleman, a hard student, and a first-honor man. You are now to respect him as a grave Professor.

The ladies smiled, and bowed to Waring, as if much impressed with his new dignity; and the gentlemen took their seats in the carriage.

"So you accept the chair, Mr. Waring?" said Miss Godolphin.

Waring bowed.

"Yes," said Mr. Clarendon, "we gave him no chance to decline. The Board elected him and forthwith adjourned, appealing to his well-known love for the College, to induce him to accept."

"We are very much pleased," said Mrs. Habersham, "to learn that Mr. Waring is to be with us. I feel quite an interest in securing such acquisitions for our society."

"Nothing," said Waring, "could be more agreeable to me, than such an arrangement. I love the College, and I love the town."

"And of course the people in it," said Mr. Clarendon.

"Of course," replied Waring, "and the people in it. I should be very ungrateful if I could be indifferent to them."

"Where is your friend Mr. De Vane, Mr. Waring?" inquired Miss Godolphin. "We were wishing to meet you both."

"It is impossible to say," replied Waring, "where Mr. De Vane is to be found at this moment. He had walked out when I called for him some two hours since, and it may be that this fine evening has tempted him to seek recreation in the public garden after a day's study."

"Yes," said Mr. Clarendon, "I'll venture to say that he is about this time holding a professional conversation with his friend Swan, about the cedars of Lebanon, or the hyssop on the wall, or some new plant just introduced into the public garden. Swan thinks him a prodigy, and has no idea that King Solomon was at all better instructed in any department of knowledge than De Vane."

The ladies laughed, and Mrs. Habersham instructed the coachman to drive to the garden.

"Our object at this time in seeking Mr. De Vane, is to invite him to join us to-morrow evening. To-day we were quite surprised at receiving the card of Mlle. Vesperini, a celebrated cantatrice whom we met abroad. She is here but for a day or two, and we wish some of our friends to enjoy the pleasure of meeting one who may be called the queen of song."

Mr. Clarendon and Mr. Waring expressed their gratification.

The carriage was approaching the garden. It was thronged with visitors. Gay groups were seated and engaged in animated conversation. Others filled the broad walks. As the carriage drew up opposite one of the principal gates, De Vane and Miss Wordsworth emerged from it, and observing the party who had just arrived, they approached them.

"Ah!" exclaimed Mr. Clarendon gayly. "Mr. De Vane, like your great progenitor, you have just quitted the garden abounding with delights. Not expelled, I trust! But at least, like him, you have an angel to walk by your side."

Esther blushed deeply.

"Yes," replied De Vane, "with such a guide, I am content to explore the great world."

"We are fortunate in meeting you, Mr. De Vane," said Miss Godolphin, "and to find you, too, with Miss Wordsworth. We called at Mr. Springfield's for her, as we set out to drive."

Esther expressed her regret at not having been at home to receive the ladies.

"Not at all," replied Miss Godolphin; "it is far better as it is. We are to receive, to-morrow evening, Mlle. Vesperini, a celebrated cantatrice, and I lay my commands on you, Mr. De Vane, to escort Miss Wordsworth. You are both indispensable, and you must come together."

De Vane bowed, and said that with Miss Wordsworth's permission, he would undertake to execute Miss Godolphin's command. Esther expressed her approval of the arrangement, and the carriage dashed on.

"How fortunate," exclaimed Miss Godolphin, "I met the very persons I most wished to see! They will enjoy Mlle. Vesperini's singing."

"There are no two persons," said Mr. Clarendon, "who will appreciate it more."

"Do you know, Mr. Clarendon, that I think musical people deserve the highest honors? In Europe, especially on the Continent, they take rank with the nobility. They are guests of princes. People of the highest rank receive them into their houses as friends. It is the homage that wealth and rank pay to genius."

"Yes," said Mr. Clarendon, "when in Europe, I often observed it. In Ireland, I met at the house of Mrs. Grant, of Laggan, a young Irish lady of extraordinary accomplishments. She was fascinating, and her singing was unrivaled. On the Continent, too, I more than once met families from Ireland, and the ladies were in every instance superior."

"This lady is very young—certainly not yet twenty-five," said Miss Godolphin; "and she is attended by an uncle—a man of good fortune, who glories in the celebrity of his young relative. He was with her when I met her in Paris."

"In that respect," said Mr. Clarendon, "the taste, or rather the conventionalism of Europe differs widely from our own. Persons of position and wealth suffer their relatives to enter public life in a way which we should utterly condemn. Their love for the fine arts is such, that it gives art an elevated rank. Mrs. Siddons was not only received everywhere, but she was sought, and sought eagerly, in the most aristocratic circles. And even when the stage proper is condemned, that is, the theatre, persons of genius are encouraged to appear in public as *artistes*, in song, in recitation, or in reading."

"I think well of it," said Miss Godolphin. "Genius should always be tributary to the advancement of society."

"There is a great deal of stiffness in this country," said Mr. Clarendon, "and the avenues to distinction are too few. Politics is almost the only pursuit for our men, and our women have none. Especially ought we in this Southern country to encourage such entertainments as Mrs. Habersham proposes to give us. They are innocent, and they must, while they prove entertaining, give to society a heightened refinement. We do not encourage the stage; indeed, we proscribe it, and I think very properly. It becomes, therefore, a high social duty, to contribute in some other way to the development of genius and the advancement of art."

"I am delighted to hear you speak in this way," said Miss Godolphin. "Our entertainments are generally flat, stale, and unprofitable. What we call parties, are often intolerable. Dancing may do for very young people, but surely not for those who have grown to any consciousness of what a serious affair life is. And then what have we left?"

"Nothing but music and conversation," said Waring; "but they are every thing."

"Yes," said Miss Godolphin, "I enjoyed myself more at your entertainment, Mr. Clarendon, given to the Duke of Saxe-Weimar, than any thing of the kind I have attended in this country."

Mr. Clarendon bowed.

"I think, Miss Godolphin," he said, "that receptions

where guests of congenial tastes are expected to call through the evening, and where only light refreshments are introduced, far more rational than large entertainments, where every thing is done upon an extravagant scale."

"Oh! and a thousand times more agreeable. In Paris, and Brussels, and other capitals on the Continent, no other evening entertainments are known, except occasionally a great ball."

"The ambassadors give their dinners," said Mr. Clarendon, "to the gentlemen; and the receptions are really refreshing, for they bring together people of taste, and cultivation, and refinement; and conversation goes on in a way perfectly charming."

"We must try to make our little capital very agreeable, Mr. Clarendon," said Mrs. Habersham, "and next winter I shall do what I can in that way."

The drive was a delightful one, and the carriage drawing up before Mr. Clarendon's door, he took leave of the ladies with thanks for such an agreeable hour.

Waring accompanied them to their residence, and Mrs. Habersham insisting that he should not walk, the carriage took him to Mrs. Bowen's door, where he was warmly received by that good lady, who was delighted to observe his growing intimacy with Miss Godolphin.

De Vane and Esther, after quitting the party in the carriage, walked leisurely to Mr. Springfield's.

"How animated Miss Godolphin is becoming!" said De Vane. "Waring and I passed an evening there lately, and we found her really bright."

"I have observed it. She is very fascinating. I can not account for the sadness which we sometimes observe in her; but even that heightens my interest in her. When she forgets her sorrow, she is brilliant."

"The suddenness with which she relapses into sadness,"

said De Vane, "is strange. It is like a cloud suddenly passing over the sun."

"Or a bright particular star," said Esther, "becoming dim by some fleecy vail, which the eye can only perceive by the lessening radiance of the orb."

"Your figure is perfect," said De Vane. "It is nothing known to us, which can explain the fact; but it is still a fact, that, at times, when Miss Godolphin seems brightest, she suddenly sinks into dejection. She is a person, too, of such intellectual strength, that it makes it the more difficult to account for, and she is not at all capricious. Her opinions are fixed, her tastes are pure, and her character is resolute. There is some painful memory, probably, known only to herself, which throws its shadow across the path of her life. She is a wonderfully interesting person, and I should be glad to see her happier than she seems to be."

"If there be any secret sorrow," said Esther, "it must have been caused by something that befell her in Europe. Her history, up to the time of her going abroad, is well known; and she was then as bright and joyous as possible, having nothing whatever to cloud her happiness but the loss of relatives."

"It is beautiful," said De Vane, "to see her when she is animated. She is magnificent, splendidly beautiful, and full of graceful majesty. She looks a queen."

"I have often thought so," said Esther. "She is singularly free from affectation, and her unstudied attitudes have at times startled me by their classical beauty, and, I may say, sublimity."

"The Guilfords, of Virginia," said De Vane, "were with her in Europe. I have heard her speak of them, and when I make my visit to that State, which I think of doing next month, I may be able to find a solution of what is certainly a mystery."

"You go to Virginia next month?" said Esther.

"Yes, I must make my father and aunt a visit. It has been my purpose to do so for some months. Almost three years have gone by since I saw them, and it is proper that I should make them a visit which they think has been already too long delayed."

"It is certainly proper," said Esther, "and must, I think, make you very happy."

"It will certainly be pleasing," he said, "to revisit relatives so dear to me, and to see the spot where very early years were passed. But I do not feel that Virginia is my home. I do not know how it is, but this is the only place in all the world where I would consent to live. It holds me by a powerful attraction; and no matter where I may be, when I quit here I shall feel that I am an exile."

He spoke with great animation, and his face beamed as he uttered the words.

"But," said Esther, "may not a return to your Virginia home revive the slumbering attachment to that place which has been so dear to you?"

"No," said he, "never. I honor and love Virginia, and cherish ancestral recollections: but here I have been for the first time conscious of my own faculties; here I have received the Promethean heat which wakes me to conscious manhood; here I have learned to turn upon the world and survey it, to compare places, study society, and know for myself what it is all worth. In my native State, I should be involved in all the meshes of conventionalism. The very fact of residing upon an estate which has come down to me through more than one generation, while it conferred consideration, would commit me to all the rules which society there recognizes as so imperious, and I could not be myself. If I had never gone from home, it might have been different; but it is too late now. I have seen the world in its largest outlines. I have learned to despise its little conventional ways. I would to-morrow relinquish my claim to my estate before I would consent to hold it and ignore my manhood."

Esther was startled by his earnestness. She had never before seen him so roused. She did not know that he had lately received letters from home, appealing to his ancestral pride, and urging him to return and fix his residence in Virginia; that Mrs. Vane, after some playful criticism upon his own letters, in which he had betrayed more plainly than before his admiration of Esther, had warned him against being ensnared by his Methodist friends, who might be good people enough in their way, but who could not, of course, be suitable to his matured tastes, or do for intimate associates; and had at some length, and with evident seriousness, portrayed the charms of the beautiful Clara Guilford, and hinted at the advantages which such an alliance would yield him.

He continued: "I am not unambitious, but I trust that the passion with me is an honest and honorable one. I desire distinction, but it must be earned—not inherited; earned, too, by a career of usefulness—not bought with money, nor obtained by the mean arts which degrade so many public men. I am satisfied that the dearth of high qualities which we must all acknowledge, is the result of the conventional rules of life, now becoming so strong in this country. Vigor and manliness are disappearing. Wealth is worshipped. The high places of the Republic are looked to as the rewards of the abject followers of some petty popular potentate, and the very road to the unseen world which we are assured awaits the good, is hedged in by aristocratic forms, which make no provision for the poor and the outcast. I wish to be a man. I will not consent to be dwarfed by the forms of society."

He was splendid in his enthusiasm. Esther had never before seen him roused in this way. His very form seemed to dilate with the grandeur of conscious manhood, and his youthful, vigorous frame seemed fired by an inspiration which it could not contain. She had never looked into the nature of the interest which she felt in De Vane. She was conscious of a very deep interest in him. She had never loved, and she had never before met one who even roused her admiration. De Vane had never spoken to her of love, had never even hinted it to her; but she, of course, had seen that he sought her society, and his admiration for her was too marked not to be observed by herself, as well as by others. Mrs. Springfield had seen it, but had never spoken to Esther on the subject. Comprehending her well, she knew that it was not at all required; for while she knew her ardor, she knew too that she possessed self-control, and would never permit herself to become too deeply interested in any one, until she ascertained that her sense of duty would suffer nothing from the attachment. Waring, too, had been very attentive to Esther, and she believed that her niece felt a certain interest in him. She thought it unnecessary to speak to her about either.

Now Esther was troubled. She was really agitated by the consciousness of her sympathy with De Vane, and she turned her eyes upon him for a moment, lustrous with the light of her awakened soul, and could not restrain a glance of boundless admiration for the nobleness of the sentiments which he uttered. He walked by her side for some moments in silence. Neither could venture to speak. De Vane was at that moment conscious of an intenser regard for Esther than he had ever before experienced; but he was not prepared to speak to her of his sentiments. They were not, indeed, sufficiently defined, and he had no present purpose in regard to her; though, if he had analyzed his heart, he might have found in its depths the wish to walk by the side of the gloriously beautiful being who was with him now, through all the paths of future life.

Yet he had great respect for his father. He would be reluctant to wound even his pride, to offend his aristocratic tastes; and to say to him that he, his son, wished to take for a wife this young disciple of a despised sect, this daughter of a Methodist preacher, who even now resided in the family of a lay preacher of that denomination, would, he knew, shock him greatly. If he could see Esther first, if he could know her worth, her splendid intellectual endowments, her accomplishments, her great soul; if he could but be made acquainted with her, without learning in advance her religious sentiments or her connections, he was sure that all would be well. But there was the trouble: how could this be done? The problem troubled him. Then, too, his aunt. Her pride of birth, her aristocratic tastes, her earnest wish to see him lead the life of a Virginia gentleman—all this troubled him. He himself comprehended Esther. He knew how superior she was to all others with whom he compared her, and he despised the paltry considerations that others esteemed so weighty. He had no present purpose; he could form none. He must visit his home, survey the ground, test his interest in Esther, before speaking to her.

That soul, which he knew had never been wakened by the voice of human passion, must not be roused until the voice of true and immortal love broke its pure slumber. The star of hope must not rise in the heavens, to be obscured by mists, but must mount the skies when they were serene and cloudless.

"I am to call for you, Miss Wordsworth, to-morrow evening, you remember," said De Vane.

"Yes," said Esther." "I wish to hear Mlle. Vesperini. I have long desired it. She is said to be peerless in song."

"I share your enthusiasm," said he. "You know my love of music; but your singing has spoiled me for that of any other person."

"I thank you for your appreciation, but I fear that I am indebted only to your kindness. You are too generous to be critical."

"I plume myself upon my taste," said he playfully; "and nothing but something like perfection can satisfy me."

They had reached Mrs. Springfield's residence, and De Vane, declining Esther's invitation to go in, bade her good evening, and walked away.

He found Waring seated in the piazza with Mrs. Bowen, awaiting his return.

"I hope you had a pleasant drive, Professor," said De Vane.

"It could not be otherwise," replied Waring, "surrounded as I was; and I need not inquire as to your walk. If it had not been agreeable, you would not have lingered so long on the way."

"Delightful!" said De Vane; "but have I been long?"

"Mrs. Bowen has been waiting tea for you—I will not undertake to say how long."

"Never mind, Mr. De Vane," said the good lady, perfectly happy in the presence of her two favorites. "Mr. Waring has just come in, and as he came in the carriage of course he got home first."

## CHAPTER XIX.

> "A BREATHLESS awe, like the swift change,
> Unseen but felt, in youthful slumbers;
> Wild, sweet, but uncommunicably strange,
> Thou breathest now in fast-ascending numbers."
>
> SHELLEY.

THE cloudless splendor of a summer evening favored the musical entertainment to which Mrs. Habersham had invited her friends. There was a delicious coolness in the air, peculiar to a Southern climate after the fervors of the day have declined ; and the evening breeze, fanning the shrubbery with which the town abounded, bestowed a fragrance which nothing but natural flowers could impart to it. What a tribute to the senses, when sweet odors mingle with sweet sounds ! The South is the home of both ; and in every household under our brilliant skies, flowers and music should be cultivated. Glorious land, lying midway between the frozen north and the burning tropics, may thy people ever encourage the industry which covers thy fields with fruitful harvests, and the arts which shed refinement upon thy happy homes !

The parlor, which had been open to receive the guests, was pretty well filled when De Vane and Esther arrived. They had driven to Mrs. Habersham's, and Mr. and Mrs. Springfield were to come at a late hour.

Miss Godolphin received them with animation, and expressed her gratification at their presence.

"I would cross the Atlantic myself," she said, "to hear noble Vesperini."

"So would I," said Esther, "most gladly, if she be what she is represented to be in the musical world."

"No description can do her justice," said Miss Godolphin. "She has genius, soul, cultivation. One must have all to be perfect."

Mr. Clarendon advanced, and said: "Ah! ladies, we are to have a great treat to-night, a foreign wonder, as Comus said, when entranced by music from some unseen fair one; but I shall be slow to believe that you will have to lay your garlands at her feet."

"Wait till you hear her, Mr. Clarendon," said Miss Godolphin. "She is really a wonder; and you will be ready to exclaim with Comus, I am quite sure:

'Can any mortal mixture of earth's mould
Breathe such divine enchanting ravishment?'"

"I have been ready to make that exclamation, De Vane, about Miss Godolphin and Miss Wordsworth any time these six months past. Yet I'm bound to believe them mortal, when I recover myself sufficiently to reason about it."

"Ah! Mr. Clarendon, you are very cruel," said Miss Godolphin, "to turn your satire upon us in this way. Is he not, Miss Wordsworth?"

"Satire!" said he. "Upon my soul, I was never more sincere in all my life. De Vane, have you not heard me often say something very like this?"

"Something very like it," said De Vane; "and it was only last evening that you pronounced me fortunate in being under the guidance of an angel."

"I did not suppose, Mr. De Vane," said Esther, "that you would take part against us."

"But, in all seriousness, ladies," said Mr. Clarendon, "I do not expect to hear any music from this celebrated

Mlle. Vesperini at all more pleasing to me than I have heard from each of you within a month. After all, music is not mere artistic skill, that may heighten its effect; but there is in the living voice a power to move the soul, which no instrument, however cunningly touched, can ever rival."

"Quite true," said Miss Wordsworth; "but it is said that Mlle. Vesperini's voice is perfection."

"That may be," said Mr. Clarendon, "artistic perfection, but a voice must possess a living sympathy if it wake the soul."

"That is the peculiar charm of this lady's voice," said Miss Godolphin; "she is what may be called eloquent in song. You know how much we have admired that, in Miss Wordsworth's singing. And I predict for *her* greater success than Mlle. Vesperini has attained, if she will be loyal to the art."

Esther flushed, and De Vane said: "I beg, Miss Godolphin, to lay my tribute at Miss Wordsworth's feet too. When her grand triumphs come, she will remember us as her early friends."

"So you are coming over to my position," said Mr. Clarendon. "To make my triumph complete, I shall say that I long ago discovered the yet undeveloped powers of both these ladies; the one before her visit to Europe, and the other some twelve months since."

The room was nearly filled, and among those who had just entered was Waring, upon whose arm a lady of extraordinary beauty was leaning. She was the daughter of Dr. Dahlgreen. Almost majestic in the fair proportions of her youthful but well-developed figure, she was very graceful, and attracted attention by her sweet manners. Her eyes were very fine, full of expression, in which soul and intellect were blended. She had just returned after an absence of some months, having been on a visit to a married sister residing in the upper part of the State. Miss Godolphin went forward to receive her, not having met her since her return from Europe.

Esther informed De Vane of this, and explained to him that she was well known to his friend, Mr. Waring.

"I never heard him speak of her," said De Vane. "It is strange."

"Oh! no," said Esther, "she has been absent for months, and you have been in society so little, that you have not met her."

"Ah! yes, she must have left the town last winter."

"Yes, in November, I think," said Esther. "We all admire her greatly, and I am glad to see that she has returned. Let us speak with her;" and, advancing to the group about Miss Dahlgreen, Esther and herself greeted each other warmly. De Vane was presented by Waring, who said:

"This, Miss Dahlgreen, is my friend, of whom you have heard me speak."

She bowed gracefully to De Vane, who said:

"You must have come to town to-day, Miss Dahlgreen, as I had not heard of your arrival."

"Only to-day," she said, "and I sent for my friend, Mr. Waring, to escort me, when I found that my father would not be able to accompany me."

At this moment, Mlle. Vesperini entered the room, and came rapidly to Miss Godolphin, attended by her uncle, who walked behind her.

She was very animated, and bowed low, speaking with marked gentleness in her tones, which, even in conversation, were very sweet. She was just the medium height, a little disposed to what we style *embonpoint*, but well formed and perfectly graceful. The sweetness of her manner was winning; and as she threw a glance about the room, she seemed to spread light through it. Her hair was brushed back from her face, and gathered in heavy rolls on either side. A wreath of green leaves encircled her head, and rich curls fell from the back part of it on her neck. Her dress was of white silk, small flounces of lace covering it nearly to the waist, and a brilliant necklace of emeralds encircled her neck.

Several gentlemen, with ladies on their arms, were presented to her, and Mr. Clarendon took charge of her, and conducted her through the room.

Very soon after her arrival, the doors of a large room opposite the parlor were thrown open, and the tables were seen covered with fruits, flowers, and iced cream. And from time to time parties entered it and partook of the refreshments.

"What impression does she make on you, Mr. De Vane?" asked Esther.

"She is very bright," he answered, "and I am pleased. Has she real warmth, do you suppose?"

"I should think so," said Esther; "but it is impossible to judge her so soon. She has musical eyes. Did you observe their color?"

"No," said he. "Are they not dark?"

"Oh! no; they have a greenish hue, which is said to be observed in all great singers."

"Indeed!" said De Vane. "I must observe her mor closely. Your theory is a new one to me. I do not dis cover it in your eyes." And he looked down into theii glorious depths. "Yours are the purest violet I ever saw."

"Are they?" said Esther, blushing. "Then I fear that I want the magic color."

"You want nothing else, then, to make you peerless in song. Do you know that you bring tears to my eyes before I am conscious of it?"

"Certainly no higher tribute than tears can be paid to music," she said.

Waring came up with Miss Dahlgreen.

"We have just been presented to the celebrated cantatrice," said Miss Dahlgreen. "Will you not speak with her?"

"Yes," said Esther, "we intend doing so. Do you find ner agreeable?"

"Very much so," she answered, "very much so. Her face is a very sweet one."

"Let us speak with her," said De Vane; and advancing with Esther to the chair where she was seated, Mr. Clarendon presented them.

Mlle. Vesperini rose from her seat, and bowed with marked cordiality to them. Esther's beauty impressed her, and she could scarcely restrain her exclamations of pleasure.

"And do you reside here?" she asked.

"Yes," said Esther.

"And is this your native place?"

"No," said Esther, "Georgia is my native State; but I have been here nearly all my life."

"Ah!" said Mlle. Vesperini. "You are so English—I should have pronounced you English if I had met you in any part of the world but here. Here one meets the several races represented, and that, too, in perfection," she said, with a bright smile.

"Miss Wordsworth," said De Vane, "has near relatives in England, as most of us in this country have."

"Ah! yes," she said, "it is so. I find them everywhere. And is Miss Wordsworth related to the poet of that name?"

"Yes," said Mr. Clarendon, "quite nearly, I think."

"I had not learned that before," said De Vane.

"You must visit Europe, Miss Wordsworth," said Mlle. Vesperini. "It will delight you."

"When I can do so," said Esther, "I shall be very happy to make the visit."

"Go to Rome, Miss Wordsworth—go to Rome. There is the seat of the arts, as it was of empire for a thousand years!"

She spoke with great animation.

"Paris," she continued, "is gay—appreciative, too. Vienna is grand but cold; St. Petersburgh, magnificent but half barbarous; yet London is great but stiff. Florence—Naples—pictures in the one, palaces and the bay in the other; but Rome—Rome is imperial still!"

"Bravo!" exclaimed Mr. Clarendon, with enthusiasm. "Bravo!"

"You think with me, then?" said she, turning to him.

"A thousand times yes," he answered.

"I am happy," she said. "Go to Rome, Miss Wordsworth, and forget the degeneracy of every thing modern, except the arts. Go to Rome, and let music fill your soul and make you immortal."

De Vane's face was bright, his enthusiasm was roused. Here stood a woman ablaze with the love of her art—the priestess of an art nothing less than divine—and urging another woman, whose beauty filled her soul with a strange ardor, to visit the temple where that art found its highest interpretation.

"You have music in you," she continued. "I read your soul. You can interpret music—you can serve music Go to Rome—imperial, sublime, eternal Rome!"

She was impassioned, and her face glowed with the enthusiasm for her art which flamed up within her.

Esther, catching the fervor of the rapt priestess, was resplendent, like the Parsee in the presence of the sun, and she was conscious of a high sympathy with the extraordinary woman who stood before her.

"I am curious to know," said Mr. Clarendon, "how you

made the discovery that my young friend is like yourself—full of music."

"I saw it in her organization—heard it in her voice—read it as one reads the mysteries of an art which laymen never comprehend."

Miss Godolphin came into the group. "Here, too, is one," said Mlle. Vesperini, "whose soul loves music. If she had been European, she would have been an *artiste;* but in this new country, your civilization does nothing for the arts; you give them no rank, no rewards, no encouragement. When Miss Godolphin was in Paris, I read her soul; but she would not listen to me. She had been to Rome—had heard the great *artistes*—and was then pursuing the art with wonderful enthusiasm; but when I spoke to her of entering into its service, she shrank from it. Caste was roused; her nationality arrested her ardor; and she refused to enter a temple where the glories or heaven fill its highest dome."

"I well remember your friendly interest in me," said Miss Godolphin, "nor can I ever forget it."

"Friendly interest! It was my love for music. I would have led you to the shrine, where you should have ministered forever."

Professor Niles and his wife came up to the circle which had gathered about Mlle. Vesperini, and they entered into conversation with her. They spoke of the great musical celebrities of Europe, with whose fortunes they were familiar.

Malibran was mentioned. "She is angelic!" exclaimed Mlle. Vesperini. "She has just reäppeared in Paris, in the grand opera, *Semiramide.* She is glorious! Poor child! she came to your country to find a sad fate. She should never have married."

"But," said Miss Godolphin, "she did not marry an American. Malibran is a French banker in New-York."

"Ah! you vindicate your country, just as you were accustomed to do in Paris," she said, shaking her brilliant fan playfully. "*Artistes* must not sell themselves. If you could have heard Malibran as I heard her in London, when she first appeared, in the part of *Rosina* in *Il Barbiere de Seviglio*, you would have pronounced her divine. She was just eighteen. Ah! *artistes* should never sell them selves. Gold may buy talent of any kind, but genius—inspiration—never!"

She uttered the last words with startling energy.

"No," said Miss Godolphin; "the best part of our nature can never be bought."

There was a deep tenderness in her tones; and the lashes fell over her large, dark eyes.

"Do you return to Europe presently?" asked Madam Niles.

"Yes; in a month. I go first to Ireland. To me, Ireland is every thing in the summer. However it may be with others, that is my season. My home is just on a little lake, that to me is more than the ocean."

"Your country," said Professor Niles, "is very beautiful. Its rural aspect was to me enchanting, especially where, from its coves, one could catch glimpses of the sea."

"If my country were like yours—free," she said, "it would be glorious."

"You like Paris?" asked Madam Niles.

"Yes. It is brilliant. To pass the gay season there is every thing. You meet all the world; and nowhere else is the opera alive, but in Paris. But I would not make it my home; rather would I pass from Italy to Ireland, and from Ireland to Italy again, taking Paris *en route*."

"We heard of you in Florence," said Madam Niles, "but did not have the pleasure of seeing you. It was four years since."

"Ah!" exclaimed Mlle. Vesperini; "I was there studying pictures."

"So we were," said Professor Niles; "and one might pass a lifetime there in that pursuit."

"Florence is very pleasant," she said, "for one who wishes to rest; but there is no life there. It is to me but a dreary spot."

Then turning to Esther, she said: "You will at some time visit Europe? Go while you are yet young—before your fervor is at all chilled—and while the love of art is a passion with you."

"It is not at all certain," said Esther, "that I shall go abroad; but if ever I feel that I can do so, I shall remember your counsel."

"It is possible, Mlle. Vesperini," said De Vane, "that I may cross the Atlantic some time next year, and it would be very agreeable to me to meet you in Rome. My veneration for the Eternal City is not less than your own."

"Ah! I shall be very happy to meet you. I shall expect you next year?"

"My plans of travel are not at all settled," he said; "but I have such a tour in view as would take me into Italy some time next year."

"Cross the Alps in October—not before, not after—descend into Italy in October."

At this moment, the doors opening from the parlor into the small drawing-room where De Vane and Waring had been received upon their late visit, were thrown open. Its exquisite and graceful adornments impressed every one. The instruments of music, the pictures, the tasteful and rare furniture, the profusion of natural flowers, lent it an air of enchantment.

"Oh! how charming!" exclaimed Mlle. Vesperini. "This is Parisian."

De Vane offered her his arm, and conducted her into

the room. She declined to be seated, but stood looking at the objects of art, which were distributed with fine taste and met the view everywhere.

Mr. Clarendon advanced, with Miss Dahlgreen on his arm, and invited her to give them some music.

With perfect grace she bowed, and took her seat at the harp, touching the chords lightly. She changed the tone of two or three of them, and then asked Miss Dahlgreen if she would prefer any particular song.

"I wish rather," Miss Dahlgreen said, "to leave that to your taste."

Esther stood near, with Waring and Miss Godolphin, and she observed with pleasure that Mr. Springfield and her aunt, with Mrs. Habersham, were favorably placed to enjoy the music.

Mlle. Vesperini, with a low, tender touch to the strings, sang from the Italian, *Domini O me Felici*, the liquid tones blending with those of the instrument, and producing perfect harmony. Every word was distinctly uttered, and the sweetness of the voice was indescribable. When the song ceased, so perfect was the stillness in the room, that the rustling of the dress of the cantatrice, as her arm, falling from the strings, rested upon it, was the first thing that woke the audience to consciousness.

She did not attempt to rise, but smiling to Esther, she desired her to come to her.

A murmur of applause went round the room, and Miss Godolphin, turning to Waring, said: "That is music."

"Yes," said he.

"Miss Wordsworth," said Mlle. Vesperini, "I am about to sing again. You heard me speak of Madame Malibran: would you wish to hear something from the opera in which she sang when I first heard her in London?"

"I should be delighted—thank you," said Esther.

"I will sing it for you," said Mlle. Vesperini. "I am sure that it will please you. I sometimes sing it in public."

Again she touched the strings, and this time with more power, and she sang. The full, glorious volume of sound floated out in the air, sometimes rising in strength and filling the room, and then sinking with a gentle, prolonged cadence, as if melting into silence, until at the close a burst of passionate energy died away into a tender, almost wailing sadness, that entered into the soul, waking its deepest sympathy.

"O Mlle. Vesperini!" exclaimed Miss Godolphin, "how you have interpreted music this evening! I feel as if I never comprehended its power before."

She smiled and bowed. Quite a number came to thank her; and as Esther did so, her eyes dripping with tears, she could only whisper: "Thank you!"

"The tribute of your tears to the music, Miss Wordsworth, is the highest that can be paid."

She spoke as if she were really the mere interpreter of the art, and she accepted the homage everywhere offered her as if it were due only to that. She was but the priestess at the shrine, standing in the midst of the worshipers.

She was about to rise from her seat, when Mr. Clarendon came to ask her to sing something in our own language.

She yielded at once, and asked him if he would name something. He appealed to Miss Godolphin, but she advised that it should be left to Mlle. Vesperini's own preference.

"Then," said she, "I will go to my country. I will find something in Irish song to express what I feel for Ireland."

Sweeping the chords of the instrument until they seemed to breathe with sadness, she sang, with a depth of pathos that could not be surpassed, Moore's lines describing, in touching eloquence, the condition of his ill-governed country—

"The harp that once through Tara's halls;"

and as she poured her soul into the song, she transported all who heard her with her own passion. The eloquence of the utterance was irresistible. The manner in which she gave the intenseness of her sentiment to the two closing lines was startling.

"Bravo! Bravo!" exclaimed Mr. Clarendon, approaching her as she rose from her seat, while a storm of applause greeted her on every side.

De Vane was electrified. His eyes blazed with enthusiasm, and he exclaimed: "That song is in the language of sadness; but the very voice of lamentation over departed glory, if it could be heard throughout Ireland, would rouse her sons to deliver, or perish with her."

Mlle. Vesperini caught the words as she was passing, and bowed low to him. Every one spoke with animation of the performance, and as Mr. Clarendon took Mlle. Vesperini to the refreshment-room, he expressed his own high appreciation of her music.

"I enjoy it myself," said she. "Music is to me every thing. Oh! I should be so desolate without it."

"Miss Wordsworth," said De Vane, "do you observe that painting?"

They stood in front of the large picture representing the daughter of Herodias bearing the head of the Baptist to her mother.

Esther stood in perfect silence for some moments. "It is very wonderful," she said. "It resembles a picture of my mother, which I have, as closely as if one were copied from the other. It is very, very wonderful."

"It is a perfect likeness of yourself," said De Vane; "perfect—features, form, expression, every thing."

She became very pale. "I have never seen this before," she said. "I must know its history."

"Let us pass on now," said De Vane, observing her emotion; and entering the refreshment-room, he handed her an ice. Others joined them, and in the animated conversation that followed, the impression of sadness made by a picture so vividly recalling her mother seemed to pass off. Some time after, Mlle. Vesperini came to her, and said:

"I am going to ask you to sing. Of course you will not refuse me."

She colored to the temples. She was really distressed.

"Can you not excuse me?" she said. "Not after your singing, surely not after that. Will you not excuse me?"

"I really wish to hear you," said Mlle. Vesperini. "Do oblige me."

"Of course," said Esther, "every one must know that in singing this evening I yield my wishes to yours." And putting her arm in that of Mlle. Vesperini, with a graceful expression in her manner, of deference to so celebrated an artist, she accompanied her to the drawing-room. She took her seat at the harp, and her attitude was that of perfect grace. Never had her beauty been more resplendent. There was nothing of embarrassment in her manner, but something of consciousness was seen in her expression—a slight indication of her sense of the very severe task which she was about to undertake.

Her dress was becoming to her; it was snowy white, and fell in rich folds about her person. She wore a necklace of pearls, and in her hair the crimson passion-flower was twisted with violets.

After touching lightly the strings of the instrument, which seemed to breathe under her snowy fingers, she sang:

"I know that my Redeemer liveth."

Her voice, gaining strength and increasing in power as she advanced, rose upon the air. It was as full of sublime and thrilling sympathy with the world's great hope of immortality, as if an angel, unseen by others, stood before her in revealing light, and warmed her soul with the love that fills the hearts of seraphs; and as the dying cadences were lost in silence, every one felt that something celestial lingered near them.

Mlle. Vesperini's eyes were swimming in tears. In her ardor, she rushed to Esther's chair, threw an arm about her, and said: "Oh! that you were with me in Rome."

"Ah! Mlle. Vesperini," said Mr. Clarendon, brushing his eyes, "we could not give her up."

De Vane's face was radiant. Turning to Waring, he said:

"What a triumph!"

"Yes," said Miss Godolphin, "she is glorious. Her song, too, is characteristic of herself. She could have chosen nothing so appropriate."

There were some present who had never heard Esther before, and the rapturous applause that greeted her, proved how well she was appreciated. She rose from her seat, conducted by Mlle. Vesperini, and approached the group where Waring and De Vane were standing.

De Vane greeted her warmly, and said: "I will not attempt to thank you—I can not."

"Nothing can be finer than that in the way of uttering thanks," said Mlle. Vesperini, smiling.

Waring gave Esther his hand silently. Miss Godolphin was exultant; she said:

"I am not taken by surprise. I knew you before; but I am delighted that Mlle. Vesperini has heard you."

More music was called for. The love for it seemed to grow by that it fed on. Miss Dahlgreen urged Miss Godolphin to sing.

"Oh! no," she said. "Mlle. Vesperini has heard me. I am at home here, and can be heard at any time. Will you not favor us, Miss Dahlgreen?"

"Not this evening, thank you," she replied. "I only

sing to cheer my friends at home; and for some time past have bestowed too little attention on music."

"You must not appeal to me," said Waring, as she looked toward him. "I heard you last fall, and I was so charmed, that I threatened, you remember, to visit you every week, to hear you."

"Yes, you are very good, Mr. Waring, I know; but I really sing very little."

Miss Godolphin took her seat at the piano, and Mlle. Vesperini and Esther undertook to accompany her in singing.

It was done with great effect, each voice at times sustaining a single part, and again blending in strong and deep harmony.

Miss Godolphin's voice was one of great power, and in cultivation almost rivaled that of Mlle. Vesperini. Rarely, in any circles, had such music been heard; and the little capital could boast at once of its beauty, its genius, its eloquence, its arts, and its statesmanship.

The flying hours were swiftly passing. Looking out from the gallery which ran on the side of the drawing-room, and into which its windows opened, the stars were seen in their bright courses, and the moon flooded the garden with its radiance.

Mlle. Vesperini was prevailed on to sing once more—to sing one of those favorite melodies, which the genius of her countryman, Moore, had produced.

She sat at the harp. Its tones were sadder than ever: they seemed to steal from a broken heart; and the voice of the cantatrice, in tenderest sympathy with them, floated upon the air.

She sang those tender lines, written in the highest conception of love desolate, and mourning the young heroic dead—

"She is far from the land where her young hero sleeps;"

and the gush of emotion which she could not restrain, was as thrilling as if she herself were the young maiden whose heart had been crushed by the blow which destroyed her lover, lamenting at once his fate and her own.

De Vane was standing near Miss Godolphin, and he had observed that from the moment the artist's fingers had struck from the chords of the harp the air which had just died in their trembling tones, she grew pale, as the song was uttered in such passionate eloquence. She seemed scarcely conscious; and when it ceased, she reeled and was falling, when he caught her and placed her in a chair. Scarcely any one had observed her emotion, for their eyes were fixed on Mlle. Vesperini, and De Vane, with perfect self-possession and delicacy, shielded her from those about him. Her head rested for a moment on his arm, pale as if death had robbed those classical features forever of their glowing beauty. Then, with a deep sigh, she woke to consciousness, and the warm blood, returning, suffused her very brow.

She looked up to De Vane's face, and murmured: "Thank you."

"Let me bring you an ice," he said.

"No," she replied, "I will go with you; and passing her arm through that of De Vane, they went into the refreshment-room, almost unobserved. Not wholly so, for Waring had witnessed the scene; but with full sympathy with De Vane, he had placed himself so as to protect them from the view of others.

After a little time, De Vane returned to the drawing-room, and said to Esther that Miss Godolphin wished her to excuse her absence to Mlle. Vesperini, and say to her that she would join her very soon.

Esther approached Mlle. Vesperini, and delivered the message. Miss Dahlgreen came forward, and expressed her thanks to Mlle. Vesperini for the pleasure which she had afforded them all.

"Ah!" she replied, "you do not know how I have enjoyed the evening. This place is charming. I know nothing like it in this country. I shall carry away with me such impressions, and cherish such recollections! It is charming."

"We are much pleased to hear you say so," said Miss Dahlgreen. "One who has seen so much that is attractive in the world, in pronouncing so warmly her approval of us, must know how we prize the tribute."

Miss Godolphin entered the room, and engaged in conversation with them.

"A thousand thanks to you, Miss Godolphin," said Mlle. Vesperini, "for this charming evening. I wish that I could linger with you, but the wheels will to-morrow bear me away."

"Not to-morrow," said Mrs. Habersham. "We did hope to have you with us longer."

"To-morrow evening, madame, I shall be compelled to fly. Ireland calls me—I must see my home."

Then followed the leave-taking. The guests departed; but long lingered in their memory the sounds that had floated over their souls, and the words of song which had awakened within them a new and strong sympathy with the divine art.

"Let us walk, Miss Wordsworth," said De Vane; "the night is fine."

"I fear, Esther," said Mrs. Springfield, "that you will take cold. It may be better that Mr. De Vane and yourself should join us in the carriage."

Esther decided to walk, and De Vane wrapping her in her ample shawl, they enjoyed the fresh air of the balmy night.

## CHAPTER XX.

. . . . "PEACE hath her victories
No less renowned than war. New foes arise,
Threatening to bind our souls with secular chains."
JOHN MILTON.

A VERY large number of persons called the next day, and left their cards for Mlle. Vesperini. She was out driving, attracted by the verdure, which gave an aspect of rural beauty to the town and its environs. Every one was disposed to acknowledge the claim of the celebrated cantatrice to their consideration; a claim which her genius, her purity of character, and her fine manners, made it any thing but a task to meet by such attentions as her brief stay afforded them the opportunity to tender. The town, distinguished for its refinement, was attractive to strangers, and European travelers embraced it in their tour, and spoke of it everywhere in terms which were not more glowing than they were just. The College shed about it an intellectual influence which was very marked, while the highest courts in the State being held there, and the annual assembling of the Legislature, made it a place of far greater interest and importance than its numerical population or its commercial activity would have conferred on it, if it had been left dependent on these alone. Long may its College prosper! Long may it be the seat of a government distinguished for intelligence, statesmanship, and dignity!

De Vane's visits to Mr. Springfield's became more frequent, and he could no longer conceal from himself his growing interest in Esther. They were much together. Books, music, art—all interested them. Not a word of love was spoken, not a hint of the slightest change in their relations. They walked side by side, and knew and trusted each other more fully every day. The rich, vigorous mind of De Vane stimulated Esther in her studies, and she habitually consulted him in reference to her course of reading. By a reflex influence, too, she guided his tastes, and brought to his view such works as she felt satisfied would conduct him to that central stand-point in all learning which would enable him to see knowledge in its highest relations—relations which, seeming to be bounded by the horizon of the visible world, really stretched out illimitably and embraced the universe. She was far too wise to obtrude her views upon him, and even when he sought a conversation with her upon the great questions of morals, she suggested rather than argued. His pride of character she well knew. She had said to him that he was very proud, and she scrupulously forbore to put him in the attitude of defending opinions which he sometimes expressed, by combating them—opinions very odious to her, too. But she would content herself with calling his attention to certain other views which ought fairly to be examined in connection with them. She was very wise, and her influence over him was far greater than he ever supposed it to be. As an angel, invisible to our mortal eyes, may walk by our side and guide our steps, so she, quite unconsciously to him, walked with him, and often influenced him where he might have erred. The nobleness of his nature was such that he loved the true, the good; though, as he had ever remarked of himself, he loved the beautiful intensely, and his tastes being offended would sometimes make him turn away from what was both good and true. There was a grandeur in his character which elevated him very far above commonplace men, and his integrity was thorough. What his future was to be could not be decided: he was but upon the threshold of life. Who can read the horoscope of a young man of intellect, ardor, and ambition?

The political contest through which the country was passing was deepening in interest, and it roused the energies of the State. Mr. Clarendon felt the deepest interest in the election of General Jackson, and he exerted all the power of his magnificent mind to bring it about. Mr. Adams was conducting the administration upon principles which he could not approve, and Mr. Clay was developing his system for the protection of American industry with great boldness. Much as Mr. Clarendon admired the personal qualities of those distinguished statesmen—the one a scholar, the other almost peerless as an orator—he could not give his sanction to a system false in itself as a measure of national policy, and as hurtful to the South as it was unfair to every other interest in the country but the manufactures which it sought to protect, while it was a flagrant violation of the Constitution.

General Jackson, too, was heroic in his character, remarkable for self-reliance, and eminently fitted to lead the way to a complete popular victory. He was of the people; they loved him, believed in him, and would follow him without hesitation, either in the red path of battle, or in the political contest, hardly less fierce, in which he was now engaged. His previous defeat was not the result of the want of popular confidence; but several eminent men being candidates for the Presidency, the vote of the electoral colleges was so divided that no one of the aspirants obtained a majority. General Jackson led the way in the splendid course which opened to the coveted place; but, by a provision of the Constitution, the election devolved upon the House of Representatives in the event of a failure of the electoral colleges to give to some one person a majority of the whole vote. General Jackson, of Tennessee, John Quincy Adams, of Massachusetts, and William H. Crawford, of Georgia, were the three who stood highest in the list of candidates by the popular vote. Mr. Clay, of Kentucky, fell short of the requisite number, and could not go before the House of Representatives; but, being the leading member of that body, his influence over it was controlling. It is well known that, if Mr. Crawford's health had not suddenly failed, he would have been the choice of the House; but a shadow passed over his grand intellect, and unfitted him for the labors of that eminent position. As an eagle, rising upon strong wing from his mountain eyrie toward some loftier and sublimer peak, from which he might with undazzled eye look out upon the boundless plain, sinks suddenly with drooping wing, and seeks the humbler resting-place from which he had soared, so this really great man sank in the very moment of anticipated triumph, when he had almost reached the highest flight of his ambition; and returning to the State which still loved and honored him, passed the remainder of his life in the discharge of humbler duties. Mr. Adams was the choice of the House—a result due to Mr. Clay's influence.

Now, the recurrence of another election brought with it still intense strife. The friends of Mr. Adams and of Mr. Clay employed all their means to secure the reëlection of the President, that he might, in accordance with the usage, then unbroken, of a service of eight years, except in the single instance of his own father, fill the measure of his ambition and his fame; while the supporters of General Jackson, roused and fired, put out all their energies in his behalf. By midsummer the contest had become a very animated one. Mr. Clarendon entered into it with ardor; he insisted that the contest involved principles of the largest interest and importance; that it was a struggle not for men, but for the ascendency of the friends of the Constitution over its enemies; that the structure of the Government was such as to make it essential to adhere to the doctrines advanced by the friends of the rights of the States, and not to surrender it to the control of those statesmen who sought to convert it into a grand imperial consolidated system, which would merge the rights of the States in the power and glory of the empire.

Into these views De Vane fully entered. He wrote and spoke for them with power, and attracted attention by the vigor and earnestness with which he advocated truths that he believed to be essential to the prosperity and glory of the country. There was an elevation and dignity about his manner, his tone, his style of thought, that separated him widely from commonplace politicians; and he was already, in character, in breadth of view, and in his whole bearing, entitled to the name of statesman.

He was about to visit Virginia. His father had expressed a decided wish that he should do so. Still he lingered—he scarcely knew why; but he found it not at all easy to complete his arrangements for his journey. He was much at Mr. Springfield's; and he had explained to Mrs. Springfield and to Esther his plans. He was to visit his home, pass the summer, or what was left of it, in the mountains, and return in October to pursue his studies. Waring, too, had been consulted. He approved his views, and urged him to adhere to his resolution as to his future residence. It was Waring's plan for the summer vacation, to remain at home, and fit himself, by diligent study, to enter upon his duties at the opening of the ensuing session of the College; and he was already quite advanced in his preparation for a course of lectures, upon the subjects embraced in his department.

Esther had relaxed somewhat her course of training for

the little girls, thinking that, in the heat of the summer months, it might be better for them to be employed with the needle, and with drawing and painting, than to be confined to books. The arrangement, too, afforded her the relaxation which she wished; and as Mrs. Green was very competent to instruct her little charge in needle-work, one of the more advanced pupils was to undertake the task of looking after their progress in the arts, as Esther playfully styled them. She made them a daily morning call, joined in their devotions, and looked into their little wants. The garden which supplied the table with vegetables was well looked after by "Uncle Jacob," as they all called the old servant. He prided himself upon having the earliest, the best, and the latest fruits and vegetables in the town.

One evening, when the sun was just sinking behind the western hills, De Vane sat at the melodeon in Waring's room, touching its keys with an air of abstraction. Waring had walked out. He was alone, and the thought of his journey, now soon to be undertaken, depressed him. What changes had come over him, since he last saw his home, when very young, full of ardor, and impressed with the stateliness of the aristocratic life which had surrounded him! Now how little there was in all that to attract him! He did not undervalue rank, nor wealth, nor power; but he had learned to estimate them at what they were worth. He had learned to distinguish the real from the ideal; to prize truth, and goodness, and refinement, wherever he found them. His tastes were purer, simpler than before; and, while his ambition was none the less, it had addressed itself to the attainment of grander objects, by nobler means. He saw now, that the aim of aristocratic appointments, which made the social distinctions of life so broad, was to perpetuate high qualities, by preserving one class from deterioration, providing for it the means of culture, which should insure a proper training, and make the mind, the heart, the tastes, the manners, what they should be. But he saw how all this had failed; how the aristocratic class was becoming enfeebled; and how the humbler class was advancing in intellectual power and moral excellence. He saw how much there was of beauty, of refinement of mind, of goodness, in those whom the aristocratic professed to despise. The young patrician's brow darkened as these thoughts came over him. Was Waring his friend? One of the noblest men the world ever saw; full of intellect, of strength, of generous sympathy, of manly virtue, of refinement, of sensibility, of a heroic love of truth—was such a man to be despised because he lacked wealth; because he had taught, to enable his sister to enjoy the little estate left to them, not large enough for both, but sufficient for her; because he belonged to a religious sect despised by many; and because he stepped forward into the work of the ministry among this people, under the promptings of a great heart, and an imperious sense of duty—was such a man to be looked down upon as a plebeian?

Was Mr. Springfield to be despised—a man of the highest order, whose mind, heart, education, tastes, manners, elevated him above tens of thousands of those who talked of race, and family, and caste?

Esther, a peerless woman, glorious in person, in intellect, in soul; a ministering angel on earth, turning away from the frivolous and little objects which so many of her age prized; bestowing her abounding means in the rearing, and support, and culture of the helpless; full of all generous qualities; accomplished to a degree which threw the attainments of the tribe of elegant high-born triflers into the shade; with a soul full of truth—was she to be looked down upon because she was the daughter of a Methodist preacher, as he had heard him styled? Because she was herself a Methodist, was she to be despised? or if not despised, treated with a condescending patronage more insulting still?

The young patrician's lips were very firmly compressed, his eyes grew larger, and in their dark depths the blaze of irrepressible indignation flamed.

He struck the keys of the instrument, and there rolled from it a lofty strain, which seemed to seek the heavens, grand, solemn, awe-inspiring; then it swelled into an anthem, which filled the room with its volume.

Waring had returned, and was standing in the door of the room, his arms crossed upon his breast. He would not disturb De Vane. He stood and observed him. He saw that he was roused. And as the music from the fine instrument rolled away, his face expressed the admiration and intent with which he regarded the young patrician.

The music ceased. De Vane closed the instrument, and rose from his seat. His face was calmer, but a high sentiment was expressed in his features.

Waring had not moved, and De Vane, turning toward the door, for the first time became aware of his presence.

"O Waring! you have returned. Where on earth have you been wandering?"

"Not quite beyond this dusty world, but still in a pleasant part of it. I have been in the public garden."

"Indeed! And did you meet any agreeable people?"

"Several," said Waring.

"Now, you intend," said De Vane, "that I shall ask after them particularly. Why not be a generous fellow at once? You need not stand upon your dignity. It's vacation now."

Waring smiled, and said: "The garden was unusually thronged, and I met a number of persons—some of them very agreeable."

"Was Miss Godolphin there?"

"She was," said Waring, "and asked after you particularly."

"I hope you gave a good account of me."

"Yes," said Waring, "I told her that you were still studying faithfully—law in the morning, and other matters in the evening, perhaps not so profitable; but that I thought you were becoming a little more humanized, for you were somewhat more inclined than formerly to visit the ladies. At which report of you she seemed quite pleased."

"I'm very much obliged to you both," said De Vane.

"Yes, and perhaps you will be still more pleased to learn that Miss Wordsworth was with her."

"Indeed!" said De Vane, looking slightly conscious.

"Oh! yes," said Waring, "and I am instructed to inform you that Miss Godolphin takes Miss Wordsworth with her to tea, and that you are expected to join them without any unnecessary delay."

"You are a gracious messenger," said De Vane; "and may I inquire if you are to honor the ladies with your presence?"

"I am to have the honor of accompanying you," he replied; "so let us walk."

As they descended the stairs, they saw Mrs. Bowen, and explained to her that they would not remain for tea, and she said:

"Well, I'm glad to see you go out; not that I don't like to have you here, but I know that you will enjoy yourselves much better."

"Thank you, Mrs. Bowen," said De Vane. "I enjoy your house very much, but I must take Professor Waring out sometimes, to see the ladies."

"Ah! yes, I understand it," she said; "it's all right."

They bade her good evening, and walked away. A few minutes' walk brought them to Mrs. Habersham's; and they were shown into a small drawing-room, where they found the ladies.

"You observe, ladies," said Waring, "that I have carried out my instructions."

"Faithfully," said Miss Godolphin, "for which we are obliged. Not finding you in the walk which you sometimes take, Mr. De Vane," she continued, "we asked Mr. Waring to be so good as to invite you to join this evening in a cup of tea, quietly, and we are very glad to see you."

"I am most happy to come," said De Vane, bowing. "My friend here deserted me this evening in some way, and left me to the solitude of my room. If I had known that he was going in search of you, I should have joined him."

"I am sure he had no such purpose," said Miss Godolphin; "but taking a turn through the walks of the public garden, after a visit to Leasowes, with Miss Wordsworth, we had the good fortune to meet Mr. Waring."

"Of course," said De Vane. "Fortunate man! I must hereafter keep close by his side."

Esther was much amused, and Miss Godolphin exclaimed: "A willful man will have his way."

A rich silver tea-service was brought in by a footman, and small tables were placed by the chair of each guest; he then, after placing on the table a silver waiter, filled with light *gâteaux* and *confitures*, withdrew. Mrs. Habersham took her seat near the tea-service, and made the tea, the gentlemen passing it to the ladies, and taking their own cups. Servants were excluded from the room, both at breakfast and tea, at Mrs. Habersham's; the European style being adopted, which leaves the family free to indulge in conversation without restraint.

After tea, Mrs. Habersham withdrew, and the conversation was of books, especially of some which had lately appeared. Sir Walter Scott was giving to the press at that time those entertaining books which have been so widely diffused throughout the world, and which have contributed so much to cheer the hours of many, who, without them, would have been listless, or would have turned to amusements less innocent than reading pages which are full of refinement, of taste, and of culture. He has almost dramatized history; and often, with a slender thread of fiction, has guided the mind through an extended view of real events and actual objects. His poetical and his prose works were both discussed.

"His poetry is very pleasing," said Miss Godolphin, "but it possesses no depth of sentiment, no passion. It charms by its descriptions and its narrations."

De Vane said: "He abandoned the field of poetry to explore another, which he has shown to be very attractive. His historical novels are charming. They possess a dramatic interest, which is so attractive to all classes."

"The great charm of Scott," said Miss Godolphin, "is his genial nature, his kindliness. One feels safe under his guidance; and no matter where he may lead you, he will, you are sure, protect you, and bring you back from lake, or mountain height, or tournament, or battle, safely. He is your friend all the way that you journey in his company."

Esther spoke of the Bride of Lammermoor as evincing more of depth of sentiment than any of his tales which she had read, and said: "It depresses me sadly to read it. There is scarcely any thing of the kind which affects me so much."

"It is not to be wondered at," said De Vane. "It is intensely sad. Every incident in the progress of the story throws its sombre shadow over the future. The scene at the fountain is full of this—the fluttering raven falling at the feet of Ravenswood and Miss Ashton, pierced with an arrow, the blood staining her white dress. I do not wonder that the book depresses you. Never read it."

"The declining fortunes," said Miss Godolphin, "of Ravenswood, his pride, his dignity, his nobleness, are to me very affecting. It is dreadful to witness the struggle between a noble, generous, proud spirit, and the adverse fortunes which he encounters in striving to uphold the claims of his house. Such a social spectacle is at any time heart-rending."

"No man," said Waring, "should carry on such a struggle. It can only occur where society is organized upon a basis too artificial to be stable. Every man should be willing to work for his living, when it becomes necessary to do so. He is the happier for it, and far more respectable."

"Yes," said Miss Godolphin, "in this country that is quite true; but in a country where no labor is reputable but military service, it is not so. Indeed, even in this country, there is sometimes a painful yielding to declining fortunes in families accustomed to wealth."

"But," said Waring, "it ought not to be so anywhere. Labor ought always to be reputable. Self-reliance, independence—these are heroic qualities, and these ought to be encouraged. I have seen young men, whose fathers were loaded with debt, and were struggling to bear up under its burdens, too, I will not say proud—I will not degrade the term by such an application of it—too mean to work, and actually seeking to obtain credit upon the account of these very fathers, when it required some address to do it. That spectacle humiliates me."

He spoke with energy, and De Vane looked at him with admiration.

"I quite agree with you, Mr. Waring," said Miss Godolphin, "in that view. You can not state it too strongly for me. But when the blow first falls—when the extent of the calamity is not known—when the hope of better times has not yet died out, and when the persons are hardly fitted for the rough service of life, ah! then the blasts of adversity are keenly felt."

"There are doubtless such cases," said Waring. "But I am very impatient at the attempt that I see sometimes made, in this country, to put labor under the ban. I honor it, and if there be any one to whom I would bow reverently and take off my hat, it is to a mechanic, with bent form and stiffened frame, who is making his way with feeble steps toward a home which he has worn out his life in trying to make a happy one."

Miss Godolphin's eyes filled with tears. "Ah! Mr. Waring," she said, "I honor the sentiment, as much as you do the bent laborer. You are not more sturdily American than I am."

"I have never doubted that," said he. "You are too earnest to sympathize with a heartless social system, that wishes to degrade industry, and stamp self-reliance as plebeian. But," he continued, after a moment's pause, "while I have known such cases, Miss Godolphin, as those to which you refer, where the sudden reverses of life have brought great wretchedness, I have witnessed other instances which were more deplorable still; instances where daughters, thoroughly educated, and competent to teach, had disdained the slightest exertion when misfortunes came that brought distress, and painful, exhausting toil upon the father who had supplied them with every luxury in their better days. How much better, how much happier, how much more respectable they would have been, if with their hands they had ministered to the wants of the family, and solaced the anxieties that bowed the form of one whose cup was made still more bitter by the thought that he could no longer meet the wishes and gratify the tastes of those who hung about him! I love and honor independence unspeakably."

"Miss Godolphin's criticism," said De Vane, "or rather her appreciative remark as to the unhappy condition of Ravenswood, is a perfectly just one. His position, and the country and the times in which he lived, made it impossible that he could do any thing to better his fortunes, except as a soldier; and sad as it was to see the quicksands of Kelpie's Flow close over him and his horse, as he rode to meet Douglas Ashton, I experienced a sense of relief too. I could not bear to see him struggling in the midst of life-long humiliations. Better death than that. His own mournful words spake the nobleness of his nature, when he said to the faithful Caleb: 'You have no longer a master. Why, old man, would you cling to a falling tower?'"

Esther had said nothing for some time. She was deeply interested in the discussion which had been going on, and as De Vane made his last remark, she fixed her eyes upon him with unconscious earnestness. She sympathized profoundly with him, and she comprehended how a grand nature like his might, under some circumstances, grow weary of life, if there were not something to cheer the spirit beyond the visible objects of time.

"Do you then, Mr. De Vane," she said, "not agree with Hamlet, that we should

'rather bear those ills we have,
Than fly to others that we know not of'?"

"Ah! he spoke of taking one's own life," said De Vane. "That, I think, is never to be done, certainly never to be looked to, as an escape from the weariness of life. But I spoke of perishing by some casualty."

"Even then," she said, "sudden death is terrible; for it precipitates us into

> 'The undiscovered country, from whose bourn
> No traveler returns.'"

De Vane looked grave. Waring said nothing, but smiled.

"Death, under any circumstances," said Miss Godolphin, "is appalling."

"Far from it," said Waring. I have seen it under circumstances which made it luminous and triumphant."

"So have I—once," said De Vane.

A silence—stillness—reigned for some moments.

At length Miss Godolphin said: "That Bride of Lammermoor has saddened us all. Poor Lucy Ashton! Let us turn to something gayer."

She rose, and rang for a servant. "Bring us some ices," she said.

He presently returned with refreshments, and left the room again.

"How delicious ices are!" said Esther; "water-ices especially!"

"Yes," said Miss Godolphin. "I find them refreshing in mid-winter."

After some general conversation, Esther said:

"Miss Godolphin, when I was last here, Mr. De Vane called my attention to a picture in the drawing-room where we were that evening, which greatly interested me. Will you give me its history?"

Miss Godolphin looked at De Vane quickly.

"I said nothing to Miss Wordsworth of its history," he said. "I pointed it out to her, but we left the room soon after, and I made no explanations."

"Then you know its history?" said Esther, turning to him with surprise.

"Only what I have told him," said Miss Godolphin, "and you shall soon learn that. It so happened that when we were in Naples the last winter we passed in Europe, we visited the studio of an eminent artist from our own country, and we saw the picture there. My aunt purchased several of his paintings—some of them very costly—and I two or three. Struck with the beauty and exquisite finish of the large picture to which you refer—that which represents Salome, the daughter of Herodias, bearing the head of John the Baptist to her mother—I offered to purchase it. The artist refused to sell it, and said he valued it highly, not only as one of his very best pictures, but because it was associated with recollections that endeared it to him. He made no further explanation, and, of course, I could ask for none. Some days after I called again, and was standing before the picture which so powerfully attracted me, when the artist came to me, and said that I seemed really to value the painting which I was examining; that he had painted it in Rome, during the last season; that it was endeared to him by associations of the strongest kind; that nothing could induce him to sell it, but that he had the means of reproducing it, if he should desire to do so at some future time; and that as I appreciated it, he would present it to me if I would accept it, adding that it would be seen in that part of his native country where he most desired to be favorably known. I, of course, thanked him warmly, and did not refuse it. He said he would have it forwarded to my address. A few weeks since, it arrived, and when it was hung, I then saw the wonderful resemblance which Salome bore to yourself. This is the history of the picture. Let us go and see it."

Rising from her seat, she rang for a servant, and ordered the green drawing-room to be lighted.

"It is very strange," said Esther. "It must, of course, be an accidental resemblance."

"I should suppose so," said Miss Godolphin, "if the resemblance were less striking, and limited to the features; but the fidelity of the picture to features, form, hair, expression, is so remarkable, that I confess I think a mystery surrounds it which we do not yet comprehend."

Speaking with great earnestness, she rose and conducted the party into the drawing-room with green silk hangings and furniture. It was octagonal in form, and on one of the panels, suspended by a rich, heavy cord of green silk, with tassels touching the elaborate frame, was the picture. The room was well lighted; and as the party entered it, the figure of the Jewish maiden, with her flowing white robes and crimson shawl, her face turned upon the spectators, seemed to breathe with life and emotion, and the resemblance to Esther was so perfect as to be absolutely startling. She herself stood in mute astonishment, and as she fixed her lustrous eyes upon the picture, they swam in tears, and her lips parting, unconsciously she said, scarcely loud enough to be heard even by De Vane, upon whose arm she rested: "Oh! how like my mother!"

Her emotion was observed, and too much respect was felt for it, to disturb her fixed gaze upon the picture.

After some moments she said: "I have in my possession, Miss Godolphin, a portrait which you have never seen. It is of my mother, and hangs in my own chamber. It was painted for her when she was of my age, and the name of the artist is unknown to me, but the picture is of the highest style of art."

"It is strange," said Miss Godolphin. "I confess myself wholly unable to explain it."

"The picture is a glorious one," said De Vane. "I never saw one so fine."

"It is one of extraordinary beauty," said Waring, "and I now see that the resemblance to Miss Wordsworth is even more faithful than I had supposed it to be, when I first saw it."

Miss Godolphin conducted them to the other paintings

which adorned the walls; and as they reached her own portrait, they stood to examine it.

"It is superb," said De Vane. "It impressed me the first time I saw it. Not only is the likeness remarkable, but the whole painting is wonderfully fine."

"How little good taste is usually shown in portraits!" said Waring. "The awkwardness, stiffness, and conceit make them unbearable; but this is free from faults."

"The criticism," said Miss Godolphin, "is a very just one. A difficulty sometimes occurs as to costume. The changing styles, not only of different ages, but those which occur in the course of a very few years, give to portraits, in some instances, a quaint and even a ludicrous appearance."

"There should," said De Vane, "be as little of modern costume introduced in a picture as possible. The drapery should be loose and flowing. The nearest approximation to the classical style is the best; best in every way, for it is quite certain that the standard of perfection in the arts was attained under the skies of Greece."

"Your remark," said Esther, "is especially true of statuary. The drapery should be flowing. The toga was the most becoming garment ever worn by your sex."

"Perfectly true," said De Vane, "and I should be pleased to go back to it. How shocking it is to see buttons, for instance, either in bronze or marble, on the skirts of ladies, more or less ample!"

"I am not at all sure that I agree with you," said Waring. "I do not think it appropriate to see modern heroes and statesmen represented in ancient costume, and especially half-nude.

"I am astonished at you," said De Vane. "The nearer nude you produce the statue, the more closely do you approach the well-established principles of art. Art has principles as well defined, and laws as binding, as any of the sciences; and you can not depart from them without detriment to the subject."

"I should subordinate every thing," said Waring, "to higher laws than those of taste; and I am not at all sure that by exhibiting the half-nude form of a hero—certainly of a statesman, and to go higher still, of an apostle—you do not impair the impression of dignity which it is the wish of the artist to create."

"Rank heresy!" said De Vane. "Bless my soul! Waring, you must positively review your impressions of art. Look at all the representations of the human form in sculpture or painting—from the time of Phidias and Apollo till now—and you will find them more or less nude. If you exclude the ancients as heathens—as I suspect you are inclined to do—then take the artists from the time when the Christian era dawned, and when every thing began to adjust itself to the new order of thought and emotion, and you will find my view confirmed. Take the sculpture, the paintings of those days, the pictures of the apostles, of saints of both sexes, and see if you will not find a universal concurrence in the principles of taste, especially in the grand principle, that the human form must be presented with as little drapery as is consistent with cultivated taste."

"There is one exception to the principle which you lay down, Mr. De Vane," said Miss Godolphin. "The blessed Virgin is everywhere in full drapery. I do not know that I can recall another instance in which your law is not well settled in its application to the works of the great masters, both in sculpture and painting."

"And the exception which you state," said Waring, "is so fully sustained by the sentiment of the world, that it proves it to be well founded. It rests upon a principle of our nature, and it is only education which can accustom the eye to any great departure from it."

"Suppose Hercules, throttling the Nemean lion," said De Vane, "or Laocoon and his sons in the folds of the serpent, were represented in drapery, would not the impression be destroyed? Or the dying gladiator—would it not impair the effect? I admit that in painting, the adjustment of drapery is more tractable, and therefore to be more modified, to suit even an uncultivated taste. But at all events, let us not insist on coats and vests for gentlemen, or a very literal copying even of the dresses of our ladies, either in sculpture or painting."

They all laughed, and were passing to another picture, when a servant entered, and approaching Miss Godolphin, informed her that Miss Wordsworth's carriage had arrived. All exclaimed against such an early departure; but upon looking at the clock, it was discovered that the hour was really a late one.

It was agreed that on the evening after the next, which would be Thursday, they should meet again at Mrs. Springfield's.

Waring and De Vane both drove with Esther to her door, and then took leave of her, declining to be taken home in the carriage.

## CHAPTER XXI.

"And would we aught behold of higher worth
Than that inanimate cold world allowed
To the poor, loveless, ever-anxious crowd—
Ah! from the soul itself must issue forth
A light, a glory, a fair luminous cloud
Enveloping the earth."

SAMUEL TAYLOR COLERIDGE.

THE arrangements for De Vane's departure were nearly completed. He must go, reluctant as he was to quit the enchanted circle in which he moved, giving and receiving pleasure. His sense of duty imperiously exerted its control over him. Such was his organization, that strong as his passions were, they were under the dominion of his principles. The tide might swell with apparently resistless power, and the waves lash the resounding shore, but they were stayed by a law of his nature that they could not overcome. The sensibility which characterized him, made him seem, to a casual observer, too warm for steady resistance to his inclinations; but those who knew him comprehended how firmly he could plant himself when he made up his mind that it was his duty to hold his position. He was easily influenced by his tastes, and attracted or repelled by what pleased or offended his sense of the beautiful; but when an appeal was made to his sense of right, the decision was made in obedience to that. He must return home, and he decided to leave the following Monday. The invitation for Thursday evening cheered him. He would once more enjoy a visit to a family to which he had become strongly attached; for, independent of his very deep interest in Esther, his respect and regard for Mr. and Mrs. Springfield were strong. He retained his room at Mrs. Bowen's, assuring her that he should re-enter it in October, and giving directions that his books and furniture should be looked after during his absence. His room was his home—he loved it—and he could not think of tearing himself away from a place so dear to him as the town where he had passed the happiest years of his life, without holding his claim upon one spot—that he might think of, in his absence, as his own. How the soul clings to inanimate objects, and invests them with its own light!

When Thursday evening came, De Vane and Waring took their walk, turning their steps toward the College. They walked through the deserted campus, and felt the sadness of its loneliness. They lingered but a little while, and then returned, going directly to Mr. Springfield's.

Miss Godolphin was already there. The house was a delightful one, full of objects of grace and beauty—books, engravings, statuettes, instruments of music. The latest reviews were laid upon the table. The snowy muslin curtains, through which the summer air came freshly, gave an appearance of lightness and purity which was exhilarating, and the chintz-covered furniture was tasteful and elegant.

There is a wonderful charm about some homes. The moment you enter them, you feel refreshed; while others, with heavy magnificence, are sombre and uninviting.

Mrs. Springfield received them.

"We are happy to see you," she said; "but you should have come earlier. The evenings are short."

"I said so to Mr. De Vane," said Waring, "but he lingered about the College campus, looking once more at the scenes of his former triumphs, a little longer than we intended to do."

"Ah! Mr. De Vane," said Miss Godolphin, "you will leave us? I shall not flatter you by saying how much we shall regret you."

"If any thing," said De Vane, "could cheer me in leaving this place, it would be the thought that my absence would be felt by any one."

"That is a very modest speech, Mr. De Vane," said Miss Godolphin. "You must know, of course, how much we shall lose in giving you up, especially at this season."

De Vane bowed, and said: "My absence will be but for some three months—scarcely that, indeed; and I shall hasten my return, in the hope of enjoying society which has been so agreeable to me. My friend, Mr. Waring, is to keep me informed, too, of movements here."

"Very well," said Miss Godolphin; "we shall get our accounts of you through him, and quite regularly, I hope."

"You are very good," said De Vane; "and I shall promise myself the happiness of hearing, in the same way, often from those of whom I shall think so constantly when absent."

"Yes," said Waring, "I undertake to write faithfully whatever is said to me here, and to report your messages."

"So that is arranged," said Mrs. Springfield. "I am very glad that it is so. In the mean while, we shall exert ourselves to make the weeks pass as agreeably as possible."

"For my part," said Waring, "I take no pleasure in summer travel. To me it is much more agreeable to be at home. This business of seeking pleasure is very irksome."

"How perfectly I agree with you!" said Esther. "Above all things, to rush into crowded hotels, or to stay at thronged watering-places, is to me the most wearisome way of life that I have ever yet seen."

"Nothing short of dreadful," said Miss Godolphin.

"It is true," said Esther, "one meets very agreeable people at some of those places; but the manner of life is very, very distasteful to me."

"Far better get a farm-house in the country, hid away in some mountain gorge, where you hear the songs of birds, the lowing of cattle, the clear human voice breaking the stillness of the air; and see fruits, and flowers, and the sweet face of nature; and get pure milk and fresh eggs," said Miss Godolphin, laughing.

"Your picture is a delightful one," said Waring.

"Yes," said Esther, "and a true picture. We found it so last summer. To add to our comforts, too, we had good horses, and could ride upon the side of the mountain, or plunge into the clear, rushing stream—not too deep, but yet suggestive of danger—and dash along the roads winding through sequestered vales, without the fear of being remarked about as too wild."

'Glorious!" said De Vane. "And you ride on horseback, do you?"

"Ride!" said Esther. "Why, of course I do. Is not that a part of the education of a Southern lady?"

"And yet I have never seen you," said he. "How I have suffered the spring to glide by without making that discovery."

"I do not ride in town—at least, very rarely," she replied.

"And you ride, too, Miss Godolphin," said De Vane, "I am to presume, after what Miss Wordsworth has said?"

"Certainly; and we intend to perfect ourselves in that way during your absence, as the town will be pretty much deserted."

"Pardon me, ladies," said De Vane; "I really supposed that our mountain region only furnished rivals for Diana Vernon. I am greatly pleased to make this discovery;

and when I return, I shall hope to join you. October is a glorious month for equestrian exercise."

"Very well," said Miss Godolphin. "We shall hold ourselves in readiness, and you must prepare for break-neck adventures, for we shall be fearless equestriennes by that time."

"I hope, ladies," said Waring, "that you will, in the mean while, permit me sometimes to join you."

"We shall be most happy," said Esther, "to have you with us."

"You are making my leave-taking, ladies," said De Vane, "a harder task for me than it was before."

"Very well," said Miss Godolphin; "if gentlemen will go on their summer rambles, we must seek what compensation we may."

She was very bright; and De Vane observed how much more cheerful she was when in the presence of those who were with her this evening, than when in larger and gayer circles.

Mr. Springfield, who had been out riding, came in, and all rose to meet him.

"I must ask you to pardon me," said he; "I rode somewhat farther than I intended, and was detained a little while on the road."

"By nothing disagreeable to you, I hope?" said Mrs. Springfield.

"I crossed the river," said he, "and upon my return, just before I reached the ferry, I met young Walden, so much intoxicated as to be unable to sit on his horse; and I rode back with him to his mother's."

"Sad—sad!" exclaimed Waring. "I had hoped that he had reformed. I must look after him again."

"It is the vice of our times," said Mr. Springfield, "and it must be arrested, or our young men will be destroyed."

Mrs. Springfield invited them to tea, and she conducted

them to the table. Mr. Springfield preferred the custom of sitting at the table, even at the evening meal. For his own part, he said, he enjoyed it more than any other; and it was often, at his house, the most prolonged sitting of the day. Boiled fowls, warm bread, cream, fruits, and flowers made it an attractive meal; and De Vane sympathized so fully with Mr. Springfield's tastes, that he enjoyed supper nowhere so much as at his house.

"This recalls," said Miss Godolphin, "so vividly our way of living when we passed the summer in Switzerland. We took a cottage, and kept house regularly. Never did we live so delightfully. The cream, the butter, the fowls, the fruits, were delicious; and as the sun went down behind the Alps, throwing shadows over us long before night, we were accustomed to spread our table in the little gallery, about which the shrubbery grew, and take our evening meal. The lowing of herds and the song of the mountaineers broke the solemn stillness of the hour. Oh! how superior it was to life in Paris, or in Florence, or in Naples! Nature, in her grandeur, and in her simple beauty too, was about us, and there was nothing to remind us of the great, noisy, dusty, confused world."

"I can imagine it must be charming," said Mr. Springfield, "after your description. Such an episode in life I wish very much, at some time, to enjoy myself."

"And you would not accept it as a permanent arrangement?" she asked.

"Oh! no," he said. "What would become of one's duties? If every one who could do it, chose some happy retreat, where the sad voice of humanity could not disturb his repose, what would become of our fellows? our kindred? of feebler pilgrims than ourselves, fainting by the wayside, and wanting a strong arm to lift them up and help them along the rough paths of life?"

Miss Godolphin looked at him earnestly, and Waring

observed De Vane's face beam as Mr. Springfield said this, in that manly, direct way, which has nothing of cant in it, and which makes every one instantly sympathize with the sincerity of the speaker.

"But," he continued, "I should be very much pleased to take such recreation as that, and it enters into my plans for the future."

"Are there many, sir, who feel as you do?" asked Miss Godolphin.

"Many, I trust," said he, "and, it is to be hoped, much more intensely. How Howard transcends us all: traversing Europe—not to enter its palaces, or visit its picture-galleries, or linger in delightful retreats; but, in the language of Burke, to gauge the depths of human misery, to let light and hope into dungeons, where they had long been strangers!"

"His was a sublime life," said Waring. "I am disposed to think, however, that there are many engaged in humane and benevolent activities little known to us, many whose lives are good and useful, without being grand."

"I do not doubt it," said Mr. Springfield. "It is in that way that the harmony of life is made up, and that in its completeness it grows into a resemblance of the wide-spread world of nature. Miss Godolphin, you must have some of these peaches. Let me select you one."

"Thank you," said she. "They are very fine. This country of ours abounds with luxuries."

"It is a goodly land," he said, "and this town is growing up into great beauty. Skirted, too, with its sand-hills, we find summer retreats without going far from home."

"I observe," said Waring, "that they are building up rapidly. The environs promise to be attractive. It would not surprise me to see permanent residences built up on our sand-hills."

"That is already done," said Mrs. Springfield. "Some of our friends intend to reside there permanently."

"It is much better to do so," said Mr. Springfield, "than to migrate every summer. Home society should be cultivated, and an extended travel resorted to for health and recreation."

"I am quite of your opinion," said Miss Godolphin.

Returning to the library, they found Mr. Clarendon there, and upon Mrs. Springfield's expressing her regret that she had not been informed of his coming, that he might have joined them at the table, he said: "My dear madam, I would not allow myself to be announced. I did not even ring your bell, but entering, found the house thrown open, and walked in unasked."

"You did just what you should have done," said Mr. Springfield, "but you stopped too soon. Will you not come now and take some fruit?"

He declined, and resumed his seat. The ladies gathered about him, and an animated conversation commenced. He was a welcome visitor everywhere. His large mind and large heart were appreciated, and there was a blended stateliness and warmth in his manners singularly captivating. His conversational powers, when he thought proper to indulge them, fell but little short of his oratory. De Vane resembled him in both respects, and the sympathy between them was strong. Esther was his special favorite, and he often called to sit an hour with her.

"I feel myself slighted," said Mr. Clarendon, addressing Esther and Miss Godolphin. "I am half inclined to think that you invited these two young gentlemen to meet you this evening, and overlooked me." He assumed the look of an injured man, and laid his hand on Esther's arm.

"Of course we could never overlook you, Mr. Clarendon. It happened that we met at Mrs. Habersham's an evening or two since, and it was arranged, before we separated, that we should meet here this evening. We are very glad that you have done us the honor to join us."

"Then," said he, "these young gentlemen have no rights here this evening that I may not enjoy?"

"None whatever," said Miss Godolphin.

Mr. Clarendon kissed the hand of each of them, and said: "Then I offer my homage."

"Waring," said he, "is it true that De Vane is to set upon his travels shortly?"

"He insists that he is serious in that purpose," said Waring, "and I must say that his preparations begin to look very much as if it were so."

"He has been trying to make that impression on me," said Mr. Clarendon, "for some weeks, but I have never yet been able to bring myself quite up to the line of faith. It must require a greater share of heroism than we usually find in these degenerate times."

All laughed heartily, and De Vane said:

"You do not overestimate the task, Mr. Clarendon; but I can not turn away from it, and I have therefore of late addressed myself to it with what resolution I am able to command."

"Telemachus quitting the island without being precipitated from it by his Mentor," said Mr. Clarendon.

There was no replying to this, and De Vane could only bow his acquiescence.

"While seated here," said Mr. Clarendon, "I took up the January number of the Edinburgh Review, Mr. Springfield. Do you find it a good one?"

"There is one article," he answered, "which I read with interest. It is a notice of The Songs of Scotland, by Allan Cunningham, and the writer proceeds to inquire into the utility of poetry."

"As if it could be questioned," said De Vane.

"In this time of practical truth," said Mr. Clarendon,

"every thing is questioned which is not convertible into gold and silver. Burke said long ago, the age of chivalry is gone. That of sophists, economists, and calculators has succeeded, and the glory of Europe is extinguished forever. How can you expect poetry to be esteemed as of any value ?"

"What a magnificent passage that is of Burke's !" said De Vane. "The finest he ever uttered, I think."

"Very eloquent," said Mr. Clarendon.

"The picture of the young Queen of France, glittering above the horizon like the morning star, is poetry, and that too of a high order," said De Vane.

"Let us turn to it," said Mr. Springfield, taking down from a shelf a volume of Burke's works; and handing it to De Vane, he requested him to find the passage and read it. He did so, with great effect.

"Glorious !" said Esther.

"Splendidly beautiful !" exclaimed Miss Godolphin.

"If Mr. De Vane will pardon me," said Mr. Springfield, "I will say that I never before so fully appreciated it."

"Does the reviewer," said Mr. Clarendon, addressing himself to Mr. Springfield, "vindicate the utility of poetry ?"

"Fully, it seems to me," he said. "I am particularly pleased that he introduces Lord Bacon as an advocate for it, who commends it as being subservient to the imagination—as logic is to the understanding—and says its office is no other than to apply and commend the dictates of reason to the imagination, for the better moving the appetite and will. The reviewer remarks, being an ally of reason and logic therefore, according to Lord Bacon, it is not to be despised."

"Good !" said Mr. Clarendon, "very good !"

"The authority of Lord Bacon is further cited," said Mr. Springfield, "in this way : The end of poetry is to fill the imagination with observations and resemblances which may second reason, and not oppress and betray it, for these abuses of art come in but *ex obliquo*, for prevention, not for practice. The reviewer adds: 'All this being the case, it seems that all speculations for putting down poetry must necessarily be vain and useless. They are formed perhaps for man as he ought to be, but certainly not for man as he is. They are, in short, like that dream of Plato, which has been a dream, and nothing more, for two thousand years. That celebrated Greek denied admittance to a poet in his ideal republic, and his republic has remained ideal."

"Excellently well put," said Mr. Clarendon; "and he might have added the testimony of Swift, recorded in verse:

'Not empire to the rising sun,
By valor, conduct, fortune won;
Not greatest wisdom in debates,
Or framing laws for ruling states;
Such heavenly influence require,
As how to strike the muse's lyre.'"

"I was greatly interested, a few evenings since," said De Vane, "in taking up a periodical, to find an article on Milton, by Dr. Channing. It is admirable throughout. He says that those who are accustomed to think of poetry as light reading, may think of the writings of Milton as only contributions to public amusement, but that such was not the thought of the great poet himself. Of all God's gifts of intellect, he esteemed poetical genius the most transcendent. He esteemed it in himself a kind of inspiration, and wrote his great works with the conscious dignity of a prophet. Dr. Channing himself adds that he agrees with Milton in his estimate of poetry. The great New-England scholar unhesitatingly assigns to the poetical faculty the first rank in his classification of the intellectual powers."

"He has just written," said Waring, "a powerful paper on Napoleon, and one which will repay the time expended in reading it."

"It is drawn out," said De Vane, "by Sir Walter Scott's life of the great captain."

"I have not yet read Scott's book," said Mr. Clarendon, "but I must do so."

"It is conceived in no generous or magnanimous spirit," said De Vane; "nor do I think it even just. He is thoroughly imbued with the sentiment of those who made war upon Napoleon, until they overthrew him."

"He should not have undertaken such a work," said Mr. Springfield.

"But, ladies," said Mr. Clarendon, "we must know your estimate of poetry. What do you say, Miss Godolphin? Is Lord Byron right?"

"Of course," said she, "you would not expect me to venture to oppose such authority as that of the great philosopher."

"You can not be excused," said Mr. Clarendon; "philosophers, heroes, statesmen, all yield to your sex."

"I agree, then," she said, "that the utility of poetry is unquestionable; that it is charming, no one doubts."

"And you, Miss Wordsworth, what say you? Are we in this age to yield ourselves to the dominion of the imagination, or to retain our sober senses?"

"We may do both, I think," said Esther. "Poetry of the highest order, such as Milton's, is consistent with the noblest of our faculties, and is but a felicitous expression of the deductions of reason."

"I pronounce that opinion an end of controversy," said Mr. Clarendon, "and I regret that I have no wreath to crown you with."

Miss Godolphin was seated near De Vane, and breaking from a vase near her a light vine brilliant with wild flowers, she twisted it into a wreath and put it into the hands of De Vane, who, rising, laid it gently on the head of Esther. It flung its crimson flowers about her curls, and seemed to have been designed as an ornament for the brow which it graced. Mr. Clarendon applauded, and Esther, blushing deeply said: "I accept the wreath as a tribute to poetry, of which I happened to speak with ardor."

"The wreath is yours fairly, and poetry is fortunate in its representative. A crown was never more worthily bestowed," said De Vane in low tones, as he stood near her. She made no reply, but a conscious expression flitted over her features.

"I have sometimes been at a loss to determine," said Waring, "whether poetry surpasses the arts in the power of expression."

"It is a beautiful field of inquiry," said Miss Godolphin, "and one might hesitate to decide between the contending claims of objects which so deeply interest us."

"I think with you, Miss Godolphin," said Mr. Clarendon; "it is one of those questions upon which a great deal may be said on both sides. Any one who visits the Louvre will find the power of art in expression so potent as to awake emotions which are rarely appealed to elsewhere."

"But," said Esther, "can any thing equal the power of language?"

"I thank you," said De Vane, "for that question; I was about to ask it myself; for I can not believe that any art can rival language in the power of expression—the language of passion, I mean, which poetry is."

"Now, Miss Godolphin," said Mr. Clarendon, "it becomes you to sit arbitress between these contending parties, for I believe you have not committed yourself."

"Not as yet," she said.

"Nor have I," said he; "but I incline to the arts."

"So do I," said Waring; "but it is not easy to decide between objects of so much interest, as Miss Godolphin felicitously says."

"I have never seen the original of the Dying Gladiator," said De Vane, "but there is in my home a very superior copy, large and finely executed. My father brought it from Rome. I have often admired it, studied it, thought that I entered into all the sentiments which it was intended to express, and I was profoundly affected by it. Some time since, in reading Childe Harold, I found a description of the scene which art had essayed to suggest, so far transcending the work itself, which, mute yet powerful, had awakened in me strong emotions, that I felt as if I had never comprehended it before."

"Repeat the lines, if you please," said Mrs. Springfield, who was deeply interested in the conversation.

De Vane bowed to her, and said: "I think I can recall them:

'I see before me the gladiator lie:
He leans upon his hand; his manly brow
Consents to death, but conquers agony,
And his drooped head sinks gradually low;
And through his side the last drops, ebbing slow
From the red gash, fall heavy, one by one,
Like the first of a thunder-shower; and now
The arena swims around him—he is gone,
Ere ceased the inhuman shout which hailed the wretch who won.

'He heard it, but he heeded not—his eyes
Were with his heart, and that was far away:
He recked not of the life he lost—nor prize;
But where his rude hut by the Danube lay,
*There* were his young barbarians all at play—
*There* was their Dacian mother—he, their sire,
Butchered to make a Roman holiday:
All this rushed with his blood. . . . .'"

Miss Godolphin's eyes were liquid, and the tears rolled down the cheeks of Esther.

"The lines are surpassingly fine," said Mrs. Clarendon, whose eyes were moist.

"A finer illustration of the power of descriptive verse," said Mr. Springfield, "it would be hard to find."

"Indeed it would," said Waring.

"Now," said De Vane, "you observe the power of poetry in expression. The sculptor represents a dying man, full of manliness; the gash, the dripping blood, the drooping head, are all seen. But the poet comes in, and he invests the dying form with the deepest moral interest. The tenderest sympathies of our nature are appealed to. The dying man is a father. By the distant Danube, his boys, all unconscious of his fate, are at play; and their Dacian mother, widowed already, does not know it, but for long days will look for his coming, but look in vain."

Every one who heard him, exhibited emotion. Unconsciously, he threw the power of his own eloquence into the description, and it was irresistible.

"I very well remember," said Mr. Clarendon, "to have seen the statue; and I must confess that my sensibilities were never touched as they have just now been by your description."

"I saw it, too," said Miss Godolphin, "not a great while since, and it never moved me as the words uttered by Mr. De Vane have done. I looked at it as a work of art. Its moral aspect had not occurred to me."

"It was injured at one time," said Mr. Clarendon. "The right arm is a restoration by Michael Angelo."

"Still," said Waring, "what are the lines but a description of a work of art? Did not the statue awaken in a man of genius the very sentiments it was intended to embody?"

"Oh! no," said De Vane, "the artist, it is believed, only

intended to express his idea of manly death; of a dying man exhibiting all of life that was left in him, in its grandest form. The power of expression in the poetry far transcends that of the statue itself."

"Walking one day," said Mr. Clarendon, "through the Louvre, I entered the Spanish gallery, and my attention was arrested by the figure of a prostrate man in deep grief. I stood, and studied the painting; it was one of great power; and it proved to be a representation of the repenting grief of St. Peter. The conception of the artist was a high triumph of genius. I had been accustomed to depict the apostle as bowed down with the weight of his grief, unable to lift his head, and his whole form prostrate. This was the picture of my imagination. Not so that of the Spanish painter. He represents St. Peter kneeling; his body drooping forward, but the *face upturned*, as if the eyes were seeking some revealing light which might shed the faintest gleam over the darkness of his spirit; and his mouth was open, the muscles too much relaxed by the anguish of his soul to support the lower jaw. The hands were clasped, but not upraised; and the whole expression was that of unutterable but not rayless grief. Sorrow had deepened into agony, which could be expressed in no way but by the attitude, the tears, the uplifted face of the apostle, wounded by a look from his Lord. Now, I had again and again read the account of the fall of St. Peter, as it stands in the inspired record, and I had read, too, what sacred poetry could utter in delineating it; but none of its lines rivaled the simple, touching narrative of the Evangelist, who informs us that when the Lord turned and looked upon Peter, he went out and wept bitterly. Still, I must say, that account, affecting as it is, did not awaken in me the emotions excited by the picture in the Spanish gallery of the Louvre."

Every one was moved by the statement of Mr. Clarendon. His fine manner and extraordinarily earnest tones made a deep impression.

"After all," said Mr. Springfield, "Miss Godolphin will find it a hard task to decide between the power of poetry and art."

"Oh! yes," said she, "I must decline it."

A servant entered with ices and fruits; and Mr. Clarendon said:

"We revel in luxuries this evening. Poetry, the arts, fruits, flowers, ices. The ancients never equaled us with all their boasted civilization."

"I am afraid that you will rouse my friend De Vane into opposition again," said Waring, "if you exalt modern civilization to any thing like equality with that of the ancients."

"Ah! yes," said Mr. Clarendon; "but I shall put him on the defensive this time, if he seeks strife; and until he can cite some authority to show that any thing the ancients possessed could rival these peaches, and this iced sherbet, I shall decline to argue."

"Preferring, I suppose," said De Vane, "to enjoy the gifts that come from the gods, without inquiring whether they are partial in their favors."

"No," said Mr. Clarendon, "I have learned to prize what I possess, and to live with contentment, imbued with the spirit of those fine lines which your Professor of Moral Philosophy at the College sometimes quotes:

'To be resigned when ills betide,
Patient when favors are denied,
Thankful for favors given—
This, dear Chloe, is wisdom's part,
This is that incense of the heart
Whose fragrance smells to heaven.'"

"Except," said De Vane, "in politics."

"Oh!" said Mr. Clarendon, "I meant to be understood of the gifts bestowed upon our physical nature. I fear that I am any thing but contented with my lot in other respects; and I am especially impatient under this prone Administration, which, however, if it should please Heaven, we shall soon expel."

"Things are looking well, then?" said Mr. Springfield.

"Everywhere, even in New-England," replied Mr. Clarendon; "and New-York is sure for us."

"I am anxious to see General Jackson," said Miss Godolphin. "I learn that he is a real hero."

"He is," said Mr. Clarendon, "in his character and his exploits both."

"I have seen him," said De Vane. "He called at my father's residence, just before I left home, on his return from Washington, having gone some considerable distance out of his way to confer with my father upon public affairs."

"Do describe him to us," exclaimed Miss Godolphin.

"His appearance impressed me. I was returning from an evening's shooting, and as I approached the house, I saw standing by the side of my father, in the gallery of the house, which was open to the western sky, a tall, somewhat slightly-built gentleman, dressed in black. He was without a hat, and the declining light of the evening fell upon his person. His hair, somewhat gray, stood up from his forehead. He wore a pair of gold-framed glasses, and another pair, thrown up above the forehead, rested on his hair. His eyes, were piercing, and their fire could be read through his glasses. The face and head were long; and there was a character of unmistakable firmness seated upon his features. As I approached the house, my father called to me, and advancing, he presented me to General Jackson, who received me with an air of courtly dignity. I was very much impressed by the stately elegance of his manners, for I had expected to meet a rough Western soldier."

"Thank you," said Miss Godolphin. "You have heightened my interest in him."

"He is distinguished," said Mr. Clarendon, "for courtly grace. There is said to be something very fascinating in his manners."

Mr. Clarendon rose and took leave. Soon after, Miss Godolphin's carriage was announced, and Waring accompanying her to it, and driving with her to Mrs. Habersham's, De Vane lingered a little while longer, as if reluctant to quit a place which had become so dear to him."

As he rose to leave, Mr. Springfield said to him:

"I hope we shall see you again, Mr. De Vane, before you leave for Virginia."

"Yes, thank you," said he, "I shall call. It is my intention to start on Monday, and I shall call in the mean while. Good night!"

He bowed very low, and walked away alone, saddened by the thought of his coming leave-taking.

## CHAPTER XXII.

"FAREWELL! thou art too dear for my possessing,
And like enough thou know'st thy estimate."
SHAKESPEARE.

To turn away from the presence of those who are dear to us, even when it is believed that the separation will be for but a few weeks, is no light task. The uncertainties that attend us in life, at every step, admonish us that great changes may occur before we tread again the same walks, or wander through the same grounds, or seat ourselves in old familiar spots; and the shadow of indefinable dread, dread of we know not what, steals over our souls. Who has turned away from home without pausing to look back, to re-take upon the heart the tracery of the place in all its features? Who has said "Farewell!" to one really loved without looking earnestly, if but for a moment, into the dear eyes, as if the soul might be read in their clear depths? Who that has stood upon the vessel's deck, as the swift winds bore it away from the shore, looking back to see a loved form growing fainter every moment, and watching the fading away of the signals which are thrown out to us when the voice can no longer speak what the soul longs to utter—who has not felt how hard it is to say FAREWELL? Who can say what may happen before we meet again? O Life! what sadness there is in thy mutations! Who could read thy heart-history without sinking under its revelations? Nothing but trust—trust in the constancy of those we love, trust in the unslumbering watchfulness of Him who careth even for the sparrow—can comfort us. Are ye not of more value than many sparrows?

On Saturday morning, De Vane called at Mr. Springfield's, to take leave of the family. Neither that gentleman nor Esther was at home, but Mrs. Springfield was. De Vane entered, and was informed by her that Mr. Springfield had gone a mile or two into the country, and that Esther was passing the day at Leasowes.

He entered into conversation with Mrs. Springfield with his accustomed freedom. His respect, his affection for her—for he had learned to regard her with a sentiment which was strong enough to be called affection—always made him frank with her, when they were alone. Her fine, cultivated mind, and the refinement and gentleness which gave an indescribable charm to her manners, made her a most agreeable person to every one, but especially so to a young, high-toned, ardent man, who could say to her much that he would not utter to one less qualified to comprehend and to sympathize with him.

"And you leave us on Monday, Mr. De Vane?" she said.

"On Monday, madam, I am sorry to say. I have been so long here, that I have learned to love this place, and I can never feel at home anywhere else."

"Perhaps, when you re-visit Virginia," she said, "you may find all your early attachments revive."

"No," said he, "that is impossible. If I had not changed, it might be so; the impressions made upon me here might give way to impressions which objects there will make. But I myself am changed. I came here young, with views, tastes, and habits formed in the midst of those who make their own world, who lead a life so artificial as to unfit them for participating in the tasks of real life. Here I have learned to look upon the world as it is; to comprehend that the true grandeur of life does not consist in surrendering the soul to the frigid conventionalisms of society, in the indulgence of exclusive ideas, but in the manly discharge of the great duties of humanity. Here my mind has been awakened. My view of the world is as much enlarged as if the mists which heretofore allowed me to see but a small part of the landscape had been swept away, and the whole wide extent of hill and valley, and mountain and plain, sketched before me, flooded with the sunlight. I shall re-visit Virginia, but I shall never again be the person I was when I took leave of my home to come to this place."

He spoke with great animation. He had risen from his seat, and unconsciously elevated himself to his full height. Mrs. Springfield smiled. She saw with the highest satisfaction this irrepressible exhibition of the noble nature of the young patrician, whose soul was asserting its right to sympathy with the great world, and contending against the restraints with which ancestral pride would bind it.

"Still, Mr. De Vane," she said, "you will find, upon your return to the home of your youth, so much to interest you, that it will be no easy task to tear yourself away from it once more. At your age, we are ardent. We yield a ready sympathy with those persons whose tastes are agreeable to us, and who are actually present. The impressions made by other objects begin to fade, and we, after a while, almost wonder that their influence over us should have been so strong."

"Ah! madam," said De Vane, "you judge me by the commonplace code of the world. I have no right to complain of it. You do not know me. But my own consciousness vindicates me from meriting any such accusation."

Mrs. Springfield saw that she had wounded him, and she hastened to assure him that she did not rank him with that light class of young persons who change with the skies under which they pass.

"You well know, Mr. De Vane," she said, "my estimate of you. But you are about to undergo an ordeal the full severity of which you yourself can not comprehend, until you find yourself in the midst of the objects which will appeal so powerfully to your affections, your tastes, your ambition."

"Pardon me, madam," said De Vane, "I comprehend all. You must remember that my aunt, Mrs. De Vane, has kept me well informed of all that transpires at home. She has all the while contributed what she could to strengthen my early tastes, to remind me of the claims of my family upon me, and to maintain over me the influence of *caste*. I recall very vividly all the past. I have never lost the vision of aristocratic splendor which filled my youthful mind. But I assure you, that I myself have undergone a great change. The great world has been revealed to me, and I can never unlearn what I have learned."

"Still," said Mrs. Springfield, "you must not forget that the young Abyssinian Prince, after seeing the great world as you have done, returned to his happy valley."

"True," said De Vane, "but that was because he saw the world only as one views a panorama. He took no part in it. It was not the actual, the living, breathing world that he saw, but a succession of pictures. The world that the young Prince saw was but little more than an exhibition of the paintings of the great masters. I have walked through the actual world. I comprehend it. I disdain the idle, luxurious life which our aristocracy lead. I intend to take part in the real struggle of humanity, and strive to help forward the crowded ranks who, like pilgrims, are seeking some happier clime. There are tasks that must be done. I am not unambitious, but I aspire to wear honors won by own exertions. I could not content myself to sit down and enjoy what better and truer men even than myself had achieved for me."

Mrs. Springfield looked at him, with a respect and admiration that her face revealed, without replying immediately to what he had said.

He walked across the floor, and stood before the portrait of Esther. The morning light touched the picture, and the canvas glowed with life. De Vane fixed his eyes on it, and seemed unconscious of the presence of Mrs. Springfield. He stood before it for minutes, absorbed, motionless. The peerless beauty of Esther seemed to hold him entranced. At length he breathed deeply, turned away from the picture, and resumed his seat without uttering a word.

Mrs. Springfield spoke. "How long do you suppose, Mr. De Vane, you will be absent from us?"

"I propose," said he, "to return in October. I shall acquaint my father with my wish to make my residence in this place. It will require some little time to arrange my affairs in Virginia; but so soon as I can dispose of them, I shall return here. This is to be my home."

"We shall be very happy to have you with us, Mr. De Vane," she replied. "You know our appreciation of you."

De Vane bowed. After some further conversation, he rose to take leave.

"Will you not come to us this evening?" asked Mrs. Springfield.

"With great pleasure, madam," he replied. "My friend, Mr. Waring, will doubtless accompany me."

"We shall be most happy to see you," said Mrs. Springfield.

De Vane walked away from the house. He greatly desired to see Esther alone, before leaving for Virginia. He had no well-defined purpose in seeking a private interview, but still he was unwilling to quit the place without conversing with her under less restraint than he must be subject to if he met her in the presence of others. He directed his steps to Leasowes. Entering the grounds, he walked directly to the cottage. Mrs. Green received him. Esther was not in, but Mrs. Green informed him that she was somewhere in the grounds; that she had taken Mary Sinclair with her, and walked out some half-hour since. De Vane went in search of her. He turned his steps toward the fountain; and as he approached it, he saw Esther and little Mary seated side by side. Esther instantly rose to meet him.

"Pardon me," said De Vane, "for trespassing upon you, Miss Wordsworth. You know that I leave for Virginia on Monday, and I could not tear myself away without once more visiting Leasowes. The place has become very dear to me."

"You know, Mr. De Vane," she replied, "how welcome you are here. You are never an intruder."

"Thanks," said De Vane. "There is no spot in the world that I visit with so much pleasure."

Esther rewarded him with her brightest smile. She invited him to be seated. "No," said he. "If agreeable to you, let us walk through the grounds. It will be some months before I can enjoy that privilege again."

Esther took Mary by the hand, and they turned their steps toward the cottage. She excused herself for a moment, and entering the house with the little girl, she presently returned alone, with her hat, and a light shawl thrown about her shoulders.

"Come, Mr. De Vane," she said, "let us see what improvements Jacob has been projecting since you were here."

They turned their steps toward the more highly cultivated parts of the grounds. They were in their full glory. Brilliant flowers grew in the midst of the beds. The rarest and most beautiful shrubbery fringed the walks, and the highest taste was displayed in the arrangement of the grounds. One might lose himself in the labyrinthine walks.

"Really," said De Vane, "this place is enchanting. It wants only statuary to make it perfect."

"It has occurred to me," said Esther, "to place some few statues in some parts of the grounds. If I should ever visit Europe, I may then make the selections."

"Visit Europe you certainly will," said De Vane. "With your tastes, Miss Wordsworth, you can not resist the attractions that such a tour offers."

"I do not know, Mr. De Vane," she replied. "There is so much to bind me here, that I can not hope very soon to gratify my tastes."

"You wrong yourself, Miss Wordsworth," said De Vane. "Your life must not be passed in this way."

Esther turned upon him her full glance.

"Have you forgotten, Mr. De Vane, the obligations that rest upon me?"

"Oh! no," he answered; "but surely, all the brightness of your life is not to be obscured in this spot, beautiful as it is."

"I have no fixed plans for the future," said Esther; "none beyond the simple performance of duties which are too sacred to be neglected."

"You will, I trust, take brighter views of life," said De Vane. "The tasks which you perform here are beautiful; and I should be uncandid if I did not say, that my admiration is yielded to you as it has never been to any one, when I see you at Leasowes. Still, I should be very sorry to know that all your days were to be passed here."

He turned to Esther as he uttered these words, and his face revealed even more than his language had disclosed. He fixed his ardent gaze upon her, as if his soul would utter its emotions in a glance, while the lips refused to breathe the passion which fired it.

Esther was deeply agitated. This frank declaration of his admiration for her, just uttered by De Vane, startled her. She made no reply.

"Yes, Miss Wordsworth," he continued, "I am too selfish to wish to see you always engaged as you now are, beautiful as the tasks that employ you must be acknowledged to be by all who can appreciate the high qualities that prompt you to discharge them. I am too selfish for that. I would appeal to you, too, in behalf of the great world. You must help to make that brighter. You must walk through it, that other eyes may see you and bless you."

"I thank you, Mr. De Vane," at length Esther said, "for all your kindness. Here I feel that I am safe. These duties have been enjoined upon me in a way that renders it impossible to disregard them. I am a little afraid of the great world of which you speak."

She spoke with trembling earnestness; and as she uttered these words, she looked into the face of De Vane, with a gentleness so perfect, and a truthfulness so clear, that he felt as if he walked by the side of a being who, if not celestial, had at least the purity of those whose robes have never been sullied by the dust of the world's crowded ways.

They walked on for some moments in silence. Their walk conducted toward the gate that opened into the town. The silence was at length broken by De Vane.

"Miss Wordsworth," he said, "I know the frankness of your nature. I am about to speak to you freely—as freely as I am at liberty to do at this moment. As you know, I am just now about to re-visit my home—the home of my youth—my ancestral home. But it is my fixed purpose to return here; and if I can secure the approval of my father, I shall make this my residence. Separated from you for some weeks to come, as I must be, I will not withhold the expression of my great regard for you. A purer friendship never warmed the heart of any man than that which I cherish for you. May I hope that you will not regard me with entire indifference, and that you will permit me to call you my friend?"

Esther colored deeply. She hesitated for a moment, and then said with a steady voice:

"Yes, Mr. De Vane, I am sincerely your friend. I should be ungrateful if I were not so."

"Thank you," said De Vane. "There is surely no consideration that can entitle me to your gratitude, Miss Wordsworth. It is I who should speak of gratitude. You have shed a brightness over my life. But I do not like the word. I am speaking of friendship. I should prize your friendship unspeakably."

"I have already said to you, Mr. De Vane," said Esther, "that I am your friend. For yourself and Mr. Waring, I entertain a sentiment that certainly deserves the name; and as the circle of my friends is not very large, I prize those who belong to it."

De Vane was a little disappointed in this reply. He regarded Waring as he did no other man on earth; but to hear Miss Wordsworth associate him with himself in one common sentiment of friendship, was a little chilling to him. Still he could not complain of it; nor could he make any explanation. He had not spoken of love. That was quite another thing. He dared not speak of it. He well knew the settled purpose of General De Vane; his aristocratic tastes, his ancestral pride, his hopes of his son, his plans of life for him. He comprehended, too, Mrs. De Vane's tastes, prejudices, preferences, pride, and ambition. All this rose before him at the moment. Could he disregard it? Was he to make a rash declaration of love to a young girl who walked by his side in her maidenly purity, belonging to a class so widely different from the aristocratic circle in which he had been reared ?

The surges of his passion swept furiously against the restraints that he placed on himself. Like the North Sea dashing against the dykes of Holland, his passion shook the barriers that kept it back. Would the wild waves break over the obstructions ? It seemed impossible to shut them out. De Vane burned to know the real sentiments of Esther respecting him. Did she love him ? Or was it only friendship ? What would he give to resolve the doubt ! There stood the young priestess, glowing with almost unearthly beauty. Was she cold ? Or did the hidden flame of passion burn in the deep of her soul ? They had reached the gate. Unconsciously they both stood, and they were silent.

De Vane struggled with his passion. What right had he to ask this young bright being who stood by his side to speak to him of love ? Would he darken her woman's sky ? Would he humiliate her by inviting her to walk with him through life, when she must encounter the scorn of his imperious father, the reproaches even of his aunt ? He was by no means sure of the state of Esther's heart. She might regard him simply as a friend. He could not trifle with her. He had too much principle to make an experiment of such a nature as would induce her to reveal her real sentiments, without being ready to bind himself to her, if she were willing, by an indissoluble engagement. His own pride, his lofty sense of honor, his profound respect for Esther—all made it impossible that he should advance a single step beyond the line that he had reached. The struggle was over. PRINCIPLE had triumphed over PASSION.

"I thank you, Miss Wordsworth," said De Vane, "for having admitted me to the circle of your friends. I shall bear with me to Virginia the consciousness that, in quitting these happy grounds, I leave behind me one who will sometimes recall the hours that we have passed together in these walks."

"Yes, Mr. De Vane, you may rest assured that I am your friend," said Esther.

"And when I return, may I reënter this portal," said De Vane, "confident that I shall still find a friend here?"

"You need not doubt it," said Esther. "I am not subject to change."

"Thank you," said De Vane, "thank you."

They passed through the gate into the great world.

In the evening, De Vane and Waring walked to Mr. Springfield's. They were expected.

Every thing was arranged with perfect taste, and the rooms wore their most cheerful aspect. Mrs. Springfield, with womanly tact, sought to surround De Vane, on this last evening, with bright objects—objects that he would recall with pleasure after his departure. Flowers, fruits, and the innumerable pleasing things that belong to such a household, were in profusion. The supper was an abounding one.

After it was ended, all assembled in the library, and engaged in cheerful conversation.

"So, Mr. De Vane," said Mr. Springfield, "you will leave us. We shall regret your absence, and hope that you will return to us as early as possible."

"You may rest assured of that, sir," said De Vane. "The journey will, of course, consume some time; and as I intend to fix my residence here, it will require some weeks to put my affairs in Virginia in such a condition that I may leave them."

"It is quite settled, then, is it," asked Mr. Springfield, "that you will make this your future home?"

"So far as I can settle it," said De Vane, "the question

is disposed of. I anticipate great opposition to my plan on the part of my father. He is very decided, I may say inflexible, upon most subjects; but I do not despair of being able to obtain his consent that I may fix my residence here. I hold that questions of that kind are to be disposed of by every one for himself. They concern our happiness too much to suffer us to submit them to the decision of others."

"I quite agree with you," said Mr. Springfield. "I think that all such matters are to be decided by one's self. In the light of all the surroundings, certainly the wishes of friends are not to be disregarded; but after all, we can only determine for ourselves what will be agreeable to us."

"So I think," said Waring. "I would not live in a palace on compulsion. It would be but a splendid prison."

"So say I," said De Vane. "Splendor is nothing without liberty. And with my views of life, to compel me to sit down upon a plantation in Virginia and see my slaves toil for my benefit, adding year after year to the increase of an estate already too large, would be intolerable. They write to me about the glories of such an existence; they describe in glowing terms the society, made up of the best blood of the country, of the sports which are introduced to break the monotony of country life; but really they have failed to awaken in me any desire to lead such a life."

"It must be admitted," said Mr. Springfield, "that such an existence seems to ignore the higher objects of our being."

"Not only so," said Waring, "but I should die from *ennui*."

"Yes," said De Vane, "I firmly believe that some degree of labor is essential to happiness. For my own part, my mind is quite made up to make my own living. I intend to labor; to have the honest consciousness, when I see the sun descending behind the western sky, that I have contributed by my own exertions to pay my own way in the world. In no other way could I feel that I was a man."

All smiled at the energy with which De Vane uttered these words.

"What will General De Vane say to all that?" asked Waring.

"Of course he will object," said De Vane. "But I have one appeal to make to him—I shall lay before him my views, my plans, my sentiments, my hopes, my principles. For, after all, with me this is a principle, and I shall remind him that he chose his own path in life; he fixed his residence just where he pleased. Therefore, I may well appeal to his sense of right, to allow me to do the same thing. His ancestral pride will give way before his strong sense of right and his manliness."

"I certainly hope so," said Waring. "We shall await the result of your visit with great anxiety. I say we, for you have friends here beside myself, who will be profoundly interested in your return."

De Vane could not resist the impulse which prompted him to look toward Esther. Her face was glowing.

"Yes," said Mrs. Springfield; "Mr. De Vane well knows that he has friends here, and I trust that he will count this household among the number."

"A thousand thanks, madam, for the assurance," said De Vane, with emotion. "I shall often recall this spot in my travels, and whatever I may meet in Virginia, nothing can efface the happy memories that must be forever associated with it."

The evening advanced. De Vane did not ask for music. He was too sad to wish to hear it. Esther felt a great relief at being spared the performance. For, though she had not analyzed her heart, she was conscious of an interest in De Vane too deep to permit her to associate him with any of the commonplace things of life. If she sang, her emotion would be too visible. Indeed, to ask her to do so would be like calling on the Jewish maiden to take her harp from the willows, and strike its chords with joyous notes, in the midst of her exile.

The hour for leave-taking came. De Vane was seated near Mr. Springfield. He rose and extended his hand to that gentleman, thanking him for all his kindness.

"I am indebted to you, sir, for many happy hours," said he. "I promise myself a long enjoyment of such scenes hereafter."

"God bless you, sir!" said Mr. Springfield. "We shall all welcome you upon your return."

De Vane turned to Mrs. Springfield, and said: "To you, madam, I do not know how to express my thanks. You have done so much for me, that I shall always regard you as associated with my best and happiest days. Farewell, madam!"

Mrs. Springfield gave him her hand, and said: "Farewell, Mr. De Vane. Come to us again as soon as possible."

Esther had risen from her seat. She stood self-possessed, and yet her eyes were lit with all the ardor of her soul. De Vane advanced to her, took her hand, stood for a moment silent, and then said: "Miss Wordsworth, farewell!" Esther said not a word.

Waring said "Good-night!" to the group, and walked to the door. De Vane turned for a moment, made a stately bow, and then passed out.

The door closed on the young patrician! Shall he ever enter it again? Time and the Future alone can reveal his destiny!

# DE VANE:

## A Story of

# PLEBEIANS AND PATRICIANS.

BY

HON. HENRY W. HILLIARD,

EX-MEMBER OF UNITED STATES HOUSE OF REPRESENTATIVES FROM ALABAMA.

"The rank is but the guinea's stamp,
The man 's the gowd for a' that."
BURNS.

---

*TWO VOLUMES IN ONE.—VOL. II.*

---

New-York:
BLELOCK & COMPANY, 19 BEEKMAN STREET.

18[illegible]5.

JOHN A. GRAY & GREEN,
Printers,
16 & 18 Jacob Street, New-York.

# DE VANE.

## A Story of

# PLEBEIANS AND PATRICIANS.

## CHAPTER I.

"Fast silent tears were flowing,
When something stood behind!
A hand was on my shoulder—
I knew its touch was kind."
Richard Monckton Milnes.

The flying post-horses dashed away from Mrs. Bowen's door—four superb blood bays; and the driver's French horn poured a loud and cheerful blast upon the morning air. The coach bore De Vane away. Five other passengers were seated with him, and much as he regretted to quit a place unspeakably dear to him, there was a degree of exhilaration imparted to him by the rapid motion of the dashing coach and four.

Waving his hand to Waring, he was gone. Would he return? Would he withstand the appeals of his aunt? Could he prevail on his father to yield to his wish to make his home in that Southern town? Or would he feel the rekindling of early passion, submit himself to the sway of ambition, and remain in his ancestral home? Who could say? Waring was sad, for he was very strongly attached to his young friend. He saw in him grand qualities, and capabilities for high tasks.

Esther went as usual to Leasowes. She walked slowly; but she did not stop by the way. Whatever may have been her emotions, she resolutely walked forward to her duties. Assembling about her the little girls, she read to them the Scriptures, and then kneeling, read one of those prayers prepared for such occasions by a woman eminent for her piety and her learning. All the morning she passed with them, directed their pursuits, and gave them some instructions in drawing. Then, joining them in their midday meal, she spoke to them of those subjects which she knew would interest them.

Soon after, Mrs. Springfield called for her, and entering the carriage, they drove away. At Esther's suggestion, they visited a poor family in the sand-hills, and returning, called at Mrs. Gildersleeve's. Esther requested Mrs. Springfield to leave her there, saying that she would be at home by evening; and her aunt drove away, comprehending her feelings.

When Esther came in the evening, she was very calm, and spoke of her visit. "I found Mrs. Gildersleeve," she said, "quite cheerful. She is beginning to take an interest in the things that engaged her formerly, and she has a niece with her, just arrived—a nice little girl."

"I am glad to hear it," said Mrs. Springfield. "She has been very desolate since the death of Eva."

"Oh! yes," said Esther. "I have grieved for her. She is comfortable, too, and finds her needlework ample for her support."

"That is fortunate," said Mrs. Springfield. "Occupation is essential to happiness, and Mrs. Gildersleeve is too proud to accept from others any thing beyond what she needs."

"I thought the sand-hills appeared attractive to-day," said Esther. "Warm as the weather is, the clear streams and the spreading shade-trees were inviting. I think we might find it agreeable to pass our summers there."

"Mr. Springfield thinks of it," she replied; "and we must select a pleasant site, if he should decide to make it a summer home."

"Let it be in a valley," said Esther, "by a clear stream, and not on a hill. I do not admire hills for residences. And we shall then be able to command the comforts that are essential to a country home."

Mr. Springfield came in, and the subject was further discussed.

"I think," said he, "that I might prefer to build on the other side of the river, some twelve miles from the town. There we should find the finest water, extraordinary facilities for bathing, the purest air, and good society."

"Is it not too far?" asked Mrs. Springfield.

"Oh! no," he said. "We should furnish our summer house, and go to it; and return whenever we found it agreeable."

It was decided that they should at some time visit the place, and see what it offered in the way of advantages for a summer residence.

So far, the name of De Vane had not been uttered by any one of the family. Mrs. Springfield forbore to do so, from consideration for Esther; and yet she did not doubt that, while the conversation turned upon other subjects, the thought that filled the heart of her niece was in some way associated with him.

The sun had gone down, and the still twilight had succeeded—twilight, that brings with it so many memories. How full of self-searching is that space which divides day from night—neither day nor night; shadowy, quiet, dreamy; too late to carry on the business of the day, too early to kindle the lights for the night! In the town, the noise of business lulls, and occasional sounds only are heard, the roll of wheels at intervals, or the tread of passers-by on the sidewalk seeking their homes; in the country, the buzz of insects, the lowing of cattle, the song of the herdsman. Even from the days of the patriarchs, the hour has invited to repose. Isaac went out to meditate in the field at the eventide.

Esther retired to her own chamber. The blinds were open, the serene summer sky was spread out before her—the sky which she had often looked up to, standing by the side of De Vane. There was the opal hue which he so much admired, and burning in the midst of it was the evening-star, lustrous, as if just kindled for the first time in the firmament by some celestial messenger, as the promise of some new advent of love to a sin-stricken world. Esther gazed upon it in deep musing. She felt very lonely, and for the first time since De Vane's departure tears stole into her eyes, and soon she wept as if the very fountains of her nature were broken up. Never before had she wept in this way. She bowed her head upon the bed, and poured out her soul. Presently she started; a hand was laid upon her shoulder, and looking up, she saw Mrs. Springfield. Her aunt took a chair near her. Esther laid her head in her lap, like a little child, and wept without restraint.

Mrs. Springfield said nothing for some time. Her own tears came to her eyes, but she checked them. At length Esther became more tranquil, and Mrs. Springfield said to her:

"My child, may I not know what makes you unhappy?"

For some moments Esther made no reply. She then threw her arms around Mrs. Springfield's neck, and kissed her.

"Has any thing been said to you, Esther, to make you unhappy?"

"Oh! no, no!" she replied. "Nothing, nothing; but I felt to-day weary and sad, and I could not restrain my tears when this quiet hour came on."

"Esther, my own child," said Mrs. Springfield, "are you disappointed? Is your heart wounded?"

She rallied instantly. The very thought that any one, even her aunt, should suppose that she had been disappointed in her hopes, roused her. The thought that any one should suppose, even for a moment, that De Vane was capable of wounding her, appealed to her spirit in a way that made it impossible she could weep any longer.

"No, aunt," she said, "neither disappointed nor wounded. I was oppressed with a sense of loneliness, which you will easily comprehend."

"I do comprehend it, my child," she said. "But I can not express my admiration of the nobleness of Mr. De Vane in returning to Virginia as he has done, under a sense of duty which alone could take him away. I comprehend his feelings too, for I saw him when you did not, under circumstances which revealed his heart quite as plainly as if he had told me all he felt."

Mrs. Springfield then related to Esther what had taken place when De Vane called on Saturday morning. His emphatic statement of his purpose to return to the town in October and fix his residence there, his earnest utterance of his views of life, and his standing in fixed and unconscious gaze upon her portrait. Esther felt the light of morning already spreading over her soul, and once more embracing her aunt, she kissed her tenderly.

Mrs. Springfield had acted with as much tact as delicacy. She saw Esther's depression. She well knew why she sought solitude as the evening came on, and she wished to assure her of her sympathy, without wounding her sensibility, or drawing from her any disclosures which she might not freely wish to make. She knew that she could trust every thing to Esther, but she knew too what a relief it would be to her to know that in herself she had not only a friend who would counsel in the affairs of every-day life, but who could sympathize with those emotions which are of far higher moment with all properly-organized natures than any or all of those things which the world calls real.

Mrs. Springfield left her alone and descended to the library, where Esther joined her before a great while, without any visible traces of the recent tears. Waring came in, and was warmly welcomed. All were pleased to see him, and with that subtle perception of proprieties which belongs to fine natures, he exerted himself to be cheerful, and to make others so. Without any false delicacy, he went directly to the subject which he knew really was the one of interest with his friends.

"Well, Mrs. Springfield," he said, "I am deserted and desolate; my *Fidus Achates* has gone."

"Really gone!" said Mrs. Springfield. "We shall all sympathize with you, for we found his society very agreeable."

"Yes," said Mr. Springfield, "I became very strongly attached to Mr. De Vane; his fine mind and noble nature refreshed me. Do you suppose that he will carry out his purpose and made this his residence?"

"It is his purpose, undoubtedly, to do so," said Waring. "He is perfectly settled in it, and his firmness is great when he once takes a position. There is so much of the heroic in him, that resistance only rouses his strength. But he is about to pass through a very severe ordeal. Returning to the home of his youth, early impressions may be revivified. The slumbering pride of ancestral state and consideration may be awakened, and the sense of duty which is so powerful in him may bring him to yield his wishes to those of General De Vane. Still, his wishes are so strong, his attachment to this place so deep, and his love of independence so uncompromising, that I have great hope of his coming back to us."

"General De Vane," said Mr. Springfield, "is, I have learned, extreme in his aristocratic tastes and opinions. Perhaps few, even in Virginia, carry them so far, and I can hardly suppose that he will consent for his son to leave him, and especially to come here and enter upon a laborious profession."

"Yes," said Waring, "it is very much to be feared that he will never give his consent to that. He is very wealthy, and there is no necessity for any exertion on the part of his son; but he will never induce George De Vane to lead the life of an idle man. A more powerful organization for working I never saw. I mean, I never knew any man whose taste for occupation was stronger, or whose scorn for indolence was more intense. No wealth could tempt him to drift through life, and his love of his race is such, that a stiff, formal social system can never hold him. We feel his absence, and yet I'll venture to say that there are some two or three laboring men in the town who fancy that no one can regret him as they do—Hobbs, for instance, the blacksmith. I think it quite likely that tears may have washed away some of the coal-dust from his face when De Vane bade him good-by, for he did call at his shop to shake hands with him on Saturday."

"He's a noble fellow," said Mr. Springfield.

"I trust that he will become a Christian," said Mrs. Springfield. "A large heart like his would be very happy if full of love to the Lord, who gave his own life for him."

"I regret," said Mr. Springfield, "that he is skeptical."

"He can not be said to be so," said Waring, "in the common acceptation of that word. He is full of doubt, but his earnest nature illumines the very clouds which surround him, and he is too warm to content himself with the frigid rationalism which satisfies some minds."

"I rejoice to hear you say so," said Mr. Springfield.

"I regret," said Waring, "more than I can express, that De Vane is not a Christian. He is just now bewildered with the mists of neology. The Germans, by their luminous vapors, have involved him, but his strong, earnest nature will make its way out of them. I love him so much, that, while I can not claim him as a believer, I do claim him as a disciple of the principles of Christianity. He reminds me of Abou Ben Abhem in the exquisite poem of Leigh Hunt.

"I have not seen it," said Mr. Springfield.

"Do repeat the lines for us, Mr. Waring," said Mrs. Springfield.

Esther had said nothing, but her eyes were fixed on Waring, as her aunt made the request, with eager interest. He observed it, and looking at her, uttered the lines:

"ABOU BEN ADHEM (may his tribe increase!)
Awoke one night from a deep dream of peace,
And saw, within the moonlight in his room,
Making it rich, and like a lily in bloom,
An angel writing in a book of gold.
Exceeding peace had made Ben Adhem bold,
And to the presence in the room he said:
'What writest thou?' The vision raised its head,
And with a look made of all sweet accord,
Answered: 'The names of those who love the Lord.'
'And is mine one?' said Abou. 'Nay, not so,'
Replied the angel. Abou spoke more low,
But cheerly still, and said: 'I pray thee, then,
Write me as one that loves his fellow-men.'
The angel wrote, and vanished. The next night
It came again, with a great wakening light,
And showed the names whom love of God had blessed,
And lo! Ben Adhem's name led all the rest."

"It *is* exquisite!" exclaimed Esther.

"Perfectly beautiful!" said Mrs. Springfield. "We are obliged to you for making us acquainted with it."

"And for giving us such hope of our young friend Mr. De Vane," said Mr. Springfield.

"It reminds me," said Esther, "of our discussion as to the comparative merits of poetry and the arts. If Mr. De Vane were here, I think he would insist that the poem which you have just repeated does much toward establishing his proposition in favor of the power of poetical description."

Waring smiled. "I had no idea," said he, "that I was furnishing an argument against myself."

"But you must admit," said Esther, "that it is a powerful one. Could any painting, or piece of sculpture, teach the beautiful lesson which the poem does, so exquisitely and so briefly?"

"I shall decline all argument upon that point," said Waring, "until I can bring in my allies, Miss Godolphin and Mr. Clarendon."

"That is yielding the field," said Esther, "for I am all alone; at least, the only ally who was with me in our late contest is absent."

"I shall report to him," said Waring, "in my first letter, how gallantly you maintained the position."

"And do give him our best wishes," said Mr. Springfield.

"And assure him of our regrets at his absence," said Mrs. Springfield.

"I shall make him very happy in doing so," said Waring.

"Have you seen Miss Godolphin very lately?" asked Esther.

"Not since I met her here," said Waring. "I think that Mrs. Habersham is about to go to her place in the country."

"Some four miles from town," said Mr. Springfield. "It is a place of great beauty, and I do not wonder at their retreating to it, though the health of the town is excellent."

"I have never seen it," said Waring.

"But you will visit it now, of course," said Mrs. Springfield, playfully.

"I shall be so much engaged with books," said Waring pleasantly, "that I shall have but little leisure for the ladies. Still, if Miss Wordsworth will accompany me, I shall be ready to visit so interesting a person as Miss Godolphin."

"Of course," said Esther, "I could not refuse to contribute to your happiness in that way. When shall we go?"

"I must first ascertain," said Waring, "if they have gone."

"And, of course, in pursuing so important an inquiry, you will not intrust any thing to an agent, but will call in person. Otherwise I should offer to look into the affair myself."

"Do, Miss Wordsworth," said Waring, "and then arrange the time of our excursion, and I shall feel quite obliged."

"Very good," said Esther. "I am very prompt, and will call to-morrow morning."

"Thanks," said Waring.

"She is," said Mr. Springfield, "a person of extraordinary attractions, and I do not wonder, Mr. Waring, that you should wish to visit her. I find her really fascinating. When she was with us, a few evenings since, she displayed wonderful resources."

"She is a superior person," said Waring, "in every way. Her intellect, her character, her accomplishments, and her beauty, are all of rare perfection. She is, too, so earnest, that it is impossible not to feel an interest in her. I can not feel any thing like a deep interest in any one who lacks depth of character. Miss Godolphin has it."

"She has," said Esther. "Her nature is a very earnest one, and I find myself powerfully attracted by her. We must visit her, Mr. Waring."

"I shall always be at your service," he said; "and when she returns to town, in October, we can arrange a plan for seeing her often."

The mention of October seemed to give general satisfaction.

"How refreshing it is," said Mrs. Springfield, "to look forward to the fall! It is to me the most agreeable of the seasons."

"Oh! incomparably so," said Esther. "I love autumn, and hail it as the crowning glory of the year."

"I must express my preference for spring," said Mr. Springfield.

"Spring," said Waring, "is beautiful, full of delights, and rich in promise; but I must agree with Miss Wordsworth in her preference for autumn."

"I enjoy spring," said Mrs. Springfield, "from sympathy with my husband's tastes. I have often seen him rejoice in the opening spring with the gladness of a boy."

"I do love its promise, and catch the joy with which it fills all nature, animate and unconscious nature," said Mr. Springfield.

"But," said Esther, "the autumn brings the matured promise; the ripened fruits, the waving harvests, and many-colored leaves, which give such a mellow beauty to the aspect of nature. Then one feels a languor in spring; but in autumn the air invigorates, and the bright, frosty mornings, when the crisp leaves crackle under your feet, impart an elasticity to your spirits, which is never experienced at any other season."

"And does not the decay of nature sadden you?" said Mr. Springfield.

"At times one does feel, when looking upon the falling leaves, and hearing the solemn winds breathing through the ever-green pines, a touch of melancholy sympathy with nature; but there are so many autumnal glories that you forget the sadness, and wrap yourself up gladly to walk out under the sparkling stars, which seem to grow brighter in the cool air. Then, too, enjoying the ripened fruits, and seeing gathered harvests, and drawing near the early fires, you anticipate the magnificence of winter."

"Now, Mr. Springfield," said Waring, "Miss Wordsworth sings the glories of autumn in a way to make one enjoy it. It is, I am happy to know, not a great way off, and we shall expect to see her grow very bright when her favorite season revisits us."

Esther looked up at him quickly, but she could detect no mischief in his composed features, and she said: "I hope we shall all be bright and happy."

"Poets," said Mr. Springfield, "sing the glories of the varying year. But Esther, I believe, is consistent; she has from her childhood, by a sort of perverseness it may be, rejoiced in the fall of the year."

"Ever since I saw the first crimson leaf from a sweet green tree, in the early autumn, and the red dogwood berries sprinkled with frost," she said.

"When are we to take our equestrian excursions," said Waring, "which we arranged some little time since?"

"Oh! I must look after that to-morrow, when I see Miss Godolphin," said Esther. "She is said to ride superbly."

"If she can excel you, Esther," said Mr. Springfield, "she must indeed be accomplished. Do you know, Mr. Waring, that last summer she dashed away from me in that wild mountain region of Virginia, and defied me to follow her? I actually found it at times difficult to keep the saddle."

"I did not know she was so wild," said Waring. "Who would have supposed it?"

"Get her over into the country," said Mr. Springfield, "and she becomes transformed."

"I fear," said Esther, "that you will frighten Mr. Waring, and that he will refuse to accompany me."

"I only wish to put him on his guard," said Mr. Springfield, "so that he may be sure of his horse, and tighten his girths."

"I am a good horseman," said Waring, "and I shall prepare myself. There are some hedges in the neighborhood, and any number of rail fences."

"My horse," said Esther, "has not yet arrived. He is at the plantation, enjoying *otium cum dignitate*, literally. No human being is allowed to use him except my own servant, who has charge of him. I must have him sent to me."

"And is he active and fleet?" asked Waring.

"Both," said Esther, "or I should not have named him Manfred."

"I must provide myself, then, with his equal; for I do not intend to be outridden by any young lady in all the State."

"Until Manfred arrives, my uncle will, I am sure, let me have his horse."

"Oh! yes, my dear Esther, with pleasure, provided you reserve your dashing adventures until Manfred does arrive. I am suited in a saddle-horse. He never stumbles, and never shies, and he is about the only horse I know that is free from those faults; so that I can not afford to have him impaled on a rail, or blown by a four hours' ride."

"I shall treat him as tenderly," said Esther, "as if he were an Arabian."

"Like Manfred," said Mr. Springfield; "and very fortunate it is for him that he has good blood in him, for he has had to encounter some sore trials, to flesh and blood both."

"I shall wait on you, then," said Waring, "very soon, to learn the result of your interview with Miss Godolphin."

"Yes," said Esther.

Conversation followed upon general subjects, and afterward Mr. Springfield and Waring interchanged their views upon some questions affecting the Church: a question of a class which they never overlooked, and about which they uniformly agreed, sometimes having to encounter serious opposition from other official members.

Mrs. Springfield was happy to see that Waring's opportune presence had cheered Esther, and in her heart she thanked him.

When he took his leave, the house was a brighter one than when he had entered it; and he bore with him the love and confidence of those who knew how to prize his pure and generous nature.

## CHAPTER II.

"WHAT! may it be, that even in heavenly place
That busy Archer his sharp arrows tries?
Sure, if that long with love acquainted eyes
Can judge of love, thou feel'st a lover's case;
I read it in thy looks, thy languished grace."

SIR PHILIP SIDNEY.

IN accordance with her promise, Esther called the next day at Mrs. Habersham's, and found Miss Godolphin at home. They had not yet removed to the country, but were preparing to do so; Mrs. Habersham having gone, when Esther called, to make arrangements for their comfortable reception. Miss Godolphin was seated in a small boudoir, surrounded by needle-work and books; and as she rose to receive Esther, she said:

"I welcome you to my own retreat, where I work, and play, and read, and write, just as I may feel inclined."

"It is a charming place," said Esther; "and I do not wonder that you pass your hours here. This window gives you a view of the garden, and I can not imagine a more cheerful spot."

"See this crape-myrtle," said Miss Godolphin, rising and putting aside the rich lace curtain that draped the sash. "Is it not perfectly beautiful? The color of the flower is perfect."

"It is indeed beautiful!" said Esther. "And the rich deep bloom of the oleander imparts an Oriental aspect to the place. How can you give it up?"

"You have not seen our country place," she said. "That

is a wilderness of delights, and you know we have both avowed our preference for the country."

"When do you go?" asked Esther.

"Probably on Saturday," she said. "My aunt is to decide to-day. I wish that you would accompany us. We should be delighted to have you."

"Thank you," said Esther. "I shall hope to see you often, but I could not at this time be absent from town."

"That Leasowes of yours," said Miss Godolphin, "is absolutely engrossing. The place is perfectly delightful—a garden of the Hesperides, as I heard Mr. De Vane describe it in conversation one evening. But you must be rescued from it, and given to the great world."

"I find it a charming retreat," said Esther, "from the great world; and when walking through its sequestered paths, feel the refreshing influence of nature upon my spirit. Then as to the little girls, they are my friends, and it sometimes saddens me to think that they have to encounter the great world."

"I shall certainly exert myself," said Miss Godolphin, "to have you drawn away from it. Leave it for a time to good Mrs. Green—for she is good. I called there some days since to see you. You were not there, and the refreshing coolness of the spot was so inviting, that when Mrs. Green asked me to stay, I sat with her for at least an hour in the little end-gallery, shaded by wild orange-trees; and she talked to me in such a way about this world, its trials and its hopes, and the Lord, who, in his goodness, was training us for a better world, where there would be peace, and where no partings would sadden us, nor death enter to wound us, that I wept like one of your little girls, and really wished that I could rest on the old saint's lap, as I did, when a child, upon my mother's."

Esther's eyes filled with tears. She was profoundly affected by the picture which Miss Godolphin had painted—this bright, proud, splendid creature, listening to the happy talk of Mrs. Green, in her natural simple way, about Jesus and heaven, until, in sympathy with the faith and hope of the Christian pilgrim, she had wept like a child.

"Yes," said Esther, "Mrs. Green is really good; and I often sit with her, to hear her speak of the better country."

"O Miss Wordsworth!" said Miss Godolphin, "I envy you your faith and your peace."

"My dear Miss Godolphin," said Esther, "they may be yours."

Miss Godolphin fixed her large, dark, soul-lit eyes on Esther's face, and said: "How I long for rest! The world is so shallow, so heartless, so unsatisfying! I have seen it, young as I am, in its glory; and I do not hate it, but I am sick of it. Its frivolous pleasures, its silly amusements, its soulless rivalries—oh! how I despise them!"

"You know," said Esther, "that there is One who has said: 'My peace I give unto you; not as the world giveth, give I unto you.'"

"How beautiful!" said Miss Godolphin. "'Not as the world giveth.' We all know how hollow that is. I must study those words, for I want peace."

Esther was deeply affected. The appealing face of Miss Godolphin, over whose classical features the shadow of some great trouble seemed to rest, which, while it did not cloud its beauty, touched it with suffering and heightened its power, was irresistible. "My dear Miss Godolphin," she said gently, "will you suffer me to try to guide you to the feet of One who will give you that peace? I am very weak myself, and my own feet want strengthening; but I speak only what I know, when I say that there is peace in believing."

"Believing!" said Miss Godolphin. "Oh! that I could believe. I have tried, I have struggled. In Rome I was accustomed to go to the places of worship where I witnessed all that was most impressive in the form of religion. I saw and heard, and was impressed, but I could not believe. The music transported me. I rose to the highest heavens upon its ascending melodies. My imagination was lighted up by all the glories of an invisible world. The pomp and splendor of the service bore me away, and I floated with the perfumed incense into the very courts of heaven. The *Miserere* subdued me and filled me with anguish. I felt the unutterable sorrow that breathed in its deep tones—tones deeper than the sepulchre, deeper than the ocean, deep as the rayless abode of lost spirits; but I never believed, never trusted, never felt true penitence, nor was my soul even once lighted up with hope—never!"

"No," said Esther, "that is not the place to find peace. I do not doubt that many sincerely worship in the midst of the imposing forms which you describe; but your nature seeks the simpler forms of majestic truth. You do not need that any ministry to the senses should move you. You are too earnest for that. It can not, of course, instruct you; but you will find in the outlines of truth all that is necessary to induce you to explore the recesses of its lofty temple. The simplest aspects of nature are the grandest. A great mountain standing out against the sky, fills us with awe, while a wide-spread landscape of variegated beauty only charms us. It is refreshing to me to read the words of my Lord; to think of him as standing, not in the midst of the temple, glorious as it was, but as seated upon the mountain-side, still more glorious, or standing upon the shore of the sea, or walking through the green fields, teaching his disciples. They may exclude the Lord from their temples, but they can not shut him out from nature."

"And do you read the teachings of the Lord, as you find them in the Scriptures, with comfort?"

"Unspeakable comfort," said Esther. "And I do find in the word of inspired truth the peace which the world can neither give nor take away."

"You must help me," said Miss Godolphin. "Let me be with you as much as possible—do!"

"You do not know how happy it will make me," said Esther, "to be with you—to seek with you the right way. It will help me, I am sure."

"Since I heard Bishop McKendree," said Miss Godolphin, "I have been longing to talk with some one on this subject. The venerable appearance of the man at once impressed me, and the simple, majestic beauty of his discourse opened to my view, for a moment, the survey of another world. I did so much desire to speak with him; but not knowing you as I do now, I could not call."

"How I regret that I did not know your wish!" said Esther. "He was with us for some days, and we should have been very happy to see you."

"I do not doubt it," she said; "but it is so rarely that I hear one who affects me as he did, that I lament his going without my hearing from him in conversation so much that I wish to know. With you I can speak freely—I can open my heart; you can fully sympathize with me. I do feel so desolate—so desolate!"

"Often," said Esther, "have I wished to speak with you, for I have felt the deepest interest in you; but I feared that you might not comprehend me, and that I should offend rather than help you."

"Oh! no; no fear of that. Why, Miss Wordsworth, if you knew what I have suffered, what a dreary world I live in, you would comprehend how welcome true sympathy is. My aunt is every thing to me that she can be. She loves me as she loves no other being; but she herself is bewildered. She has no light to cheer her own spirit;

and the thought of death fills her with the deepest gloom. You are to be my guide. I shall cling to you."

"Oh! that I were stronger!" said Esther. "I have sat by the hour and listened to the conversation of Mr. Springfield and Mr. Waring, and felt an eager desire that the whole world could have the truth presented just as they spoke of it. No argument, no display, but conversation; bringing to bear upon the great subject the largest views, in a natural, unstudied way, that lighted it up indescribably, just as one hears other subjects spoken of—the arts, commerce, politics, the events of life—without a tinge of doubt coloring their remarks, or the lightest fleecy vail of mist clouding their vision."

"Delightful!" exclaimed Miss Godolphin. "I do not wish any one to attempt to argue me into believing. It would be hopeless. But to hear Christians speak of the things which belong to religion, as if they felt them to be real, has always had a great charm for me. I love that good Mrs. Green, since I heard her speak as she did, in a way that I can not describe to you; and I feel, at times, like running round there, and begging her to let me come to her every day, to hear her talk of the better country, and of the road that leads to it."

"She will be delighted to see you," said Esther, smiling. "There is a great charm about naturalness, and I do not wonder that it gives you pleasure to hear the happy talk of my old friend."

"She must give me some of her time," said Miss Godolphin. "If it were not for leaving my aunt inconsolable, I should offer myself to Mrs. Green as a pupil, and take my place among her other orphans."

"And yet you would take me away into the great world!" said Esther, smiling.

"Oh! I only meant," said Miss Godolphin, "that I desired to see more of you—to have you more with us; and

I really think that you would help to make the great world better and happier."

"I shall certainly be very happy to be more with you," said Esther. "I am afraid of the great world."

"What is called the fashionable world," said Miss Godolphin, "is to me not only unattractive, but repellent. It is to the last degree distasteful to me. I have walked through its vain mask, and feel now like one who, sitting out a gay ball, stands in the cold gray light of morning, when the music has ceased and the guests have gone, looking at the decorated room, lately so brilliant, now vacant and chilling; and I ask myself if it can be possible that these same people will ever return to resume their revelry."

"Society," said Esther, "ought to be organized upon a different basis. Social enjoyment there ought to be, but surely it may be had without making society itself the worse for it. Life is too serious, too momentous an affair, to allow us to pass through it seeking amusement merely. Our tastes may be cultivated, refined, ministered to by the arts, by music, by literature, by conversation; and we may indulge in whatever entertains us, without making us frivolous, or without degrading us, by lessening our love for the pure, beautiful objects which are within our reach."

"Oh! yes," said Miss Godolphin, "we need not live in solitude, nor ignore society, nor become misanthropic."

"Visiting," said Esther, "as it is usually conducted, seems to me very unsatisfactory."

"Odious!" said Miss Godolphin; "and I carry it on chiefly by cards; for I will not lend myself to the paltry ceremonies which consist of calling, and sitting for a few moments, and talking commonplaces, and hurrying to some other parlor to repeat the same senseless form. I will not. In Europe they arrange things beautifully, for there society is admitted to be artificial, and it has its laws, perfectly well understood. In the first place, when a stranger goes to reside in a place, he is expected to make the first call, on such persons as he may desire to open social relations with—reversing our rule, and very properly too, I think; for it may not be known that such a person has arrived, or it may not be his wish to enter society. So, the new-comer makes the first call, and leaves his card at such doors as he may wish afterward to enter as a visitor there. Those who desire to recognize social relations with the new-comer, may return the call, either by sending a card, the most frigid of all modes of recognition, or by driving to the door and leaving a card, which is respectful but stately; or by calling in person, and sending in a card with one of the corners turned down, which means that you are willing to see the person hereafter; or by ringing the door-bell, sending in your name, and asking for the person—all of which is perfectly well understood by all well-bred people in Europe. And for my part, I admire the system, and shall act upon it here."

"A very large circle of merely formal people is neither profitable nor agreeable," said Esther.

"Forms," said Miss Godolphin, "are not to be overlooked. They have their importance. But within the circle of form there must be a smaller one of real interest and heart attachment. I am pleased with our society here. It is unusually good; but with the large number of young persons who surround us, it is not to be expected that we can know them all intimately."

"I shall hope to see you often," said Esther, "even when you go to the country."

"Oh! yes," she said; "the distance is very short. We shall drive in almost daily, and we shall insist upon keeping you with us part of the time."

Esther expressed her thanks, and said:

"Our friend, Mr. Waring, was projecting some riding excursions only last evening, and it is his wish that you should join us in them."

"Oh! thank you," said she, "I shall be very happy if you will consent to take me as one of the party, and will join you at any time."

"I have said to Mr. Waring that I must wait for the coming of my own horse. I shall order him to be brought to me without delay."

"Is he far from here? Will it require some time to get him here?"

"But a few days," said Esther. "He is just now enjoying country life, and I should have had him brought to me in the spring, but I was so occupied that I did not do so."

"In the mean time," said Miss Godolphin, "we can supply you, perhaps. We have at our country place two or three good saddle-horses, I believe."

"I must wait for Manfred, thank you," said Esther. "We know each other."

"When Mr. De Vane returns," said Miss Godolphin, "he must find us fearless horsewomen. Those Virginia gentlemen, especially from the mountains, do ride superbly."

"Of course, then," said Esther, "we must be diligent in the mean while; and I promised Mr. Waring to see you to-day on this important matter."

"Ah!" said Miss Godolphin, looking at Esther quickly, "does Mr. Waring wish me to join you before Mr. De Vane's return?"

"He is quite earnest about it," said Esther.

Miss Godolphin looked gratified, and said:

"Any one might find it a sufficient attraction to attend you and Mr. Waring," she said, "independent of the pleasure of being on horseback; but I fancied that he was so engrossed by you and his friend Mr. De Vane, that he had no room for any one else in his heart."

Esther laughed, and said: "We are good friends, it is true—tried friends; and his attachment to Mr. De Vane is great; but I do not think we fill his entire heart."

"I never witnessed any thing like his friendship for that young Virginian," said Miss Godolphin. "I believe he would lay down his life for him to-morrow; and as to yourself, I have heard it said that he entertains for you the grand passion."

"For me!" exclaimed Esther, coloring to the temples. "Why, he is to me as a brother. I have known him since I was a child."

Miss Godolphin's eyes rested on her, with an earnest look. "That is just what Mr. Clarendon said," she remarked. "He vindicated you promptly, and added that you had never loved any one."

The receding blood again rushed to Esther's face, and she said in low tones: "I thank Mr. Clarendon."

"Do you think, Miss Wordsworth, that men are capable of true, unswerving, lifelong attachments?"

"Really," said Esther, "I have not studied the philosophy that would enable me to answer that question."

"Lord Bacon's philosophy," said Miss Godolphin, "the philosophy of observation and experience—the philosophy of life—makes me doubt it."

Esther's face was troubled. An indefinable shadow passed over her spirit.

"Observe," said Miss Godolphin, "I am only skeptical. My faith, or rather my rejection of faith, is not confirmed."

"It is to be hoped," said Esther, "that you will adopt a brighter creed. It is dreadful to doubt; and I should think, to doubt the loyalty of those we love, would make one most miserable."

For a minute or two Miss Godolphin said nothing. She

seemed lost in thought, unconscious of the presence of Esther. She looked out upon the garden. The perfume of its flowers came through the open window, and the glancing sunbeams played over the deep-green leaves of the oleander.

Where had the thoughts of Miss Godolphin wandered? What converse was she holding with her own heart, as memory threw its broad light over the past?

"And Mr. Waring is your friend?" she said at length. "He looks like a true man. You are happy, Miss Wordsworth, in the possession of such a friend."

"I prize him highly," said Esther. "He is a true man—noble, generous, sincere, earnest. His mind and his heart are both grand."

Miss Godolphin's face expressed interest, and Esther proceeded to give a statement of Waring's course—his attachment to his sister; his unselfish relinquishment of his share of the joint estate inherited by them, for her benefit; his engaging in teaching; his career in college; and his pure, fervent faith as a Christian.

Miss Godolphin's face exhibited varying emotions, as Esther continued, with an unconscious glow, to recite her knowledge of her friend's history; and when she ceased to speak, there was silence for a moment.

"Miss Wordsworth," said Miss Godolphin, "such a man is godlike! How immeasurably he transcends those who boast of rank, and plume themselves upon the possession of wealth! Such a man throws a crowned king into eclipse, and vindicates the claim of men to that trust and consideration which our sex always wish to repose in them."

Esther was almost startled by her enthusiasm. She said: "You can not overrate Mr. Waring, Miss Godolphin; he is pure gold."

It was understood, before Esther left Miss Godolphin,

that arrangements should be made as early as possible for their equestrian excursions; and when they separated, each felt a deeper interest in the other, and both resolved, that for the future they would seek each other oftener, and indulge a more unrestricted intercourse than they had hitherto enjoyed.

When Thursday evening came, Waring appeared punctually in Mr. Springfield's library, and joined the family at tea. It had long been his habit to pass that evening with them, and he prized the privilege.

As he entered, seeing Esther seated on a *fauteuil*, he advanced to her, and said gayly: "What tidings do you bring?"

She smiled, and said: "Are you very much interested in knowing?"

"I think I may venture to say that I am. The sketch which you drew, when I was here last, of our horseback adventures, has so impressed me, that I find the forms of fair ladies galloping over my pages in the highest equestrian style, when I attempt to read."

"Indeed!" said Esther. "Day-dreams! You are really interested."

"I must confess it honestly; and you will, as a humane person, relieve my anxiety as speedily as possible."

"Then," said Esther, "I am happy to say that my tidings are good. Miss Godolphln graciously consents to join us, whenever we notify her that we are ready."

Waring's face lighted up, and Esther was surprised to see the pleasure which her announcement gave.

"And they have not yet gone to the country, then?" he said.

"Not yet," said Esther. "They will probably go on Saturday; but the distance is so short, that it is only a suburban residence; and I have promised to visit Miss Godolphin often.

"There is a wonderful fascination about her," said Waring; "and I think that you will find her as unworldly as she is charming."

"She is remarkably so," said Esther, "and that is her great charm. Comprehending the great world as she does—having seen it in its many-sidedness, to use a German phrase—she is as simple in her tastes as if she had never left her native place. She is, of course, cultivated as she could not have been if she had remained at home, but her tastes are as pure and fresh as possible. She hates fashionable life, and loves the true, the simple, and the beautiful."

Waring listened with evident satisfaction to Esther's glowing tribute to her friend—for such she now felt her to be. The sympathy between them became perfect, from the moment Miss Godolphin spoke to her upon the subject of religion, as she had done.

"Few come back from the grand tour," said Waring, "with such tastes. With all her genius and accomplishments, there is nothing of pretension or false manner about her. She is a very superior person."

"We all admire her," said Mr. Springfield, "as every one must who can appreciate qualities so rare as hers."

"Do you know her religious views?" asked Waring, addressing himself to Esther.

"We had quite a free conversation on that subject when I was last with her," she said, "and I was distressed to find her so much bewildered; but she is earnest and humble, and I hope that she will soon emerge from the clouds which surround her."

Waring made no reply, but seemed to be lost in thought. Mrs. Springfield had not been present when the conversation was going on, but she now entered the room, and that roused Waring from his prolonged reverie. He rose, and took his seat near her.

"Mrs. Springfield," said he, "I am so lonely now, that I hail the evenings that permit me to come here."

"And why not come every evening? We should be very happy to see you."

"Oh! my books would suffer. I must do something to help me on the road."

"The days are so long," said Mrs. Springfield, "that you might very well close your books with the going down of the sun."

"Labor is the law of my life, you know, and I do not know that it will ever be otherwise with me."

They were invited to the tea-table, and the evening passed off cheerfully.

Esther that night revolved a subject which Waring's conversation and manner suggested. She began, for the first time, to suspect that he was deeply interested in Miss Godolphin. She was inclined to believe that the busy archer was trying his arrows upon the young Professor. Could he have the boldness to try his archery in that direction? to venture to pierce that manly and hitherto impenetrable breast?

With a woman's instinct, she could very well conceive that the brilliant, inexplicable, beautiful being whose sky was sometimes overcast by fleeting clouds, luminous from the very glory that they obscured, was the very person to attract a nature like that of this pure, elevated, unworldly man, who had never yet been brought under the dominion of that passion which exempts so few from its control.

## CHAPTER III.

"O PURE of heart! thou need'st not ask of me
What this strong music in the soul may be—
What and wherein it doth exist;
This light, this glory, this fair luminous mist,
This beautiful and beauty-making power.
We in ourselves rejoice."

SAMUEL TAYLOR COLERIDGE.

THE deepening splendors of summer were beginning to catch the tint of early autumn. Waring had received a letter from De Vane, announcing his arrival, and giving a detailed account of his reception, and of the impressions made on him by re-visiting early scenes. He had not yet made any visits, and had seen but few of the gentlemen of the neighborhood. General De Vane had welcomed him warmly, and expressed his gratification at his appearance; for he was full of health and vigor. Mrs. De Vane was as much moved as a mother upon welcoming home once more a long-absent son. The family servants greeted him joyously. Even his English pointer had recognized him, and inanimate objects seemed to be conscious of the return of their young lord. Mr. Guilford, his stately neighbor, had called, and invited him to visit him.

Evidently De Vane's welcome had been a gratifying one, and he was more pleased than he had expected to be, in returning to his ancestral home; but he sent kind messages to friends, and especially to Mr. Springfield and his family.

Waring read, and re-read, the long letter, and then sat down to think over it. It was natural that a young man of family and fortune, re-visiting his home, should be pleased with the cordial welcome that greeted him, and conscious of the consideration extended to him. All this was natural, and Waring felt that it was so. Still there was a shade of disappointment at finding in the language of his friend somewhat more of warmth than he had looked for in describing home scenes. He did not reply to the letter immediately, but deferred that until he could read his own impressions more clearly.

In the mean while, he had been much with Esther and Miss Godolphin. Manfred had arrived—Esther's saddle-horse—and was in fine condition. He was a pure white, with mane and tail as fine and glossy as silk, and showed in his limbs and in his delicately-formed head his Arabian blood. Full of intelligence, he was spirited and yet docile, and was especially tractable by his mistress, who managed him with perfect skill. Waring had engaged the horse which De Vane had been accustomed to ride, and Miss Godolphin had her own—a blood bay, with mane and tail and legs black and glossy as a raven's plumage. Esther, yielding to Miss Godolphin's repeated and earnest invitation, was passing a week or two with her friend at Miss Habersham's country-seat, and Waring was accustomed often to ride out early and pass the mornings with the ladies, who joined him on horseback. A servant always accompanied them, who, mounted on one of Mrs. Habersham's horses, opened gates for them when they rode into inclosures, and held their horses, if they desired at any time to seat themselves upon the bank of the clear stream which meandered through the grounds, giving the place its name, Clear Brook.

After receiving De Vane's letter, Waring rode out to Clear Brook. The ladies had, after an early breakfast, mounted their horses and gone on their accustomed ride.

Waring, acquainted with the grounds, went in pursuit of them, and soon overtook them.

"You are welcome, Mr. Waring," said Miss Godolphin; "and the pleasure is not lessened by its being an unexpected one. You should have notified us, and breakfast would have waited for you."

"Thank you," said he. "My good friend Mrs. Bowen never scolds me, except when I go out before breakfast, which she insists will ruin my health, if I persist in it. So I took my coffee before I mounted my horse."

"What a day!" said Esther. "These woods are glorious at this season, and the light falling through them reminds one of descriptions of great cathedrals, where the sunbeams pour through windows of stained glass."

"Yes," said Miss Godolphin; "but never yet did cathedral equal this. See those crimson leaves, and that wild vine throwing its boundless luxuriance over that towering oak, and the yellow richness of that young poplar. I prefer this to any thing in the way of architectural splendor that I have ever seen."

"Art can never rival this," said Waring; "and it is a happy faculty of our being that enables us to sympathize with nature."

"Sympathy with nature," said Miss Godolphin, "is a part of my being. Everywhere, in the gentlest or grandest aspects of visible creation, I find something that appeals to me, and awakens within me a living sympathy. What should I do without nature? I rejoice in her smiles, and share her sorrows when they come upon her."

"It is most fortunate, too," said Waring, "that whatever may be our mood, we can turn to natural objects with interest."

"Yes," said Miss Godolphin, "that is generally true. When artificial objects have ceased to delight us, and even offend by their intrusive presence, we can still turn to natural scenes, and find something to refresh, if not to cheer us."

"I find," said Esther, "that writers whose love of nature leads them to describe its charms, interpret the aspects of the visible world so as to make them harmonize with their own emotions."

"I have observed it," said Waring.

"For," continued Esther, "a happy soul finds nature happy. It was while Adam and Eve stood in their unsinning purity, that they saw the beauties of Paradise and the glories of the outspread heavens. They sang their morning hymn of praise in full sympathy with the gladness of nature."

"Yes," said Miss Godolphin, "it is so. Nature smiles or weeps as we smile or weep. But we may be so wretched as to be indifferent even to the harshest visitations of the elements, and defy nature even in storms. The great master of human nature comprehended this when he made poor old Lear indifferent to the storm. In reply to Kent, who tells him:

> 'The tyranny of the open night's too rough
> For nature to endure.'

Lear says:

> 'Thou think'st 'tis much, that this contentious storm
> Invades us to the skin: so 'tis to thee:
> But where the greater malady is fixed,
> The lesser is scarce felt. . . .
> . . . . . When the mind's free,
> The body's delicate: the tempest in my mind
> Doth from my senses take all feeling else,
> Save what beats there.' "

She uttered the lines in a way that made them enter the souls of her friends who rode with her. They had checked the horses for a few minutes, when Esther called their attention to the beauty of the scene; and as she finished the lines, she sat the very impersonation of sadness.

Waring said, after a silence of some moments: "Still it is possible to triumph over nature, not by sadness only, not by the benumbing power of deep grief, which makes us defy it, but we can illumine its darkest aspects with the light of our own spirits. In the language of an Eastern hymn, we may say in mid-winter to the frozen earth:

'Awake, thou wintry earth!
Fling off thy sadness!
Fair vernal flowers laugh forth
Your ancient gladness!
Christ is risen!'

The soul rejoicing in the triumph of its Lord, may spread a luminous glory over all the visible world."

"I was crossing the Alps," said Miss Godolphin, "in early spring. The morning was one of extraordinary mildness, and the mountains were in their glory. Still I could feel no sympathy with the splendid scene—far more splendid than the traveler usually witnesses in going over that pass. Toward evening a thunder-storm came on, wild and terrific in its sublime strength, and I assure you, I felt no more apprehension than I do at this moment. Indeed, I was too much oppressed even to sympathize with the surpassing power of the elements in their strife, as I did more than once after that time. Can you help me, Mr. Waring, to find that power which enables one to triumph over storms within the soul, as well as to defy those which spread their fury over the earth?"

"Have you not read, Miss Godolphin, the account, given in language of simple beauty, of the storm which suddenly came down on the Galilean Sea, when those who were driven before its fury in the little boat which could not resist it, began to be overwhelmed with fear? that when the tempest was at its height, their fear was increased by seeing a form treading the waters as if they had been marble beneath His feet, and that then a clear, calm voice was heard through the roar of winds and waves, saying, 'It is I, be not afraid,' and that presently both the commotion in the elements was stilled by him, and the commotion within human hearts, not less wild, subsided? He can give us a peace which nothing can disturb, and he alone."

"Yes, Mr. Waring," she said, "I have read it? I read that book more than I ever did. Miss Wordsworth's example is not lost upon me."

There was a gentle dignity in her manner as she uttered these words; so far from the slightest attempt at effect, so full of truthful earnestness, that Waring and Esther were both much impressed with it. They rode on. Waring did not press the conversation; he comprehended too well that it was unsafe to disturb the process through which Miss Godolphin's soul was passing, by too much of human counsel. He could not understand her troubles, for he did not know her history; but he saw that her spirit was in a state of unrest, and he hoped that after it flew over the wide waste of shoreless waters, exhausted and weary, it would fold its wings at last at the feet of Him who invited all to come to him and find rest.

After riding for some distance in silence, he informed the ladies that he had received a letter from De Vane.

"Indeed!" exclaimed Miss Godolphin with animation. "And what does he write?"

"He had arrived at home," said Waring, "but had been there too short a time to do more than glance at the surroundings. He had received some calls, but had returned none; nor had any thing been said upon the subject of his return to this State. He charged me with kind messages to his friends, and, of course, names you both as embraced in that phrase."

"I shall accept no general tender of regards in that way," said Miss Godolphin, smiling. "I never did value any such expression."

Esther looked at Waring earnestly, but said nothing.

"Oh! but you must understand me," said Waring. "He does name you both, asks after you specially, and alludes to you more than once as his friends."

"Still," said Miss Godolphin, "the message must be very intensive to make me appropriate any part of it. What do you say, Esther?"

It was the first time he had heard her call Miss Wordsworth by that name, and it pleased him; it proved a growing intimacy, which he hoped would become still closer.

"I feel very much as you do," said Esther. "We value words from friends which are intended for us alone."

"Then, Mr. Waring," said Miss Godolphin, "you are instructed to make known to your friend, Mr. De Vane, that if he desires us to treat his messages with any consideration, they must be direct, and mean something."

Waring laughed. "Oh! I am sure they do mean much. You do my friend injustice."

"Seriously, though," said Miss Godolphin, "what does he say of his impressions? Does his heart warm once more for his home? and does he look back already upon us as if he saw us in perspective?"

"He is evidently gratified with his reception," said Waring. "It is natural that it should be so, and would be strange if it were otherwise."

"Of course," said Miss Godolphin. "The 'young laird' returning to his ancestral halls, must be received with the honor due to his rank."

"That is it precisely," said Waring. "And if I had explained for an hour, I could not have given so proper a statement of the case."

"Will he return?" she asked abruptly.

"I have not permitted myself to doubt it," said Waring. "I have all the while known that the most powerful inducements to stay would be presented to De Vane upon his reaching home. I told him so, and tried to prepare him in advance for the ordeal; and he uniformly insisted that his mind was made up and his purpose fixed. I see no reason yet to doubt it. I have the greatest confidence in the basis of his character—he is a true man. His tastes sometimes govern him, and he is impressible; but when he takes his position, after considering it well, he will hold it. He had taken his position in regard to his future residence before leaving here, after the fullest consideration, and I think he will hold it in the face of every thing that can be brought to bear upon him."

"Wait till we see his next letter," said Miss Godolphin.

Esther said not a word, but her heightened color disclosed the interest which she felt in the conversation.

Upon reaching the house, Waring excused himself and returned to town.

De Vane had said nothing to him before leaving for Virginia as to his sentiments in regard to Esther, nor had he in his letter made any allusion to the subject. His scrupulous regard for Esther made him forbear to do so, just as it had repressed any declaration to Esther of an attachment which he felt to be powerful. His sense of duty to his father, too, made him feel that it was imperative on him first to consult him in regard to his plans of life, and to endeavor to bring him to his own views, before committing himself to others.

Still, Waring saw how deep his interest in Esther really was, and he comprehended too that she was not insensible to the regard which the manner of De Vane so plainly exhibited for her. As he rode slowly toward the town, these thoughts troubled him. The delicate threads which influences about these two bright young beings were weaving into the strong cords of fate, who could see?—two beings so deeply loved by him, so full of generous and high qualities. He breathed a silent prayer that all might be overruled for their good.

The weeks flew by. Esther returned to town, resumed her morning visits at Leasowes, and advanced steadily in the path of duty. September had come. Walking one evening in the public garden, the gardener respectfully took off his hat as she was passing a bed where he was clipping a border of box, and spoke to her. She spoke to him pleasantly, and was passing on, when he said:

"If you please, madam, I was wanting to inquire if you have heard any thing lately about the young gentleman who used to walk with you sometimes?"

Esther's face flushed instantly—how the tumultuous blood flashed over it! The suddenness of the question startled her, and the unconscious gardener stood waiting for a reply.

"No," she said, after a moment's hesitation, "I have not heard any thing very lately from him, but he is expected to return in October."

"I wish he was here now," said the man. "A finer gentleman never trod these walks. It did me good always to see his face; it was as welcome as the sun after a shower."

Esther could scarcely repress her tears. The gardener stepped on the bed of flowers, and selecting some half-dozen of the rarest, presented them to her, saying: "It will be a bright day when he comes back to us, and I'm glad October is not far off."

"Thank you for the flowers," said Esther, "they are really beautiful," and bowing to the gardener, she walked on. It seemed that she was to have De Vane that evening brought to her memory by another friend of his;

for calling at Leasowes, for a moment, she met "Uncle Jacob," who seemed disposed for conversation.

"Mighty pretty flowers you've got there, Missis," he said.

"Yes, Uncle Jacob, they have just been presented to me by the public gardener, Mr. Swan."

"I think we can beat 'em," said Jacob, roused at once by a spirit of rivalry. "Last time Marster De Vane was here, he said mine was the finest garden he seen anywhere about. Wish he'd come back again."

Esther was amused. "Yes, Uncle Jacob," she said, "yours is a fine garden. You do look after it well."

"Just what Marster De Vane told me," said the old man, highly gratified.

Esther passed on. She returned home, and when sitting in the library the same evening, with Mr. and Mrs. Springfield, after tea, her servant Antony, a smart, well-dressed man, who attended to her horse and went on errands for her, came to the door, and said:

"Missis, Mr. Hobbs says you must have Manfred shod like Mr. De Vane had his horse shod when he was here. If you don't, he'll cut hisself some time."

"Very well, Antony," she said; "ask Mr. Hobbs to have him shod in that way."

"He says too, Missis, that he'd like mightily to know if any body's heard from him lately, and that he never missed any body as much in his life."

"Why, Antony," said Mrs. Springfield, "how did Mr. Hobbs happen to say that to you?"

"I don't know, ma'am," he answered, "but he says that Mr. De Vane used to come here mighty often, and he thought mebby you'd all know when he was comin' back."

Mr. Springfield, who raised his eyes from his book to look at Antony, was much amused.

"Tell your friend Mr. Hobbs," said Mrs. Springfield,

"that we hope to see him again early in October. Perhaps he can content himself until that time."

Antony disappeared. It occurred to Esther that it was a remarkable evening, and it of course fixed her thoughts more intensely than before upon the young Virginian.

"We should hear something of Mr. De Vane," said Mr. Springfield. "Has Mr. Waring had a letter recently, do you know, Esther?"

"I do not know, uncle," she said. "He has not said any thing to me upon the subject."

She felt anxious. Her solicitude was heightened by the events of the day. How vividly such things recall the absent! Who has not experienced a series of small things, nothing in themselves, but so linked together as to startle us by their conjunction?

Mr. Springfield sat musing for five minutes, and then was roused by a rap at the library-door, when, upon an invitation to enter, Waring walked in. Esther started. She felt that he had heard from De Vane. She had that kind of subtle, incomprehensible impression which we sometimes experience in moments when the sensibilities are unusually quick, and the spirit scarcely requires the ministry of the senses to enable it to perceive objects.

"Good evening, Mr. Waring," said Mr. Springfield, rising to receive him. "I am glad to see you."

"We are all glad to see you," said Mrs. Springfield, giving him her hand.

Esther came forward and extended hers, when Waring, turning to her, said: "Are you not well? You're looking pale."

"Perfectly well," said Esther, now coloring, "and I too am very glad to see you."

Waring sat down.

"Have you had tea?" asked Mrs. Springfield.

"Yes, thank you," he said, "and should have joined

you, but calling at the post-office, I found a very long letter from De Vane, and walked to my own room to read it."

"Good tidings from him, I hope," said Mr. Springfield.

"Yes," said Waring. "He is very well, and begs to be remembered in the kindest terms to you all."

Mr. Springfield bowed.

"I do not know that I can do better than to read you that paragraph of his letter," said Waring.

"We shall be pleased to hear it," said Mr. Springfield.

Waring took from his pocket the letter—it must have covered ten pages—and detaching the last sheet, he proceeded to read it.

"Having disposed of these affairs, I now turn to other subjects far more agreeable to me. You know, my dear Waring, my strong attachments draw me to the town, where, for more than three years, I resided; where I first came to the consciousness of manhood, and felt that my soul and intellect had both opened under the influences which were forming me—for really it was a formative process through which I passed. My attachment to the place is strong—to my friends there, so strong, that I feel it would be impossible for me to be happy away from there. Upon coming here, I was so warmly greeted, that early memories revived powerfully; and I could not, for some weeks, bring myself to make known to my father and to my aunt my plans of life. They seemed to have taken it for granted, upon my return, that I had yielded to their wishes. It seemed cruel to undeceive them; but I at length went over the whole ground with Mrs. De Vane, and satisfied her, at one sitting, that I was immovable. She saw it, and felt that to keep me here, merely in obedience to an arbitrary wish of my father, would be to sacrifice me. She is a very superior woman; and when she became satisfied that my happiness and my success in life were both involved, she addressed herself to the great task of bringing my father over to my views. Then came the great struggle that I have already described to you—a struggle far the most painful of my life. It is ended. My father acquiesces; says I am a modern man; that I have been, in that Southern college, subjected to influences which bring me into full sympathy with the progress of the age, and that, as he has had his career, it is proper that I should be suffered to shape mine.

"The struggle is ended, and I shall return to you early in October. I have not written of late, because I was unwilling to do so until I saw the end; and it is possible that you, and others whose esteem is prized by me beyond measure, may have misinterpreted my silence. I have never wavered for an hour. I have, in the first part of my letter, given you a full statement of all that was offered to tempt me to make this my home—for I wish you to comprehend me—but I have not at any time swerved from my purpose. Do, then, make this known to my friends—of course, I mean to Mr. Springfield, whose good opinion you know I prize; to Mrs. Springfield, whose fine mind and true heart have done so much for me—more than she herself can know; and to Miss Wordsworth. Nor do I wish to be misjudged by Miss Godolphin. Good Mrs. Bowen, I am sure, has never had her faith in me shaken. Before quitting here, I shall make my arrangements to have my interests looked after for me, and this will detain me some little time; still, you may expect me early in October. Intending to travel with my own horses, I shall be somewhat longer on the way. When I do arrive, I shall make the melodeon discourse its most triumphant music. Once more, I say, I have had a great struggle, but it is over.

"I am to make a political speech at Charlottesville on Saturday, being invited to do so by the citizens. Virginia is safe for General Jackson. The Hamiltons, our Methodist neighbors, have just called. I shall go to meet them. They are far the most agreeable people I have seen since my return, and they remind me vividly of our friends, the Springfields. Adieu.

"Always your friend, GEORGE DE VANE.

"P. S.—The Hamiltons sat an hour. Perfectly charming people; and they sympathize wholly with my plans of life.

"I forgot to mention that I have a horse for you—one of the best Virginia breed—and anticipate equestrian exercises, with two friends known to us both, on my return.

"G. D. V."

"There," said Waring, "I have done my duty."

"Yes," said Mr. Springfield, "we are all greatly indebted to you. Your friend is really a noble fellow."

"I know," said Waring, "what he has had to encounter. I almost trembled for the issue."

"You will write him again?" asked Mr. Springfield.

"Without delay," said Waring.

"Then," said Mrs. Springfield, "do offer him our congratulations, and assure him of a warm welcome upon his coming."

There was a spice of mischief in Waring's composition, grave as he was; and turning to Esther, he said:

"And has Miss Wordsworth no message for my friend, Mr. De Vane?"

Esther's face was radiant, and her smile bright as a sunbeam.

"Only to thank him for not having forgotten us," she said.

Never had a letter diffused greater joy; and Waring's own heart was full of gladness. He had read aloud but a small part of it. De Vane had given him an extended history of his trials and contests; of his meeting his early friend, Clara Guilford; of Mrs. De Vane's plans for his future; of her criticism of Esther; and warning him against the designs of his Methodist friends upon him; and he hinted at the knowledge which he had obtained of the history of a *friend* of theirs, which would, perhaps, explain the mystery of her sadness. All this, of course, Waring kept to himself, as it was intended by the writer that he should, and as his own sense of propriety would have prompted him to do.

"Then," said Mr. Springfield, "it is a settled thing, that Mr. De Vane is to reside amongst us. I must express my very great gratification. I have, from the first hour of our acquaintance, entertained a high opinion of him. He wants but one thing to make his character complete."

"You think," said Waring, "he is just where the young ruler was, who came kneeling, and asking the way to life."

"Yes," said Mr. Springfield.

"He will find it," said Waring. "It may require years to disentangle him from the meshes of German rationalism; but I can not believe that any nature so noble, and that loves truth so profoundly, can finally wander out of the way—never."

"I agree with you," said Mrs. Springfield. "I have often conversed with Mr. De Vane upon that great subject, and he is earnest in seeking the right way. He has some very wrong opinions, and he will never be argued out of them; but he will be led in the right way."

"Thank you," said Waring warmly, "for your appreciation of my friend."

"We may look for him, I suppose," said Mrs. Springfield, "in the course of a few weeks?"

"I suppose," said Waring, "that he ought to arrive early in October, unless some unexpected detention should occur."

"He is to travel through a fine country," said Mr. Springfield. "We passed over the greater part of the road last fall."

"I wish," said Waring, "that you could have been present this evening, when I informed Mrs. Bowen of De Vane's decision, and told her of his speedy coming. She absolutely wept for joy; and I do not doubt that she will to-morrow morning commence preparations for having his room in readiness, just as if he were coming to-morrow night."

"He inspires very strong sentiments, I suppose," said Mr. Springfield, "where he is well known; sentiments of esteem and affection, which only a great nature like his can awaken."

"How is Miss Godolphin, Mr. Waring?" asked Mrs. Springfield.

"Really, my dear madam, I can not say. It has been some days since I saw her."

"Some days!" said Esther. "It seems to me that it was only day before yesterday. Have you forgotten our meeting at the book-store?"

Mrs. Springfield laughed heartily, and said: "Why, Waring, has it come to that? However, I suppose two days may seem a long while to a young gentleman under some circumstances. Angels' visits, few and far between —is that the line?"

"It is hardly deferential enough," said Esther, "to treat a grave Professor in this way, when it is barely two weeks before he enters upon his duties."

"By the way, so it is," said he, "only about two weeks before I shall have to be very stately, and work hard too."

"And renounce riding on horseback?" asked Mr. Springfield.

"Never!" said Waring. "One may be allowed that for the benefit of his health and spirits."

"Surely!" said Esther.

"Of course!" said Mrs. Springfield.

"Good night!" said Waring, and rising, and shaking hands warmly with his friends, he walked away in high spirits.

## CHAPTER IV.

"PAST, present, future, all appeared
In harmony united,
Like guests that meet, and some from far,
By cordial love united."

WORDSWORTH.

OCTOBER came, rich with autumnal glories. Neither fruits nor flowers had disappeared, for in that mild climate they graced even the stern reign of winter. There was a refreshing coolness in the morning air, and the leaves, touched by early frost, wore the varied hues which give such a charm to the woods in the fall of the year, as to make us cease to regret the spring. Gold and crimson, intermingled with the never-fading deep green, met the view everywhere. The evenings were delightful, and fires were kindled, to temper the slight chilliness which succeeded the lessening days. Absentees returned to town; and carriages, which had been put away for the hot season, were now drawn out, and rolled once more through the streets. The doors of the College were thrown open, and students were coming in from all parts of the State. The town was beginning to wear a cheerful aspect, and to resume its animation. Friends, meeting on the streets, greeted each other warmly; and within-doors pleasant sounds were heard, which spoke of reünited households, and all the routine of home life was once more resumed.

Waring entered upon his duties, and wore for the first time the robes of a professor. His colleagues greeted him cordially, and he undertook his new tasks with energy and heartiness. Quite a number of the students were acquainted with him. They were members of some one of the less advanced classes when he graduated, and, feeling the greatest respect for his character and talents, they impressed the new-comers with a high idea of his qualifications. In no college in all the world was there a higher respect felt for a first-honor man than in that, where he had but a little while before received that distinction; and the *éclât* which attended him on that occasion secured for him a favorable reception from the students with whom he was to walk as a professor—younger himself than some of those who surrounded him, to hear his lectures.

Mrs. Habersham had returned to town, and Waring called to pay his respects. He was received both by Mrs. Habersham and Miss Godolphin with marked kindness. They respected and trusted him, and the visits of no one gave them more pleasure than those of the young Professor. His interest in Miss Godolphin was deepening, and yet he found in her manner at times something so inexplicable that his ardor was checked, and his heart, full of generous sympathy, was disturbed. It was impossible for him to conceive what had thrown a shadow over the brilliant morning of a life which had so much to give it splendor; yet he felt himself powerfully attracted to her, and he resolved to study the varying phases of a character which so deeply interested him, before it became impossible to withdraw from its contemplation, without the loss of his own happiness.

"How does the College open?" asked Miss Godolphin. "Prosperously?"

"Never with higher promise," he said. "We have a larger number of students than we have had at any time; and we must recommend to the Trustees to erect for us additional buildings."

"You want a new chapel," she said.

"Yes; we must have one; and we are enlarging our library. We should have a building suited to it."

"I hope," she said, "that the Legislature will be generous."

"You must help us with them," said Waring. "Exert your influence, and secure for us a large appropriation."

"If I can do any thing, you may count upon me," she replied.

"I am very sure that you can do much. One of the leading members is, I am sorry to learn, earnestly opposed to classical learning, and thinks nothing can save the country but common-schools."

"Ah! well, we must put out all our strength against him, and urge Mr. De Vane to activity when he returns."

"Yes," said Waring, "and Mr. Le Grande is a member of the House, whose splendid scholarship will be of immense importance to us, himself at once an advocate for classical learning, and a noble illustration of the advantage which it confers. A graduate, too, of our College."

"I hope to hear him this winter. He is said to be very eloquent. I was so unfortunate as to miss his great speech at the last session."

"His eloquence," said Waring, "is rich and massive, formed upon the classical models. He rivals them in the fertility of his genius and the stateliness of his style. Some passages in his orations are worthy of the palmiest periods of Roman eloquence. It is really refreshing to hear him speak. There is nothing commonplace, nothing of rant, and yet an affluent style, which bears you away."

"I must hear him," said Miss Godolphin. "It is delightful to hear such oratory."

"Yes," said Waring; "to escape the platitudes of some speakers, and the mannerism of others, is, as you say, delightful."

"The Legislature of this State is a superior body, I believe," she said.

"Very," said Waring. "There are several members of the Senate, and of the House, who would adorn any parliamentary body in the world."

"Then, too," said Miss Godolphin, "we have eminent men not in public life, who are equal to any that fill the coveted places; for instance, Mr. Clarendon, and Mr. Hallam—not to mention others."

"Yes," said Waring, "Mr. Hallam, at the bar, would rank high anywhere; and Mr. Clarendon, at the bar, and before the people, is, in my judgment, unrivaled. He is imperial."

"So I have heard Mr. De Vane describe him," said Miss Godolphin.

"If you wish to kindle De Vane's enthusiasm," said Waring, "just bring up Mr. Clarendon. His appreciation of his friend is charming."

"And when are we to have Mr. De Vane with us?" she asked.

"Very soon, probably next week. He is on his way—he was detained a little time looking after his affairs. It seems that General De Vane, to secure his regular visits to Virginia, has set apart a planting interest for him in that State. He relies upon the conscientiousness of his son, to make him look after it, to some extent, in person. He is on the way, and I hope to see him within the next ten days—possibly within less time he may be here."

"I am sincerely glad," said Miss Godolphin; "indeed I am. He is a wonderfully agreeable person; and he has vindicated his manliness by adhering to his resolution to make this place his home, and to engage in the actual life-struggle."

"He deserves all your commendation," said Waring. "He has passed through an ordeal which few could endure as he has borne it. His tastes and his ambition were both powerfully appealed to, and all his ancestral pride brought to bear upon his resolution; but he has decided to be a MAN rather than an aristocrat."

"You certainly could give him no higher praise than that," said Miss Godolphin.

"None, in my estimate of character," said Waring. "It fills me with admiration to see a true man—one who can bear himself with that fine air that is at once dignified and gentle, without pretension or stiffness, as if unconscious of rank or distinctions, whether inherited or conferred. The high breeding of De Vane is seen in his bearing; but the nobleness of his nature is such, that he can not be spoiled. His principles are well settled, and they will triumph whenever they are tested."

"There is, I think, much to attract him here," said Miss Godolphin. "He seems to be really attracted to the place."

"He is," said Waring, "and yet I could not dismiss all anxiety about him when I thought of the Virginia home, the father, the aunt, the wealth, the consideration, the strong feeling of caste in which he was educated. When I received his letter announcing his intention to return, it filled me with the exultation with which one hears the news of a victory; and I assure you that it required as much true heroism to resist the temptations to lead a life of luxurious and aristocratic ease, and to break away from the enticements which surrounded him in that Virginia home of his, as it does to enable one to achieve a triumph in battle against heavy odds."

"Still," said Miss Godolphin, "we must not underrate our attractions here; and I am sure that Mr. De Vane knows how to appreciate them."

There was something of archness in her manner of saying this, which implied much more than the words.

"But," she added, "I entirely agree with you in thinking that he deserves the highest commendation for carrying out his resolution to renounce a life of ease and inaction, for a career of active labor."

"Upon his return," said Waring, "I shall bring him to you, that he may make his acknowledgments for your appreciation of him."

"Do," said Miss Godolphin. "We shall be very glad to see him."

Some time after, when the evening was pretty well advanced, Waring returned to his solitary room, to think of the mystery attending Miss Godolphin, who, sometimes very sad, had been this evening brighter than he had seen her.

The unusually large number of students entering the College, gave great animation to the town; and as they took their evening walks, they spread through the streets their own brightness.

Doctor Hume was unusually active, and Blanche ambled with him in the most amiable way, from the College grounds to the post-office, the book-stores, the printing-offices, and other points, where he habitually called. Whatever distrusts may have been entertained as to his orthodoxy, no one who knew him could regard him unkindly. His own genial nature shone through his face, and gave warmth to his manners; and he forbore to press his peculiar religious views upon the students.

Leasowes was once more a scene of regular industry, and Esther had resumed her accustomed labors with her pupils. She was never brighter. The activity of her step showed the gladness of her nature. Her smile warmed the little circle of orphaned girls far more than the sunlight, and her voice filled the walks which she trod with joyous notes. Never were the waters which flashed in the fountain brighter; and as they filled the marble basin into which they fell, the liquid crystal, overflowing its edges, gave new freshness to the turf which lined the little stream that glided away into the overshadowing shrubbery.

De Vane had not yet arrived, but he was expected daily. Mrs. Bowen, as Waring had predicted, had really gone to work promptly, to put his room in perfect order. Carpets, curtains, chairs, books, every thing looked as fresh as if De Vane had stepped out of it but an hour before. Every morning she walked in to survey it, and to adjust the curtains and dust the furniture; and she enjoyed it next to a visit to Waring, who still retained his room, preferring it to any which could be provided for him at the College. She was becoming very impatient at the delay in De Vane's return, and on Saturday morning walked into Waring's room, after making her usual visit to his friend's, just opposite.

"Mr. Waring," she said, "when *is* Mr. De Vane coming? I'm afraid something has happened to him on the road."

"Oh! no," said Waring. "The road is a long one, and it requires some time to make the journey. He is not coming in the stage-coach, you know, but is traveling with his own horses and servant, and that, you know, requires more time. I think, however, we shall see him here now very soon."

"Well," said Mrs. Bowen, "I hope the good Lord will take care of him, and bring him safely. I do want to see him."

"Every thing is ready for him in his room, I suppose," said Waring.

"Oh! yes," said Mrs. Bowen. "I've tried to put things to rights. I've put the table just where he used to have it, and the chairs and the books just as he liked to have them. I hope he'll be pleased."

"You may be sure of that," said Waring. "He was always pleased with your arrangements in his room. I have often heard him say that he could not feel at home anywhere but here."

The good old lady was immensely gratified, and her eyes were moist as she said:

"Well, I do love to work for Mr. De Vane, and to put his things in order, he is so easy to please."

"I never heard him make the first complaint. He doesn't like to have his books moved, I know, and I never disturb them, further than to brush the dust off of them; and I leave his pens and papers just where he lets them stay."

Waring smiled. He saw that Mrs. Bowen had learned to respect De Vane's rights; for, while scrupulously neat in every thing, he would leave his books in apparent confusion, and he was annoyed if one removed them. Sometimes they covered tables, sofa, chairs, and floor, for days together, when he was pursuing some particular branch of study. Then would come a general clearing up, and the books were replaced on the shelves. No one but a student can realize the luxury of being permitted to leave books and papers scattered in this apparent confusion, with the certainty that they will not be disturbed by the ruthless hand of careful housekeeping.

Waring passed the evening at Mr. Springfield's, taking tea with the family.

"Well, Professor," said Mr. Springfield, as he entered, "we are glad to see you. How do affairs go on at the College?"

"Thank you," said Waring, "well. We are more prosperous than ever before."

"And what does Dr. Hume say to the new arrangement?"

"He is very amiable," said Waring; "and is really so

good a friend, that he would make no objection if he disapproved it. But I do not think he does. He is a man of liberal spirit, and contends for perfect freedom of opinion."

"He seems to be deeply interested in politics," said Mr. Springfield, "and is intensely of the State Rights school of thinkers."

"Yes," said Waring, "he at times utters some startling opinions, which may yet be as formidable as dragon's teeth, and, if wide-spread, will yield great armies."

"So I think," said Mr. Springfield; "but I agree with him in politics at least. It is of the first importance, to resist the tendency to consolidation in the Government, which is beginning to manifest itself. If it should go on for a few years as it is now doing, the whole character of the Government will be changed."

"That is true," said Waring. "But if every Southern State would resist the encroachments of the Federal Government, as Georgia has done, we should have very little trouble."

"Yes," said Mr. Springfield, "Georgia has done nobly; and the emphatic announcement, that, the argument being exhausted, it was the purpose of the people to stand by their arms, seems to have been accepted as an authentic utterance of the will of the State."

"Have you read Dr. Hume's new work on Political Economy?" asked Waring.

"No," replied Mr. Springfield. "It was sent to me by Mr. Müller, some days since, but I have not yet had leisure to look into it."

"You will be pleased with it," said Waring. "But some of his propositions may startle you. Pursuing the idea that money is but the representative of property, having no real value in itself, he conducts you to the conclusion that the imports of a nation are the best measure of its wealth; and that a country is enriched by importing, no matter how little it may export."

"A very sound proposition, certainly," said Mr. Springfield, "if a country can produce a sufficient supply of the precious metals to pay for the articles which it buys from abroad; but I can never believe that a nation, any more than an individual, can be enriched by running in debt."

"The book," said Waring, "is remarkable for its clearness; and you will like it. I quite agree with its author, that a mere hoarding of money can never increase the real wealth of an individual or a nation."

"Certainly not," said Mr. Springfield.

At this moment, Mrs. Springfield and Esther, who had just returned from a drive, entered the room, and expressed their gratification at meeting Waring. They went in to tea, and the conversation became general.

"We found our drive," said Esther, "a delightful one. There is a refreshing coolness in the air."

"I do not remember to have seen a finer season," said Waring. "The early frost has touched the leaves with the richest hues, and the crisp earth under one's tread is exhilarating. In what direction did you drive?"

"We took the upper road," said Esther. "It is undulating, and, I think, affords the finest view of our environs."

"Much," said Waring. "That bold little stream that pours its noisy waters over the road, always refreshes me."

"For my part," said Mr. Springfield, "I prefer the river. Either to drive to the mill, and from there proceed down to the ferry, or to go directly from the town, down the river-road, some three or four miles, is, at this season, especially pleasing to me."

"I wonder," said Mrs. Springfield, "that you can overlook the beauties of the road leading to Mrs. Habersham's country-seat. The environs in that direction, I think much the finest."

"If it were not," said Mr. Springfield, "that you must traverse a mile or two of sand, I might agree with you."

"Yes, but you have the tall pines as a compensation," said Esther. "Let others boast of the oak, and describe its spreading majesty as they may, but the pine is my tree. How it lifts it lofty head above the surrounding forest, so stately, so still, so silent, unless the wind sweeps through it, and then it sends out its deep solemn tone, as if the spirit of humanity dwelt there! Often in summer mornings, when the bright sky was cloudless, and the earth bathed in its light, have I sat under the pine trees, listening to their sad music. Far up in the air, birds were floating, and not a sound was heard to break the solemn tone of the strain which sounded like the wail of the distant sea; and many a summer evening have I stood to see the sun go down behind a pine forest, sending his fierce beams athwart the dark-green branches, until they seemed to blaze. I love the pine. It is a dear tree."

She spoke with an enthusiasm kindled by the recollection of early scenes, and her face beamed.

"Thank you for your tribute to the pine," said Waring. "It is associated with my school-days. I often wandered through the stately pine forests, impressed by the scenes which you describe, watching the clear streams, and climbing the chalk-hills."

"I love the pine," said Esther, "as the Arab loves the palm-tree. Both rise with stately glory, and catch the earliest light of day. It is very common to hear persons speak of the majestic oak: to me the pine is far more impressive; and when winter comes, and strips the oak of its glories, the pine stands in undiminished grandeur, defying storms and ice, like a true man meeting adversity, unchanged and unchangeable."

"If you emblazon your arms at any time upon your coach, Esther," said Mr. Springfield playfully, "you must add the pine. I think it would do well to place it in the centre, and group the other objects about it, or omit them altogether."

"I should be content with the pine alone," said Esther.

"Mrs. Habersham's place," said Waring, "is skirted on one side by a remarkably fine grove of young pines; and I thought, as I rode through it, on my late visit there, that I did not know any woods more beautiful—a sad beauty though it is. One feels a sense of loneliness in the pine woods, more intense than he experiences elsewhere."

"I love trees which change their foliage," said Mr. Springfield. "It is beautiful to witness the fall of the leaves, when you look to the reproduction of the departed glories of the forest in the coming spring. Nature impresses us in all her aspects, and especially in the varying seasons. The year is the type of time, and to me its course is nothing short of sublime, when I look upon it, as chronicling the advance of time toward eternity—the finite foreshadowing the infinite."

"Still," said Esther, "I love to see some trees standing with unchanging verdure and undecaying beauty in the midst of the general decline in the glories of the forest. It is so consoling to feel that all things do not acknowledge the power of mutability—resisting that sway which Spenser, in the Faerie Queene, describes as potential over every thing under the heaven's rule, and which made him loathe

'This state of life so tickle,
And love of things so vain to cast away;
Whose flowering guide, so fading and so fickle,
Short Time shall soon cut down with his consuming-sickle.'"

"And do you read the Faerie Queene?" asked Waring

"With real pleasure," said Esther; "some parts of it, at least."

"His pathetic description of patient waiting is one of the strongest to be found in any language. It was evoked by his personal disappointments."

"Royal favor," said Mr. Springfield, "is almost as uncertain as popular applause."

"When are we to see Mr. De Vane?" asked Mrs. Springfield.

"I look for him every day now," said Waring. "He must be quite near here, unless something has detained him on the road."

"He does not travel by the public conveyances, I believe," she said.

"No," said Waring, "he comes with his servant and his own horses, and this, of course, makes the journey somewhat tedious."

"He will find it more agreeable, however," said Mr. Springfield, "especially traveling through the district of country which he will traverse in coming here."

"I suppose," said Mrs. Springfield, "that Mrs. Bowen is ready to receive him?"

"Ready!" said Waring. "I wish you could see his room. No mother ever looked for the return of an absent son with greater eagerness. It would not surprise me to find him upon my return, this evening."

But Waring, returning, soon after this conversation, to Mrs. Bowen's, did not find his friend. He had not yet arrived.

## CHAPTER V.

"THAT is my home of love: if I have ranged,
Like him that travels, I return again."

SHAKESPEARE.

ON the following Wednesday evening, about sunset, a traveler was seen entering the town, driving in an elegant sulky, a very fine, large bay horse; while a servant, mounted on another closely resembling him, followed. The servant led a loose horse of extraordinary beauty—a chestnut sorrel, with heavy mane and tail. All the horses were of the best Virginia breed, and in form and action displayed their fine qualities. All the appointments about the traveler's harness, the dark livery of the servant, the trappings of the horses, displayed taste, and were unmistakably aristocratic. His own dress was simply elegant—rather plain than showy. He drove directly to Mrs. Bowen's; and as he approached the house, he saw a gentleman seated in the portico, enjoying the freshness of the quiet evening air. It was Waring.

Waring was seated with his face turned away from the street by which the traveler approached Mrs. Bowen's house, and it was not until he stopped directly in front of it, that he turned to observe him. He then instantly started up, and rushing out, exclaimed:

"What! De Vane, have you actually arrived at last?"

"I am happy to say that I am here bodily," replied De Vane, extending his hand, which Waring shook heartily. "What with moving accidents by flood and field, I thought at times that I should never reach here. How are all our friends ?"

"Well," said Waring, "very well, and looking for you daily. You are somewhat behind time. But come in."

"Where is Cæsar ?" said De Vane. "I must send him to show my man the way to the livery-stable."

Cæsar appeared — an active black man, Mrs. Bowen's chief reliance in the conduct of all out-door affairs—and very cordially extended his hand to De Vane, and gave him a generous welcome. De Vane instructed him to show his servant Tully to the livery-stable, and Cæsar, after unstrapping De Vane's trunk, protected from dust and rain by a heavy bear's skin, and taking his traveling articles into the house, mounted into the sulky and drove to the stable, followed by his classical namesake.

Mrs. Bowen met De Vane as he entered the house, and gave his hand an energetic shaking, while tears of joy rolled down her cheeks. "I'm so glad to see you, Mr. De Vane," she said. "I began to be uneasy about you."

"Why," said De Vane, "I was detained some two or three days in Virginia longer than I supposed I should be, and then I found one or two mountain streams so much swollen by late rains, that I was kept some few days waiting for them to run down, and finally had to swim them, with bag and baggage. But here I am, safe, at last, Mrs. Bowen."

"Thank the Lord for it !" she said. "And your room is ready for you, and has been for weeks."

"Ah ! thank you," said De Vane. "Then I will go to it, and get some of this dust off; and when my servant returns from the stable, please send him to me."

Waring accompanied him to his room, and they talked over their affairs. Both had a great deal to say—many questions to ask and answer. Waring gave him an account of affairs that particularly interested him ; and upon

De Vane's asking after Mr. Springfield and his family, he gave him a full statement of Esther's doings, comprehending, of course, that it would gratify him. In reply to De Vane's inquiries, Waring spoke, too, of Mrs. Habersham and Miss Godolphin, representing the interest which both had expressed in De Vane, and their gratification at learning that it was his purpose to fix his residence here.

The conversation was a long and satisfactory one. The past, the present, and the future, all were discussed, and when Cæsar came to invite them to supper, the friends had not yet concluded their interview; but they descended promptly to the table. Mrs. Bowen had made ample preparation for De Vane, fancying, of course, as good old ladies will do, when an absent one returns, that he had been half-starved on the journey. A beef-steak, two boiled fowls, and at least a dozen varieties of hot bread, smoked on the luxurious table. Knowing that De Vane disdained tea, clear, amber-colored coffee, with rich cream, appeared, and De Vane and Waring both partook of the bounties in a way to gratify Mrs. Bowen.

"This coffee, Mrs. Bowen," said De Vane, "excels any that I have seen since I left your house. The gods might throw away their nectar for it."

"I know you always liked it," said the gratified old lady, "and I'm glad to see you drinking it once more. It's the real Old Government Java."

"That it is," said De Vane, "and I would not give it for all the Mocha in the world."

"Nor I," said Waring. "The flavor is perfect."

"And then, too," said De Vane, "there is a great deal in the making. How do you succeed in having it so uniformly good?"

"Why," said Mrs. Bowen, "I pick it myself before it is parched, so as to take out every bad grain. Then I have it stirred while it is parching, to keep it from burning.

Then I grind it every time I want to use any, and instead of the French way, I take the old-fashioned way of boiling it in the tin pot which is brought on the table. Then I put the sugar in the cup, pour in the cream, stir it well, and stir it while I pour the coffee in the cup."

"It's a regular science," said De Vane, "and if ever I go to housekeeping, I must get you to instruct me."

"Oh! I'll do that, you may be sure," said Mrs. Bowen, "if you set up housekeeping anywhere about here."

"Well, that is understood," said De Vane; "and as to the place of my keeping house, that may be considered as settled, too, for I intend to make this place my home."

"So Mr. Waring told me, some time ago," she said, "and I was mighty glad to hear it, as I've no doubt others will be, too."

"Thank you," said De Vane.

"I suppose," said Waring, "that though you have settled the question as to where you will set up your household gods, you have not yet fixed upon the time."

"Oh! no," said De Vane, "that is quite uncertain."

"You do not propose to set up a bachelor's establishment, I presume?" said Waring.

"Oh! no," replied De Vane. "I do not approve that way of living; and Mrs. Bowen must take care of me until I find some one who will consent to share my fortunes with me, through the journey of life."

"I'll be very glad to have you here," said Mrs. Bowen, "but I think gentlemen ought not to put off marrying too long."

"You agree with Dr. Franklin," said Waring.

"Yes, sir," she said. "He was a wise man, and gave good advice about most things."

"He was an intensely selfish old fellow, in my opinion," said De Vane; "and reduced every thing in heaven and earth, to the standard of his utilitarian philosophy."

"He aspired simply to be a philosopher," said Waring.

"The high-priest of selfishness!" said De Vane. "Still, he may be right about marriage."

"He was not without sentiment," said Waring. "Upon one of his visits to Boston, he caused marble monuments to be placed over the graves of his parents, and they may be seen now in the burying-ground lying on one of the principal streets of that city."

"Of course," said De Vane, "a philosopher would hardly overlook such a duty as to pay respect to the memory of a parent, but I detest the philosophy that instructs a man to do right, simply because it is profitable to do so."

"There certainly should be a higher sentiment than that in our moral code," said Waring.

"Yes," said De Vane. "I would not have a man run up a calculation every time a moral question addresses itself to him, that he may ascertain what he will make or lose by taking one side or the other of it."

"He was an economist in all things," said Waring.

"Yes," said De Vane. "You may take his Poor Richard Almanacs, and all that class of his writings, into the account, and you will find it a mere code of selfishness. His appeal to the passions, to go to bed early and rise early, was not based upon any moral or æsthetical view, but upon the idea that they would save a certain amount of money by employing the light of the sun, rather than that of candles."

"But," said Waring, "after all, that was sensible enough."

"Sensible enough," said De Vane; "but that is just what I object to in it. The inevitable money question is introduced into every thing. He was essentially material in his ideas—of the earth, earthy. Even in the great debates upon the Federal Constitution, when two rival sections were in conflict about the largest questions—questions involving principles essential to the perpetuity of free institutions—his idea was not to ascertain which was really the true principle, and insist upon it until it triumphed; but he was for a compromise, and he could employ no better figure than one taken from mechanics. If, in making a broad table, you can not make the joints fit, you must take a little from each edge; just as if moral questions were to be treated as deal planks."

Waring laughed. "I have often observed," he said, "how poorly figures taken from physics illustrate moral propositions. Still, as Mrs. Bowen teaches the same philosophy in regard to early marriages that Dr. Franklin does, we must admit that it is worth consideration."

"Certainly," said De Vane. "I am ready to accept Mrs. Bowen as authority upon any question. I have always found her a good adviser."

"I'm obliged to you, Mr. De Vane," she said. "I always wish to advise for the best; and as to marrying early in life, I'm sure that I'm right."

"You must be more earnest in your exhortations, then, to Waring," he said. "He is suffering the time to slip."

"I've been thinking of that," said Mrs. Bowen, "and I'm glad that you've mentioned it."

"Much obliged," said Waring. "I shall take the subject into serious consideration."

"Are you going out to preaching to-night, Mr. Waring?" asked Mrs. Bowen.

"No, not this evening," said Waring. "I will stay with De Vane, as he has been absent so long."

"So this is the evening for your preaching," said De Vane. "I had forgotten it. Every Wednesday evening, I believe, you set apart for that service."

"Yes," said Waring; "that is our usage."

"Well," said Mrs. Bowen, "I must let Mr. Springfield know that you have arrived, Mr. De Vane. The last time I saw him, he asked me about you."

"Thank you," said De Vane. "If he should ask after me this evening, do give him my best regards, and say that I will soon call on him."

Mrs. Bowen rose from the table, put on her bonnet and shawl, and calling for a servant-girl, started for the church, which was only some three blocks from her house.

The gentlemen went up to Waring's room, to continue their conversation, which lasted deep into the night.

At breakfast the next morning, Mrs. Bowen informed De Vane that she had met Mr. Springfield at church the previous evening, and that, upon his asking after him, she had delivered his message.

"He seemed very glad to hear that you had arrived," said Mrs. Bowen, "and said that he should be happy to see you at his house."

"Very much obliged," said De Vane. "What do you say, Waring, to our calling this evening?"

"I shall be happy to join you," said Waring.

So it was arranged that they should pass the evening at Mr. Springfield's. Waring went to the College to look after his duties, and De Vane proceeded to arrange his room in a way to suit him, unpacking his trunk, and distributing his books in a home fashion.

In the afternoon, he invited Waring to walk with him, and taking the livery-stable in their way, they entered it, and examined De Vane's horses. Waring, who sympathized with De Vane in his taste for horses, was greatly pleased with them, pronouncing them quite equal, if not superior, to any he had seen.

"I observe," said he, "that the two bays are closely matched."

"Yes," said De Vane. "I train my horses to harness. It is a mistake to suppose that their gaits are injured by it, unless they are used to draw burdens, or in heavy carriages; but if worked only in a sulky, or in some light vehicle, I am satisfied that their action is improved by it. I do not suffer any horse of mine to pace, as it is called. A firm, clear trot is much to be preferred. It is my intention to keep a light barouche, and we shall enjoy evening drives."

"How could you select horses so closely resembling each other?" asked Waring.

"They are full brothers," said De Vane. "This one, which you observe is slightly the larger of the two, is one year older than the other. They are of the best English breed, imported by my father into Virginia."

"They are very superior," said Waring.

"Bring out the sorrel," said De Vane to his servant.

He entered the stall, and led out a beautiful horse, not quite so large as the bays, but in other respects fully equal to them.

"There," said De Vane, "is the most faultless horse that I know. Observe his shoulder; the slope is perfect, and the fore-arm, long and broad, secures fine action, while the arched loin and well-muscled hind-legs give him great power and speed."

Waring expressed the highest admiration for him.

"Do you observe his halter?" said De Vane.

Waring stepped forward to the head of the horse, and saw his own name worked on the morocco head-band.

"You have named him for me," he said. "It is a compliment."

"He is yours," said De Vane. "I brought him out for you, and I hope that you will like him."

"You are not serious," said Waring, "in taking all this trouble for me, and in making me such a splendid gift?"

"I assure you," said De Vane, "I was never more serious, and the gift would be a very poor compensation for the great obligations under which you have brought me by your trouble with me for some years. But the gift is not intended as a compensation, but merely as an acknowledgment of my sense of your kindness."

"I accept the horse, De Vane, frankly, as a mark of your friendship, not as any acknowledgment of an obligation; for you are under none to me. But the gift is a valuable one, and if our relations were other than they are, I could not accept it," said Waring.

"The horse," said De Vane, "came from my own place, and his blood is of the best in Virginia."

"Is he named?" asked Waring.

"Yes," said De Vane; "Ivanhoe—resembling his namesake in all high qualities."

Waring caressed the horse, who seemed to recognize him as a friend, by that subtle instinct which animals often exhibit, and from that hour the strongest attachment grew up between them.

The gentlemen extended their walk to other parts of the town, and entered the public garden. The fine evening drew many promenaders to its walks, and among them Mr. and Mrs. Clarendon. De Vane advanced to speak with them.

"We welcome you, sir," said Mr. Clarendon, grasping his hand warmly, "to your home and to your friends."

"Thank you, sir," said De Vane. "I am most happy to meet you once more, and to see Mrs. Clarendon in improved health. You are enjoying this pure air, I hope, madam?"

"Yes," said Mrs. Clarendon; "it is delightful, and I welcome you once more to a place which I know you love so well."

De Vane bowed.

"I think, madam," said Waring, "that we must not suffer him to wander from us again. We all felt his absence."

"Very much," she replied, "and I am gratified to learn that Mr. De Vane is to make this place his home."

"That is quite settled, is it, De Vane?" asked Mr. Clarendon.

"Quite settled," he replied. "And you can well understand how my interest in the place deepens, from the fact that it is a settled question that this is to be my residence."

"I congratulate you, De Vane," said Mr. Clarendon. "You have chosen wisely. Much as I love our native State—the glorious Old Dominion—I know no place in the world so attractive to me as this; and, as I said to you some time since, I know you, and I am confident that this is the place for you."

"Thank you," said De Vane. "I quite agree with you; and you will allow me to say, that the wish to be near you was one of the chief considerations that influenced my decision in fixing upon this place as my home."

Mr. Clarendon bowed.

Mrs. Clarendon said: "Then, Mr. De Vane, we shall hope to see much of you. You must come to us as you would to your home. I think Mr. Clarendon was really unhappy while you were absent, and was immensely gratified when he learned, through Mr. Waring, that after a full survey of your ancestral home, you had decided to return to us."

"I am very much gratified to hear you say so, madam," said De Vane. "Mr. Clarendon well knows how much his counsels have influenced me."

"You have done wisely, sir," said Mr. Clarendon, taking out his handsome snuff-box, and extending it to De Vane. "You have done wisely, sir, and time will prove it."

"I shall reënter the office on Monday," said De Vane, "and go to work. My vacation has been quite long enough."

"So it has," said Mr. Clarendon, "and I shall expect you."

"In the mean while," said Mrs. Clarendon, "we shall hope to see you."

De Vane bowed.

"Come with him, Professor Waring," said Mrs. Clarendon.

"Thank you," said Waring, "I shall be happy to do so."

Other persons approaching, Waring and De Vane lifted their hats and passed on. Seating themselves, at the end of the walk, upon one of the benches, they surveyed the animated scene, and a glow of the highest satisfaction overspread De Vane's face.

"This is a charming place, Waring," said he. "I really know no place where the same elegance and refinement are to be found. The place is large enough to be free from the petty annoyances of a village, and it is not so large as to be troubled with the vices of a city. It is full, too, of animation; never dull, never languid, but always cheerful."

"So I think," said Waring; "and my attachment to it has become so strong, that I fear I could not live with contentment elsewhere."

"Of course not," said De Vane; "that is not to be thought of. This is our abiding place."

At that moment the gardener came up, his face beaming, his hat in his hand, and, bowing very low to De Vane, said:

"How do you do, sir? I'm very glad to see you back once more."

"Ah! Mr. Swan, I'm glad to see you," said De Vane, shaking hands with him. "How have you been through the summer?"

"Very well, I thank you, sir," he replied. "You're looking very hearty."

"Oh! yes, thank you," said De Vane, "my health is

excellent. I see that you still keep your garden in fine order."

"I'm very much obliged to you, sir, for saying so. Let me cut one or two of my roses for you." And walking to one of the beds, he clipped some two or three of the finest flowers, and returning with them, handed them to De Vane.

"I know that you are fond of flowers, sir," he said, "and you see how fine these are."

"Very fine, indeed. Thank you," said De Vane, placing them in his vest.

"And you will stay here now, sir?" asked the gardener, with real interest.

"Yes," said De Vane; "this is now my home, and I shall be often a visitor to your garden."

"You will always be welcome, sir," said Mr. Swan, bowing low; and bidding good evening to the gentlemen, he walked away.

"That is one of your prime favorites, De Vane, I believe?" said Waring.

"Yes," said De Vane, "I like him. He is a capital gardener, and understands his business thoroughly. It would surprise you to hear him talk of botany."

"Your friend Hobbs, the blacksmith, is anxious to see you," said Waring. "He has asked after you several times."

"Yes," said De Vane, "he is a good friend of mine, and is really an artist. I must see him, and get him to look after my horses' shoes at once."

"Let us take a turn through the garden," said Waring, "and then return. As we are to pass the evening at Mr. Springfield's, let us go early."

Rising, they walked through a serpentine path, and emerged, at the end of it, into the street. They met a number of persons, who stopped to congratulate De Vane upon his return, and when they reached Mrs. Bowen's, the candles were already lighted.

"Shall we go before taking tea?" asked De Vane.

"Oh! yes," said Waring. "Mrs. Springfield will certainly expect us."

"Then," said De Vane, "I will detain you but a moment;" and going to his room to make some change in his dress, Waring explained to Mrs. Bowen that they were going out for the evening, and that they might not return very early.

"Very well," said Mrs. Bowen. "I understand. And you are right to go early, for I know that Mr. Springfield will expect you."

## CHAPTER VI.

> "SHE is most fair, and thereunto
> Her life doth rightly harmonize;
> Feeling or thought that was not true
> Ne'er made less beautiful the blue
> Unclouded heaven of her eyes."
>
> LOWELL.

WARING and De Vane were received at the door by Mr. Springfield, who gave the young Virginian a warm welcome, and conducted them to the library. Mrs. Springfield and Esther were seated near a bright wood fire, which threw its cheerful light over the objects in the room, and tempered the cool October air. The picture warmed De Vane's heart instantly, and the cheerful, tasteful elegance of the room recalled the past vividly.

Mrs. Springfield advanced to meet him with cordial greetings, and, taking his hand, said: "We are very happy to see you, Mr. De Vane; we welcome you with our hearts."

De Vane bowed very low, and said: "I shall not undertake to say, madam, how happy I am to return. I thank you for your welcome."

Esther remained standing at her chair, from which she had risen as De Vane entered. Never had she appeared more splendidly beautiful. Her face was radiant. She was dressed in rich dark colors; and in her hair a single crimson rose was worn, lending its fragrance and beauty to her own charms.

De Vane advanced to her, and gave her his hand, saying: "You see, Miss Wordsworth, that I have made good my words. I have really been able to resist the attractions of my Virginia home, and I am here once more."

Esther smiled brightly, and said: "We must all thank you, Mr. De Vane, for your loyalty to this place. Your friends are very happy to see you here."

Waring observed them closely, and he saw how earnestly they both spoke. He saw the mutual consciousness when their eyes met; and he did not doubt from that moment that their interest in each other was too deep to be evanescent. For good or for evil they had met, and all their future was to take its coloring from that meeting. He saw this with blended satisfaction and anxiety. He knew both De Vane and Esther well, and he comprehended how many perils surrounded their path—the aristocratic prejudice of General De Vane; the high self-respect of Esther, and her firm religious sentiments, both of which he felt would be able to control her action, even against her affections; and he could not dismiss from his own heart a troubled interest in the fortunes of two beings who were so dear to him.

De Vane seated himself, and said: "I can never be other than loyal to this place; it is now my home, and henceforth I am bound to it by every tie of interest and affection."

"Content to give up your Virginia mountains?" said Waring playfully.

"Reserving the privilege," replied De Vane, "of making them an occasional visit."

"We must give Mr. De Vane the greater credit," said Esther, "in deciding to reside here, because he has given up so beautiful a country as the mountain region of Virginia."

"Thank you for your generosity," said De Vane; "you

have answered Mr. Waring so well that I need say nothing more in vindication of myself."

"Mr. Waring knows," said Mr. Springfield, "that in fixing upon this as our residence, we too, yielded up much that is dear to us. Georgia is a great State, and that part of it where we resided possesses many attractions."

"Yes," said Waring, "I have often said so to Mr. De Vane, but he always insisted that nothing could rival the scenery of his Virginia home."

"I remember," said Esther, "that he was very eloquent in praise of it, some months since, when we all met at Leasowes."

"Yes," said De Vane, "I well remember the conversation; and I think Mr. Waring was equally enthusiastic in speaking of Georgia. He said something about mountains and cataracts, and seemed somewhat disposed to dispute the claims of Niagara to possess sublimity."

"Then," said Mrs. Springfield, "I think that we may all congratulate each other upon finding a place like this, which can compensate us for giving up homes endeared to us by early associations, and the charms of nature."

"Did you find the journey a pleasant one, Mr. De Vane?" asked Mr. Springfield.

"The first part of it quite otherwise," said De Vane. "The mountain streams were so much swollen as to impede my progress seriously, but after that I enjoyed the travel."

"You did not take the stage-coach, I believe?" said Mr. Springfield.

"No," said De Vane; "I traveled with my own horses, which I found much more agreeable to me."

"Oh! very much more so," said Mr. Springfield.

"We enjoyed the journey," said Mrs. Springfield, "greatly. We found every part of it agreeable to us. The season was a fine one."

"And the most agreeable part of it," said Esther, "was in traversing the mountain roads. The streams were clear and beautiful, and we drove through many of them, the wheels passing over the graveled beds, without the slightest obstruction. We found the farm-houses, too, positively delightful resting-places: the coldest water, the purest milk, the sweetest butter, and the most delicious fruits refreshed us after the day's travel."

"And the cheapness of every thing," said Mr. Springfield, "was as remarkable as its quality. We had four horses and our servants, and I could travel at much less expense than I can stay at home."

"That is remarkable," said Waring. "I found it so in the eastern part of Tennessee, a country singularly beautiful. If it were on the Continent of Europe, it would be as attractive to travelers as Switzerland."

"It will yet become so," said De Vane. "It is just now somewhat inaccessible, and at times almost impassable. When a thunder-storm overtakes one, in some of those mountain gorges, miles away from any human habitation, it is a wild sort of thing. I should think the ladies might find it inconvenient."

"We encountered one," said Esther, "and I really enjoyed it. It was terrific, but yet sublime. And it recalled vividly Lord Byron's description of a storm on the Alps, which I had read but a little while before."

"And you had no fear?" asked De Vane.

"I was awed," said Esther, "but I was unconscious of fear. The sublimity of the scene filled my soul. And when the storm passed away, and the sun came forth in his glory, like a monarch to resume his throne after a battle, throwing his splendor over mountain-peaks, and filling the valley through which we drove with his yellow beams, I felt that I had never seen any thing half so lovely."

De Vane listened to her description with the deepest interest. Her face glowed with animation, and the dark splendors of her deep blue eyes was almost dazzling.

"Had you any shelter to protect you from the fury of the storm?" asked Waring.

"None whatever," she replied, "except a projecting rock from the mountain-side, which actually trembled with the reverberations, and heightened the effect of the scene, making one realize the sublime descriptions of the prophets, which represent the earth as conscious of the dread majesty of its Maker, when he looks upon it, and touches the hills."

"I well remember it," said Mr. Springfield. "The horses shook with fear, and it was no easy matter to control them."

"I observed the same effect upon mine," said De Vane; "and they could only be restrained from breaking away by my voice, which seemed to reässure them, as I spoke to them in firm, cheerful tones, from time to time. They would draw nearer to me, as if for protection."

"Your friend and my friend, Mrs. Bowen, seemed very happy that you have arrived safely," said Mr. Springfield, smiling.

"Oh! yes," said De Vane, "she gave me a warm welcome; and upon entering my room, I saw that I had not been forgotten during my absence."

"You may be quite sure of that," said Waring. "I think that for at least a month past your room has been dusted every morning, just as if you were expected by sunset."

They all laughed, and Mrs. Springfield said: "She is a most excellent person, and you are fortunate, Mr. De Vane, in having so good a friend."

"So I think, madam," said De Vane. "I prize her highly."

"I think," said Mr. Springfield, "it would be hard for

her to decide whether she was more partial to Mr. De Vane or to Mr. Waring."

"It certainly would," said Mrs. Springfield, "for she speaks of you both in terms which imply perfection in both."

"She is really very kind," said Waring; "and I have no thought of leaving her hospitable home until I set up my own."

"And have you decided when that is to be?" asked Mrs. Springfield.

"Oh! no," said Waring; "that is yet in the mists of the future."

"And will only be disclosed, I suppose," said De Vane, "when the Maid of the Mist reveals herself in a rainbow of hope."

"Ah!" said Waring, "you have been reading Sir Walter Scott."

"A very good way of parrying the point," said De Vane.

"We must insist upon his being more explicit," said Mrs. Springfield.

De Vane observed that Esther heard the conversation, playful as it was, with interest. She was silent, but aroused and attentive.

"Has he been at all demonstrative in any direction since I left, Miss Wordsworth?" inquired De Vane.

"Have I Mr. Waring's permission," said Esther, "to report him during the summer?"

"I think," said Waring, "that we should first call upon Mr. De Vane to give an account of himself during his absence. It is usual for travelers to entertain their friends upon their return home with a recital of their adventures. That, at least, is the classical style, and so true a friend to the classics as Mr. De Vane, can not, I am sure, resist the examples of Ulysses and Æneas."

"It would require a summer's day or a winter's evening at least," said De Vane, "to relate my adventures, and I insist that so simple a thing as a reply to my question might be disposed of at once. The adroitness of my friend in turning the examination from himself to me rather heightens my interest in the subject."

"So soon as you obtain Mr. Waring's permission," said Esther, "I shall be happy to relate all that I know of his adventures during the summer."

"We will wait," said Waring, "until we go out for an evening's ride, and then you are at liberty to give an account to Mr. De Vane of our summer doings, provided he in the mean while shall enlighten us as to his own movements."

"What if I have nothing to disclose?" said De Vane.

"That supposition is hardly to be tolerated," said Waring. "Virginia the place and Mr. De Vane the man, these two being known to us, we can not permit ourselves to believe that three months could pass by without events well worthy to be recounted."

"The proposition is stated in a very scholarly way," said De Vane, "and is so complimentary to me, that if there were any thing of interest to relate, I should at once, like Æneas in the presence of the Carthaginian queen, begin the narration. But mine was a simple visit to an old home, where I wandered upon the mountains and roamed through the forests, and saw some few friends of the family, and almost felt myself a boy once more."

"Some fair ladies, of course, you met," said Waring.

"Yes," said De Vane, "the Guilfords, of whom you have heard me speak, and the Hamiltons, who reside near us."

"I remember that you spoke of the Hamiltons in one of your letters," said Waring.

"They are charming people," said De Vane; "much the

most agreeable I met. Elegance without pretension, wealth without pride, piety without bigotry, accomplishments without folly—these are their characteristics."

"They must be charming," said Mrs. Springfield. "I have heard Bishop Mc Kendree speak of them in similar terms."

"They are dear friends of the Bishop, I know, madam," said De Vane. "They have a son at this time in Europe, at the University at Heidelberg. Two daughters are with them. The elder of the two—about eighteen years of age, I suppose—is faultlessly beautiful, and resembling Miss Godolphin so closely that I was constantly reminded of her."

"She must indeed be beautiful," said Esther.

"Very much so," said De Vane.

"You spoke of the Guilfords," said Waring.

"Yes," said De Vane, "they are intimate with my aunt, Mrs. De Vane, and I saw them often."

"I have heard Miss Godolphin describe Miss Clara Guilford as very beautiful and accomplished," said Waring.

"She is so," said De Vane, "highly so. A more brilliant person one rarely meets, and she possesses the quality of preserving her American habits, notwithstanding her very decided taste for European life. She rides on horseback, over mountains and plains, in the most fearless way, and I found it actually exhilarating to accompany her in some of her daring feats. We rode one morning, after a very early breakfast, to Monticello, Mr. Jefferson's seat, and finding one of the gates which lay in our way fastened, she drew back a few steps, and dashing forward, leaped the fence, her horse clearing it magnificently. I, of course, followed, and found it somewhat of an exploit."

"Fine," said Waring, "fine; and yet she prefers Europe to America?"

"She prefers England," said De Vane, "and I think she will never live in this country with any thing like satisfaction. She is thoroughly aristocratic, and has many near relatives in England—some of them of very high rank."

"She is very unlike Miss Godolphin, then," said Esther. "She is wholly American, and yet I believe is nearly related to some of the noble families of England."

"And I admire her for it," said De Vane. "Miss Godolphin is a superior person."

"She is indeed," said Esther. "I have been much with her through the summer, and I have learned to love her as much as I admire her. She will be very much pleased to meet you, Mr. De Vane."

"I shall take an early day to call on her," said De Vane. "I bear messages to her from Miss Guilford, which I must deliver in person."

"They met in Europe, I believe," said Esther. "I have heard Miss Godolphin speak of her."

"They were much together while abroad," said De Vane, "and under circumstances of extraordinary interest. Miss Guilford gave me an extended account of their travels."

"And yet," said Waring, "the one returns to this country estranged from home, while the other loves it more intensely than ever."

"Miss Godolphin," said De Vane, "is a person of great depth of character. She has had a large experience of life for one so young, and it has not resulted in making her artificial, but rather in deepening and strengthening the nobler qualities of her nature."

"Is not that a common experience?" said Esther.

"I think not," said De Vane. "Very much depends upon organization, however. A noble poet—Lord Byron—tells us,

'The tree of knowledge is not that of life.'

His doctrine is that a knowledge of the world exposes its heartlessness, and disgusts us with life."

"A life of dissipation, a life passed amidst scenes which ignore the restraints of Christianity and civilization alike, must disgust us with the world," said Waring, "because it first disgusts us with ourselves. It is a sorrow that worketh death."

"That is a very harsh judgment upon the noble poet," said De Vane. "I firmly believe that Byron was sadly sinned against. The truth is, when society rises up against a man who has violated some of its conventionalisms, it is terrific in its persecution. I regard the whole history of Lord Byron's life with compassion. He felt that his race was making war upon him, and he replied to their assaults with scorn and indignation. But there breaks through all this, at times, the cry of a wounded spirit. Is it not his own sadness that he describes in those lines of inconsolable sorrow, too deep for the ministering tenderness of heaven or earth to read—

'It is that settled ceaseless gloom
The fabled Hebrew wanderer bore,
Which will not look beyond the tomb,
Yet dares not hope for rest before'?"

"It is dreadful," said Esther. "What wretchedness that must be which neither heaven nor earth can minister to! I confess that I am strongly disposed to pity Lord Byron. Such genius, such unhappiness, such a splendid wreck so early in life! There was great tenderness in his nature. It seems to have been perverted by the misguiding hand of his own mother."

"Yes," said De Vane, "your judgment is just. If he had married differently, his life would have been a different one. His wife is evidently a cold person—wholly under the dominion of the rules of society, which are called practical, too often but another name for selfishness. The mother and the wife both helped to ruin him. There was no sympathy with his real nature, and his infirmities grew to be crimes against society."

"And do you believe," said Waring, "that there was any real tenderness in his nature? He was harsh and vindictive. The rules of society which he violated, are essential to its protection."

"There certainly was great tenderness in his nature," said Esther. "The opening lines of one of the cantos of his Childe Harold attest it unmistakably:

> 'Ada, sole daughter of my house and heart,
> Is thy face like thy mother's,
> My fair child?'

It has been some time since I read the lines, but I believe I quote them correctly; and I well remember how this blending of the names of daughter and mother affected me when I read them, and thought of his exile and his desolateness—destined never again to see wife or child."

De Vane heard this beautiful, pure being vindicate the claims of the noble but ruined man to the forbearance of society, and the tender judgment of a world that survived him, with the deepest admiration for her courage and her truth; and even Waring found his heart touched with a new sympathy for the man whose genius he had admired, but whose course he unsparingly condemned, because he thought it likely to mislead others.

A servant entered, and announced to Mrs. Springfield that supper was on the table. And De Vane, giving his arm to Esther, said:

"We must, at some future time, renew this discussion."

"Then," said Waring, as they took their seats, "I must find an ally in Miss Godolphin. If I do not misinterpret a remark of hers, she will join me in condemnation of the noble poet."

"I have the impression," said De Vane, "that she has seen him. I am very sure that she is familiar with his history. And I think Miss Guilford informed me that Miss Godolphin had met Lord Byron, when she was very young."

"The critics have treated him with such unfairness," said Mr. Springfield, "that I find myself strongly inclined to search for some ground upon which a man of such splendid abilities may be vindicated against his accusers."

"His reply to the critics," said Waring, "makes one half inclined to pity them."

"It is somewhat strange," said Mr. Springfield, "that Sir Walter Scott not only admired Lord Byron, but felt for him a sincere friendship."

"Yes," said De Vane, "and Lord Byron felt a true regard for Sir Walter; and their friendship is in itself a proof that Lord Byron possessed redeeming qualities; for Sir Walter Scott was a pure man, and no friendship could have existed on his part toward any man totally abandoned."

"So I think," said Mr. Springfield.

"Miss Godolphin," said Mrs. Springfield, "went to Europe some five or six years since, and she may have met Lord Byron."

"Yes," said De Vane. "He was then in Italy, projecting his enterprise in behalf of the Greeks; and I know that some persons, very nearly related to Miss Godolphin, accompanied him into Greece."

Esther fixed her eyes searchingly upon De Vane's face, as if she would read his whole meaning. It was clear that he had touched a topic which interested her, one in some way connected with the history of Miss Godolphin; and she waited with anxiety to see if he would add any thing which might make it plain that he was acquainted with it. But he said nothing more.

"She was the brightest young person at that time," said Mrs. Springfield, "that I had ever known. Animated, vivacious, joyous; and so young, yet so cultivated. She is even more beautiful now than she was then, for her extreme youth was full of promise only, which has now matured into perfection. She is splendidly beautiful, but there is a shadow upon her brightness which I do not comprehend."

De Vane said not a word.

Mr. Springfield said: "I think Miss Godolphin is fast regaining her cheerfulness. She may have lost some near relative abroad, which plunged her into grief; but whatever may have caused her sadness, it is evidently passing away."

"Yes, I think so," said Mrs. Springfield.

"Did you carry out your purpose, Miss Wordsworth," asked De Vane, "of taking rides in the saddle?"

"Oh! yes," she replied. I was in the country for some time with Miss Godolphin, and it was our habit to ride on horseback daily."

"Yes, sir," said Waring. "I am happy to be able to assure you that the ladies both ride excellently. They, of course, ride with grace, and they manage their steeds with admirable skill."

"I must thank you," said Esther. "I can assure you, Mr. De Vane, that it is more than Mr. Waring ever said to us."

"I am bound to make a faithful report to my friend, Mr. De Vane," said Waring, "of your progress during his absence. I think I promised something of the kind, did I not?"

Esther's conscious blush was her only reply; but De Vane said:

"I believe it was understood that you were to keep me informed of events that interested our friends; but he really wrote so rarely, Miss Wordsworth, that I did not know but I might be forgotten before my return."

"Wrote so rarely, indeed!" said Waring. "I think I wrote punctually, every Thursday morning; but I was absolutely neglected. Whether I must attribute it to politics, or to the Virginia ladies, or whatever else, I can not say; but I received only some two or three letters from him through the whole summer."

"You know, Waring," said De Vane, "how unjust that accusation is. I assure you, Mrs. Springfield, that I was so engrossed with business, that I found but little leisure for writing to friends; for when I was disengaged from actual occupation, I found it necessary to ramble through the woods to refresh myself. It would have been any thing but a kindness to inflict letters upon a friend, written in moments of weariness. And besides this, I was for some weeks engaged in a struggle to free myself from restraints about me, which threatened to become life-long, unless I was vigorous in resisting them; and it would have been selfish to write under circumstances, when I must have recited to a friend what would not have been agreeable to him."

"We are so happy to have you with us again, Mr. De Vane," said Mrs. Springfield, "that we may very well excuse your silence, while engaged in preparations for your return."

"So I think," said Mr. Springfield.

"Well," said Waring, "as a general amnesty seems to be agreed on, I shall not be so unamiable as to disturb it."

"I hope," said De Vane, "that the horseback riding is not to be relinquished."

"By no means," said Esther. "We must enjoy this fine season. The evenings are cool and bracing."

"I shall enjoy the rides more than I have ever done," said Waring; "for my friend, Mr. De Vane, has generously brought me from Virginia a very fine horse."

"That is a treasure," said Mr. Springfield.

"Does he equal Manfred?" asked Esther.

"I think he does, fully," said Waring; "and that is high praise, you know."

"Manfred?" said De Vane. "I have not the honor of his acquaintance."

"No," said Waring; "he arrived after your departure. He is Miss Wordsworth's Arabian."

"Then I hope soon to be introduced to him. Is he an Arabian?" said De Vane.

"Yes," said Mr. Springfield, "and a very fine animal. Having a decided taste for horses, I have taken great trouble to secure the best breeds; and I have bestowed the same care on Esther's plantation that I have on my own. We own several imported horses, and among them is Manfred."

"I sympathize strongly with your taste," said De Vane. "I must show you two of my own horses. They are of our very best blood, imported into Virginia from England, and I think an improvement on the original stock."

"They are very fine," said Waring; "but I think that Mr. De Vane, with his accustomed generosity, has presented to me the finest of the three."

"I am glad that you think so," said De Vane; "but it would be no easy task to decide between the rival claims of three animals really so fine."

"I shall take great pleasure in seeing them," said Mr. Springfield. "The taste for fine horses is one which I think grows on us. I doubt if we ever lose it. I believe that Esther has it as intensely as I have."

"I believe so," said Esther. "I care little for fine carriages, or luxurious vehicles of any shape. I like them simply neat. But I do love fine horses."

"You are very unlike the Spanish ladies, then," said De Vane. "They rejoice in splendid equipages—the harness loaded with plate—and content themselves with mules to draw them."

"Some of them are very fine, though," said Waring. "The Andalusian race is said to rival the finest horses."

"Nothing," said De Vane, "can ever rival a blooded horse; and I could not be induced either to ride or drive any other. But we must arrange for an equestrian excursion very soon, Miss Wordsworth."

"With pleasure," said Esther. "But we must first see Miss Godolphin."

"Of course," said De Vane. "When shall we call, Mr. Waring?"

"At any moment that it may be agreeable to you," said Waring.

"Very good," replied De Vane. "Then it shall be early."

"You will find Mr. Waring," said Esther, "ready to accompany you, I am sure, at any time."

"Ah! he is not reluctant, then, to place himself in danger," said De Vane.

"He has shown some courage in that way during the summer," said Esther, "and I suppose has lost nothing of his spirit."

"I think, Professor," said Mr. Springfield, "that your friends are so much interested in you, they observe your movements."

"I regard it as a compliment," said Waring; "and I frankly admit that one who visits Miss Godolphin often, will find it no easy task to remain indifferent to her charms; but I have so long escaped danger, that I am not easily alarmed."

"Take care, Mr. Waring," said Mrs. Springfield. "I think Miss Godolphin very fascinating."

"I freely confess that," said Waring.

"No one can dispute it who knows her," said De Vane. "She is very attractive."

"She has made a great impression since her return from Europe," said Mrs. Springfield. "I hear every one speak of her in terms of the highest admiration."

"The real nobleness of her nature can only be appreciated by those who know her well," said Esther.

"And has Mr. Waring learned to know her well?" asked De Vane.

"He must answer for himself," said Esther. "He certainly has had the opportunity to learn her real character."

"Come," said Mrs. Springfield, "I shall protest against Professor Waring's being so closely pressed."

"Thank you, madam," said Waring. "It is not the first time you have shown yourself my friend."

"Mrs. Springfield has rescued you at a very critical conjuncture," said De Vane, laughing. "At some time, Miss Wordsworth, we must attack him when he is not supported by his allies."

Rising, they returned to the library, where the conversation became general, turning upon the state of the country, at that time much excited by the presidential canvass, just drawing toward its close.

After some time, De Vane requested Esther to give them some music; and conducting her to the piano, she took up some new sheets of music, which had been placed there that day for the first time.

"What shall I sing, Mr. De Vane?" asked Esther.

"You must do me the favor to make your own selection," he replied.

"Then," she said, "I will sing one of the songs of Lord

Byron, of whom we have just been speaking. I never saw the music before to-day, but it rivals the lines, and that is great praise."

"Ah! and what are the lines?" asked De Vane.

"They are one of the Hebrew melodies of the noble poet; sad, of course, but exquisitely tender and beautiful," said Esther. "He calls them Herod's Lament for Mariamne; and they are founded upon the account in Jewish history of the murder of that beautiful woman, by a misinterpreted order of Herod, upon his departure for battle."

She sang the lines with matchless pathos, giving to them a depth and tenderness which were irresistible. When she ceased, every one in the room was in tears, De Vane striving in vain to repress his emotion.

"Wonderful!" exclaimed Waring. "Absolutely wonderful! I never comprehended the anguish which Herod must have felt, until now. It is the saddest incident in history—the murder of the beautiful Mariamne, and the impotent rage and self-accusing remorse of Herod upon his return."

"I do not know," said De Vane, "whether the lines or the music affect us most. There is wonderful pathos in both. Thanks, Miss Wordsworth: I have once more heard *music*."

Esther rose from the instrument, and soon after the gentlemen took their leave.

"Waring," said De Vane, "Miss Wordsworth is the most extraordinary person I have ever known. Her accomplishments alone would make her peerless; but when you regard her character, she is absolutely wonderful. I have compared her with others, and when absent from her, thought that some might rival her in personal charms and accomplishments; but since I have seen her once more, I do not hesitate to pronounce her superior to any woman on earth."

"I am not surprised to hear you speak of her in such terms," said Waring. "She is a very lovely person, and her whole life is as remarkable as her beauty and her accomplishments."

"You heard me speak of Miss Guilford this evening," said De Vane. "It was the aim of my aunt to bring about our marriage. Her soul was interested in it. I never witnessed so intense a desire on the part of any one to accomplish an object; and we were thrown with each other on every occasion. We rode together, walked together, read the same books, conversed without reserve; each studied the other; and I found her a splendidly beautiful and accomplished woman. She evidently regarded me as lawful spoil, and looked upon me as her captive from the first hour we met. But while she interested me, and filled me with admiration, my heart was as tranquil as if I had been studying a historical personage, or looking daily upon a being of another realm, with whom it was impossible to feel a living sympathy."

"I felt a little nervous about you," said Waring, "though I said nothing of it in my letters to you."

"There was not the slightest occasion for it," said De Vane. "My aunt, who is really a noble woman, at length became satisfied that I could never love Clara Guilford; and she has too much heart to wish me to marry one whom I could not love, so that she reluctantly relinquished her scheme. She then spoke to me about Miss Wordsworth, remarking that I had written of her in glowing terms, and that she feared for me. She spoke with kindness, but perfect frankness, and said that it would make my father very unhappy if he supposed it possible that I could ever form such a connection; that she knew he would never require me to marry any woman who was distasteful to me; but that she was equally sure he would never give his consent to my marrying any one at all inferior to me in social position. Wealth he cared nothing about. We had that. But social position he did value. I then gave my aunt an account of Miss Wordsworth throughout; described her as she is—her beauty of person, her accomplishments, her intellect, her character, her self-sacrificing life, her freshness, her soul. In short, I said to her all that you can imagine I would say of such a woman; and I saw that my aunt was interested. 'But then,' said she, 'she is a Methodist, and the daughter of a Methodist preacher, and your father will never tolerate that.' I insisted that such a prejudice was unworthy of any one, and that I was sure my father was too noble to suffer it to sway him, if he could but know Miss Wordsworth. I spoke of Mr. and Mrs. Springfield, and of yourself, Waring; and she became deeply interested. From day to day she spoke of the matter to me; asked minutely about Miss Wordsworth, and, indeed, about you all; and I saw that she was fast coming over to my side. She has great confidence in two things—my pride and my truthfulness. Miss Guilford had described Miss Godolphin to my aunt, and when she found that she was intimate with Miss Wordsworth, who was at that time actually her guest, as you wrote me, it effected quite a revolution in her sentiments. I said to my aunt that I felt the greatest interest in Miss Wordsworth, but that I had never made up my own mind in regard to our future relations, and that, of course, I had never spoken to her on the subject, nor could I know how she regarded me. My aunt seemed to fancy that Miss Wordsworth was too much engrossed with her benevolent and romantic scheme, as she called it, at Leasowes, ever to relinquish it, and that she could not make any man a good wife, unless she abandoned it, so far, at least, as to intrust it to others. But I became satisfied that I should find a warm supporter in Mrs. De Vane, if it ever became necessary to appeal to her, in a contest with my father, respecting Miss Wordsworth.

"I have spoken to you, Waring, with great frankness. My interview with Miss Wordsworth has reäwakened all my interest in her. She is transcendently lovely; and she is the only woman who really ever made any impression upon my heart."

In their conversation, they had unconsciously extended their walk far beyond their lodgings. They stood now near the College grounds; and the scattered lights in the windows showed that some of the students were yet busy with their books.

"De Vane," said Waring, "I am very glad that you have spoken to me. From the first day that we met each other within those walls, that now stand out against the starlit sky, I have felt an interest in you, which has deepened into unchanging friendship. My regard for Miss Wordsworth is as great as it is for yourself. Never until this evening, did I comprehend the nature of the interest which you feel in her. Allow me to say, that when you met, I observed you, and I became satisfied instantly, that what I had supposed might be only admiration, was something deeper and intenser. It has filled me with anxiety. I speak frankly; for I am too deeply interested in you to speak with indifference, or in the language of complaint. You might well hope to interest any woman. But there are great barriers between yourself and Miss Wordsworth. She is as proud as you are. A loftier spirit I never knew. She would suffer martyrdom rather than yield to a sentiment which she thought should be checked and restrained."

"But what barriers can there be?" exclaimed De Vane impatiently.

"The aristocratic position and unyielding prejudices of

General De Vane, and your own want of sympathy with the religious views of Miss Wordsworth."

De Vane was silent. He put his arm in that of Waring, and they retraced their steps.

Rising clouds swept over the heavens. The whole Southern sky was dark, and as the night-breeze strengthened, the stars began to disappear. In spite of his own judgment, De Vane felt saddened by the aspect of the heavens. That lurking belief in the sympathy of nature with our fortunes, and of its power to foreshadow coming events, which we all experience, caused him to turn his eyes anxiously upon the darkening sky; and he found more to cheer him than he would admit to himself, when the freshening wind drove the clouds before it, and he saw through the rifts a star shedding its radiance calmly amidst the surrounding gloom, and lighting the Southern horizon with its lustre, when blankness covered the face of every other planet that burned in the firmament.

## CHAPTER VII.

> WHAT is your substance, whereof are you made,
> That millions of strange shadows on you tend?
> Since every one hath, every one, one shade,
> And you, but one, can every shadow lend.
>
> SHAKESPEARE.

THE next morning, when De Vane and Waring were seated at the breakfast-table, Mr. Swan, the public gardener, entered, bearing a most elaborate bouquet. Advancing to De Vane, he made him a set speech, expressing his gratification at his return, wishing him the greatest prosperity, and concluding by asking him to be so condescending as to accept the flowers which he had gathered from his garden. De Vane thanked him for his kindness, and assured him that he appreciated the flowers, which were really beautiful; and then Mr. Swan, making a bow which was intended to be magnificent, retired.

"Those flowers are rare and beautiful," said Waring; "and Mr. Swan is certainly an admirer."

"Yes," said Mrs. Bowen, "that Mr. Swan is really a nice man; he seems to be very well disposed."

"He is quite an ardent friend of Mr. De Vane," said Waring; "and that, of course, argues a certain degree of merit in the man himself."

"Thank you," said De Vane. "But Mr. Swan is really a good man; he loves his calling, and extends his regards naturally to any one who sympathizes with his taste. I was able to explain to him, at one time, the history of a tulip of extraordinary beauty, very rarely seen in this country, and he has been my friend from that hour."

"Ranking you for wisdom with King Solomon himself," said Waring, "who spoke of trees, from the cedar-tree that is Lebanon, even unto the hyssop that springeth out of the wall."

"Then he greatly overrates my knowledge," said De Vane, laughing.

After breakfast, De Vane called Cæsar to him, and instructed him to show his servant the way to Mr. Springfield's. He then handed to Tully a small silver waiter, upon which the bouquet was placed, with a note addressed to Miss Wordsworth, and directed him to deliver it to her servant.

Tully, returning some time after, brought a note on his waiter, which he presented to his master. It was the first note that De Vane had ever received from Esther, and its perfectly graceful and faultless style, while it did not surprise—certainly charmed him. He placed it with his treasures.

In the evening, Waring proposed to De Vane that they should walk to the river, and they turned their steps in that direction. Reaching the mill, they stood to admire the scene. The flashing water flew in silver spray from the wheel; the river rushed over the rocks, which strove in vain to impede its course. Evergreen trees hung over its banks, and the vine dipped its red berries in the stream, while the sunbeams flamed over the picture, giving it a warm coloring.

"How beautiful this is!" said Waring. "Do you remember, De Vane, that we took this very walk about twelve months since?"

"Perfectly well," said De Vane; "and every thing vividly recalls it. It seems a great while, when I look back, and yet but twelve months have gone by; but what eventful months! I can scarcely recognize myself. The truth is, we date the length of existence by our emotions."

"True, most true," said Waring. "We have no actual measure of time but consciousness."

Following the windings of the stream, they came to the road leading from the ferry; and involuntarily both paused, and both were silent. With De Vane memory was busy, and Waring respected his emotions. The past rose before them both. The brilliant evening, the glowing western sky, the waters reddening under the glancing sunlight, the ferry-boat still plying between the rising banks—all were before them once more. De Vane saw through the luminous past the traveling-carriage, the party following it as it ascended the hill, and Esther in her glorious youthful beauty; and he felt that his real existence had taken its conscious vitality from that moment.

"Yes, it is true," said De Vane. "We live only as the soul receives its impressions. It sheds its own inherent light upon the outward world."

He spoke unconsciously. His eyes were fixed upon the stream, which flowed swiftly on its shining way, in itself a picture of human life: sometimes brightened by the splendors of the sun, then darkened by overhanging shadows; but, whether in sunshine or shadow, gliding onward to the wide sea.

Turning away from the scenery which so much interested them, they retraced their steps; and just as they were crossing the main street, near the State House, the splendid equipage of Mrs. Habersham drove up. Mrs. Habersham and Miss Godolphin both recognized De Vane, and the coachman being ordered to draw up his horses, the gentlemen advanced to the carriage.

"We are delighted to see you, Mr. De Vane," said Miss Godolphin, extending her hand to him, "and we give you a warm welcome."

Mrs. Habersham, too, shook his hand with real pleasure, and said: "Yes Mr. De Vane, we are happy to see you once more."

De Vane made his acknowledgments for their graciousness, and Waring coming up, they entered into conversation with the ladies, which was closed, after some minutes, by an invitation to them to pass the evening at Mrs. Habersham's, an invitation readily accepted; and the spirited horses dashed away once more.

"How resplendent Miss Godolphin is!" said De Vane. "I never saw her looking so well."

"She is brilliant," said Waring.

"Have you seen much of her through the summer?" asked De Vane.

"Yes," replied Waring. "I have been much with her. She is deeply interested in the subject of religion, and is an earnest seeker after the right way. With all her intellect, she is child-like—not childish, which is a widely different thing, but simple, truthful, guileless."

De Vane heard Waring's glowing tribute with interest, and he observed how much his ardor in speaking of Miss Godolphin had increased, since his recent intercourse with her had enabled him to study her character more closely. It was not to be wondered at; no one could know her without coming within the range of her fascination. Early in the evening they made their visit. They were received by Mrs. Habersham and Miss Godolphin with marked cordiality, and the tea service was immediately brought in. The elegance, indeed the splendor of every thing—the furniture, the pictures, the statuary—imparted an aristocratic aspect to the house, rarely seen in this country; and the tastes of both the ladies were understood to partake of the same character. A certain hauteur appeared in the manner of Mrs. Habersham, and there was a stateliness about Miss Godolphin that repelled many, who thought her pride quite equal to that of her aunt. They recognized De Vane as a peer from the first; and they had learned to appreciate Waring—to comprehend the elevation of his character and the high order of his abilities—by an intercourse with him which had now become so well established, that he was always received as a friend. His fine sense, his large attainments, his pure and yet warm nature, had won upon them both; and Miss Godolphin had unconsciously become deeply interested in him. All unacquainted with the cause of her occasional sadness, Waring saw so much to admire in the high qualities of Miss Godolphin, that he found a strange pleasure in her society; and his visits of late had become so frequent, as to attract the observation of his friends. Mr. and Mrs. Springfield, of course, could not be ignorant of his growing interest in her, and they had once or twice spoken to him playfully in regard to it. This evening De Vane became satisfied that his friend's interest in Miss Godolphin was really deep, and he felt that he could no longer forbear to disclose to him all that he had learned respecting her history from Miss Guilford during his late visit to Virginia. It so happened that the conversation turned upon subjects which touched European events.

"And you met the Guilfords, Mr. De Vane, when in Virginia, did you not?" asked Miss Godolphin.

"Often, very often. They are near neighbors, and Mrs. De Vane and Mrs. Guilford have long been friends," replied De Vane.

"We traveled with them so long in Europe," said Miss Godolphin, "that we knew them well. Not only were we with them on the Continent, but we were much together in England. Are her tastes as English as ever?"

"Quite," said De Vane. "She is to go out again early next spring."

"It does not surprise me," said Miss Godolphin. "She

can never be happy in this country. England is, in all respects, suited to her tastes."

"That is the conclusion that I reached," said De Vane.

"She is a person of extraordinary beauty," said Miss Godolphin, "and her accomplishments are rare. I felt a little curious to know how you withstood her attractions."

"I am so patriotic," said De Vane, "that I found myself in perpetual antagonism with Miss Guilford. Our disputes ran so high, that Mrs. De Vane found it necessary sometimes to interfere, for the preservation of amicable relations. She charged me with a want of loyalty to my caste, and I retorted by charging upon her a want of loyalty to the country; so that you may imagine the disputes ran high."

Miss Godolphin laughed heartily. "And so you were not ensnared?" she said.

"Oh! no," said De Vane. "There was a state of quasi-hostilities between us all the while, and she at length gave me up to my degenerate tastes."

"Clara Guilford," said Miss Godolphin, "is a splendid person—intellectual, accomplished, full of animation and energy; but she is wholly unsuited to this country. Nothing short of a visit to Europe every year or two will content her; and where one is so wholly dependent upon society for happiness, I can not believe that there is much heart. Yet she certainly is not destitute of feeling."

"No," said De Vane. "She possesses sensibility—a high degree of it; and it may be that she is not incapable of forming a very strong attachment. But I should fear that her tastes would interfere with it. She loves rank, splendor, the great world; and if she should encounter a reverse, if an eclipse should come over her fortunes, I do not know how she would bear it."

"I never thought her capable of feeling what I should call a strong attachment," said Miss Godolphin.

Mrs. Habersham and Waring had been in conversation,

but as Miss Godolphin said this, he fixed his eyes on her with a steadfast gaze, and was silent.

Mrs. Habersham observed this, and said:

"Who are you discussing, Hortensia? You must permit Mr. Waring and myself to share it."

"I was speaking with Mr. De Vane," she said, "of a friend of ours in Virginia. Do you not remember Clara Guilford?"

"Perfectly well," said Mrs. Habersham; "the most brilliant person we met in Europe."

"So I remember you thought her," said Miss Godolphin. "Mr. De Vane has been much with her through the summer, and has returned unscathed by her charms."

"That is very wonderful," said Mrs. Habersham. "I never met a more attractive person. How did you escape, Mr. De Vane?"

"It must be, madam, some defect in myself, some insensibility to such charms; or it may be that I was shielded by some invisible goddess, as Æneas was sometimes protected when in danger."

"There may be much truth in what you say," said Miss Godolphin mischievously.

"Nothing else can account for it," said Mrs. Habersham. "Do you not say so, Mr. Waring?"

"The extreme danger that Mr. De Vane was in, and the extraordinary escape which he has made, would seem to authorize such a conjecture," said Waring. "Mr. De Vane well knows that one of the rules of dramatic classical art is, never to introduce a celestial being, without something worthy of such interference should demand it; and I suppose the rule has not been violated in his case."

"But who is the celestial being that interposed?" asked Miss Godolphin.

"Some one it must have been that felt a deep interest in Mr. De Vane's welfare," said Waring.

"And lovely enough to rank with celestials, of course," said Miss Godolphin.

"It seems to me that you are combining against Mr. De Vane," said Mrs. Habersham. "I must really take part with him."

"Very well, aunt," said Miss Godolphin; "if you think it necessary to succor one who is aided by some celestial being."

"I am grateful to you, Mrs. Habersham, for your friendly sympathy," said De Vane.

"I did not understand their object when I made my remark as to the mode of your escape from Miss Guilford's charms, Mr. De Vane, I assure you. Hortensia is, I see, somewhat disposed to persecute you this evening."

"No one can be more innocent than I am, aunt. Mr. De Vane himself first suggested the nature of the assistance he had received; and I was only curious to know something of the *personnel* of a being at once so benevolent and so charming. Are you sure about her wings?"

"To all of which I can say nothing," said De Vane. "If I am indebted to celestial aid at all for my escape from the charms of Miss Guilford, the being who succored me was invisible. I only intended to assure you, in the most emphatic way, of my insensibility. Of that, there can be no doubt."

"Perhaps the revealing future may yet bring to our view the friendly goddess," said Miss Godolphin.

"If so," said De Vane, "I shall gratefully acknowledge her kind offices, and submit myself unfalteringly to her guidance."

"You could not do better, I assure you, than to do so," said Waring. "It sometimes happens in life, it may be, that an impression made on us, of which we are ourselves scarcely conscious, renders us insensible to the attractions of all the world besides, however it may array itself afterward."

Miss Godolphin's face was a study. The light which illumined it had been unusually brilliant—never more so. It was the cloudless sky of a summer day; but now a cloud stole over it, dimming its splendor. She was silent. Waring observed it, and was embarrassed. De Vane saw that the subject must be changed, and he said to Miss Godolphin that he had heard, since his arrival, of her growing taste for equestrian excursions.

"Mr. Waring informs me," he said, "that he had the pleasure of joining you in several rides during the summer."

"Yes," she replied, "Mr. Waring was good enough to accompany Miss Wordsworth and myself several times; and when in the country, we often rode the whole morning without any one to attend us. We found it delightful."

"I hope that you will not discontinue the habit," said De Vane. "I have been promising myself the pleasure of attending you frequently. Miss Wordsworth assures me that she will be ready to accompany us."

"Thank you," said Miss Godolphin. "I shall be happy to join you at any time."

"Then," said De Vane, "we will make an early arrangement for a ride. Mr. Waring will, of course, join us?"

"With the greatest pleasure," said Waring. "The fall is beautiful; and in fine weather, I much prefer the saddle to a carriage of any description."

It was settled that during the next week they should begin their excursions.

De Vane requested Miss Godolphin to give them some music.

"Do you prefer the harp or the piano?" she asked.

"Which shall it be, Mr. Waring?" said De Vane.

"With Miss Godolphin's voice, I prefer the harp," said Waring.

She instantly rose, and took her seat by the instrument.

Her fingers swept its chords with marvelous skill; and after playing a symphony of exquisite beauty, she sang those lines of Moore, so full of tender sympathy,

"Has sorrow thy young days shaded?"

And the deep, almost spiritual tenderness of her tones affected those who heard her indescribably. It was as if an angel, saddened by some scene of the past, forgot for a moment the bliss of heaven, and touched the harp attuned for celestial melody, with the tones of earthly sorrow. As the last lines were uttered by her, her clasped hands, half hidden by the drapery of her dress, disclosed the strength of her own emotions. For some minutes she did not move, and then rising slowly, she seated herself near Mrs. Habersham.

"Thank you," said De Vane. "There are no songs like those of Moore. Their beauty and tenderness are inimitable."

"It is wonderful," said Miss Godolphin, "that a person so gay as Moore should have been able to write as he does. He must have suffered."

"One would suppose so," said Waring. "It is said that a comedian in Paris, who drew immense crowds night after night, to witness his unrivaled gayeties, called on an eminent physician, to consult him in regard to a depression of spirits which he could not shake off, and which he therefore thought must be the result of physical disorganization. He called *incognito;* and the physician, unable to discover any symptoms of disease, advised him to visit the theatre, and witness the performances of the celebrated Monsieur Vaudeville, then attracting such audiences. 'Alas!' exclaimed the actor, 'I am that very Monsieur Vaudeville.' So little can we judge of the interior nature by outward gayety. It may be so with Moore."

"Moore sings his own songs exquisitely," said Miss Godolphin. "We heard him in London. He sat down quickly when invited to sing, ran his fingers over the keys of the instrument, and then sang like an *improvisatore*, giving the fullest effect to every sentiment, by his manner of uttering the words. I remember that on one occasion, in the presence of a somewhat large company, he sang one of his melodies with such resistless pathos, that every one sympathized with him; and when it was ended, he rose from his seat, bowed to the lady whose reception he graced with his presence, and glided from the room. Something was said by one of the party, within my hearing, of an early attachment between himself and the lady at whose house we were entertained."

"There is enough in the condition of his country to awaken his patriotism," said De Vane. "I wonder that he has not written more on that subject than he has. Some of his national songs are very fine."

"He is much in England," said Miss Godolphin, "and welcomed by the aristocratic circles, not only of London, but in the country; and this, of course, while it does not lessen his loyalty to Ireland, softens the asperity which characterizes all that is written by most men of genius in that country."

"Yet," said Waring, "nothing can be finer than some of his tributes to Ireland."

"Oh! unquestionably," said De Vane. "Some of them would rouse Ireland to flame, if they could be sung or recited throughout the country, as the ancient bards rehearsed their poems in the midst of their countrymen.

After some formal conversation upon local topics, the gentlemen took their leave of the ladies, and walked slowly homeward.

"You must have observed, De Vane," said Waring, "how sudden the change in Miss Godolphin's spirits was, and it was evidently caused by the conversation upon the subject of some reigning attachment, which made it impossible for one who had experienced it to feel any deep interest in another afterward. What does it mean? Can it be possible that she has loved, and loved hopelessly? One can hardly suppose so. And yet there are circumstances which, at times, almost satisfy me that it is so. What do you think of it?"

"There are recollections," said De Vane, "which sadden Miss Godolphin. I learned her history from Miss Guilford. It is proper that I should make known to you what has been stated to me. I should have written to you in regard to it, but I was unwilling to commit to paper statements of such extreme delicacy connected with the name of a lady.

"It seems that when Miss Godolphin went to Europe, now nearly five years since, when she was very young, that she passed the first six months in England with her relatives. She was much admired, and received attentions from several gentlemen, who saw her at the residence of her uncle, Sir George Godolphin. His only son, at that time barely twenty-two years of age, became very strongly attached to Miss Godolphin, and addressed her. She rejected him; and finding her stay under the same roof with her cousin embarrassing to both, she prevailed on Mrs. Habersham to go to the Continent. Passing through Paris, after a brief visit to that city, they proceeded to Italy, and took up their residence there. Lord Byron was at that time residing near the place where they had fixed their own residence, and was projecting his enterprise for aiding Greece in her great struggle for independence. He saw the ladies, and sometimes visited them. At this time young Godolphin, unable to conquer his passion, came to Italy, and renewed his suit to Miss Godolphin. He urged her to reconsider her resolution—to permit him to hope—to subject him to any probation, that he might satisfy her of the unconquerable strength of his love. She was touched by his ardor and constancy, but still steadily refused to contract any engagement with him. Young Godolphin remained with them, joined them in their excursions, and made the acquaintance of Lord Byron. Miss Godolphin herself had caught the enthusiastic interest in the fortunes of Greece which filled the soul of the noble poet; and she expressed the wish in the presence of her cousin, that she could do something to aid that heroic people, struggling for liberty. Inflamed with the hope of acquiring some real interest in the heart of Miss Godolphin, by offering his services to Greece, and sharing, too, the enthusiasm which fired Lord Byron, he devoted himself to the same cause.

"Miss Godolphin encouraged his purpose, and for the first time really regarded him with admiration. Young, noble, accomplished, and generous, he might well interest any woman. His fortune was very large, and he employed much of it in the cause which he had espoused. The whole energy of his nature was enlisted—for he never did any thing by halves.

"He accompanied Lord Byron when he entered Greece, and perished in an engagement in which he took part, soon after the death of the noble poet. Sir George Godolphin was overwhelmed with grief, when the tidings of the death of his son reached him; and wrote to Miss Godolphin, reproaching her in bitter terms, as the cause of the desolation of his house.

"She was plunged into deep grief. Her own spirit gave the keenest edge to the accusations of Sir George. She felt that she had inflamed the ambition of the generous man who loved her so ardently, and she could not still the voice of her own soul, which spake to her in tones of anguish, of the fatal effects of her visit to the house of her uncle, then so bright and happy, now so dark and desolate. If she could have brought herself to yield to the passionate entreaties of her cousin, all might have been averted; but then she did not love him. She might have done so in time; but she had searched her young, true heart, and found it impossible to promise him any thing which could encourage him. Then ambition, rising up within him, while love was yet unconquered, impelled him to the step which sacrificed his own life, brought darkness upon the stately towers of his ancestral home, and threw a rayless shadow upon the morning of her life.

"You comprehend now, much that has seemed so mysterious to us in the manner of Miss Godolphin."

"Yes, yes," said Waring, "I see it all. Self-accusing, full of remorse, she has mourned young Godolphin as none but the most generous natures can mourn the dead. The youth, the ardor, the enthusiasm, the self-sacrificing spirit of the man whom she could not love while living, all conspire to make her love his memory."

"It is the settled opinion of Miss Guilford," said De Vane, "that Miss Godolphin not only never loved her cousin, but that she never could have done so. She observed their intercourse, and knew the sentiments of Miss Godolphin well. She attributes her sadness, which was much greater formerly than it is now, to remorse. She fancies that the fate of young Godolphin was caused by herself, and she has tortured herself, as a generous and strong nature will do, under such circumstances. She is satisfied that this is the true solution of Miss Godolphin's grief. She had brilliant offers while abroad, from English gentlemen, and from her own countrymen, but she rejected them in every instance, unhesitatingly."

De Vane was full and emphatic in this statement, from a desire to relieve Waring of that apprehension which he knew he must entertain of the nature of Miss Godolphin's sadness. He saw how deep his interest in her was—too deep now to be concealed; and from a generous sympathy with his friend, he sought to remove the slightest ground for the belief that she had ever loved.

"Thank you, De Vane, for your kindness," said Waring. "I comprehend Miss Godolphin now. She is an extraordinary woman, whose glorious nature has been too long darkened by sorrow—sorrow that she should never have indulged. I am greatly relieved. I confess to you that my interest in her is very strong. Her generous reception of me from the first hour of our acquaintance; her glorious scorn of all little and contemptible conventionalisms; her grand love of truth wherever she sees it; her beautiful appreciation of what is good, whether in high life or humble life—all this, and much more, has won me, in spite of my reserve and caution. Still I could not banish some distrust. I feared that she had loved, and loved hopelessly; and to one of my nature, this would have been intolerable. I am greatly relieved. I did not comprehend until now, the extent of my interest in Miss Godolphin."

"I rejoice to be able to contribute any thing to your happiness," said De Vane. "I have observed your interest in Miss Godolphin, and I felt it my duty to make known to you the statement which I had from Miss Guilford. She speaks with enthusiasm of Miss Godolphin, and wonders that any one can withstand her charms."

"So do I," said Waring earnestly and quickly, and with perfect simplicity.

"It does not surprise me to hear you say so," said De Vane. "But fortunately, the fatal arrows from one quiver do not pierce all hearts, otherwise the world would be in a hopeless state."

"Certainly," said Waring, laughing, "certainly—you are right."

"So excuse me for not attempting to rival you," said De Vane.

"I am, De Vane, under great obligations to you for your forbearance," said Waring. "I do not know how Miss Godolphin may regard my presumption, but I certainly can never regard any other woman than herself, as entitled to the homage of my heart."

"Presumption, indeed!" said De Vane. "Any woman on earth might feel herself honored by your addresses. If I do not misinterpret Miss Godolphin, she is capable of appreciating you. She is a noble woman, and her soul rises above the distinctions which some regard as so vast and so important."

They had reached home; but neither felt inclined to sleep. They sat down in Waring's room, and De Vane, opening the melodeon—which he had not touched since his return—played a grand old piece. Through the notes there rolled the exultant tone of youth and hope; and as he concluded it, the volume of sound, rising beyond the limits of the apartment, floated out upon the night air, and was borne toward the heavens, which, bending over the earth, seemed to sympathize with human hearts, and to cheer all souls which could look away from the present and the actual, to the invisible but still real and revealing future.

## CHAPTER VIII.

"She her throne makes Reason climb,
While wild passions captive lie,
And each article of time,
Her pure thoughts to heaven fly;
All her vows religious be,
And she vows her love to me."
William Habington.

Some engagement took Waring to the College, the next morning, Saturday as it was, and De Vane walked to Leasowes. He had not visited it since his return, and he felt a strong inclination to walk through the grounds. It was not at all certain that he should meet Esther, as it was only occasionally that she visited the place on Saturday; but he wished to visit walks so endeared to him by associations. He entered the grounds at about ten o'clock in the forenoon, and turning to the right, walked slowly through the wild orange trees, whose branches, trimmed in a tasteful way, suffered the sunlight to fall upon the graveled walks, as through the windows of a cathedral upon its paved floor. No one was visible; and seating himself at length upon one of the iron settees, he recalled the morning when, walking by the side of Esther by this very spot, he had named her place Leasowes. The warmth of his manner had, on that occasion, startled her. He had observed it, and he had restrained himself afterward, up to the very hour of his departure from Virginia. Even then he had asked no more than to be admitted upon a footing of friendship—friendship in a high sense, but only friendship. His future was at that time all uncertain. His residence had not then been fixed—at least, his own selection was open to objections which his father might urge—nor had he then satisfied himself as to the nature and strength of his sentiments respecting Esther. But now no question could be raised as to where his home was to be, nor could he longer doubt that he loved with all the energy of his nature. Why, then, should he longer delay a frank declaration of his love? Why should he leave himself in doubt as to Esther's interest in him? Why hesitate to obey the strong promptings of his own heart?

After sitting for a half-hour almost unconscious of his surroundings, he heard voices in a neighboring walk, and he instantly recognized them. Miss Godolphin and Esther were in earnest conversation. He heard his own name mentioned by Miss Godolphin, and he at once rose and walked away, feeling that he ought not to hear a conversation which was not intended for his ear. Passing into another walk, he pursued it until it emerged at the base of the hill where the fountain was throwing its bright waters into the pure morning sunlight, and he seated himself upon the very spot which he occupied when he had last met Esther here. Again memory was busy. The past was recalled; and the beautiful, clear truthfulness of Esther, her modest yet noble utterance of her sentiment, her glowing beauty—all were before him. He had risen from his seat, and was looking over the railing that surrounded the marble basin into which the waters of the fountain fell, perfectly abstracted from all the objects about him, when he was startled by a voice very near him: "Good morning! Mr. De Vane. I welcome you once more to Leasowes."

He started, and turning, saw Esther. There she stood in her resplendent beauty, more elaborately and elegantly dressed than was usual with her when at Leasowes, and her manner so playful and bright, that De Vane felt he had never seen her when she appeared so lovely.

"I owe you an apology, Miss Wordsworth," he said, "for trespassing upon your seclusion here without your permission, but I could not resist my wish to visit this spot once more."

"Permission!" said Esther. "Do you not remember that I gave you an invitation long since to visit Leasowes whenever you found it agreeable to do so?"

"Perfectly well," said De Vane; "but as I have been an exile for the last three months, I should have sought anew your gracious permission before entering your realm."

"I am not so arbitrary a sovereign as to require a new pledge of loyalty every three months from friends."

"Thank you," said De Vane, "for not doubting my loyalty. It has been unswerving, I assure you. I am delighted to meet you alone, that I may say so with all the ardor which my nature prompts."

Esther colored, and then became very pale, but she made no reply. De Vane's manner, much more than his language, startled and embarrassed her.

"I am very fortunate, Miss Wordsworth, in meeting you here. I was by no means sure that I should find you."

"I have been driving with Miss Godolphin this morning," she replied, "and she had put me down here but a short time since. We had walked some little time through the grounds, when she left me, that I might pay a flying visit to my little girls; and as I entered the house, I saw you, and came to welcome you."

"Miss Wordsworth, it would be impossible to conceal my interest in you, if I desired to do so. Long before my departure for Virginia it must have been known to you, but I was not at liberty to speak of it. Every thing was unsettled—my residence, my whole future. Now every thing is understood—I am to reside here, and whatever plans may have been laid out for me by others, of course are disposed of by my fixing upon this place as my residence, and deciding to take part in the active employments of life. I am at liberty to speak to you. I know my own heart, and you are enthroned in it for all the future."

Again Esther's face was flushed to the temples, and she was evidently deeply moved. Her emotion did not permit her to speak. De Vane, ardent as he was, treated her with the profoundest respect. She had seated herself, and he stood before her, his arms folded and his lips compressed.

"Speak to me, Miss Wordsworth, speak to me. I love you deeply, passionately, unchangeably. Will you permit me to love you? Will you say that I may indulge a sentiment which it would be impossible to conquer? Or are you too cold to experience the glow of earthly passion?"

Esther raised her glowing face, and far down in her fathomless eyes he read a soul capable of profoundest sentiment.

"I do not know how to answer you, Mr. De Vane. Coldness is no part of my nature."

De Vane sat down by her side, and took her hand; it trembled.

"And may I hope, Esther, that you do not regard me with indifference?"

"I should always reproach myself, Mr. De Vane, if I were to speak to you now in any other way than with perfect frankness. I do not regard you with indifference, but I fear to trust my own heart."

"And why should you fear, Esther? What is there to inspire distrust?"

"Oh! much, very much. The solemn injunction of a dying mother binds me to duties which might be distasteful to you. Your views of religion differ widely from mine; and while I honor you too much to believe you capable of sharing the prejudice, yet I know that your father and your aunt regard me as belonging to a despised people."

"And what are their prejudices to us?" said De Vane. "When they come to know you, they will honor and love you."

"Still," said Esther, "I could never consent to introduce unhappiness into any family. It was but a few moments since that I was with Miss Godolphin. She spoke of you, of your father, and of your aunt, and I saw our relations as I had never seen them before. Never, never could I be happy if I were to darken any house, especially such a house as yours, so full of ancestral pride, all of which is centered on you."

"But, Esther, dearest Esther, do you not regard my happiness? Would you sacrifice me on the cruel altar of family pride? Then, too, you overrate the barrier to which you refer. It will at once give way when you are known."

"I would not sacrifice you, Mr. De Vane, to any false sentiment of my own. It is due to truth to say that I prize the love with which you have honored me, but in the face of an unhappy father you would read my condemnation; and if your magnanimity did not permit you to reproach me, your heart would suggest accusations against me. Then, too, the want of sympathy in our religious views would deprive me of the consolation which I should so much need if I saw you made unhappy because of me."

"O Esther! do not torture yourself and me by such apprehensions. My dearest Esther, these are only summer clouds, which will pass over, and leave us a cloudless heaven."

"Still, Mr. De Vane," she said, "while I must be loyal to truth, and say as I do that my own heart pleads for you, I must say too, with perfect sincerity, that while these barriers exist, we can only be friends."

Tears filled her eyes, and after trembling for a moment upon the dark lashes, rolled down her cheeks. She could no longer restrain herself. She wept as if the fountains of feeling so long repressed had broken from the control under which she had hitherto held them, and would have their way. Her young, pure, generous heart suffered in the fierce struggle between love and duty, and she could not still its throbbings. De Vane was deeply affected. His respect for her was as great as his love. The perfect purity of her character, the nobleness of her nature, which, disdaining all false sentiments, prompted her to avow her regard for him; while the majestic sense of duty which reigned within her prevented her from yielding to his wishes, and forbade her to enter into any engagement with him; all this filled him with a sentiment almost of veneration for the woman whom he regarded with a feeling amounting to adoration. He held her hand in silence for some moments, suffered the violence of her emotions to subside, and then spoke to her cheerfully:

"Well, dearest Esther, all that I ask is, that you will give me time to remove these barriers. We understand each other. I can trust you without vows. There is no possibility of change on my part, and all will yet be well with us."

"O change! There can be no change in me. I am not subject to change even in friendship, and I have never known what it was to feel an interest in any one such as I feel in you. Do not urge me, Mr. De Vane. You are right, you can trust me without vows. We comprehend each other now, and we must trust each other for all the future."

De Vane bowed his head, and kissed her hand—the first touch of lips, warmed by passion, which she had ever felt.

She withdrew her hand, and rose from her seat. They stood by the fountain; its waters flashed in the sunlight, and fell in sparkling spray; and as the breeze swept it lightly, a rainbow spanned the little basin.

"See, Esther," said De Vane, "you think that a cloud rests upon our future; there is our bow of promise. It spans your own fountain."

A smile, bright as sunlight, overspread her face, and her eyes shone through the lingering tears with a richer lustre than that which gilded the falling waters of the fountain.

They turned into one of the walks, and De Vane said:

"You refuse, Esther, to bind yourself to me by vows, but you have made me transcendently happy by avowing your interest in me. Your decision is not the result of indifference. I shall labor to remove the barriers which to you seem so formidable; when that is done, I hope to claim you as my own."

"You may underrate the magnitude of the obstacles to which I refer, Mr. De Vane," she replied. "I have spoken with perfect frankness, but I can promise nothing whatever. I am your friend, and it is impossible that I can be more, until I become satisfied that my duty—I mean, until I am able to feel that considerations which affect us both make it proper that I should yield to your wishes."

"And is this all that you can say to me, Esther?"

"All," she replied.

"It must then be my task to satisfy your distrust, and to make you feel that you can become mine without doing violence to your own sense of duty. I repeat, I am yours unchangeably. I bind myself to perfect loyalty to you, for all the future."

She walked by his side in silence. They reached a part of the grounds where the walk, emerging into a broader one, brought them into view of the house; and

Esther, turning to him, said: "I must take leave of you now. I have yet a commission to execute with my little girls."

"Then I must bid you good morning. A thousand thanks, Esther, for your frankness. It would have made me very unhappy to distrust you. I shall soon see you again. Good morning!"

"Good morning!" said Esther, extending her hand to him.

He clasped it warmly, and, turning away, passed out from Leasowes into the great, busy world. His emotions were not sufficiently well defined to enable him to feel either exhilarated or depressed. He was deeply moved. The whole grand nature of the man was roused. His abounding love swept, like a rising flood, every thing before it; but the sky which overarched it, was not cloudless. Like a landscape through which the Rhine pours its rejoicing waters, bright with the summer's sun, and yet sometimes darkened and turned out of its course by overshadowing mountains, so the current of his soul ran. He felt that he was loved, and yet he was not accepted. Great barriers rose between him and the woman he adored. Could they ever be removed? He had striven to cheer Esther, but he could not conceal from himself the difficulties in his way. His father's indomitable pride of family, his utter prejudice against the religious sect to which Esther belonged; Esther's own womanly pride and self-respect, and her gentle but unswerving sense of duty; al. this troubled him. Still he was loved, and there was rapture in the thought. He walked into the main street, and entered the book-store of Mr. Müller. The richly-bound volumes on the shelves, the new tempting books on the table, attracted and cheered him. How vividly he recalled his meeting and conversation with Esther, upon this very spot, twelve months before! A beautiful edition of

Milton's poetical works, in two volumes, just imported from England, lay before him, and, turning its pages, he found the passage to which he had called the attention of Waring at that time. He read it again—it charmed him; and, stepping to the counter, he requested Mr. Müller to have the volumes sent to his room.

"This is a splendid edition, Mr. De Vane," said Mr. Müller. "The finest I have ever seen. But I thought you had Milton's works entire—a very handsome edition that I imported for you, some time since."

"Yes," said De Vane; "I have the set to which you refer, but I intend these volumes for a friend."

"I hope your friend will appreciate them, sir. There is nothing like them in this country, and they are so expensive that I was afraid to duplicate them."

De Vane returned to his lodgings, and wrote a note to Esther, to accompany the edition of Milton which he had just purchased:

"I send you, Esther, the accompanying volumes. Please accept them. The Paradise Lost is succeeded by the Paradise Regained. Woman cheered man in his expulsion from the Eastern garden, and helped him to find his way to a brighter realm. I can not look forward to the path which my feet must tread through this wide world, with any thing like hope, unless you consent to walk by my side. Cheerfully then should I pursue it, with an humble trust that with such companionship, and Providence my guide, I should attain that blissful seat of which Milton sings. Always yours,

"George De Vane.

"Saturday morning."

He sent Tully with the package, who, returning after some time, reported that he had waited for Miss Wordsworth, as she was not in when he first called at the house, and he handed his master a note. De Vane opened it, and read:

"Thanks. ESTHER WORDSWORTH."

He laid it away, counting it, brief as it was, a precious thing.

Waring came in, and asked him what he had been doing with himself all the morning.

"I have been walking," said De Vane.

"That is very indefinite," said Waring. "Where have you been walking? I went to the College a little while, and when I came back you were gone. Cæsar was ignorant of your whereabouts, and Tully was as obscure as an oracle."

"Oh!" said De Vane laughing, "I did not confide to them my plans when I walked out, and of course they could only offer conjectures as to my locality."

"Yes, and I met Miss Godolphin driving, and she could give no account of you. She said she had just been at Leasowes, and you were not there."

"Indeed!" said De Vane. "Was she searching for me?"

"Oh! I suppose not," said Waring; "but not finding you on the street, I fancied that you might have called on the ladies, but she assured me that she had just left Miss Wordsworth, and that she had not seen you."

"So I am discharged from that suspicion," said De Vane; "acquitted upon the strength of circumstantial evidence. But what did Miss Godolphin have to say for herself?"

"Nothing very special," said Waring. "She was in her carriage, and I stood conversing with her on the side of the street."

"So, when I am taking my morning walk, you are looking up the ladies," said De Vane. "You must take me with you hereafter."

"I should have been happy to do so this time; but I had no idea that I should have the good fortune to fall in with any of them."

"Waring," said De Vane, "let us take a ride this evening. Our horses are rested, and it will do them good, as well as ourselves, to take the exercise."

"Very good," said Waring. "Then I will go to Tomlinson's at once, and purchase my bridle and saddle."

"I will go with you," said De Vane. "I think I comprehend those things."

So they went to Tomlinson's, and looked through the establishment. Waring selected a light bridle and an English saddle, under De Vane's counsel, and they were sent forthwith to the livery-stable, for Ivanhoe.

The evening came, and De Vane and Waring mounted their horses. They took the road leading to Mrs. Habersham's country-seat, Clearbrook.

The ride exhilarated them. Never had Waring felt the same activity in a horse that he found in Ivanhoe. The clear springy walk, the vigor and elasticity of motion, the perfect ease with which the animal moved, whether in a slow gait or in a gallop, made the exercise delightful.

"He is superb, De Vane!" exclaimed Waring.

"I am pleased that you like him," said De Vane. "There are few finer horses."

"I know none," said Waring. "I positively believe him to be superior to Manfred."

"I have not yet seen Manfred, you know," said De Vane. "Is he really very fine?"

"Beautiful," said Waring. "I thought him unrivaled, until I saw Ivanhoe."

"The horse I am riding," said De Vane, "is a thoroughbred. Have you observed his action?"

"It is fine," said Waring, "his stride is remarkable."

"Yes," said De Vane, "and active as he is, he possesses uncommon power. See how his shoulder slopes; and his long arm, and shortness from the knee to the lower joint, with his muscle, mark him as a fast horse."

He was a superb animal, and the ease with which De Vane controlled him, showed him to be a perfect horseman.

The stream which flows through Mrs. Habersham's grounds, winds across the road, and is so transparent that its golden sands may be seen at the bottom, while its waters wash the axles of vehicles passing through it; and those who rode or drove from the town usually passed through it in their excursions, and then, after a shorter or longer advance upon the road beyond, just as their inclinations prompted, returned. Just as De Vane and Waring reached the stream, a light open carriage drove into it. Miss Godolphin and Esther were seated in the carriage, and the gentlemen drew up their horses, to allow the vehicle to pass.

"Ah! gentlemen, why were you not an hour earlier?" exclaimed Miss Godolphin. "We have made a delightful visit to Clearbrook."

"How unkind not to invite us!" said Waring.

"Unkind, indeed! How ungallant not to invite us to join you on horseback!" she exclaimed. "I could not have supposed, Mr. De Vane, that you would overlook us."

De Vane bowed low, something of a conscious look appearing in Esther's face, as their eyes met, and he said:

"I assure you, Miss Godolphin, that it would have afforded us both the greatest pleasure to join you in a ride if we had supposed that it would be agreeable to you to permit us to do so this evening. We are just exercising our horses, and hope early next week to attend you."

"Shall we pardon them, Miss Wordsworth, and suffer them to show by their good conduct that they merit it?"

"I think," said Esther, "that we must accept the invitation to ride next week. Shall we not?"

"Very well, gentlemen," said Miss Godolphin, "will you have the kindness to name the day when we shall go forth *au cheval?*"

"Would Tuesday be agreeable to you?" asked De Vane.

"Let it be Tuesday, then, Miss Wordsworth, if you have no engagements with which it will interfere."

"None whatever," said Esther.

"Then, gentlemen, it shall be Tuesday."

De Vane and Waring both bowed.

"What a very fine horse you are riding, Mr. De Vane," said Miss Godolphin. "He looks English."

"It shows how admirable your judgment is," said De Vane. "He is of the best English blood."

"He is superb," she said.

"And yours is a beautiful creature, Mr. Waring," said Esther. "I really think him almost equal to Manfred."

"Ah! Mr. De Vane, do you hear that?" said Waring. "You are not to carry off the honors without my contesting the matter with you."

"You have always borne the honors away from me," said De Vane.

"But he shall not do so this time, without a divided vote," said Miss Godolphin. "Mr. Waring's horse is beautiful; but I give the preference to the bay."

"The best judges, ladies, are divided in opinion in regard to the two horses, just as you are," said De Vane.

"Mr. De Vane's judgment and taste," said Waring, "were shown in the selection of both. He was generous enough to present this horse to me; and if he had offered me the choice, I should certainly have selected him."

"Ah!" said Miss Godolphin, bowing to De Vane, "your

judgment, your taste, and—what is worth far more than either—your friendship, Mr. De Vane, are all shown, in presenting to Mr. Waring so beautiful an animal, and one which he so entirely approves."

De Vane lifted his hat in acknowledgment of the compliment.

The ladies then bowed to the gentlemen, and drove on.

Waring and De Vane rode through the stream, and passing some short distance beyond, turned their horses' heads toward the town.

"Miss Godolphin and Miss Wordsworth seem to pass much of their time with each other," said De Vane.

"Yes," replied Waring. "It has been so throughout the summer; and I am happy to observe it. Miss Wordsworth's influence over Miss Godolphin is steadily increasing, and it must be for good. I said to you, some days since, that Miss Godolphin felt great concern upon the subject of religion, and I attribute it to the influence of her friend. Miss Wordsworth sent to England for a copy of Lady Huntingdon's Life, which she presented to Miss Godolphin, and she has read it with the greatest interest."

"Miss Wordsworth," said De Vane, "is a Methodist, and holds the views of that people conscientiously and firmly; but, I trust, she is not bigoted."

"Not in the least so," said Waring; "no one can be further from it. But she holds with the tenacity of perfect conviction and indubitable faith, the doctrine that one who enters the kingdom of heaven must repent, and believe in the Lord Jesus Christ. She comprehends that no superficial work will do; that there must be forgiveness of sins and a change of heart before one can be acceptable to God."

"And is that essential, Waring? May not a pure life and good deeds be acceptable to the Deity, without absolute conformity to a creed?"

"De Vane," said Waring, "read the third of St. John's

Gospel. Read it searchingly, and you will be satisfied that your question can be answered only in one way: 'Except a man be born again, he can not see the kingdom of God.' You will observe that when the Jewish ruler, who seems to have been a man of singular candor and directness, exclaimed impatiently against what appeared to him an impossibility, unless the doctrine of the transmigration of souls were true, our Lord corrects his error by assuring him that what is born of flesh must be flesh, and that what is born of the spirit must be spirit. In other words, if it were possible for a man to be reproduced, inheriting his fallen nature, and living under any improvement of his physical condition, any degree of high-toned civilization, that could bring him into no nearer relation to God, who is not only good but holy; and that it was a spiritual birth to which he referred—a thorough change, to be wrought in us by his Spirit: so that it might be said of our moral nature, Old things are passed away, behold all things are become new."

De Vane rode for some time in silence. He was profoundly impressed by the fresh, clear view of conversion which Waring had presented. Waring had quite too thorough a knowledge of human nature and of De Vane's peculiar line of thought to attempt to subdue him by mere authority, by referring to miracles as authenticating the divine mission of our Lord, and demanding that his teachings should be accepted upon that basis. He comprehended how thoroughly De Vane was imbued with the German idea of accounting for our Lord's miracles upon natural grounds; as, for instance, explaining that stupendous work of feeding five thousand persons—faint, weary, and hungering for food—by supposing that a caravan, opportunely passing with a large supply of bread, furnished it to the apostles for the use of the Master. And how fully he was acquainted with the acute philosophy of Hume, which involved all reliance upon human testimony in impenetrable clouds, and made even the eternal granite a quagmire under the tread of human feet seeking some stable foundation for their hope of immortality; and he therefore preferred to rest his argument upon the incontestable basis that, God being holy and man sinful, there could be no reconciliation without a change of nature; for without it, there could be no harmony.

"In the same connection," Waring proceeded to say, "you will observe that our Lord says, by way of encouragement to the ruler, who had sought an interview with him by night, 'For God so loved the world, that he gave his only-begotten Son, that whosoever believeth in him should not perish, but have everlasting life;' and thus revealed to him the single condition of salvation—trust in the great sacrifice offered for the sins of the whole world."

"You speak of a sacrifice," said De Vane. "Where is its necessity? God is an absolute sovereign. Why might he not pardon unconditionally, and save the whole race?"

"Ah!" said Waring, "that is the grandest problem in the universe. We may not comprehend its whole extent, no more than we can see the entire disk of an orb like Jupiter, or the extent of a belt like that which encircles Saturn; but of this we may be quite sure, while God is an absolute, he is not an arbitrary Sovereign. His government is a moral one, and the considerations which demanded a sacrifice for a guilty world relate to the whole realm of intelligent being embraced within the divine administration. Where all are sinners, as our race are, to grant no pardon would be to exterminate the beings just introduced into the circle of creation; to grant unconditional and universal pardon would be to inaugurate universal license to sin and rebellion, and to overthrow all government; and to select a part of the race capriciously, as objects of the divine compassion, would inspire no respect for the government, nor veneration for the Sovereign. The only plan is that of the Gospel. By offering as a victim the Son of God, who suffered vicariously, the just for the unjust, every thing is preserved: the divine administration is vindicated; sin is punished in the most impressive and dread form; and the offenders are encouraged to love and trust the Almighty Father, who gives such a signal proof of reverence for his own law and love for our race."

Again De Vane was silent. At length he said:

"These are dread subjects; they are to be studied profoundly. You do not think me capable, Waring, of regarding them lightly?"

"Of course not," said Waring. "Your trouble is in asserting the supremacy of reason over subjects which lie beyond the range of its largest powers. Depend upon it, we need a revelation to instruct us in invisible things, and we must limit reason to an investigation of the claims of any disclosure which professes to be of divine origin, and not venture to examine the truths revealed to us for our instruction by any standard within our own minds."

They were entering the town, and the descending sun filled the heavens with its glory. The tall pines were ablaze with its lingering beams, and the clouds, like huge castles or vast mountains, wore deeper splendors than ever gilded the scenery, even of Eastern climes. The horsemen rode on silently, both feeling that disposition to meditation which we all experience under the deepening shadows of twilight, as we see night descend upon the earth.

## CHAPTER IX.

"PERFECT let us walk before Thee—
Walk in white
To the sight
Of thy heavenly glory!"
CHARLES WESLEY.

SUCH was the confidence between Esther and Mrs. Springfield, that nothing affecting the happiness of either could occur without being made known to the other.

Of course, Esther communicated to her aunt what had taken place on Saturday. She suffered the Sabbath to pass before she mentioned the subject, seeking in the mean while that guidance which the Father gives to all humble and trusting souls. Mrs. Springfield was deeply affected when she learned that Esther, adhering firmly to her sense of duty, had declined to enter into any engagement with De Vane. She comprehended the struggle through which her niece had passed. She interpreted her heart rightly, and knew how loyal it was to De Vane, at the very moment when she restrained its promptings, and silenced, if she could not still, its throbbings. She heartily approved Esther's course, and said so to her, cheering her, at the same time, with the assurance that doubtless all would yet be well, but that, in any event, nothing could harm one who simply followed the path of duty, no matter how flinty it might be to our weary feet. Unselfish, pure, and wise, this noble woman counseled her niece to be brave and cheerful; and as Esther, unable to restrain her emotions, bowed her face on her aunt's knees, and wept as if her heart were breaking, Mrs. Springfield caressed her tenderly, and waited for the outburst of tears to pass away before she spoke to her. She then kissed her forehead, and said:

"Esther, you have done just what you should have done. Nothing of principle should ever be yielded in forming such a relation as that of marriage; it must be altogether pure. Remember we are a peculiar people. Let the great world form alliances from motives of ambition or worldliness. It must not be so with us. We are seeking a better country, that is, an heavenly, and we must connect ourselves in such close relations as those which marriage creates, only with those who will walk with us. But all will yet be well. I have the highest respect for Mr. De Vane, and my confidence in the nobleness of his nature satisfies me that he will find the right way, and all will be overruled for the best."

Soothed, if not cheered, Esther rose, and her aunt left her to compose herself.

Soon after, she walked to Leasowes, and entered cheerfully upon her self-appointed tasks.

De Vane wrote to Mrs. De Vane a very long letter, full of ardor, and informing her of the precise state of his relations to Esther. He described, in glowing terms, her character, with which he had already made his aunt acquainted; and he detailed at length the interview of Saturday, the gentle but decided refusal to engage herself until she was assured that she could do so consistently with her self-respect and her sense of duty. He urged Mrs. De Vane to break the matter to his father, and to impress upon him the noble nature of Miss Wordsworth, and the purity and elevation of her character. He assured her, finally, that his happiness was involved, and that he would marry no other woman under heaven, if he did not marry Miss Wordsworth.

Mailing his letter, he awaited a reply with anxiety.

In the mean while, he entered upon his studies in Mr. Clarendon's office with new energy. His life-tasks were before him, and they roused his manhood.

Mr. Clarendon was gratified to see the ardor with which he took up his professional labors, and encouraged him to the utmost of his power.

Not mercenary himself, he did not limit his view of the legal profession to its money-yielding capabilities, but took the larger and more generous view, which Cicero entertained, and which made him so eminent in defense of the innocent, and so resistless in prosecuting the guilty.

Tuesday evening came, and Waring and De Vane joined Miss Godolphin and Esther in the equestrian excursion agreed on. Without any preconcert, Waring and Miss Godolphin rode in advance, and De Vane, riding with Esther, followed them, the party taking the road that led most directly to the country; and after quitting the town, turning toward the river, they pursued its course. De Vane, with a taste for fine horses, was delighted with Manfred, and he observed the perfect skill with which Esther controlled him, spirited as he was.

"Manfred is really a fine animal," he said; "but does he never give you trouble?"

"Not now," replied Esther. "When I first rode him, he startled me by his fleetness, dashing off sometimes at great speed, as if he rejoiced in his strength; but he was never vicious, and I have taught him to yield to the rein."

"Then he suits you perfectly," said De Vane. "I have not seen a finer horse, for the saddle, for a lady's use."

Miss Godolphin rode a very handsome black horse, and she showed to the greatest advantage in her rich, dark riding-dress, and her splendid hat, with its plume—all in harmony with her style of beauty.

"I am happy to see," said De Vane, "that Miss Godolphin is brighter than she was when she returned from Europe. Do you not observe it?"

"Oh! yes," said Esther. "The shadow is, I trust, passing away. I did not know, until she spoke to me upon the subject some weeks since, what she had suffered."

"Did she explain every thing?" asked De Vane.

"With perfect unreserve she unfolded her history, and I comprehended for the first time what she must have suffered. Have you ever heard it?"

"Yes," said De Vane; "I learned it from her friend, Miss Guilford, whom I met in Virginia. You know, of course, that they were in Europe together?"

"Yes," said Esther, "I have heard her speak of Miss Guilford. But what Miss Godolphin has suffered! How dreadful to feel what she has endured for many, many months!"

"She has accused herself needlessly," said De Vane. "She was not in the least to blame. The course of Sir George Godolphin was harsh, and unworthy of him."

Waring and Miss Godolphin had reached the point in the road leading to the ferry, where the two gentlemen had first met Mr. Springfield and his family; and they drew up their horses, to await the coming of De Vane and Esther.

"We mark the progress of time by events," said Waring, as they reached the spot; "and you may, perhaps, not have forgotten, Miss Wordsworth, that some twelve months since a traveling-carriage drove up this road, and the party following it were arrested by two young gentlemen who stood in the highway?"

"Oh! yes," said Esther, coloring. "I remember it perfectly well. Has it been twelve months? It scarcely seems so long."

"Twelve months, almost to a day," said Waring. "How swiftly time flies!"

"Was it here," asked Miss Godolphin, "that you met Miss Wordsworth for the first time, Mr. De Vane?"

"Upon this very spot," said De Vane. "Mr. Waring and I were taking an evening walk, and we stood here to admire the effect of the light upon the water and the surrounding objects. Mr. Springfield and his party were just returning from their summer's travel, and we met them here. Really, in looking back to it, it seems as if I had been studying one of Claude Lorraine's pictures; and I can scarcely feel that the scene was one of real life. I feel as if I had known Mr. Springfield and his family all my life."

Miss Godolphin smiled. Unconsciously, De Vane had uttered his heart-thoughts, and only said, in different language, that his real existence had only begun on the banks of the stream which flowed before them, twelve months before. She perfectly comprehended it, but she forebore to speak her thoughts. Esther was present, and she spared her. What is life until the heart expands? Like plants that are full of verdure and brightness, but yield no fragrance, until suddenly the flower bursts into beauty; so the life, exuberant and joyous as it may seem, has no real meaning until the soul wakes to consciousness, under the power of some great sentiment.

"The scene is one of remarkable beauty," said Miss Godolphin. "Observe that light upon the rapids. The water flashes like molten silver, and the spray that rises, catching the slanting sunbeams, is like a shower of tiny pearls. See that wheel of the mill above us. How the glancing water reflects the light, as if it were draped with liquid mirrors, while the wild vines, climbing the great trees on the river-bank, catch the sunbeams, and hang over the waters like a canopy of green and gold! The whole picture is Southern."

"Very beautiful!" said Esther.

"After all," said De Vane, "I like ferry-boats better than bridges. It is a little voyage that one makes between the two banks. You are upon the water and enjoy its current, and the very exertion which it requires to overcome its swiftness, imparts a pleasing sense of triumph."

"Unless you are in haste to get over," said Waring; "then the delay is an annoyance."

"Oh! of course. I speak of pleasure excursions," said De Vane. "Business is quite another thing. But observe those two men. How vigorously they exert themselves in bringing the boat over! The carriage and the horses, and the foot-passengers, are heavy enough to make it necessary to put out strength in accomplishing the voyage; and when they reach this bank, a sense of relief will be experienced, as if another dangerous adventure in life were well over."

"On the Rhine," said Miss Godolphin, "there are bridges of boats, and when a vessel approaches, a space is made sufficiently wide for it to pass, by dropping some of the boats out of the current, and reconstructing the bridge after it has gone by, bringing the boats back to their place. The scene is full of animation, and the arrangement in every way convenient, affording a safe intercommunication between the two banks of the stream, and yet offering no obstruction to commerce."

"I think," said Waring, "I should prefer a bridge of that kind to a ferry, however picturesque."

"Oh! certainly, if you intend to apply your utilitarian philosophy to the beauties of nature," said De Vane. "But then you would do better to construct your bridges as they do on the Thames—grandly—and make them beautiful objects in the landscape, compelling the steamers to lower their smoke-pipes when they pass through the arches. But I insist upon keeping some part of the realm of nature free from the encroachments of commercial despotism."

"Well," said Miss Godolphin, "I think with Mr. De Vane. Long may our ferry-boat ply between these banks!"

"I am sorry to disturb your plans," said Waring, "but I learn that an enterprising set of people have made up their minds to throw a bridge over the river very soon."

"Then," said De Vane, "we must preserve this picture in the chambers of memory, for it is one of great beauty."

They rode on, making a circuit about the town, passing beyond the College, and returning by the way of the sand-hills.

The party rode as much together as possible, and the conversation was general and animated. They reached home exhilarated with the exercise, and full of the joy which youth feels in the present, while hope illumines the future with its strong light.

On Thursday morning, at the breakfast-table, Mrs. Bowen reminded Waring that the love-feast was to be held the next evening, informing him that it had been announced the preceding evening, at the close of the service.

"Yes," said Waring, "I might have forgotten it, if you had not named it. I thank you for reminding me."

"A love-feast!" said De Vane. "What is that?"

"It is a meeting," said Waring, "held by the Methodists once in three months, in which each one who feels disposed to relate his experience as a Christian, may do so without reserve."

"Indeed!" said De Vane. "Do explain it to me. I confess that my curiosity is roused."

"We hold," said Waring, "a conference once in the year, where the preachers assemble to report the results of their labors, and receive from the Bishop who presides, their appointments for the following year. This is called the annual conference, and it presents a scene of high moral interest. At times it rises into sublimity. A body brought together from extensive fields of labor, composed of men of intellect and character, submit themselves to the Bishop, who, surrounded by several ministers—elders in charge of districts—as a cabinet to advise him, looks out upon the whole work embraced within the bounds of the conference, and assigns them to such posts as he may think best for the great cause. A rigid examination of character is made, and the minister learns his appointment for the first time from the lips of the Bishop, who, at the close of the conference, reads out the list. Then these presiding elders hold in each of their districts—into which each conference is subdivided—a conference every three months, called a quarterly conference, composed of the official members of the circuit or station, where the proper business is transacted and character is examined. On the Friday preceding, a meeting of the members of the church is held, with the view of relating to each other their experience. Ancient usages are adhered to by us. The early Christians had their feasts of charity—the Methodists hold their feasts of love. None are admitted but Christians, and serious persons who request the privilege. The doors are rigidly closed, and the world shut out. Water and bread are handed around, and each one partakes of it, in token of good-will, felt by each toward all. Then every one rises and speaks who may be disposed, briefly stating his experience as a Christian."

De Vane listened with great interest to Waring's description, and then said, when he had concluded:

"I should be happy, Waring, to attend the love-feast to-morrow evening. Can I be permitted to do so?"

"I will inquire," said Waring. "The Presiding Elder is to be here to-morrow, and I will apply to him for a ticket."

"Thank you," said De Vane. "I really wish to attend."

Mrs. Bowen heard this with amazement. The idea that De Vane should desire to attend a love-feast, astonished her. She admired him extravagantly, and had often felt saddened by his indifference to the services of the Church. She prayed for him fervently, and was now inexpressibly thankful that he felt a desire to attend one of those meetings, peculiar to her people, and which she esteemed so highly.

Waring obtained permission for De Vane to attend the love-feast, and after early tea, they accompanied Mrs. Bowen to the Methodist meeting-house. It was soon pretty well filled, quite a large number of persons belonging to other churches having been admitted. The Presiding Elder was the Rev. William Chalmers, an educated and accomplished gentleman, and a preacher of the highest order; and his presence never failed to attract many persons, not members of the church, to his ministrations. After the introductory prayer and hymn, Mr. Chalmers explained, briefly, the nature of the meeting; and the bread and water were handed to every one in the house, all partaking.

Mr. Chalmers then rose and related his experience, which, without being too minute, was pointed and deeply interesting. He had been converted when young, and had entered upon the work of the ministry immediately upon quitting college. His first attempt to persuade others was in exhortations following the sermon of some of the preachers, and he had continued to experience a clear manifestation of the favor of God up to the present moment, enjoying a constant sense of his acceptance.

His remarks were very impressive, the good taste which characterized, and the fervor which imbued them, making them felt by every one. De Vane had never before heard any thing like it. It was as if he had been suddenly introduced into the presence of the early Christians.

After Mr. Chalmers had resumed his seat, some moments of silence ensued. Then a venerable man rose from his seat on one of the side-benches, and spoke for about five minutes. He had been a member of the Church for more than forty years, was still enjoying a clear sense of the divine approval, and was prepared, at any hour, to pass over the waters which his feet already touched, and enter the home of the blessed.

As he took his seat, a hearty "Amen!" was uttered by several of the leading members, and a single stanza of a hymn was sung.

Two or three others followed, speaking with distinctness and confidence of their sense of sins forgiven, and of assured peace.

Among the females, there now rose up one. She was tall and middle-aged, and dressed with marked simplicity and neatness. She, too, spoke for a few moments of her religious state, describing it as full of peace and hope. She was followed by a much younger person, who spoke with such marked intelligence, that every one heard her with interest. She described her conversion, the intense wretchedness which had preceded it, and the rapture which followed; stating her present peace as the result of an unswerving trust in God, and realizing, as she said, the truth of the promise, uttered by an inspired prophet, "Thou shalt keep him in perfect peace, whose mind is staid on thee;" and as she resumed her seat, great emotion was exhibited throughout the assemblage. The testimony delivered was so clear, simple, fervent, and in such perfect taste, both as regarded manner and language, that it was not only above criticism, but it found its way into the depths of every listening soul. Mr. Chalmers instantly sang a stanza, descriptive of the triumph of a renewed soul, beginning with the line,

"Ye wingéd seraphs, fly!"

and it was taken up by others, who swelled the sound until it filled the house with its exulting rapture.

"It is good to be here!" exclaimed Mr. Chalmers.

"Amen!" responded many voices.

The pastor of the church now rose, and spoke for a few minutes. He had been converted when young, and had entered the ministry at eighteen. It was to him a happy work in the midst of all its toils and responsibilities, and he had no other aim in life but to preach the Word and honor the name of the MASTER. A deep sympathy with his remarks was exhibited, and as he sat down, Mr. Chalmers exclaimed: "The Lord bless thee, my brother, and cause his face to shine upon thee!" "Amen!" was uttered all over the house. Mr. Springfield rose, and spoke for a few minutes, with marked clearness and fervor. He referred to his conversion—which had occurred just as he attained the age of twenty-one—and his abiding sense of pardon and peace. He looked to the future with hope, for he had learned to *trust*, as well as to *obey*. He was heard with deep interest. Several of the leading members of the church followed in quick succession, speaking the language of faith and hope, and several describing the manner of their conversion, referring to the hour and the place.

A very young man rose. He was from the low country, and was present casually, traveling for a few weeks with Mr. Chalmers around his district; and he felt that it would be no intrusion if he added his testimony to the goodness of his redeeming Lord. He described his awakening and his conversion, and he said: "After peace entered my soul, the whole aspect of nature was changed; the heavens were bright, and the trees seemed to wave their branches in praise of their Creator." He stated that it was his purpose to give his life to the task of inviting sinners to the Lord whom he had found so gracious, and to identify himself with the only cause which was worthy of the entire consecration of an immortal being—a cause which would display its beneficent triumphs, when heroes, and statesmen, and empires, and all human glory had disappeared.

"The Lord guide and strengthen thee, and give thee good success!" exclaimed Mr. Chalmers, which was responded to by many voices, uttering an earnest Amen!

Mr. Chalmers now rose, and remarked that it was time to bring the meeting to a close. That it had been one of marked interest, and he trusted of great profit.

A hymn was sung—

> "How happy every child of grace,
> Who knows his sins forgiven!"

and Mr. Arthur, the pastor, made the closing prayer.

The love-feast had ended; the doors were thrown open, and the congregation dispersed.

As De Vane was passing to the door, he joined Mr. Springfield and his party, and spoke to them. They received him warmly, and Mrs. Springfield expressed her satisfaction at seeing him there. "It is new to you, Mr. De Vane," she said, "and may not be agreeable to your tastes; but it is a profitable meeting to Christians."

"I do not doubt it, madam," he said. "I have been much interested in it."

Offering his arm to Esther, he walked with her, preceded by Mr. and Mrs. Springfield; and upon reaching the house, accepted an invitation to enter.

"Well, Mr. De Vane," said Mr. Springfield, "you have witnessed a meeting peculiar to us as a people, and I trust that you found nothing in it to offend you."

"On the contrary," said De Vane, "I was profoundly interested in it. I can imagine nothing more agreeable to an earnest believer in Christianity, than to hear others speak of its effects, as wrought in them. I love earnestness in every thing; and every one must concede, that if the claims of religion are to be admitted at all, they must be recognized as supreme. I can conceive of nothing so distasteful as conventionalism, and a deference to the world's opinion in matters affecting one's relations to God. No, sir; such a meeting as I have been permitted to witness this evening can never offend me."

"You must allow me to say, sir," said Mr. Springfield, "that I am highly gratified to hear you express yourself in this way. Persons of culture, unacquainted with our usages, sometimes find their taste offended by them. I am not, however, surprised to find that you are differently affected by our love-feast."

De Vane bowed, appreciating the compliment which was paid to the real nobleness of his nature.

"I was much pleased with Mr. Chalmers and Mr. Arthur," said De Vane.

"They are superior men," replied Mr. Springfield. "Mr. Chalmers was educated at your College, and is a person of fine acquirements. Both as a writer and preacher, he ranks high. You can hear him on Sunday morning, if you wish, as he is to preach at that time."

"I shall certainly avail myself of the privilege," said De Vane.

"Mr. Arthur," said Mr. Springfield, "is a Georgian; not thoroughly educated, but self-taught, and he is still rapidly improving. He is a very able preacher, and his increasing library attests his love of books and his progress in learning. His language is remarkable for its purity, and his style possesses a great charm."

"I must hear him at some time," said De Vane. "I admire him greatly. There is a manliness about his air very pleasing to me."

"I quite agree with you," said Mrs. Springfield. "He is a great favorite of mine."

"I do not know which of the two I prefer," said Esther. "I admire them both. They are charming men."

"You are fortunate in having such ministers," said De Vane.

"Very much so," said Mrs. Springfield.

After some conversation upon other subjects, De Vane rose and took leave of the family, saying that he should not fail to hear Mr. Chalmers on Sunday.

He found Waring in his room awaiting his return, and anxious to know how the meeting had impressed him.

"Well, De Vane, what do you think of a love-feast?"

"I was profoundly impressed with it," said De Vane, "and I shall hope to have the privilege of attending one sometimes. I love its earnestness."

"Just as I expected," said Waring. "I was confident that you would see it in that light. Ah! De Vane, you ought to be a Christian."

"I wish I could be one," said De Vane.

"Did you like Mr. Chalmers?" asked Waring.

"Greatly," said De Vane. "I am to hear him on Sunday. Mr. Springfield informed me that he would preach."

"Yes," said Waring, "it will delight you. He is a charming preacher. A more polished one you never heard."

Then followed a long conversation upon other subjects; and when the friends separated for the night, the town clock was striking twelve.

On Sunday morning the Methodist church was filled to overflowing, and the first people of the town pressed eagerly to hear Mr. Chalmers. Mr. and Mrs. Clarendon were both present, and were accompanied by Mrs. Habersham and Miss Godolphin. Mr. Hallam and other eminent men were scattered through the congregation. Waring took his accustomed seat, and De Vane was by his side. Mr. Chalmers rose in the pulpit, and opened the services by reading a portion of the Old and the New Testament.

His appearance was that of a man of intellect, sensibility, and refinement. His dark lambent eyes were full of expression, and his finely-chiseled features bore the ineffaceable stamp of genius and sentiment. His reading was very fine, clear, and rhetorical, and his hearers caught new views of the meaning of particular passages of the Scriptures, as he uttered them.

A hymn followed—one of remarkable beauty—which was read in a way to impress the sentiments which it embodied, almost as deeply as if it had been sung, and then the whole congregation, rising to their feet, sang it, Mr. Chalmers himself leading the music. The prayer that followed impressed De Vane, and he thought it the finest he had ever heard. Another hymn followed, sung without the lines being recited from the pulpit; and then Mr. Chalmers rose, and announcing his text, proceeded to deliver his sermon, without reference even to notes. His text was from the eightieth Psalm, first verse: "Give ear, O Shepherd of Israel, thou that leadest Joseph like a flock; thou that dwellest between the cherubims, shine forth."

It was a transcendently great discourse, blending argument, illustration, beauty, and fervor in wonderful combination and matchless power. The tenderness of the all-merciful Father; the glory of the God of hosts dwelling between the cherubims; the outshining of his nature in manifestations of love for a lost race, until at length, on Calvary, the expiring Son, encircled by the angels who bent in wondering gaze over the priceless sacrifice laid before the mercy-seat—all was described in language so perfect, so pure, so much in harmony with the sublime theme of the preacher, that all who heard him yielded ready sympathy, and wept those tears which come from the depths of the soul. Some sobbing was heard, but the prevailing tribute of the audience to the power of the discourse, was that of profuse weeping. Never in all his life had De Vane been so deeply affected. His taste, his sensibility, his judgment—all approved what he had heard, and there was no room for criticism. Mr. Arthur concluded the services in his fine, warm, natural way; and so far from impairing the effect of the discourse, heightened and strengthened it.

As the congregation were dispersing, De Vane met Mr. Clarendon and his party; his eyes were moist, and the ladies were still weeping.

"What a discourse!" said Mr. Clarendon. "I forgot the world and time and myself, until it was ended."

"You have described my own emotions," said De Vane. "It was glorious."

The ladies entered the carriage. Esther came up, to take the extended hand of Mr. Clarendon. "What do you Methodists mean?" he said. "Do you intend to captivate us all?"

"Only to make you free indeed," she replied, smiling through her tears.

De Vane shook hands with her, silently. She turned to speak to Mrs. Habersham and Miss Godolphin; and De Vane, joining Waring, who was standing near him, walked away from the Methodist chapel.

## CHAPTER X.

> "Love not! O warning! vainly said,
> In present hours as in years gone by;
> Love flings a halo round the dear one's head,
> Faultless, immortal, till they change or die.
> Love not!"
>
> Caroline Morton.

The weeks flew by swiftly. Waring was closely engaged with his duties at the College, and De Vane was pursuing his studies with diligence. He made rapid progress, and was already nearly prepared to pass the examination required for admission to the bar. Still he had no thought of making immediate application, intending to take a more extended course, before entering upon the duties of the profession. He had not received any reply to the letters which he had written to Mrs. De Vane. Occasionally Waring joined him in riding with Miss Godolphin and Esther, and they sometimes drove in the evening in De Vane's open carriage, stopping to visit friends or to walk in the public garden, just as they found it most agreeable.

One evening Waring and De Vane were riding with Miss Godolphin and Esther; they had been on an excursion to the sand-hills, and upon their return were just entering the town, when Manfred started suddenly, and plunging to the side of the road where it was precipitous, came near leaping into the ravine which skirted it. But for the admirable skill with which Esther controlled him, he would have done so; and even when restrained, he stood with expanded nostrils and dilated eyes, the very picture of terror. De Vane instantly rode to the aid of Esther, and soothed the frightened horse by speaking to him cheerfully and laying his hand firmly upon his neck.

Waring and Miss Godolphin, who were a little way in the rear, came up, and the group formed a subject for the pencil of an artist. The sun, which shed his strong red beams through the pine forest, which comes up to the very boundaries of the town, revealed a being standing on a projecting rock on the road-side, who seemed scarcely of this world. She was very tall, dark as an Indian, her black hair streaming down her shoulders like a mantle, her eyes blazing and wild with some strange passion, her dress fantastic as that of a stage-queen, and her attitude full of unconscious majesty. The sunlight fell upon her, and a very large, perfectly black greyhound stood by her side, while the party on horseback, arrested by the object before them, confronted her silently, and with almost a sense of awe. Several minutes elapsed before any one spoke: at length De Vane said:

"My good woman, why do you stand there on the road-side? Are you in want of any thing?"

The woman fixed her eyes on the face of the young man, and seemed to study it as if she would read his soul. She spoke at length, in tones so sad as almost to sound like the wailing of deep grief. "You are brave, and she is young and fair; but will that make your path bright? I have seen the past and can read the future. Clouds will darken the morning sky, though the sun be never so strong."

In spite of his own judgment, and the cool courage for which he was remarkable, De Vane could not treat the words lightly. He was distressed. Esther became very pale.

Waring and Miss Godolphin looked on for a moment in silence, but observing the effect of the woman's words on Esther, Waring rode nearer, and said:

"My good woman, who are you? What can we do for you?"

She turned her eyes on him, and then looking steadily at Miss Godolphin, who sat moveless in her dark dress on her black horse, like a queen mourning some dead loved one, she said:

"Darkness sometimes comes in the morning, and then the sun bursts forth and the sky is all bright."

Miss Godolphin trembled, she scarcely knew why; a vague terror possessed her. The innate superstition of her nature was touched, and she felt for a moment as if the strange being before her—unearthly and superhuman—could read the sealed book of fate.

"It is very strange!" said Waring. "What does she mean?"

"What can she mean?" said De Vane. "She must be some maniac who has wandered from her keepers. She may be in want." Taking out his purse, he threw a gold-piece at her feet, and said: "Perhaps you are far from home; there is something that will buy food for you until you find your people."

The woman fixed her gaze on him once more; a kindly look passed into her brilliant eyes, and she said gently: "Brave souls endure long. When storms pass by, the cloudless heavens are bright, and the earth rejoices once more."

Turning away from the spot where she stood, without stooping to take up the piece of gold which De Vane had thrown at her feet, she walked slowly into the woods and disappeared. The party rode on.

"She is a strange being," said Waring. "She must have friends near here, and if her pride revolts against the offer of money, doubtless she will return to secure it, or send some of her people for it."

"She is most extraordinary," said De Vane; "her appearance is that of an Indian woman, and yet her features are those of the white race."

"I have a faint recollection of having seen her," said Esther, "but when or where, it is impossible to say. She frightened me, I am ashamed to say, dreadfully."

"I do not wonder at it," said De Vane. "Her appearance was sudden, and it was enough to startle any one."

"She is a very strange person," said Miss Godolphin. "She really seems unearthly. Do you think, Miss Wordsworth, it is possible that you can have met her anywhere before?"

"I am confident that I have," said Esther. "It seems a mere dream, but it is too distinct to be unreal."

"What remarkable language she uses!" said De Vane. "It is really poetical."

"Do you know," said Waring, "that it is very much in the Indian style? They are poetical, as all tribes dwelling in the midst of nature are found to be, and some of the Indian tribes rise in the use of language to a highly figurative and even ornate and elegant style."

"The language of that woman," said De Vane, "reminds one of Ossian—it is lofty, figurative, and sad."

"She assumed the tone of a sibyl," said Miss Godolphin. "She spoke as if human fortunes were revealed to her."

"Yet she was as indefinite as an oracle," said Waring. "Her generalization was such that it would be easy to verify her prophecies, whatever turn human fortunes might take."

"Still," said De Vane, "there seemed to be some deep meaning in her words. I confess to a vein of superstition in my nature."

"That comes of your passion for the classics," said Waring. "Augurs and soothsayers decided the fortunes of men and states in former times."

"I confess too," said Miss Godolphin, "that I share Mr.

De Vane's respect for such predictions as we have just listened to. That woman may be endowed with supernatural vision."

"Scarcely, I should think," said Waring. "We must inquire about her."

It was understood that they were to pass the evening at Mrs. Springfield's, it being Thursday, when she received, without issuing cards of invitation.

The evening was fine, and an unusually large company assembled in the attractive drawing-rooms of Mrs. Springfield. The cheerfulness, the unpretending elegance, and the high culture which reigned in the house, made it a most agreeable one to visit. Large entertainments were never given, but at the receptions the numbers were sometimes such as to rival those brought together by regular cards of invitation.

Mrs. Habersham accompanied Miss Godolphin, and Mr. Clarendon soon sought them, and entered into conversation with them.

"O Mr. Clarendon!" said Miss Godolphin, "we had a rare adventure this evening, and I have not ceased to tremble yet."

"Indeed!" said he, opening his eyes very wide, and looking sympathetic horror; "and what shape did it come in?"

"Oh! I can not undertake to relate it, in the absence of Miss Wordsworth. She was present, and shared my terror," said Miss Godolphin.

"Then let us find her," said Mr. Clarendon, offering her his arm. They made their way into the library, where Esther was engaged in conversation with Waring; and going to the spot where she stood, Mr. Clarendon bowed, and said:

"I am here, Miss Wordsworth, to hear you repeat a tale which is to freeze my young blood, and make my hair to stand on end, like quills upon the fretful porcupine. Will you deign to speak ?"

"And has not Miss Godolphin informed you of our adventure ?" said Esther, smiling.

"Only that you have had an adventure ; but not a word further can I prevail on her to utter," said he.

"Oh ! here comes my uncle," said Esther, "and he can recite it, and enlighten you better than I can. I told him what had occurred upon my return home, and he is confident that he knows the person who startled us so much."

Mr. Springfield came up, and he was appealed to for an explanation.

"Where is Mr. De Vane ?" he asked, turning to Waring. "He should hear what I have to say."

"I am looking for him every moment," said Waring. "He received letters from Virginia just as we reached home, and he said that he would look over them, and follow me before a great while."

At that moment, De Vane entered the room, and advanced directly to the group in which Esther was standing. He looked somewhat graver than usual, and bowed with stately grace to the party awaiting his approach.

"An opportune arrival !" said Mr. Clarendon, extending his hand to him. "I await with impatience the unfolding of a tale, which can not be disclosed until you are ready to hear it. Welcome, sir !"

"I regret my late arrival on every account," said De Vane, "but I trust that I am yet in time to be enlightened by any disclosures that are to be made."

"Mr. Springfield, will you please to proceed ?" said Mr. Clarendon.

"It seems, then," said Mr. Springfield, "that our young friends were returning this evening from an excursion on horseback, when, just at the limits of the town where the pines rise in such a fine grove, Esther's horse started violently, and threatened to go over the precipice on the side of the road, when Mr. De Vane, with great coolness and judgment, soothed Manfred, and held him from doing mischief; when, looking across the road, to discover what had frightened him, a strange woman was seen standing on a projecting rock, in a queen-like attitude, and dressed quite out of the way in which civilized females are accustomed to appear; and, upon being accosted, she proceeded to utter one or two prophetic sentences, in highly figurative style. Her language was fine, her manner majestic, and the words evidently designed to convey some hidden meaning."

"What were the words?" asked Mr. Clarendon.

Esther colored deeply, and De Vane looked uneasy. Waring hesitated to say any thing, and Miss Godolphin was profoundly interested.

"Upon my soul!" said Mr. Clarendon, "I am becoming deeply interested. This begins to look as if it meant something."

Waring smiled, and said: "I suppose I must answer your question, as Mr. Springfield was not of our party when the woman appeared to us. Observing her strange demeanor, I was curious to know what she might have to say, and therefore observed her closely. In reply to a question from Mr. De Vane, as to 'Why she stood on the road-side? if she was in want of any thing?' she looked on him with the eyes of an awakened sibyl, and after a full survey both of himself and Miss Wordsworth, she said, in low, sad tones: '*You are brave, and she is young and fair; but will that make your path bright? I have seen the past, and I can read the future. Clouds will darken the morning sky, though the sun be never so strong.*' I then rode nearer, and asked her if we could do any thing for her; when, fixing upon me the same steady gaze which she had turned on De Vane, she said: '*Darkness sometimes comes in the morning, and then the sun bursts forth, and the sky is all bright.*' Upon this Mr. De Vane threw a piece of gold at her feet, which she disdained to touch, but looking kindly on him, she said, '*Brave souls endure long. When storms pass by, the cloudless heavens are bright, and the earth rejoices once more;*' when she turned away, and disappeared."

"It is very wonderful!" exclaimed Mr. Clarendon, evidently deeply impressed by what he had heard.

"I found Esther so much agitated when she reached home," said Mr. Springfield, "that I tried to soothe her, by giving her the only explanation which, I think, can apply to an incident so extraordinary. When I resided in Georgia, I became acquainted with some of the leading men of the Cherokee nation, and I learned from one of them an account so remarkable and interesting that it haunted me. An English gentleman, becoming embittered against his friends, came to this country, and entered the Cherokee nation, adopted their habits, their dress, and, in short, became one of them. He married the daughter of a chief, and lived with the people of his adoption to the day of his death. A daughter was born to him, and she was sent to Philadelphia, where she received a thorough education. Returning, to visit her people, who had made great progress in civilization, she was the object of much attention from all travelers passing through the nation, and she attracted the notice of the son of a gentleman of fortune, who actually asked her in marriage. Obstacles were interposed by her father, and the gentleman, finding him inexorable, and the daughter refusing to disobey, abandoned her. Shut up in the nation, her mind acting on itself, with so little to divert it from dwelling on her sorrow, she lost her reason, and at once became, in the estimation of her people, a prophetess. They venerated her, and exalted her into the highest rank of inspired beings. Some years since, when Esther was a child, some of the tribe came to Athens, where we were on a visit, and she accompanied them. Going out to their encampment, we met the prophetess, and she took a wonderful fancy to Esther, who, while greatly alarmed by the appearance of the Indians, seemed to approach her without fear. I think, even then, she uttered some prediction about Esther, in which cloud and sunshine were much intermixed, but I do not recall it distinctly, of course regarding it as of no moment."

"But," said Mr. Clarendon, "can it be possible she is here? Can this be the prophetess?"

"I do not know how that may be," said Mr. Springfield; "but it is possible that some wandering party of the Cherokees may may be visiting here, in prospect of the assembling of the Legislature."

De Vane, Esther, and Miss Godolphin had all listened to the conversation with the deepest interest.

"Her language," said Miss Godolphin, "was that of an educated woman. Did you ever hear any thing more impressively uttered, Mr. De Vane?"

"Never," said De Vane, "never; and her appearance was nothing short of majestic."

"It is very remarkable," said Mr. Clarendon, "that persons who profess to be able to read the future at once acquire a certain ascendency over us. I doubt if the strongest minds are not to some extent under the dominion of that subtle superstition which asserts its sway so widely as to be almost, if not quite, universal. It is one of those points where civilization and barbarism meet. Humanity, in all its conditions, desires to fathom the infinite, and to read the invisible; and we yield some deference to the claims of those who profess to be able to see coming events in the shadows which they cast before them."

"The observation is, I think," said Waring, "a perfectly just one; and I confess that I experienced this evening, when we were confronted with that extraordinary woman, a certain degree of deference and more respect for her utterances than they were at all entitled to."

"By the way," said Mr. Clarendon, "her words were very remarkable. She has uttered a prophecy almost in the language of poetry, and yet susceptible of clear interpretation."

The heightening color of Esther, the conscious look of De Vane, and the expression of Miss Godolphin's face, satisfied him that it was a subject too deeply involving the happiness of those about him to be discussed lightly; and he added: "I must look into this, and see if the prophetess can read my fortunes."

"Ah! Mr. Clarendon," said Esther, "it requires no prophetess to read your future. It is to be a brilliant one."

"And you are ascending the tripod?" said Mr. Clarendon. "I yield to such a priestess," and bending low, he kissed Esther's hand. "No sweeter language could greet me if I stood at Delphi."

The group dispersed, other persons coming forward, and Mr. Springfield turning away to attend to guests just coming in. In the course of the evening, De Vane sought a conversation with Esther, but found her so surrounded that he could only express his wish to speak with her alone, and it was understood between them that he should call the next day at twelve. He took a seat by the side of Miss Godolphin, and had a long and earnest conversation. She was eager to speak with him of his visit to Virginia, and she asked him seriously what his relations were with Miss Guilford.

"Were you jesting, Mr. De Vane, when you said, some evenings since, that she had made no impression on you?"

De Vane smiled. "And do you suppose that I am really a prisoner at large?" he replied.

"Do not evade the question," she said, "but do answer me frankly. I know that she looked forward to meeting you in Virginia with the greatest interest. She often spoke of you, and you were the subject of correspondence with your aunt. She was much admired in Europe, and I am curious to know if you have really escaped, without surrendering to charms which many thought were irresistible."

De Vane saw that she was seriously interested. He did not doubt that the interest grew out of a generous concern for her friend, Miss Wordsworth. The event of the evening had startled her; the roadside prophetess, the strange prediction in regard to the future of the persons before her—for she had evidently designed her words to be prophetic—the emotion of Esther, all satisfied her that the happiness of at least one party might be involved in the growing intercourse between De Vane and Esther, and she resolved, with true and unselfish courage, to seek a free conversation with him.

"I assure you, Miss Godolphin," he said, "that I am perfectly sincere. I found Miss Guilford's beauty resplendent, and I admired her greatly. She transcended my expectations. She is a brilliant woman; but after an unrestricted intercourse of a summer's duration, I left her without the slightest interest in her, beyond the admiration which she excited when we first met. I beg you to believe me when I assure you as a friend—and I trust that you will permit me to hold that relation to you—that it would be impossible for me to regard Miss Guilford with any stronger or tenderer sentiment than that of admiration."

He spoke earnestly. Miss Godolphin extended her hand to him, and said:

"I am honored by your friendship, Mr. De Vane; always regard me as your friend, and allow me to say that my interest in you is far deeper since this conversation than it was before."

De Vane bowed. Esther had never hinted to Miss Godolphin her interest in De Vane, nor had she at any time referred to their relations; but her observation had satisfied Miss Godolphin that a nature so noble, pure, and true as that of Esther, if impressed at all, must be so ineffaceably. Her heart, she felt, was like the plant that blooms but once, exhales its sweetness, and then dies. She had felt it to be her duty to speak to Esther some weeks since in regard to De Vane, to explain to her the peculiarities of his family, the hopes founded upon the expected alliance with Miss Guilford; and she had related to Esther, for the first time, her own past; her relations to the family of Sir George Godolphin; and the suffering which she had endured. In the conversation which had taken place at Leasowes, and in which De Vane had heard himself named, Miss Godolphin had made this communication to Esther.

At this moment several persons came to the sofa where De Vane and Miss Godolphin were seated, and spoke with them, breaking off a conversation intensely interesting to those who were engaged in it, and turning upon subjects which must have led to farther explanations, if it had continued; but society is imperious, and presently quite a general and sparkling talk sprang up, in which Miss Godolphin bore a leading part.

Music followed, Miss Godolphin taking the piano, and Esther accompanying her with her voice, in one of those grand old songs which made every thing yield before the sway of passion uttering itself in the language of poetry, and borrowing harmony to raise and spiritualize it. And so the evening wore away, and the guests departed.

Not all to sleep, however; for Waring and De Vane outsat the early hours of the night in conversation; and Miss Godolphin and Esther invoked tired nature's sweet restorer all in vain, until long after midnight, when they sank into slumbers full of dreams, in which the majestic form of the wild prophetess stood once more before them, speaking of the past and the future.

The next day, at twelve o'clock, De Vane called on Esther, and was received by her in the drawing-room.

"I hope," said he, "that you are bright to-day, and that you have suffered nothing from the adventure of yesterday."

"Not quite bright," said Esther. "I found it impossible to sleep last night. Visions of the strange woman whom we met floated before me, until daylight streamed in through the windows, bringing quite a sense of relief."

"She seemed to impress you," said De Vane; "and she was certainly an extraordinary person to meet on the roadside. I intend to ride out to the same spot this evening, to see if any trace of her can be found."

"Do," said Esther. "I feel the greatest interest in knowing more of her. My aunt agrees in thinking it must be the person whom my uncle described to us last evening."

"I do not doubt it," said De Vane. "How strange it is that such beings utter words, which seem to come freighted with supernatural meaning and emphasis! It is very remarkable that upon returning to my room last evening, my servant handed me a package of letters, and among them was one from my aunt. It is very long, but I shall put it in your hands to read, for I intend, Esther, to treat you throughout our intercourse with perfect frankness. I can give you no higher proof of my love and confidence."

He handed her the letter, and added: "Do not read it now. I shall leave it with you. You will observe that the prediction of the sibyl is speedily verified; clouds be-

19

gin to overspread our path. But let us take courage; they will not linger forever."

A deep flush overspread Esther's face, but she was silent.

"My father," continued De Vane, "does not know you, and his conventional prejudices are like the Virginia mountains, deep-seated, and shrouded often in mists and clouds, which shut out the light and warmth of the brightest and purest mornings. I am not surprised at this. I looked for it, but my aunt, like a glorious woman as she is, is for us, Esther, and that secures every thing. It delights me, and fills me with hope."

Esther looked at the address of the letter which she held in her hand. The writing had a stateliness about it, and elegance. It was thoroughly English, and, she fancied, thoroughly aristocratic.

"I am happy to know," she said, "that Mrs. De Vane regards me kindly. I am of course indebted to you for that."

"I have only described you as you are, Esther," said De Vane; "and Mrs. De Vane has great confidence in my taste and judgment. We often spoke of you when I was in Virginia; and when she became satisfied that her plans for me respecting Miss Guilford would not succeed, she began to hear my representation of you favorably. But my last letter, in which I described an interview at Leasowes, seems to have completed the conquest, and she is now earnestly our friend."

Esther smiled.

"We must be brave, Esther," he continued. "My father's confidence in Mrs. De Vane is fathomless. He knows how fastidious she is, and how thoroughly devoted she is to *caste*. I shall bring every thing right, and our sky will yet be cloudless."

"You must not suffer me, Mr. De Vane," she said, "to

introduce unhappiness into your family. I should be wretched if I saw any estrangement between you and your father. Never, never could I forgive myself if that should follow."

"My dearest Esther," said De Vane, "you must take a brighter view of our relations. I can await the passing away of the clouds. Can you not?"

"I have already said," replied Esther, "that you need not doubt my interest in you. It is too sincere to permit me to darken your home, by bringing the shadow of your father's displeasure upon you. You need not fear any change in my regard for you, but every consideration satisfies me that there should be no change in our relations without the full approbation of General De Vane."

Her soul, full of truth, shone through her eyes, and she seemed almost majestic as with tones sad and gentle, but firm and steady, she uttered these words; as a priestess of Apollo glowing with earthly love, but yet true to the vows which bound her still to minister at the altar, might repel the love who sought to lead her away from the temple where she worshiped.

"Well, Esther," said De Vane, "I can not doubt the future. I will never relinquish you; never but with life itself. Life to me without you is desolate. I scorn its highest prizes, its ambition, its glory; and as to its heartless, soulless conventionalisms, I hate and trample upon them. The paltry things that the world values, I detest; and the stately establishments which it sets up and venerates are but pyramids to hold the ashes of the dead—hollow, gloomy vaults, where every thing is cold and lifeless."

The young patrician rose from his seat, and stood in the full height of his strength and pride. He felt that he was a MAN.

"They shall never bind me," he continued, "with their

fetters, golden though they be; nor compel me to bow before their false gods. While I live in this breathing world, I will give my soul its full expansion, and whatever place the world may assign me, I shall preserve my self-respect. Ancestral honors! family alliances! what are these to me? The poor Indian exchanges his gold for glass beads, and fancies himself happy; but I will never sell my soul for the world's baubles."

His form towered, as he uttered these words with startling energy; and Esther felt that she had never seen him when he appeared so full of glorious manhood. He seemed a demi-god roused to indignation, and yet restraining the passion that shook his soul. He strode across the floor several times, and, turning to Esther, said with gentleness: "I leave Mrs. De Vane's letter with you, Esther. I can not trust myself to speak of these things just now. Good morning!"

Esther gave him her hand. He grasped it with energy, and, bowing low, walked away.

The mid-day sun was in the heavens, and drifting clouds, sweeping away to the eastward, left his disk unvailed. De Vane thought of the sibyl.

In the evening, De Vane and Waring rode to the spot, the scene of the adventure of the previous day; but they could find no trace of the strange being who had startled their party.

They rode into the neighboring woods, but they sought in vain for the prophetess or her people. The only sign of any stranger footprints to be discovered was near a spring of pure and abundant water, some half-mile from the road. There a party had evidently pitched their tents, but they were already gone, and silence reigned over the spot.

## CHAPTER XI.

"Upon her face there was the tint of grief—
The settled shadow of an inward strife—
And an unquiet drooping of the eye,
As if its lid were charged with unshed tears.
What could her grief be?"

LORD BYRON.

THE effect of the appearance of the sibyl upon Miss Godolphin's spirits, was even more marked and abiding than on Esther's. Her sadness seemed to return with increased power. She re-visited the past; and the gloom which was passing away reässerted its dominion. Like the starlit heavens over which drifting clouds fly, obscuring their glory for a time, but leaving the orbs which burn in the far depths the brighter for the passing shadow, all the splendid qualities of her nature were shining out with increasing brilliancy, as her melancholy gave way. But now, deeper gloom overspread her soul, than when she first returned from Europe. Esther observed this with great pain, and sought to attract her from the dark stream where she had seated herself, hanging her harp, like a captive Jewish maiden, upon the willows which fringed its banks. She was much with her; placed in her hands books which might interest her, and brought her under the influence, as often as possible, of those elevating and consoling views of life which cheered her own heart.

Calling one morning on her, she found her seated in her boudoir, with a letter lying before her, with its margin deeply traced with the lines of mourning, and it was wet with tears—fresh tears, though the letter was an old one; and Esther, under an impulse which she could not resist, threw herself on the sofa by the side of her friend, and put her arms around her tenderly. Miss Godolphin, inexpressibly touched by a mark of sympathy so warm, from one whose habitual self-restraint made her sometimes appear even cold, laid her head on Esther's shoulder, and wept as if the fountains of sensibility would pour out all their floods. Soothed by Esther's gentleness, she at length lifted her head—that proud, beautiful, splendid head—and kissed her friend passionately, and then, smiling through her tears, she said:

"You will think me weak, Esther, very weak. I do not know that you have seen me weep before. But I have been re-visiting the past, and it has overwhelmed me with its shadows."

She handed Esther the open letter. It was from Sir George Godolphin—that in which he reproached her with having brought sorrow and desolation upon his house. It was a cruel letter, and it had crushed her spirit.

After reading it, Esther folded it and laid it on the *escritoire.*

"Hortensia," she said, "let me speak with you freely. You are ungenerous with yourself. You have become an ally of Sir George in accusing yourself. A more cruel letter—a more unjust one—I never read. The visit to his house was at his own solicitation; his son was thrown in your way; you dealt honestly with him throughout; you left England; he followed you to the Continent; you never at any time encouraged his addresses; and when you persisted in declining to yield to his wishes, he surrendered himself to a generous but wild adventure, which bore him away from his home and his country, it seems forever."

"Yes, but I encouraged him, Esther. I cheered him on in the glorious but perilous course which he had resolved to pursue, and which would never have been entered on if I had given him any hope for the future."

"But," exclaimed Esther, "you never loved him. Why should you sacrifice yourself for a man whom you never loved, and never could have loved?"

"Oh! never, never! But still, Esther, he loved me, and but for me he would now be the caressed and honored son of a stately but now broken-hearted nobleman, who sees his hopes extinguished forever."

"Hortensia," said Esther earnestly, "have you searched your heart? Was there no love in it? no slightest interest which time might have developed?"

Miss Godolphin hesitated not a moment. She replied instantly, and with her natural energy:

"My heart required no searching. I never loved him—never, never—nor would it be possible for me to love him, if he stood before me to-day in all the strength of his young manhood."

"Then," said Esther, with a beaming smile, "you must dismiss this sadness. I assure you it ought not to darken your life a moment. I am qualified to judge the case. My interest in you has made me study it, and I am perfectly sure that there is nothing whatever with which you should reproach yourself."

"Thank you, dearest Esther," said Miss Godolphin. "You are indeed an angel visiting me in the wilderness, to comfort and guide me; and I will try to drink of the waters of consolation which you have shown me." Both smiled through their tears, for Esther had wept with her friend.

It was a beautiful picture—two young beings, so contrasted in their personal appearance, yet both surpassingly lovely; the one with her profuse fair hair falling in rich curls about her bright face, the other with her dark locks braided in heavy masses and gathered in a clasp of gold at the back of the head, leaving the full outline of her classical features visible; seated side by side, as if an angel, quitting heaven for a season, had come to visit and cheer another who was striving with passions which would not permit her yet to rise to her celestial home.

"The appearance and language of the strange woman whom we saw on the roadside," said Miss Godolphin, "in some way revived the past powerfully. The allusion to darkening young days, and the whole aspect of the extraordinary being, affected me strangely."

"I have observed it," said Esther, "and can sympathize with you, for I was startled and saddened by it myself; but I have reasoned myself out of it. There can be nothing in what she has said."

"I do not know," said Miss Godolphin. "I almost believe that some beings do, in some way, read coming events."

"Oh! no," said Esther. "It can not be."

"Of course," said Miss Godolphin, "reason rejects their claims to supernatural power; and yet it is wonderful that their predictions are sometimes verified by succeeding events. I well remember that the evening before my cousin started on that disastrous adventure, a woman, not unlike her whom we saw a few days since, came to the spot where we were standing, and looking wildly into his face, uttered a solemn warning to him, not to make the journey which he contemplated. He laughed at her words; but she repeated them, saying that if he persisted in going, sorrow would darken his father's house. Oh! I remember so vividly her appearance and her words. The brave young man flushed for a moment at the woman's earnestness, but putting a piece of gold in her hand, he turned from her, and we walked away."

"Such things are strange," said Esther. "But it is quite

impossible that one can read the future without divine enlightenment; and we know they do not possess that."

"Perhaps I am superstitious," said Miss Godolphin; "but I can not free myself from the dominion which such beings exert over me."

"Every one," said Esther, "I suppose, has a tinge of superstition, which gives its coloring to life. I am very sensible of it. I require some time to bring my reason to my aid; and for days after meeting the strange woman who startled us, I could not regain my composure."

"Is it not related of King Saul, that he consulted the Witch of Endor?" asked Miss Godolphin.

"Yes," replied Esther, "and the result was a great shock to the stately king. When the prophet appeared, he fell straightway along the earth, and was sore afraid."

"It is very wonderful," said Miss Godolphin. "What power could the witch have possessed over Samuel?"

"None whatever," said Esther. "The appearance of the prophet must have been permitted, to carry out the purposes of God, in regard to the erring monarch. The incantations of the pythoness could have had no power over a prophet of God. It was when the king heard the awful words from the lips of the prophet, that on the next day he and his sons were to be slain in battle, that, overwhelmed with such a heavy message, his strength gave way, and he fell prostrate."

"My heart always mourns over his fate," said Miss Godolphin. "I have heard Mr. Waring describe him in a way that interested and saddened me beyond expression: his early life, his modesty, his splendid person, his grand administration of the affairs of his kingdom, his declining fortunes, his clinging to the sceptre until it was torn from his grasp on a bloody field; and then his regal courage, and his death upon a mountain-side from which he could look out upon the lost battle, a disaster which his pride would not suffer him to survive."

The next day Waring called at Leasowes, and held a long conversation with Esther. He had observed the deepening gloom of Miss Godolphin, and it saddened him. The cloud which threw its shadow upon her, wrapped him too in its folds, for his interest in her had become so strong, as to control his thoughts and emotions.

Esther dealt with him frankly. She knew that De Vane had informed him of the history of Miss Godolphin, and she therefore spoke with the greater freedom. Her interest in Waring could not have been greater if he had been a brother. She was resolved that he should not be deceived in any thing, if she could prevent it; and therefore, when he spoke to her at Leasowes, she gave him a full statement of facts so far as she was herself acquainted with them.

"This I learned," she said, in concluding her statement, "from Miss Godolphin, and I am sure, that so far from wishing to conceal it from you, she would desire you to be fully informed of it.

"It corresponds perfectly," said Waring, "with what De Vane said to me; and he heard the facts from Miss Guilford. But upon one point, I wish you to speak to me without reserve. Did Miss Godolphin ever love her cousin?"

"Never," said Esther. "Of that I am fully assured. She herself spoke to me in a way to satisfy me that her heart was never interested. On that you may rely."

"Why, then," said Waring, "this sadness—this protracted grief?"

"It springs," said Esther, "from deep sensibility, and from unjust self-accusation. That is the sole cause of it, I assure you. She has suffered beyond description; but if her cousin stood before her to-day, to urge his suit, she would reject him."

Waring looked relieved.

"Thank you, my friend," he said, "thank you. I need not explain to you why I have sought this interview. Of course, you comprehend the nature of my interest in Miss Godolphin."

Esther smiled. "I think so," she said.

"I do not know how Miss Godolphin regards me. She is so brilliant, and is, in some respects, so aristocratic, that it is impossible to say how she may view me, my opinions, my creed, or my people."

Esther was silent for a moment. She felt the extreme difficulty of her position. She did not know how Miss Godolphin regarded her friend, and she thought it possible Waring's apprehensions were not unfounded.

"Miss Godolphin's nature," she said at length, "is a noble one. She has heart, but I think that her habitual sadness—produced by the fate of her cousin—has prevented her feeling an interest in any one, beyond that of friendship."

"I hope," said Waring, "that you will permit me sometimes to speak with you upon this subject."

"Most willingly," said Esther. "You know, Mr. Waring, that you are my brother."

"And you may be assured that I shall be, while I live," said Waring.

He took his leave; and Esther felt a strong desire to do what she could to make brighter and happier the path of the noble and true man, whose pure heart and great intellect were consecrated to the noblest task of life, and who, with all his learning, had the guileless simplicity of a little child.

## CHAPTER XII.

"A CHANGE came o'er the spirit of my dream;
The Wanderer was returned."
LORD BYRON.

ON Saturday morning, Esther had gone to Leasowes early, intending to pass an hour or two with the little girls before going into the town. It was her wish to visit the book-store of Mr. Müller, that she might select something to present to Mr. Springfield, upon the recurrence of his birthday—a mark of respect and affection which she never omitted.

She had been in her grounds but a half-hour, and was walking with little Mary Sinclair and one or two others, when she saw Mrs. Habersham's coach dash up to the gate. The footman threw open the door, and Miss Godolphin, leaping out, disdaining the steps, rushed through the gate, and sprang to where Esther was standing in the midst of the little group, who, dismayed at her impetuosity, gave way. She threw her arms about Esther, and exclaimed:

"O Esther! Esther! he lives! He has reached England!"

Her agitation was very great. Her face was glowing, and it beamed with a joy which Esther had never seen it wear before.

"Do you not understand?" she exclaimed. "Hubert Godolphin, my cousin, who was lost to us, is living, and has returned to England."

"Oh! is it possible?" cried Esther. "The dead is alive, and the lost is found."

"Yes," said Miss Godolphin, "that beautiful saying is realized perfectly. I have just received a letter from Sir George, overflowing with kindness. He begs me to pardon all his harshness. Oh! what a mountain has rolled from me! It really seems as if the words of the strange woman had already been fulfilled—*that the darkness which clouds the morning passes away, leaving the heavens brighter than ever before.*"

How resplendent she was, standing in the October sun, the whole face and form radiant with joy! She accompanied Esther to the house, and handed her Sir George's letter. It recounted the adventures of his son. He was dangerously wounded, but not slain in battle, and had been carried a prisoner into the mountains, where he had passed some three years, before he could effect a communication with the British Minister at Constantinople. After that, he was speedily released, returned to England, and intends now to visit the United States."

"Then we shall see him here," said Esther.

"So it seems," said Miss Godolphin. "We shall expect him daily, until his arrival. Oh! you can not imagine how happy I am."

Esther looked a little grave. She was the soul of truth. She had assured Waring that Miss Godolphin had never loved her cousin. Had she misinterpreted her own heart, when she said so to Esther? Did she really love him? Would his loyalty, under so many adverse circumstances, win her heart, if he had never succeeded in doing so hitherto?

She trembled a little for Waring; but a few weeks would decide the questions which she so rapidly addressed to herself. Her solicitude was so great, that it appeared in her manner. Miss Godolphin observed it, and said:

"You do not sympathize with me, Esther. Oh! if you could know what I have suffered, you would rejoice with me."

"I do rejoice with you, dear Hortensia, heartily," she said. "No one has felt a truer sympathy with you than myself."

She rose, and kissed Miss Godolphin fervently.

"And now," said Miss Godolphin, "I must hasten back to my aunt. These letters came only this morning, and after we had read them, I said to her that I must see you, and let you know my joy."

They embraced each other, and Miss Godolphin was about leaving the house, when, turning again to Esther, she said:

"But you are not to pass all the morning here. Will you not take a seat with me, and drive into the town?"

"With pleasure," said Esther. "Let me detain you but a moment."

Giving some directions to Mrs. Green, she accompanied Miss Godolphin to the carriage, and driving to the bookstore, she entered it, to make her selection for Mr. Springfield's library.

After looking over the shelves for some time, turning to the table where the books just received were placed, she found a fine copy of Jeremy Taylor's works, an English edition, just imported, and she directed that it should be sent to her.

She was about to leave the store, when Waring and De Vane entered it, and seeing her, walked to the alcove where she was standing.

"We are fortunate, Miss Wordsworth," said Waring. "We did not know that we should meet you here."

Esther explained the object of her coming, and showed the volumes which she had purchased.

"They are beautiful," said De Vane; "and the little

acquaintance that I have with the writings of Jeremy Taylor, makes me desire to read his works at length."

"They are most attractive," said Waring. "They are as varied and beautiful as nature."

Stepping to the counter where Mr. Müller stood, he inquired if he could duplicate the set which Miss Wordsworth had just purchased; and being informed that there was one more copy, bound in somewhat different style, he directed that it should be stamped with the words, GEORGE DE VANE, on each volume, and sent to Mrs. Bowen's.

Returning to where De Vane and Esther were standing, she said: "I have a very gratifying piece of intelligence to communicate."

Both the gentlemen looked eagerly at her, and awaited her words. She then proceeded to inform them of the facts made known to her by Miss Godolphin, in regard to her cousin, Hubert Godolphin. Both expressed their astonishment and their gratification.

"And how does it affect Miss Godolphin?" asked De Vane.

"It has filled her with joy," said Esther. "Never have I witnessed such an effect produced by a letter, as Sir George Godolphin's produced on her. It was an ample apology for all his previous want of generosity; a full atonement, so far as an acknowledgment of the kind could constitute it, for his harshness."

"And the heaven of her soul will now be cloudless," said De Vane.

"Yes," said Esther, with emphasis. "And I must inform you, also, that Hubert Godolphin is to visit his cousin immediately, and bear his father's acknowledgments in person, for past injustice."

Waring's face flushed, and De Vane looked surprised.

"It is all very strange," said De Vane. "*Mehercule!*

Waring, I believe that the sibyl saw the coming event, when she looked so steadily at Miss Godolphin, and uttered those remarkable words."

"It is simply," said Waring gently, "one of those remarkable things which sometimes occur in the moral world, to startle us."

He looked a little troubled. Esther felt for him. She had almost dreaded to make the communication to him; but she thought it better that he should hear it from her, rather than be startled by the announcement from Miss Godolphin, with her exuberant joy.

"I am somewhat curious to see a gentleman who has endured such fortunes," said De Vane. "When is he to arrive?"

"He is to be looked for daily, as he was to sail in the next vessel after that which brought his letters."

Waring was very grave; but his self-possession had returned, and he entered into cheerful conversation with De Vane and Esther upon the effect which this event must produce upon Miss Godolphin.

After speaking of books and friends, Esther left the store, and Waring and De Vane soon followed, walking slowly homeward.

"By the way, Waring," said De Vane, "let us take the shop of our friend Hobbs in the way, and give him instructions about our horses; their shoes want attention."

Waring assenting, they visited the blacksmith; and it being his habit to rest at noon, they found him deep in a book, as if utterly unconscious of forge and sledge-hammer.

"How are you, Mr. Hobbs?" said De Vane, rousing him.

"Bless my soul and body, Mr. De Vane, is that you? I'm well, thank'ee. How is it with yourself? How d'ye do, Mr. Waring?"

"We are both pretty well, Mr. Hobbs," said De Vane. "Our horseback exercise does us good."

"Nothing like it in the world, sir," said Mr. Hobbs, "but striking with the sledge-hammer; that'll cure any dyspeptic in the world."

"I suspect you are right," said Waring. "But, Mr. Hobbs, we should soon break down at that business."

"Not a bit of it," said the blacksmith. "I didn't weigh a hundred and thirty when I began the trade, and now I go hard on to two hundred."

The gentlemen both laughed as the honest blacksmith raised himself to his full height, and looked as if he could give Hercules a tight wrestle.

"What are you reading to-day, Mr. Hobbs?" asked De Vane.

"Why, sir," said he, "my boy, who is named after General Marion, brought home his life, by Weems, that Mrs. Steele, his school-teacher, gave him; and I was reading that."

"A very interesting book," said De Vane. "I like to read it myself."

"It is interesting," said the blacksmith. "Jasper and Newton gave them chaps that they attacked thunder."

"Oh! yes," said De Vane; "they were brave fellows."

"But the best thing in the book," continued the blacksmith, "is where Sergeant McDonald got *Seline* out of the clutches of that infernal old tory. I should have liked to have the shoeing of that horse. I'd have done it for McDonald all the days of his life without charging him a cent."

Perceiving that Mr. Hobbs was becoming rather animated, De Vane said: "Speaking of shoeing horses, we called to request you to pay special attention to the feet of ours. Perhaps it would be well to make their shoes somewhat lighter."

"I like a good heavy shoe on a horse, myself," said the blacksmith; "but as you so seldom drive yours, it may be just as well to make them lighter."

"Do," said De Vane; "and instead of heels, make the swell in the shoe a little fuller at the back part of the foot, and the toe thinner."

"I'll do it, sir," said Mr. Hobbs, "but the shoes won't last any time."

"Oh! never mind that," said De Vane. "We do not ride a great deal."

"That horse of yours, Mr. Waring," said the blacksmith, "is the best conditioned thing that ever I saw. He's most equal to Miss Wordsworth's horse."

"I am glad to hear you speak well of him," said Waring; "and if he equals Miss Wordsworth's horse, he must be fine."

"That horse," said the blacksmith, "has got almost as much sense as a human. I've seen Miss Wordsworth riding him, and the way he behaves himself is beautiful; and when I go to shoe him, if I just tell him to hold up his foot, he does it as natural as if he spoke English."

"I suspect he understands it," said Waring, laughing.

Bidding the blacksmith good-morning, they walked to Mrs. Bowen's.

Waring's interview with the blacksmith had done him good; and De Vane was pleased to see that he was becoming cheerful.

"That man," said Waring, "has a great amount of good in him. He sees the strong points of a book at once. If the fellow was not quite so strong in his language, I should enjoy his conversation more."

"He restrains himself in your presence," said De Vane. "If you could hear him indulge his vocabulary when I am alone with him, you would pronounce him decidedly emphatic."

"You must break the habit in him, De Vane. He has great faith in you, and you can control him."

"I have once or twice remonstrated with him," said De Vane, "but, before he knows it, he breaks out again. I must give him the names of some of the heathen gods to swear by—Vulcan, for instance."

Waring laughed, and they entered the house.

Some short time after De Vane had entered his room, Mr. Müller's messenger came with the package of books, which he said he had been directed to leave there.

"There must be some mistake," said De Vane. "I made no purchase at the book-store this morning."

"Mr. Müller said they were for you, sir," said the messenger; and setting down his basket, he laid the books on the table.

De Vane opened the package, and found his name, stamped in gold, on the back.

"Mr. Waring bought them, sir," said the messenger, "and said they were to be left here for you."

De Vane at once comprehended it, and dismissed the messenger.

He was touched by this act of kindness on the part of Waring. The selection of books, the delicacy with which it was done, and the value of the gift, were felt by him. When he met Waring in the evening, he thanked him warmly, and assured him that he could have made him no more acceptable gift.

"I trust, De Vane," he said, "that you will find your interest in the grand old preacher increase as you read his works. There is a wonderful richness in his style, and a refreshing purity pervading his teachings, of which one never grows weary."

"I shall put myself under his instructions systematically," said De Vane, "and shall endeavor to follow them faithfully."

Waring was delighted. He felt that the taste of De Vane would not only not be offended by the works which he had put into his hands, but that their beauties would allure him into far deeper researches than he could be induced to make in any theological writings less attractive. And this pure, generous, thorough Christian found, in his effort to bring his friend into the path of life, something to brighten his own spirit, just now troubled by apprehensions respecting his relations with Miss Godolphin, as the clouds which skirt the horizon are sometimes illumined with golden tints by a warm ray of light streaming upon them from the sun, which they mantle with their drapery as he sinks to rest.

## CHAPTER XIII.

> "I HAD not known her long, but loved her more
> Than I could dream of then. Oh! even now
> I dare not dwell upon my passion: more
> Than life itself I loved her, and still love."
>
> WILLIAM CROSS WILLIAMSON.

THE town was unusually gay. The assembling of the Legislature had brought there the most eminent men in the State, who were either members of that body, or who came as visitors, many of them bringing their families, to pass a few weeks at a place so attractive. Some of them took furnished houses, and entertained handsomely; brought their equipages, servants, and plate with them; and the little capital shone with a far higher splendor than many larger ones. The triumph of General Jackson was complete; and the prospect of a new administration, coming in with so much of popular favor, lent extraordinary interest to political topics.

Mr. Clarendon was in the highest spirits. He entertained magnificently, and assembled at his house, from time to time, the most brilliant people. De Vane was recognized as a man of great promise, and he received marked and flattering attentions from the leading men of the State. Mr. Le Grande was known to be his friend, and Mr. Clarendon openly predicted his future eminence. A grand career was opening before him. As a very marked compliment, he was invited by Mr. Le Grande to meet at dinner a select number of the most eminent men in the State, where the programme of the incoming Administration was discussed, its policy foreshadowed, and the members of the Cabinet were brought on the *tapis*—a political dinner, where the work of the whole political campaign was laid out. Nor was it an empty compliment paid to De Vane, for he was drawn out in conversation, and his large views were appreciated by the eminent men who sat with him. Self-possessed, and yet deferential to men of larger experience than himself, he expressed his opinions with freedom when called out; and so successfully did he represent them, that he made an impression upon that small but brilliant assemblage that never was effaced.

The session of the Legislature was one of unusual interest; and Mr. Le Grande distinguished himself by a luminous speech upon a proposition which had been brought forward to reduce the laws of the State into a code.

It being understood that he was to speak on a certain day, the galleries and lobbies were thronged, and among the number De Vane and Esther were seen favorably seated.

There, too, Mrs. Habersham and Miss Godolphin, attended by Waring, had seats. Mrs. Clarendon was present, with two or three ladies from the sea-board, attended by Mr. Clarendon.

The speech of Mr. Le Grande was made in opposition to the measure. He insisted that a great system like their law could not advantageously be embraced within a code; that the Code of Napoleon afforded no proper precedent for any such undertaking; that our law had grown up with society, advancing with its progress, accommodating itself to its wants; and that Napoleon introduced his Code really to reconstruct society, when the French Revolution had swept away every thing established, and had overthrown all barriers. The argument was fine, and it heightened the reputation even of Mr. Le Grande. The scheme was defeated.

At this session, too, a case of impeachment came up, of very great interest. It affected the privileges of an eminent citizen, whose public services and high personal qualities endeared him to the people of the State. Several of the ablest members of the House of Representatives were appointed to conduct the prosecution, the Senate being the tribunal before which it was heard. The defense was confided to Mr. Clarendon. He conducted it with so much ability, so much energy, so much grace, so much learning, that it earned for him imperishable renown. The whole trial, from the beginning to the end, was most impressive. The venerable man who took his seat day after day with meek dignity, the august tribunal before which he was arraigned, the deep sympathy felt for him by his judges, the recollection of his public services, the clouds which were already hanging their solemn drapery around the far-advanced evening of his life, the splendid array of talent in the committee selected to conduct the prosecution, and the brilliant and powerful exhibition of intellect and ardor shown by his great advocate—all contributed to make it a deeply affecting spectacle, over which a sad splendor reigned throughout. Mr. Clarendon's speech was full of learning and eloquence, rivaling the highest oratorical display which was elicited upon the trial of Warren Hastings; and if it had been delivered in Westminster Hall, on such an occasion, it would have ranked him at once with the great Parliamentary speakers whose fame is limited only by the bounds of civilization. Uttered where it was, in the presence of an audience as cultivated and appreciative as any country could furnish, it won for him the highest distinction, and inaugurated that splendid career which the whole nation subsequently witnessed. Powerful and brilliant as the defense was, it could not avert the solemn sentence which the great tribunal was compelled, from a controlling sense of duty, to deliver. But even then, the brief, subdued, but beautiful speech which the venerable man uttered as he bowed before the inexorable authority of his judges, prepared by Mr. Clarendon, melted them to tears; and the words of the President of the Senate, sonorous and full of dignity, touched with a generous sympathy, almost trembled as they conveyed the stern judgment of a court too pure to yield to passion, and too great not to be affected by such a spectacle—age and suffering appealing in vain in sight of the form of Justice holding aloft the scales in the clear light of Truth.

De Vane heard Mr. Clarendon's great speech with uncontrollable enthusiasm. It swept him like a torrent, and Esther, who was seated by his side, observed him, as the grand and ardent nature of the young Virginian, fired by the oratory of his noble friend, flamed up with full sympathy and increased admiration.

"*Mehercule!* Miss Wordsworth," he exclaimed, "the world rarely hears any thing like that. It is the revivification of the godlike speech which was uttered under the skies of Greece. It has never been excelled, in ancient or modern times."

"Glorious!" said Esther, "glorious! O Mr. De Vane! what power there is in eloquence. Neither the thunder of cannon nor the fury of the storm itself can rival it. It is, as you say, godlike."

All around them there was the greatest enthusiasm, and praises were lavished upon the orator. Presently they met Waring and his party, and the friends greeted each other in that warm way which prevails when great sentiments animate and control us.

"I'll venture to say," said Waring, addressing himself to Esther, "that De Vane has been swearing by Hercules. Has he not, now?"

She laughed, and said: "I believe I did hear some such classical exclamation, but I think it must be pardoned, and conceded as an involuntary tribute to surpassing eloquence."

"Certainly," said Miss Godolphin; "Mr. De Vane should be allowed to swear by all the gods of Olympus in witnessing such a triumph of his friend."

At this moment Mr. Clarendon, accompanied by Mr. Le Grande, came up to the group, where they stood waiting to receive him, and they offered him their congratulations. He thanked them, and said: "Would that I could have done more for the old man! His gray hairs appeal to me in a way that is positively dreadful. I suffer unspeakably."

"Then you can not save him?" exclaimed Esther.

"My dear child," said he, laying his hand kindly on hers, "I fear not."

"It is too sad," said Miss Godolphin, her eyes filling with tears.

They entered their carriages and drove away. It was as Mr. Clarendon feared it would be, but it afforded one of the finest exhibitions of the ascendency of the higher qualities of humanity which the world has ever witnessed.

In the course of the session, Mr. Hallam was elected one of the Chancellors of the State, and became associated with the venerable Chancellor De Lolme, whose learning, accomplishments, and manners had long adorned that bench, and whose elegant hospitality contributed largely to refine and elevate the tone of the society in which he lived.

Some few days after the delivery of Mr. Clarendon's great speech, De Vane met him walking toward the State House, with a gentleman whose appearance at once interested him. He was evidently a stranger, as evidently a foreigner, and there was in his manner something so distinctly aristocratic, that it was impossible to overlook it. His features, without being decidedly intellectual, were fine; his complexion was dark, as were his hair and eyes; and there was a manliness in his bearing which imparted unusual dignity to the appearance of one so young—he could scarcely be thirty. As De Vane was about to pass, after lifting his hat to Mr. Clarendon, that gentleman said:

"Excuse me, Mr. De Vane, for detaining you a moment. I wish to present you to Mr. Godolphin, son of Sir George, who has just arrived from England."

After an interchange of the usual civilities, the gentlemen separated, and De Vane walked directly to Mr. Springfield's; and upon being shown into the library, asked for Miss Wordsworth. Esther had but a moment before returned from Leasowes, and coming into the room with hat and shawl on, she said:

"Rather than keep you waiting, Mr. De Vane, I come without even stopping to take off my hat."

"Thank you," said De Vane, rising to take her extended hand. "I was anxious to see you, and I am glad that you are so prompt in coming to meet me. Do you know that Hubert Godolphin is here?"

"Indeed!" exclaimed Esther, becoming very pale. "No, I had not heard it. Have you seen him?"

"Yes," said De Vane. "I met him on the sidewalk with Mr. Clarendon, who presented me to him. Have you met Miss Godolphin this morning?"

"I have not," said Esther. "I have been all the morning at Leasowes. Do you know when Mr. Godolphin arrived?"

"Last night," said De Vane. "He brings letters of introduction to Mr. Clarendon, and he has gone with him to the State House, to present him to Mr. Le Grande, and some two or three celebrities besides. I feel the greatest anxiety to know how Miss Godolphin will receive her cousin. My interest in Waring is such, that I am positively unhappy about him. His nature has wonderful depth, and he is attached to Miss Godolphin in a way to involve his happiness for life. If he should be disappointed in her, I do not know how he could bear it. He is so noble, so gentle and yet so strong, so pure, so full of truth, and with such an intellect as to entitle him to the homage of all men; that I do not know how any woman can resist him, if he should honor her with his love."

Esther smiled at his earnestness, and said: "Your interest in Mr. Waring does not exceed my own. I have observed Miss Godolphin, and have wished to know whether her regard for our friend is that of mere friendship, or something deeper and intenser; but I have not been able to satisfy myself respecting what is at once so interesting and so delicate a subject. That she does not love Hubert Godolphin, I am confident; at least, I am very confident that she has not loved him heretofore. What his presence may effect, and this new proof of the strength of his own attachment, I can not say; but her nature is noble, and the earnestness and truth of her character really rise into grandeur."

"Then Waring is safe!" exclaimed De Vane. "No woman of a really grand nature can refuse his love."

"You must not overlook," said Esther, "the influence of caste. The tastes of Miss Godolphin might incline her to the style of life which, as the wife of the son of Sir George, she could lead, notwithstanding the contempt which she avows for mere conventional rank, unaccompanied by refinement and worth."

"Never!" said De Vane, with great vehemence, "never! I would stake a kingdom upon the loyalty of Miss Godolphin to those sentiments which I know, Esther, you prize so highly. You must not suffer yourself to believe that Waring is not prized just as highly as he would be, if he were an earl's son."

"He is, of course, by you, Mr. De Vane, and by all who

feel as you do. But after all, he belongs to a despised sect, and high as Miss Godolphin's nature is, it may be that she would hesitate to walk through life by the side of one who has consecrated himself to the task of preaching the Gospel, not only to the rich and the great, but to the poor and the outcast."

De Vane rose, and walked rapidly across the room several times. He was profoundly moved by Esther's language. He knew that she loved Waring as a sister loves an only brother, and he saw that at this critical conjuncture of his fortunes, all her pride was roused for him; he was to be measured with a patrician, the son of a nobleman; wealth, family, every thing to aid the one, while the other could only offer his own glorious nature and splendid endowments, without fortune or rank to aid him. And the very majesty of her own transcendent womanhood displayed itself in behalf of her friend. Her form rose to its full height, as she stood near the centre of the library, and her large eyes blazed with full lustre. Never had De Vane seen her more roused, never more splendidly beautiful. Her height and color gave extraordinary brilliancy to her face, and the consciousness of speaking for her friend, for her sect, for her people, for humanity in its native worth—as compared with the pride of life, and the pretension of rank, and the assumed glory of conventional and privileged classes—imparted to her an air nothing short of majestic. There she stood, a daughter of the people, and De Vane felt that in her presence the titled and the great might bow their heads, encircled with coronets, and bend their jeweled necks in homage.

"Esther," said he, "I should regard any woman with immeasurable scorn, who could weigh fortune or rank against the simple, native qualities of such a man as Waring. He absolutely ennobles the race by belonging to it. He vindicates humanity from its low estate by the glory of his nature. As to Miss Godolphin's estimate of him, we shall see what disclosures time may make. He has never yet spoken to her of love; nor will he, until this visit of her cousin has ended. He is too proud, or, perhaps I ought to say, he has too much self-respect, to enter into competition with any man for the hand of the woman he loves."

Taking Esther's hand, he bent his head and touched it with his lips, and left the house. As he walked toward Mrs. Bowen's, he revolved every thing in connection with the relations of Waring and Miss Godolphin, which could in any way affect them, and yet he could reach no satisfactory conclusion. He sympathized with Esther's anxiety, and almost shared her jealous pride for Waring; for he comprehended the full magnitude of the opposition which was to be encountered by him in seeking the hand of Miss Godolphin. His own relations with Esther were clouded by influences springing from aristocratic prejudices, and he felt how powerful they were, even when directed against one so peerless as herself. He saw, too, that his own hopes were endangered by the view which Esther was now disposed to take, of the inherent antagonism between the tastes of that aristocratic class and the opinions and habits of her own people; and he knew her well enough to comprehend that she would never consent to ally herself to a family that looked with disdain upon a people of whom she believed the world was not worthy. She would never consent to be received into an aristocratic circle as an exceptional case, with the understanding that she was to look coldly upon her people and make her religious views as little obtrusive as possible. She was at any time prepared, like the Jewish maiden, to offer up her life as a sacrifice for the glory of the despised people to which she belonged, and she would have smiled as she yielded her pure bosom to the glittering steel of the heroic hand that was to smite her; but she could never renounce them for the sake of an aristocratic or even royal alliance. She was content, too, to endure whatever reproach or contempt might be visited upon her people, and she would not have exchanged the privilege of being an humble worshiper in that chapel for a diadem, and all the splendor of the most gorgeous establishments. All this De Vane felt, and his passion deepened as he thought of her whom he had just seen in all the glow of awakened and almost indignant earnestness. He entered the house. Waring had not yet arrived. Going to his own room, he found on his table an invitation from Mr. Clarendon to meet Mr. Hubert Godolphin the next day at dinner.

Soon after, Waring entered the house, and presently came into De Vane's room. He held in his hand a note. It was an invitation from Clarendon to dinner. De Vane rose to meet his friend with more than usual respect in his manner, and offered him a seat.

"It seems," said Waring, "that Mr. Godolphin has arrived. Have you met him?"

"Yes," replied De Vane, "I met him this morning, in company with Mr. Clarendon. He came last night; and we are to join him at dinner to-morrow, when you will have the opportunity of judging for yourself, how much he is to be admired or—dreaded."

Waring smiled, and said: "I see that you do not intend to describe him. You go to Mr. Clarendon's, of course?"

"Of course," replied De Vane; "and you?"

"Yes," said Waring. "Are there to be ladies, or is it a dinner for gentlemen?"

"For gentlemen only, I suppose," said De Vane; "the object being to introduce this young Englishman, who rivals Othello, at least, in hair-breadth 'scapes, to the celebrities who are here, you being one of them."

"And you," said Waring.

"Oh!" said De Vane, laughing, "I am invited to see the dignitaries, and to make myself agreeable generally. I shall expect you to shine, Waring. You must lay aside reserve, and give them an opportunity to see something of that wealth which you so carefully conceal in general society."

Waring smiled, but made no reply.

"The truth is," said De Vane, "it is only when you are with friends—such, for instance, as Mr. Springfield, Mr. Clarendon, and myself—that you seem at all disposed to employ your capital; and while we are very much honored by your confidence, we feel a natural desire that others should know you as we do; so you must really rouse yourself."

"Such is my organization," said Waring, "that I converse freely only with those who appreciate what I have to say. You never knew any one who was so much affected by the audience he addresses, as I am. Unaffectedly, I grow warm and sympathizing when I am surrounded by those who are cultivated, and in whom genial nature has created the living soul—not a mere half-torpid faculty called by that name. Opaque bodies darken me, and dense souls oppress me."

"I have observed it," said De Vane; "but we shall not meet such people at Mr. Clarendon's. I have observed, too, that you must be drawn out, to enable you to take part in conversation in general society, even when it is composed of the most intellectual people. In short, I think you are a little proud, and do not like to display your power, unless you are invited to do so, or roused by opposition; then you are yourself. I would give a great deal to see you fairly roused to-morrow, by Mr. Le Grande, for instance, or by Dr. Hume, if he should happen to be present."

"We must hear Mr. Godolphin," said Waring. "It would hardly be proper to engross the conversation at a dinner-table where he is the honored guest."

"I am inclined to think that he would be very much obliged to you for taking that part of the entertainment off his hands," said De Vane, "if I may judge by his face. He is pleasant-looking, but not intellectual."

"Ah!" said Waring. "Did you have much conversation with him?"

"Very little," replied De Vane. "He is gentlemanlike and agreeable; but his aspect does not disclose the regnant mind."

"We must call on him," said Waring. "It is due to Miss Godolphin, that every mark of respect should be paid to her relative."

"Certainly," said De Vane. "Let us go now."

Calling at the hotel, they were informed that Mr. Godolphin had not yet returned from his walk; and leaving their cards, the gentlemen returned to Mrs. Bowen's.

When Waring and De Vane entered the drawing-room of Mr. Clarendon the next day, they found quite a large party of gentlemen already assembled; at least, it was large for a dinner at a private house, where the number should not exceed twelve or fifteen, if it is to be genial, and not strictly ceremonious and stately. The two Chancellors were there, and several of the eminent members of the Legislature—Mr. Le Grande one of them; Dr. Hume, Professor Niles, and Professor Waring, representing the College. Mr. Godolphin had not arrived, but came not a great while after, and the gentlemen present were formally presented to him by Mr. Clarendon.

Mrs. Clarendon did not make her appearance at the table, and Mr. Clarendon seated Mr. Godolphin on his right, with Mr. Le Grande for his *vis-à-vis*, placing Waring on the right of that gentleman, and De Vane on the other side of him; so that the group were able to interchange conversation with each other with ease.

On the left of Mr. Clarendon sat Chancellor De Lolme, whose elegant manners and fine conversational powers, imparted a great charm to the party. Mr. Godolphin, accustomed as he was to meet cultivated, refined, and eminent persons, soon felt that he was in the presence of men of no common order; and as the conversation became free and general, he could scarcely forbear to express his surprise and gratification; but while his own good breeding restrained any remark of the kind, he exhibited in his whole manner his appreciation of the gentlemen who surrounded him. He excelled in conversation, and was very entertaining, because thoroughly informed as to the progress of events in the actual world. As to books, he did not seem disposed to speak of them; so that when, by some remark of Mr. Le Grande, addressed to Waring, the subject of ethical philosophy, as it was treated on the Continent, in contrast with the opinions held in England and Scotland, came up, he took no part in it, but listened with marked attention to the learned and brilliant discourse of those gentlemen. De Vane's wish was fully gratified, for Waring was thoroughly roused by Mr. Le Grande, and he unconsciously displayed those rare treasures of intellect and learning, which his friends well knew him to possess, but which he usually disclosed only in genial conversation with them, or from his Professor's chair. For some time the whole party were attracted by the conversation of the two gentlemen; and as it advanced, the fascination became so complete, that it was with reluctance the guests rose from the table, after a sitting so unusually long, that they found the hour was quite late when they returned to the drawing-room to take their coffee.

Even Dr. Hume expressed his gratification, and coming to where Mr. Le Grande was standing, he said:

"I am very much obliged to you, sir, for all that you have said; and I hope at some time to hear the discussion renewed between yourself and Professor Waring; you both maintain your opinions well."

"You are very good," said Mr. Le Grande. "I think the College has great reason to be proud of the young Professor."

"So we are, sir," said Dr. Hume. "He is skilled in dialectics."

All who heard the remark smiled.

De Vane entered into conversation with Godolphin, and inquired if it was his purpose to make an extended tour through the United States.

"I think not," he replied. "I should be pleased to visit your great West; but I have been so long absent from England, that I shall return early in the spring. I wish in the mean while to pass some time in Washington, where some of my countrymen are sojourning."

"I should be pleased to show you any thing here which may interest you during your stay," said De Vane.

"You are very good," replied Mr. Godolphin. "I am charmed with the place. It quite surpasses my expectations, though it had been described to me in glowing terms by friends who reside here."

Waring came forward, and said: "We shall be happy to see you, Mr. Godolphin, at the College, during your stay here. We have a library which may interest you; for, while it is not very extensive, it is well selected.

"Thank you," he replied. "It will, I'm sure, afford me great pleasure to visit the College. You must allow me to say that it is well represented here to-day."

Waring bowed.

The next morning, cards of invitation came, both to

Waring and to De Vane, from Chancellor De Lolme, inviting them to dinner on the following day. It was the first time that Waring had been honored with an invitation to that house, and De Vane was delighted; for it was a tribute to him, as a man, from a very exclusive and aristocratic quarter, and it was the most satisfactory proof of the decided impression which his conversation on the previous day had made on the brilliant circle assembled at Mr. Clarendon's table. De Vane felt that Waring's social position was now perfectly well settled, and that from this time forth all the consideration would be extended to him which his preëminent abilities and noble qualities so richly merited.

Eager to learn what Miss Godolphin's impressions were, since the return of her cousin, De Vane walked to Leasowes about twelve o'clock, when he knew he should find Esther released from her morning's engagement with her little charge. Entering the gate, he was advancing upon one of the winding walks leading to the house, when he saw both Miss Godolphin and Esther engaged in earnest conversation, walking in one of the paths which conducted to the gate by a still wider circuit. They had not seen him, and hurriedly retracing his steps, he emerged from the grounds, and passed on to the town. He congratulated himself at not having met Miss Godolphin under circumstances so embarrassing, and he was now confident that he should be able to learn from Esther what he so much desired to know; for his interest in Waring was too deep to suffer him to wait inactively while the crisis of his fate developed itself. He resolved to call on Esther in the evening, and after a full conversation with her, to contribute what he might to protect his friend from any unnecessary pain, or, if possible, to advance his hopes.

In the evening, he called at Mr. Springfield's, and asked for Miss Wordsworth. He was shown into the drawing-room, and after some little time Esther entered. She was radiant, and De Vane felt that she had good tidings for him. He rose to meet her, and she welcomed him with her brightest smile.

"If I should ask you, Esther, in the beautiful language of the Scriptures, 'What of the night?' what would be your reply?"

"I should answer," she said, "in the same language: 'The morning cometh, and also the night.'"

"I must beg you to interpret for me," said De Vane; "for I really do not comprehend the language, couched as it is in such a figure. Do you mean that Waring's sky is to be visited with the morning light, after such a weary night of doubt and watching, and that then a still darker and longer night is to close in upon it?"

"Ah! Mr. De Vane," said Esther playfully, "you must study the Scriptures. You appealed to me by quoting the language of the sublime prophet, and I could do no less than answer in his own words."

"But really," said De Vane, "I am compelled to confess that I do not understand the beautiful but mysterious language of the prophet. Will you not condescend to enlighten me?"

"Upon the hope that I indulge, that you will look more diligently into the inspired volume, whose authority you seemed to invoke by appealing to it, I will give you the interpretation which is, I believe, generally accepted. It is understood that two captive nations appealed to the prophet, as a watchman, for some sign of hope, some appearance of coming deliverance; and he replied to their question, 'Watchman, what of the night?' in these words, 'The morning cometh, and also the night;' meaning that morning was about to dawn upon the one people, and a protracted night to settle down upon the other: the one nation was presently to be delivered, while the other was to undergo a long captivity."

"Thank you," said De Vane. "I am, then, to understand that morning is about to dawn upon our friend, and that the other is still to endure the darkness which has so long covered his sky?"

"Such is my interpretation of the signs," said Esther. "Of one thing I am quite sure, there has been no change in the sentiments of Miss Godolphin, so far as her cousin is concerned. That I am at liberty to say to you. As to the hopes of our friend, I, of course, can not speak; for not a word has ever been uttered in regard to him that would authorize me to form any opinion. I had this morning a conversation with Hortensia. She came to me at Leasowes, and communicated every thing. Mr. Godolphin renewed the offer of his hand, and she decidedly declined it. He assured her of his unchanging love, and urged her to withhold her final decision until his return to England, and then to write him. She explained to him every thing—her wretchedness at the thought of his having fallen in battle, her joy at the tidings of his return to England, her deep sense of his constancy, and her sincere friendship; but she assured him it was impossible that she could ever regard him in any other light than that of an honored friend and relative; and she implored him to conquer a passion which she insisted was only a fancy, which a year's residence in society such as he would meet in London, would easily overcome. He prevailed on her to give him the opportunity of proving his constancy by awaiting his return home, that he might assure her, from the very midst of the most brilliant circle of his own country, that he could love no woman but herself. And so the affair rests."

"I pity him from the very depths of my heart," said De Vane. "He is a noble fellow, and such constancy I have rarely known. It is wonderful. He had known his cousin but a short time in Europe; he was very young when he saw her—indeed, is still young; and yet now, after years of absence and suffering have tried his love, it is as ardent as at first."

Esther was touched by this generous tribute to one who was striving to bear away from them one so loved and prized as Miss Godolphin, and whose success would shed disastrous eclipse over the life of one so dear to him who uttered it, as she knew Waring to be—dear as an elder brother, upon whom no shadow could fall without clouding his own happiness.

"Do you know, Miss Wordsworth," said De Vane, rising, and speaking in a stately way, "that I committed a trespass this morning, for which I have yet to ask your pardon?"

"A trespass!" exclaimed Esther. "I am not conscious of it."

"Still I must sue for pardon," said De Vane. "At an hour when you were in the full possession of your prerogative as mistress of Leasowes, and before you had emerged from the sanctity which invests you there, and repels intruders, except on holidays, I actually entered your domain, and was advancing upon your seat of empire, when I saw you walking with a fair lady; and conscious of the intrusion, I retraced my steps without making myself known to you."

"Were you at Leasowes this morning?" Esther asked eagerly.

"I must confess it," said De Vane; "and seeing Miss Godolphin in conversation with you, I withdrew."

She laughed, and said: "It was very well that you did not join us, for at that moment Hortensia was speaking to me with great earnestness, and your presence would have distressed her."

"So I conjectured," said De Vane; "and like an illustrious personage whom Milton describes, I fled from the sight of happiness which I was not to share."

Esther laughed heartily, and De Vane took leave with a heart full of joy, and love, and hope.

## CHAPTER XIV.

"WHY in this furnace is my spirit proved
Like steel in tempering fire? Because I loved!
Because I loved what not to love, and see,
Was more or less than mortal, and than me."

THE LAMENT OF TASSO.

IT is a beautiful compensation in human life, that when we feel and toil for others, the pressure of our own sorrows is lighter; the soul receives strength from sympathy, and by a beneficent law of humanity, we grow strong as we strive to do good.

De Vane's solicitude for Waring was so great, that he almost forgot his own troubles; and he awaited calmly, for a time, a reply to letters which he had recently written, both to Mrs. De Vane and to General De Vane, expressing in earnest terms his love for Miss Wordsworth, and his resolution to be loyal to his own heart, no matter what opposition he might encounter. He described her to his father in manly but glowing terms, and he expressed his perfect indifference to any advantages which he might acquire by a marriage such as General De Vane projected for him. Nor could he restrain the utterance of his profound indignation against those rules of conventional life, which would exclude a person, however cultivated, refined, pure, and lovely she might be, from the circles which they governed. In the mean while, he saw Esther constantly, and their intercourse yielded the purest enjoyment. Books, conversation, music, excursions to the neighboring country, wherever objects of interest attracted them, and a thorough coöperation in doing good to those who needed their kindly offices—all gave a charm to the flying days. Their relations had undergone no change since the explanation which took place at the little fountain in the grounds of Leasowes. Esther was firm, and De Vane never for a moment swerved from his attachment or his purpose. They saw much of society, and Esther was greatly admired. Mr. Le Grande was marked in his attentions to her, expressing without reserve his appreciation of her beauty, her intellect, and her character; and others, still younger, and more disposed to possess what they so extravagantly admired, pressed their attentions upon her. But, with a gentle dignity, she kept within a charmed circle, which she did not suffer any one to overstep. Her bearing was such as to repress the language of passion, and without giving offense, she, in every instance, prevented an actual appeal to her decision, by making it plain that a declaration of love would be unacceptable.

Mr. Clarendon said to her one evening:

"Miss Wordsworth, with your glorious beauty, and all your attractions, you are like the sibyl repelling Apollo himself, who pressed her with all the ardor of the god; and you still exclaim to the great throng of your admirers: '*O profani, procul, procul este!*'"

De Vane, who was standing near, smiled as he saw Esther's eyes turn quickly toward him, but he said nothing.

The dinner at Chancellor De Lolme's brought together mainly the same guests who met at Mr. Clarendon's table, and it was an entertainment of marked elegance. The conversation turned on politics, and De Vane was drawn out by Mr. Clarendon in a way to make him the observed of some two or three gentlemen of distinction, whom he met for the first time. Waring and Mr. Le Grande did not renew their discussion, but Chancellor De

Lolme paid marked attention to the young Professor, and conversed with him for some time on a subject which deeply interested them both—the relations between ethical and political philosophy. From that time Waring became a frequent guest at the Chancellor's elegant and hospitable house.

Some days after, cards were issued for an evening party at Mrs. Habersham's, and it proved to be unusually brilliant. Eminent men from all parts of the State were present, and the families of several from the sea-board accompanied them. The handsome house, with its elegant furniture, afforded ample room and abounding means for such an entertainment. Natural flowers shed a perfume through the spacious saloons; and statuary and paintings imparted that indescribable grace which nothing can supply in their absence. There was no dancing. There never was at Mrs. Habersham's. Her own taste and that of Miss Godolphin's agreed in excluding it. But musical instruments of the rarest and most costly kind were placed in the drawing-room this evening, the harp alone occupying its accustomed place in the octagonal green room. One or two eminent professors of music were present, whose skill was so well known, that their performance alone would have attracted numbers to hear them. Esther was standing near the door, opening into the octagonal room, in conversation with Mr. Le Grande, when Mr. Clarendon advanced, Mr. Godolphin leaning on his arm, and said:

"I wish, Miss Wordsworth, to present Mr. Godolphin."

Mr. Godolphin bowed low, and said:

"I have for some time desired the honor of meeting you. You are not unknown to me, Miss Wordsworth."

Esther bowed, and a conversation followed, in which she took part, with Mr. Godolphin, Mr. Le Grande, and Mr. Clarendon. Various topics were introduced, among others the costume of the people of Europe, as compared with that of Oriental nations, and this led to some remarks as to the effect of civilization upon the fine arts. At that moment, Miss Godolphin came up to the group, and invited Esther to give them at least one song, saying, that it was the wish of those present, many of whom had never heard her, to have that gratification afforded them this evening. Mr. Godolphin offered his arm, and conducted her to the piano, at which she seated herself with apparent composure, but really under the influence of great embarrassment. The presence of so large a company, some of them total strangers to her, and the fact that the entertainment was intended to owe its chief interest to the music of the evening, awakened natural apprehension in one so full of sensibility. With perfect grace, she touched the keys of the instrument, playing first a wild exuberant piece, perfectly new to almost every one, and in which the music seemed to exert its full power in uttering the voice not of mirth, but of deep and earnest gladness; now rapid, and again slow and tender, with a joyous outburst finally, which was so exultant that it moved many to tears, from pure sympathy with its almost human passionateness.

The room rang with applause, and Mr. Godolphin, bending low, thanked her in the warmest terms.

"And now," said Miss Godolphin, "we must have the song?"

"What shall it be?" asked Esther.

"We leave the selection to yourself," she replied; "but, if perfectly agreeable to you, I should wish you to sing Judith.'

This was a new piece, almost unknown as yet in this country, describing Judith's solemn consecration of herself to the perilous task of delivering her country from the Assyrian hosts that stretched their beleaguering lines around the city where she dwelt, who trusted in shield and spear, and bow and sling, and knew not the Lord that breaketh the battles, in which she prays that their stateliness may be broken down by the hand of a woman. It was a piece of wonderful power, music and language conspiring to produce the greatest effect; and it was a piece of considerable length. Esther took the fresh sheets of music lying near, and placed them before her. Her style of dress was in harmony with the piece which she was about to play, for it was unusually rich this evening. Her golden hair was intertwined with pearls, and her faultless neck was encircled with a necklace, of exquisite workmanship, of the same precious material, from which hung a cross, formed of the largest and purest pearls, of very great value—an ornament which had been her mother's, and which she rarely wore. Her robe was white silk, trimmed heavily with the finest lace.

She was roused by her own music, as she advanced in the piece, and her voice gave out all its power as she uttered the sentiments, so heroic, so devoted, and so sublime, that the whole scene of the beleaguered city, and the surrounding heights covered with the tents and streaming with the defiant banners of the haughty Assyrians, came up to view, while the soaring spirit of the glorious woman preparing to go forth to spoil the pride of the fierce leader of the mighty host, broke forth in tones so grand, and of such imperial triumph, that all who heard them felt as if they stood in the presence of some being already inspired with authentic power, to proclaim the deliverance of her country, and the utter rout and destruction of her enemies. As the closing notes died away, and Esther's hands fell from the instrument gently, the enthusiasm of the company was such, that it did not seek to restrain itself, but everywhere exclamations of rapture were heard, which betrayed the power that the wonderful music which had just ceased, had swayed over their souls.

Esther rose from her seat, and again Mr. Godolphin, offering his arm, conducted her to a seat. Mr. Clarendon and Waring came directly to her, and tendered their thanks, and a moment after De Vane joined them.

"It occurs to me," said Mr. Clarendon, "that in a conversation in which some of us took part, some months since, when the comparative power of the fine arts, and of language in expression, was discussed, we overlooked music; and really I am not prepared to say, after what I have just heard, that it does not transcend every thing, in the utterance of the higher emotions of our nature, and in swaying the soul."

"Ah! but you must consider," said De Vane, "that we have just now heard music associated with language, and it goes far toward confirming my theory, which claims the ascendency of human speech over the fine arts in the power of expression, to observe the effect produced by the piece of music to which we have just listened; for what is music, after all, but speech in its passionate tones?"

"Very cleverly stated," said Mr. Clarendon. "But you claim rather more than I can concede, when you class music with language. The truth is, music is one of the fine arts."

"Quite true," said Waring; "and even when we listen to music unaccompanied by language, we are often profoundly moved by it; as in the *Miserere*, for instance, when the human voice can not be distinguished, and the tones float upon the air, the effect is described as very great."

"So it is," said Miss Godolphin, "for I have heard it just as you describe it; and it was wonderful how one felt it."

"Yes," said Mr. Clarendon, "I perfectly well recall it."

At this moment Miss Godolphin came up, leaning on Mr. Le Grande's arm.

"We are reöpening our discussion, Miss Godolphin,"

said De Vane, "as to the comparative power of language and of the fine arts to affect us, and Mr. Clarendon has appealed to the impression made by music as an art. Now is that allowable?"

"Why not?" she said.

"Because," replied De Vane, "it consists of sounds, and language is made up of sounds, so that music is kindred to it."

"Ah! Mr. De Vane," said Miss Godolphin, "you remember that the controversy, as it stood before, was not as to the power of uttered language to move us, but as to the capability of its descriptions—its capability of bringing to view scenes and ideas which, when realized, would affect us. And it seems to me that you vary the ground of our discussion when you add vocal sounds, which appeal to us in quite a different way."

"Very fairly done," said Mr. Clarendon. "Do you not think so, Le Grande?"

"I must be allowed to say, while I admire the skill and dialectic power of Miss Godolphin's remark," said Mr. Le Grande, "that in testing the power of language in its relations to thought and emotion, it is quite proper to take into the estimate the highest forms which it wears. Eloquence, for instance, is not dependent only upon a collocation of words, but the tones of the human voice must enter largely into it. And if this be true, music partakes in some sort of the nature of speech."

"Still," said Mr. Clarendon, "that varies the original inquiry, started some time since, as to the capability of statuary or painting to move us, and of the comparative power of verbal description to do so, when representing the same object. And I remember that one of the illustrations offered was the Dying Gladiator—the work of art appealing to us by its mute suggestions—and Lord Byron's descriptive lines, in which he introduces the rude hut on the

Danube, the boys at play, and the unconscious Dacian mother. Now, vocal utterances are not to be taken into the account in such an inquiry. Is it not so, Miss Wordsworth, for I believe you sat arbitress then?"

Esther smiled, and said: "I think you are right, Mr. Clarendon."

"The truth is," said Mr. Clarendon, laying his hand on De Vane's shoulder, "this young gentleman, seeing the complete ascendency of music established this evening, wishes to press it into the support of his theory; and I confess the same anxiety to rank it as one of the fine arts."

All laughed.

"The power of music to affect us," said Mr. Le Grande, "is nothing less than wonderful. The ancients have attested it in the fable of Orpheus moving beasts and woods, and all nations employ martial music to animate their soldiers in preparing for battle."

"There is a remarkable instance of the power of music over human passion," said Waring, "in the case of King Saul, whose wild and stormy soul could only be soothed by the harp of David, who, while yet young, swept the chords of that instrument in the presence of the monarch who at the same time hated and dreaded him, and yet was swayed by the notes that he produced."

"It is a most felicitous illustration," said Mr. Le Grande.

"I confess my own susceptibility to the influence of music," said De Vane. "It subdues or rouses me as nothing else can. Its descriptive power, too, is almost unlimited. In that very piece which we all heard with so much emotion just now, it was easy to trace the varying sentiment in the notes, as they rose, or sank, or wailed, or denounced, or triumphed, without observing the words in which the sentiment was expressed. I do not wonder at the effect produced by the Marseillaise. I never hear its notes, even upon a feeble instrument, without instantly calling before me Paris—its streets filled with armed men, torches borne by women, who join the chorus of the wild song as the deeper voices of the maddened populace shout it out, and the frantic drums rattle it forth to animate the tread of the fierce band, a band in which both sexes mingle and all ages are seen, from the boy of twelve to the gray-haired octogenarian. That hymn would bring an empire toppling down."

De Vane had unconsciously, in his animation, uttered this with amazing power, and his language, attitude, and gesture were all so striking, that the group about him regarded him with unconcealed admiration. Mr. Le Grande fixed his eyes upon him, and said:

"Mr. De Vane has just given us a great argument in support of his theory—the transcendent power of language to represent scenes which are not before us."

His face flushed with pleasure, and he bowed. Esther's face beamed as brightly as his own.

"It is to be observed, too, I think, Mr. Godolphin," said Mr. Clarendon, "that the national anthem of England breathes the majestic breadth and strength of her imperial sway. One who hears it can imagine the circling hours of the day never ceasing to light the wide extent of her realm."

"I'm very much obliged to you, I'm sure," said Mr. Godolphin. "We are loyal people, and we love our national anthem."

"We have none," said Mr. Le Grande.

"Will not Miss Godolphin give us some music now?" said Waring. "I am sure that we shall all be happy to hear her."

"You should excuse me this evening, I think," she replied. "Do you not say so, Mr. Clarendon?"

"My dear lady," said he, "you should not appeal to me,

when the question respects your being excused from singing. I am incapable of impartial justice in that matter."

Waring gave her his arm, and conducted her to the octagonal room, as a wish was expressed to hear her performance on the harp; and she seated herself by the instrument, and threw her fingers over its chords so as to produce instantly low, sweet tones, as if its spirit, sleeping before, became conscious now of the hand of an enchantress which woke it to life and tenderness. Gentle, almost wailing notes breathed forth, until, rising into higher tones, the music swelled into louder and grander circles, which filled the hearers with delight. It was as if the early morning of spring, dewy, and cheered by the song of a single bird, expanded into light and glory, until it became vocal with the glad caroling of a forest of songsters.

It was the remark everywhere throughout the thronged and rapt audience, that it was not conceivable such music could be produced from the harp, and the professors who stood near her could not repress their surprise at such a triumph in one of the most difficult instruments belonging to their art—an instrument upon which many perform, and over which they acquire some skill, but which the fewest number ever master so far as to make it yield those fluent tones which fill the soul with their ravishing melody.

Some one requested a song, and she said: "I will give you one that is destined, I think, to immortality. It is true at once to nature and to the heart."

Touching the strings again, she made them vocal under her fingers, and sang those lines of Moore, which breathe sentiments as pure as they are tender,

"'Tis the last rose of summer;"

and the depth, and richness, and passionateness of her voice entered every soul. Tears flowed freely while she sang; and as the dying cadence of her tones was mingled with the exquisite sweetness of the air, which seemed to linger over the chords like the breath of an angel, the large drops rolled down the cheeks of Mr. Clarendon, attesting the power of her music over his noble, grand, and yet gentle nature. When she had withdrawn her hand from the instrument, he advanced to her, took her hand in his, and said:

"You are right, dear lady; that song can never die, so long as nature reproduces her flowers, or human hearts cherish loved objects on earth."

It was painful to De Vane to observe the emotion of Hubert Godolphin. He was very manly, and yet he could hardly restrain the tears which welled up into his eyes. His agitation was so great, that he turned away, and walked to another room, that he might conquer it. Miss Godolphin was brilliantly beautiful this evening. The shadow that had so long dimmed the lustre of her extraordinary charms had passed away, and she was as resplendent as a tropical morning, when the glories of nature are illumined by a light undimmed by mists. Her dress was in harmony with her rejoicing spirit—rich, and adorned with all the appliances which a liberal but pure taste could bestow upon it. She wore no curls, but the diamonds flashed in her richly-braided hair, and a necklace, precious enough to ransom a queen from captivity, encircled her throat; while a dark green silk robe, trimmed with Brussels lace, displayed her form in all the stately and yet graceful elegance which so preëminently distinguished her.

It was proposed that the two ladies who had so gratified the guests by their performance, should contribute their voices in addition to the instrumental music which the two eminent professors were about to execute; and they took their places near the piano. The piece selected was from the 'Creation;' and one of the artists took his seat at the piano, while the other accompanied him on the violin; and Miss Godolphin and Esther, together with the professional performers, sustained the several parts of the piece. The effect was very great; and as the last notes of the instrument, under the vigorous touch of the German professor, died away, an outburst of applause broke forth from the delighted company, Mr. Godolphin and Mr. Clarendon shouting "Bravo! bravo!" vehemently.

"*Mehercule!*" said De Vane, turning to Waring. "Statuary, and painting, and language must look to their laurels if they compete with music in the power of expression."

Waring laughed, and advancing to the ladies, thanked them warmly for their music.

"Let us go to supper," said Miss Godolphin. "Mr. Godolphin, will you take Mrs. Habersham to the table?"

He bowed, and advancing to that lady, offered his arm. Waring conducted Miss Godolphin, and De Vane took Esther to the table. It was a magnificent entertainment, such as Mrs. Habersham's great wealth and Miss Godolphin's fine taste could supply; and it was intended as a compliment to one who had strong claims upon their consideration, and who had been accustomed to the most profuse elegance at home.

Not until a late hour did the guests depart, and every one bore away an impression of rare splendor and elegance—an evening to be remembered for its brightness; for the grace and intellect and gladness which characterized all its festivities.

Some few days after, Hubert Godolphin took leave of his cousin, and returned to Washington, to join a party of his friends, who had come over with him to visit the great Republic.

Letters came to De Vane—a very long one from his aunt and a pretty full one from his father. Mrs. De Vane urged him to yield to his father's wishes—to consent to quit his present residence, at least for a time, and to satisfy the exactions of General De Vane, by proving that his love for Esther was not the result of mere intercourse with her, but a true and vigorous sentiment, which could survive through time and absence. She did not know that General De Vane had himself written to his son, and she therefore entered fully into all the reasoning by which the counsels of that gentleman were animated.

General De Vane's letter was direct, and yet kind. Its tone may be learned from a passage taken from it, in which he treated the question of his son's wishes in regard to Miss Wordsworth:

"I am not insensible to the strength of the sentiment which you profess to feel for Miss Wordsworth. I have outlived my youth, but not my heart; and my views in regard to you, while they may have been ambitious, have never been selfish. While I ardently desire that you should marry a woman of your own class, (I do not mean to depreciate Miss Wordsworth, who, I do not doubt, is a very worthy young person,) I do not wish you to marry one whom you could neither love nor respect. The fact that the young person to whom you are just now so much attached is a friend and associate of Miss Godolphin, certainly speaks much in her favor, and she could not have the approval of Mr. Clarendon if she did not possess considerable merit. Still, she is of a people not just of our own class; and I should somewhat fear, that hereafter your tastes might be offended by the persons who would surround her. There are very good people of her persuasion—the Hamiltons, for instance—but they are rare, and there is always a certain clinging to each other, it seems to me, which might seriously offend you, when, hereafter, you come to look at things 'in a dry light,' as my Lord Bacon says. Still, I hold that every man has the right to choose the woman who is to walk by his side through life; and if you are content to subject your regard for Miss Wordsworth to a fair test, I shall waive all objection on my part to your marriage. Go to Europe in the spring, and travel there a year or two; and if, when you return, your sentiments are unchanged, I shall then respect your wishes, and offer no obstacle to their accomplishment.

"Mr. Randolph was here yesterday, on his way to Washington, and asked after you with interest. He is in high spirits, and says that he feels all the ardor of a fox-hunter intent upon being in at the death. He means to see the present administration out."

De Vane read his father's letter with mingled emotions. There was light in it, but it was remote. Time, distance, the ocean—all these rolled between him and Esther by the plan submitted to him, and, in the ardor of his nature, it seemed a vista as long as that through which Jacob saw Rachel, was opening before him. He felt a profound respect for his father; he knew the terrible strength of his ideas of *caste*. His tastes were not only aristocratic, but his sentiments were such. The whole structure of his character was exclusive; and yet he actually had brought himself to yield to the alliance, which at one time he so utterly opposed, provided it should be consummated after subjecting the parties who were to enter into it to an ordeal of time and absence. He read and re-read the letters; revolved every idea which they contained; and the deep and silent hours of midnight found him walking in his chamber, and looking in troubled anxiety over the dim, wide sea which stretched before him, as he sought to read the future.

## CHAPTER XV.

"LOVE took up the glass of time, and turned it in his glowing hands;
Every moment, lightly shaken, ran itself in golden sands.

"Love took up the harp of life, and smote on all the chords with might;
Smote the chord of self, that, trembling, passed in music out of sight."

TENNYSON.

WHEN we submit ourselves to an ordeal which is to prove us worthy of a beloved object, there is a cheerful courage which takes the place of anxiety. Conscious of our strength, we address ourselves to the tasks before us, and glory in suffering or in doing whatever awaits us. Love sheds over the objects about us its own glowing light, and the days which fly by us are gilded with its hues. The descending night, which comes to remind us that there is one day less of doubt and trial, sends its harbinger of hope, the star of evening, which glitters above the horizon, to lure us from despondency.

De Vane had represented to Esther the state of his affairs, and she cheerfully acquiesced in the arrangement proposed to test the strength and loyalty of the sentiments which he avowed. Now that General De Vane had yielded his objections to her personally, and required only that he might be satisfied of the strength of his son's attachment, she could not withhold her own assent to a plan which was to demonstrate it. Heretofore she had firmly refused to enter into any engagement with De Vane, and now she would do no more than encourage him to believe that, when his father's objections were removed, she would be ready to show her own appreciation of a regard so true and enduring. De Vane himself began to view their relations under brighter lights, and while the intervening months which must roll away before he could look upon Esther as his own, by a positive promise from her own lips that she would be his, seemed interminable; yet the thought that when they were ended, all uncertainty would have passed away with them, at length tranquillized if it did not cheer him; and he bent himself to his studies with redoubled energy, that he might be admitted to the bar before his departure for Europe. His progress was very great, and the only relaxation which he took from his intense study was a ride on horseback with Waring, or an evening drive, when the day was so inviting as to make it agreeable.

The weeks flew by rapidly. The winter was already gone before he could comprehend that its reign was over, and the signs of opening spring met his eye, as if by some enchantment the leafless trees had caught the breathing warmth of the tropics. It was arranged that he should return to Virginia in May, and by the close of that month sail from New-York for London. March was now almost gone. In April, the court before which he was to be examined opened its session, and he was introduced to the judges by Mr. Clarendon, as an applicant for license to practice. His examination was perfectly satisfactory, and he was admitted, with evident marks of consideration by the judges, to the bar. Then followed a few weeks of delightful recreation. The circling hours were bright, and in the society of Esther he enjoyed those exquisite pleasures which love and hope shed over youth—pleasures as pure as they are perfect. The early spring flowers, the deepening foliage, the songs of birds, the breath of nature laden with the perfume of the early-blooming plants, the sunsets kindling a glory in the western sky as deep and pure as if the opening portals of heaven shed there a supernal light—all this, De Vane and Esther enjoyed as we enjoy such scenes but once in life. As we advance upon the path of existence and comprehend the ways of the world; as we see so many illusions which cheered us in our youth fade away, and as the actual engrosses so much of time and lays its imperious claims upon our finest faculties; as we become acquainted with sorrow and stand in the presence of death, we feel that the sad strain which sighed over the harp of a noble poet as he swept its chords in exile and bitterness is but too true:

> "The tree of knowledge is not that of life."

But De Vane and Esther were full of youth, and joy, and hope. The light which flushed their foreheads awoke their souls to gladness, as the earliest beams of the sun, falling upon the statue of Memnon, made it vocal, and called forth music to welcome the day.

Waring's sympathy with his friend was perfect. His own spirit was refreshed; and as he saw the two young, bright beings moving in the realm of love and hope, he was accustomed to breathe a prayer that no cloud might darken a sky so full of light and joy.

So far as his own hopes were involved, every thing was uncertain. He had not breathed a word of love to Miss Godolphin; he awaited her decision as to the addresses of her cousin Hubert. Acting in perfect good faith, she withheld her final reply until he should reach England and write to her; it was then her purpose to answer him in the most formal and emphatic way. Waring saw her often, sent her books to read, some of them intended to enlighten her as to evangelical religion, and they discussed the merits of these books, and kindred subjects, when they met. Nor did he limit his reading, nor seek to restrict hers, to this subject alone. History, criticism, poetry, and general literature, all these engaged them, and Miss Godolphin learned to appreciate more and more the extraordinary mind and elevated character of a man who, consecrating himself solemnly to the work of the Christian ministry, and exercising its functions among a people upon whom the great world looked down with no patronizing aspect, was yet so cultivated, so refined, so transcendently superior to the self-appointed magnates of that class who regarded Christianity as that circle did who, when the fame of Jesus began to take hold of the heart of the people of Judea, inquired: "Have any of the rulers, or of the Pharisees, believed on him?"

The time came at length when De Vane was to take his departure. But a few days remained before he must say "Farewell!" for a time, to those who were so dear to him. The quarterly meeting for the Methodist Church was about to be held; and Waring, yielding to the earnest request of the presiding elder, consented to preach on Sunday night. De Vane was to leave on Tuesday, and that was one of the considerations which induced him to consent to preach at a time and in a place where there was so much to embarrass him.

A very large congregation assembled to hear him. Persons of all denominations flocked to the Methodist church, and filled its simple, plain seats. Mr. Clarendon attended Mrs. Habersham and Miss Godolphin, and Chancellor Hallam and several of the professors from the College were present. The subject of Waring's discourse was from that brief but noble Psalm, in which King David, after surveying the wide-spread heavens through which the moon floated, and over which countless stars shed their light, extols the glory of the Lord of the universe, and utters his adoring wonder that, bending from all the splendors of creation, he should be mindful of man, and exalt the son of man to such dignity as to visit him. He treated it with the finest effect, exhibiting man, at the first view, as a feeble being, the proudest and most heroic of the race subject to disease and death. He then presented him as an intellectual being, achieving the highest triumphs in the arts, in literature, in science—a being capable of comprehending the works of God, susceptible to the noblest emotions—love, gratitude, joy, adoration; who, while inanimate nature, in its sublimest forms and most brilliant aspects, could only reflect the majesty of the Maker, was himself so organized that he could vie with angels and archangels in swelling the pomp of worship which filled heaven with its mighty anthems and bore to the farthest verge of creation the sounding praise which made his excellent name, known throughout its amplest bounds. He then described him as an immortal being—a being whose very nature the Son of God had assumed; who, by his triumph over our enemies, had exalted the form of humanity to that high seat which the redeemed and sanctified should finally attain. And he proceeded to press, with wonderful power, the thought that the life of such a being ought to be consecrated to the noblest tasks and the highest aims; that such a being, viewed in the revealing light of divine truth, was too great for the little schemes of worldliness or the most towering objects of human ambition; and that his whole earthly existence should be in harmony with the glory which was to be his inheritance, when states and empires, and the world itself, had perished, and nothing stood but the objects which God had made to endure forever. The sweep of Waring's thought was broad and vigorous, and he bore those who heard him on its majestic tide; so that when the sermon was ended, the world and its proudest and most dazzling objects stood dwarfed in the presence of the sublime scenery which had just been brought to view. The effect was very great, and De Vane experienced, at the same time, the highest satisfaction at the glorious success of his friend in preaching the Gospel, and a deep and awful sense of the majesty of revealed truth. Never before had he so comprehended the relations of man to his higher destiny; never had he been so profoundly conscious of the momentous issues which attend life; and long after, he recalled the scene, the words, the thoughts of the preacher, and uttered two lines of the closing hymn, lines written by Montgomery:

> "'Tis not the whole of life to live,
> Nor all of death to die."

Upon the rolling seas, and in distant lands, the vision came back upon him; and he would stand and look up to the deep, limitless heavens, spreading their constellations above his head, as if they lighted the way to the throne of God, and breathe a prayer that the great Being who dwelt beyond those visible glories, would be mindful of him, and lead him in the way of truth and life.

As the congregation dispersed, De Vane joined the group, where Mr. Clarendon, Mrs. Habersham, and Miss Godolphin were standing near the door, waiting to speak with Waring; but he had passed out of another door, and walked with Mr. Springfield, who, with Mrs. Springfield and Esther, had succeeded in making their way out of the thronged avenue some moments earlier than others.

"Ah!" said Mr. Clarendon, "he has made his escape. I really did wish to thank him. I feel that we all are indebted to him."

"So I think," said Chancellor Hallam. "I confess myself under the greatest obligations to Professor Waring for that discourse."

Miss Godolphin was silent, but her face was glowing.

She was full of animation, but she did not trust her heart to express itself in words."

"And you are to leave us on Tuesday, Mr. De Vane?" asked Mr. Clarendon.

"Yes," he replied. "I regret to say that I must take my departure so early."

"But I should think," said Mrs. Habersham, "that the prospect of a visit to Europe would be very pleasing to you."

"So it is, madam," replied De Vane; "but it can not be an unalloyed pleasure, as I must leave my friends behind me."

Bidding them good-night, he walked to his lodgings, and had a long conversation with Mrs. Bowen, who was so full of joy, that she could not think of retiring to rest, until she had expressed it to some one; and she found a willing listener in De Vane, whose affection for Waring was not less than her own.

While they were engaged in conversation, Waring passed on to his room, and retired, without seeing De Vane that night.

The next day, De Vane was busily engaged in completing his arrangements for his departure. He had purchased a large, handsome lot in that part of the town which stretched between the public garden and the College, and he had already caused several out-buildings, including a stable for his horses, to be erected, thus settling the question as to his residence so plainly, that no one could doubt his purpose to make his home there. He left every thing in charge of Waring, putting his horses and servant fully at his disposal until his return; for he preferred to take public conveyances in traveling to Virginia. There was something pleasing to De Vane in leaving these objects behind him—in leaving something to remind his friends that he was gone only on a visit, and that he would return to resume the every-day life which he relinquished only for a season. The very shrubbery, which began already to grow luxuriously, and which was both rare and beautiful—having been supplied through the kindness of Mrs. Habersham, and the partiality of Mr. Swan, the public gardener—imparted a home look to his place, and helped to attach him to the spot.

Mr. Swan offered his services in looking after the place during his absence, and it was often observed afterward, that no garden in the town displayed more beauty than De Vane's, even in his absence.

In the evening, Waring and De Vane took tea at Mrs. Springfield's, where they met Mr. and Mrs. Clarendon, and Mrs. Habersham and Miss Godolphin, who were invited to join them. It was very agreeable, both to De Vane and Esther, to have pleasing associations connected with the last evening which they were to pass with each other previous to their long separation. It was better to part cheerfully, than to take leave of each other in sadness, and doubt, and gloom. They were as yet but friends—friends to be sure answering in their relation to each perfectly, that fine description of such a state in the felicitous phrase of a noble poet: "Friendship between the sexes is love full fledged, waiting for a fair day to fly." But still they were only friends, and Esther shrank from an unwitnessed leave-taking.

The evening was very bright. The supper was a happy one; all enjoyed it. Those who sat about the table were kindred spirits, and the winged hours rustled lightly as they flew over them. Conversation flowed freely. Mr. Clarendon excelled himself, and Mr. Springfield, who rivaled him in that delightful gift, was as genial as possible. Music was not attempted; it would have touched chords too deep not to bring tears. In such hours we can not enter the realm of song, without losing control of our sensibility; and when we begin to pause and listen to voices which we may not hear again for many months, if ever, the spirit of sadness spreads her mists over the soul, and we abandon ourselves to her sway, yielding our homage in passionate tears. Music was not attempted. The strings of the magic interpreter of sentiment lay mute.

Waring and De Vane lingered a few moments after the other guests had taken leave, and Mr. Springfield invited them to join in the evening prayer, which he was accustomed to offer before the family retired to rest. He read the eighty-fourth Psalm, which breathes a beautiful tribute to the peace and blessedness of the courts of the Lord, and declares with triumphant faith, "O Lord of hosts, blessed is the man that trusteth in thee;" and kneeling, he offered a fervent prayer, imploring the divine blessing upon them all, and especially commending to the care of Him who neither slumbers nor sleeps, the friend who was about to leave them for a season; entreating that he might be kept from the dangers of the land and the perils of the sea, and from whatever would harm soul or body, until, brought once more to join in worship with them, they might all mingle their praises as they bent again before the throne of grace.

As they rose from their knees, Esther's emotion was such, that she could not repress the tears that, if she were alone, would rain from her eyes; even now they glittered upon the lashes, and one or two fell like dew-drops upon the hand of De Vane, as she bent her head, while he said, cheerfully: "Esther, farewell!" He shook the hand of Mrs. Springfield tenderly and respectfully, grasped that of Mr. Springfield with energy, as that gentleman uttered a fervent "God bless you!" turned upon his steps, and was gone.

Was he ever again to enter that house where he had passed so many happy hours? That belonged to the future and the unknown. But as he walked away, with Waring, under the star-lit heavens, it seemed to him that the blessing which Mr. Springfield had implored for him, filled the air, invisible but felt; as music floats in it, unseen but not voiceless.

The next morning saw him on his way to Virginia, and again the dashing horses bore him swiftly away from a spot the dearest to him in all the world.

After his departure, Esther devoted herself to her duties at Leasowes with new activity. She found it a great resource, for occupation was essential to her; and the consciousness of doing good to the little girls, whose eyes welcomed her so brightly every morning, cheered her indescribably.

Waring often called at Mr. Springfield's; and the interest which he felt in De Vane seemed to bring the absent one nearer, as he spoke of him cheerfully and hopefully.

Some weeks after De Vane's departure, Waring came, bringing a letter for Esther, which had been received under cover to himself; and he at the same time stated that he also had a very long one addressed to him. Both were written in New-York, just previous to De Vane's going on board the ship America, a splendid vessel, which sailed regularly between that city and London. Esther instantly retired to her own room to read the letter which Waring handed her; and he remained in the library with Mr. and Mrs. Springfield, giving them a full account of his friend's movements and views.

It seems that De Vane had made but a brief stay in Virginia, and had proceeded to New-York to make arrangements for his voyage. There he met Hubert Godolphin and his party of friends, who were to sail in the same vessel with himself. He had found in this something to cheer him; for he was to go abroad with one person at least, who knew those who were so dear to him; and Mr.

Godolphin had expressed the greatest satisfaction upon learning that De Vane was to go out in the same vessel. The friends, too, who were with him, De Vane found to be most agreeable people; among them, Sir Arthur Clifford and family, who were related to the Guilfords, and who had been making them a visit. The family consisted of Sir Arthur and Lady Clifford, and two daughters, one of them some twenty years of age, and the other about four years younger. Their only son was at Oxford.

De Vane's letter to Esther was very long. It described every thing; and its last lines were written just as the vessel was about to leave the wharf. A glowing farewell, and a passionate assurance of changeless love, closed it. It filled her with happiness; and kneeling in the stillness of her own chamber, she offered a fervent prayer that the wanderer might be kept by the tender mercies of Him whose power overspreads the sea and the land, and be brought back in safety to those who would watch for his coming as they watch who wait for the morning light.

Descending to the library, she entered into conversation with Waring, who read aloud parts of his letter—not those which referred to herself, but his descriptions of persons and places.

It was his first visit to New-York, and he was delighted with the bounding activity and energy of the people; with the signs of wealth which filled the streets; with the shipping crowded at the wharves of the city, as if bringing from all parts of the globe tributes to its supremacy in the world of commerce; with the magnificent bay, opening, through gates grander than the Pillars of Hercules, into the wide sea; with the spirit of enterprise that projected the extent of the metropolis in larger lines than those which bounded the greatest cities of the Old World; and with the stately ships, launched by its own men, which already outstripped those of all other nations.

These, then, he described, as they impressed his vigorous mind; and he sketched, with power and ardor, the future of a city which was seated upon the ocean, in such relations to a continent whose exhaustless resources were far beyond the power of human calculation.

Mr. Springfield expressed his gratification at the views exhibited by De Vane in his letter to Waring, and the conversation turned upon the future of him who had gone abroad to explore the great world.

"Mr. De Vane's powers of observation," said Mr. Springfield, "are extraordinary, and his mind will be greatly enriched by foreign travel. He will profit more by one year's residence in Europe than most persons of his age would by five. He not only sees with quick perception the objects about him worthy to be observed, but he looks at them in a way to understand their value and their influence. I shall be exceedingly gratified, I am sure, to read his letters written in the midst of the scenes which will surround him for twelve months to come."

"Yes," said Waring, "he will be thoroughly educated as to some subjects which interest him by the time he returns home. His will not be an idle tour; he will study the institutions of the states of Europe closely. His tastes are aristocratic, but his principles are not all so; and he will see for himself the actual working of the political systems, which require such an expenditure of money and blood to maintain them."

"He will find himself most favorably introduced to English circles, by going to London with Mr. Hubert Godolphin," said Mr. Springfield.

"Of course he bears letters with him; but he might be slow in presenting them. Mr. Godolphin will not suffer him to avoid society."

"He will enjoy every advantage in that way," said Waring. "It is not his purpose, however, to remain more than three months in England. He goes to the Continent, to pass some time in Paris, and he will spend the winter in Italy. Classical in his tastes, he desires to spend some time in Rome; and his plan is to return through Germany to England in the following spring, so as to pass a few weeks in London during the sitting of Parliament. Since his late visit to Virginia, he has decided to return to this country by the latter part of the summer of next year."

"Indeed!" said Mrs. Springfield. "He will, then, be able to reach home—for his home is here—by October twelvemonth."

"That is his plan," said Waring.

Esther looked a little conscious, as if she had been already enlightened upon that point; but she was silent.

"Italy is, just now," said Mr. Springfield, "a country of very great interest. Her condition is, in every respect, volcanic. The internal fires not only threaten to upheave the land, but to flame up against the political system which crushes and degrades her."

"Yes," said Waring, "the shock must come. The signs of coming disturbances in France, too, are too clear to be misunderstood. Two or three years will develop a popular outburst that will shake the reigning dynasty from the height where the strong arm of united Europe has placed it, if the storm is not subverted."

"So I think," said Mr. Springfield. "Mr. De Vane visits Europe at a period of unusual interest. I feel a very strong inclination to go myself, but I must wait yet longer before I gratify that wish."

"It may be that I shall join you, when you complete your arrangements for the tour," said Waring. "I should wish to make it an extended one, passing into the East, and visiting the scenes associated with the greatest events in the history of our race."

"Let us keep it in view," said Mr. Springfield, "and we may yet accomplish it."

The ladies smiled, and Mrs. Springfield said:

"Esther and I must be of the party. We should enjoy it beyond expression."

"Of course," said Mr. Springfield, "we must take you with us. Is there any other person, Mr. Waring, that you would suggest, as necessary to complete the happiness of the party?"

All laughed, and Mrs. Springfield said:

"It is hardly fair to call upon Mr. Waring so directly to avow his preference for traveling companions."

"Oh! I was not inquiring about a companion for the journey of life," said Mr. Springfield, "but only for a tour through Europe and the East, though there is no saying how that might terminate; for if Mr. Waring found a lady friend agreeable upon such an excursion, he might be disposed to invite her to tread the still longer road with him."

At that instant the door-bell rang, and in a moment after Miss Godolphin entered the room. All rose to receive her, and Waring was so embarrassed by the suddenness of her appearance in the midst of a conversation so closely touching her, that Mr. Springfield was very much amused, and he said pleasantly:

"Ah! Miss Godolphin, it is said that the approach of an angel inclines us to speak of the celestial being; and we were just now saying to each other how happy we should be to make the grand tour, if we could take with us certain friends; and we were upon the point of naming you as you entered the room."

"Thank you, Mr. Springfield," she replied. "I should be most happy to accompany you upon any journey that you might propose, and especially to travel with you through Europe and the East."

"Very well," said he; "that is settled. Hold yourself in readiness. The time is not yet fixed, but the plan of travel is fully mapped out."

"I am delighted to hear it," she said.

"But sit down," said Mr. Springfield, "and pass the evening with us."

"Oh! thank you, no," she replied. "It is nearly sunset, and I ran in to ask Esther to drive with me to-morrow morning to see a poor woman, who, Mrs. Gildersleeve sends me word, is sick and needy."

"I shall certainly go with you," said Esther; "but you must pass the evening with us. We will send a note to Mrs. Habersham, informing her that you are here."

"There is no resisting you," she said. "Let me write the note, Esther."

Sitting down at Mr. Springfield's library-table, she wrote a note to Mrs. Habersham, explaining her detention, and dispatched it by a servant.

Then followed a gay conversation, in which the plan of travel was fully discussed, and as definitely arranged, as if it were to be undertaken the next week. She, too, had received a letter from New-York, in which Mr. De Vane's presence was named, and her cousin expressed the great pleasure which it gave him to find that he was to be a fellow-voyager across the Atlantic. She spoke of this with perfect naturalness, without the slightest embarrassment; and it was easy to see that she regarded Hubert Godolphin only as a kinsman and a friend.

Rarely had Waring passed a happier evening. All were bright; Mrs. Springfield and Esther feeling greatly cheered by the letters from De Vane, and sympathizing with Waring in his evident gratification at meeting Miss Godolphin, and in hearing her speak thus of subjects which interested him so profoundly.

Mr. Springfield was much brighter than usual, cheerful

as he was habitually; for he, too, was relieved by the tidings which came from one whose fortunes seemed so closely interwoven with those of a being so dear to him as Esther.

Waring walked to Mrs. Habersham's with Miss Godolphin, and in taking leave of her, could not forbear thanking her for the pleasure which she had conferred on him that evening, in consenting to stay, when she came only to make a moment's call.

"I have been so much engaged," said he, "of late, that I have not had the pleasure of meeting you so often as I desired, and I count it a piece of good fortune to have been able to enjoy your society this evening."

"Thank you," she replied.

It was further than Waring had ever gone before; and Miss Godolphin's voice almost trembled as she uttered her brief reply.

The "Good-night!" spoken and returned, was uttered in tones, which revealed the truth of which neither was so fully conscious before, that the dawn of a new creation was kindling its glories over their souls.

## CHAPTER XVI.

"Dead and gone is the old world's Ideal,
The old arts and old religion fled;
But I gladly live amid the Real,
And I seek a worthier Ideal.
Courage, brother, God is overhead!"
Anonymous.

The summer came, spreading its verdure all over the town. Leasowes was in its full beauty, and Esther passed most of her time there. She found in the duties which engaged her there, more to cheer her than anywhere else. There was an indefinable satisfaction in dwelling in the midst of scenes which De Vane was familiar with; and the consciousness of doing good to the little girls who were left to encounter the perils of orphanage at so early an age, yielded the richest compensation. It required but little stretch of faith to believe that in the midst of those shaded walks, angels trod, or spread their sheltering wings around the little forms that dwelt there. Waring had now made it a rule to call every Saturday morning, and make Esther a long visit, suggesting what he could to guide or lighten her tasks, and conversing with her about the past, the present, and the future.

It was Saturday. He had not yet called, and Esther, seated under the sheltering vines that ran over the front piazza, was raising her head occasionally to look toward the distant gate, when at length she saw him advancing toward the house with rapid strides, and involuntarily she rose to meet him. As she walked toward him, he held up letters in his right hand, and shook them gayly. Her heart leaped within her; for she had not had a line from De Vane since he sailed from New-York. When Waring approached near enough to be heard, he exclaimed:

"I congratulate you! Good tidings!"

The tumultuous blood rushed to her face; and as she stood for a moment, awaiting Waring's coming, he felt that he had never seen a brighter impersonation of joy, and youth, and beauty.

"Here are letters, Miss Esther," he said. "They bring good news from a far country. I waited this morning for the mails to be opened before making my visit; for I felt that I should receive something from our friend."

"Thank you," she said, earnestly, as he placed two letters in her hand.

"It seems," said Waring, "that by some mischance our letters have been detained. I have received two; one written the very day after De Vane arrived in London, and the other three weeks later, and yet they both reach me by the same mail. But I am delighted to find that our friend is not only well, but in all respects what we could wish him to be. And now, I am not going to trespass upon you. You must read your letters, and I will call and see you this evening, when we can talk over every thing."

"You are very good, Mr. Waring," said Esther. "I shall be delighted to see you."

She gave him her hand, and bidding her "Good-morning!" he walked away.

Esther was touched by the delicacy of his conduct, for she could not bear to look into her letters in his presence; and, hurrying to the little fountain which threw its bright spray over the summer flowers, she seated herself and opened her treasures. When she rose to return to the house, two hours had flown by, and Mrs. Green was wondering what she had found to detain her in the grounds so long.

"Bless me!" she exclaimed, as she saw Esther, "I did not know what had become of you. Jacob told me he had not seen you, and I should have thought you had gone home, but for your bonnet and parasol, which I saw lying just where you placed them this morning."

"No," said Esther, "I have had letters, and have been reading them at the fountain."

"I hope your friends are well, Miss Esther," said Mrs. Green, using the plural number, though she had but one person in her thoughts when she spoke.

"Oh! yes, thank you," said Esther. "My letters bring good accounts."

She had scarcely seated herself, before Miss Godolphin entered the house, who, running to Esther, embraced her ardently. Her face was beaming.

"O Esther!" she exclaimed, "I have had letters from England; and I now feel, for the first time for years, that I am as full of joy as when a child."

They entered a small apartment, which Esther had furnished as a drawing-room, and seated themselves where the summer air, breathing through the shrubbery, brought refreshing coolness with it, and the fragrance of flowers.

Miss Godolphin then proceeded to relate to Esther, the precise state of her correspondence with her cousin Hubert; her good faith in awaiting a letter from him after his return to England; her reluctance to wound him, and her distress at his persistence in a suit which she wished him to see was hopeless. His promised letter had now reached her, and it appealed to her once more earnestly to consult her heart, and try to give him room to hope that she might be able to reciprocate a sentiment which had glowed not only with ardor, but which had burned steadily through all discouragements till now; but that if she found it impossible to feel the interest in him which he so much desired, he would cease to trouble her with his importunities, and beg only that he might be regarded as a friend, ready always to serve her.

"You can not conceive, Esther," she added, "what a sense of relief this letter brings to me. I shall now write to my cousin as a friend, claim him as such, and strive to hold my ascendency over his generous nature, in that relation; for his is truly a noble and generous spirit."

"Yes," said Esther. "I do not doubt it. He must be noble and generous. But I am almost as much relieved as yourself; for, dear, dear Hortensia! I do not think that you could ever love him; and the thought of giving one's self away under a sense of gratitude, or of yielding to importunity, is to me simply dreadful. I should never quit these shades, if such a fate awaited me."

"Of course," replied Miss Godolphin, "it is not to be thought of. I have never loved my cousin, and it would be impossible for me to yield to his wishes. This I shall state to him again, and this time so emphatically as to make it final. Marriage! I shudder to think of it, where any inferior consideration induces the parties to enter into it. Wealth, position, worldly advantages—these I scorn beyond expression; and if I even loved Hubert, I should almost shrink from yielding to my own inclination, lest the splendid position which it would conduct to might in some way seem to influence me. If I ever marry, it will be because I prefer the man to whom I give my hand, to any one on earth."

In her animation, she rose from her seat, and stood in all the splendor of her beauty, her eyes flashing with the light of her awakened soul.

"You will marry, Hortensia, I hope; and marry a man whom you can love," said Esther, smiling.

Miss Godolphin's face flushed, as Esther fixed her eyes upon her, and she said playfully: "Yes, let us hope, dear Esther, that the fates may deal kindly with us. By the way, my letters say that Mr. De Vane is greatly admired in England. He is overwhelmed with attentions. Of course, you have heard from him."

"Yes," said Esther. "Mr. Waring brought me letters this morning."

"Ah!" said Miss Godolphin; "and of course you are very bright. Is he dazzled with the splendors about him?"

"Far from it, far from it," she said. "He is studying the institutions of the country, and while he admires much that he sees, he thinks that life is too artificial in the higher circles, and that the pressure of the aristocratic system upon the inferior class is too severe."

"I am delighted," said Miss Godolphin. "It is so like him. He is not the man to be misled by false lights, but I did not know how the social life of England might affect him."

"You must come and pass the evening with us," said Esther, "and we will discuss the whole subject."

"Very well," replied Miss Godolphin; "and now you must take a seat with me, and let me set you down at home."

"Is your carriage at the gate?" asked Esther.

"Yes," she said. "I drove."

"I will go with you with great pleasure," said Esther. And, taking leave of Mrs. Green and her little girls, she walked with Miss Godolphin to the carriage, and was soon set down at Mr. Springfield's.

In the evening, Waring and Miss Godolphin both came to tea, and the topics which such parts of the letters as were communicated suggested, were freely discussed. Waring's letters from De Vane were very long, and, independent of the personal interest which pervaded some of the paragraphs, which paragraphs were not read aloud, there were views of public affairs, which engaged those who sat in Mr. Springfield's library, in the most entertaining way. The freshness and vigor with which De Vane described what he saw, and the independent and manly tone in which he expressed his opinions, not only imparted a great charm to his letters, but awakened trains of thought that held the friends grouped in delightful conversation for hours.

"So," said Mr. Springfield, "our friend Mr. De Vane, with all his aristocratic training and tastes, is not pleased with the aspect of English social life. I must confess I had supposed that he would be fascinated, for whatever evils may exist, there must be refinement and culture."

"That is quite true," replied Waring, "but he has not limited his observation simply to the results of their social system, as they appear in the matured and ripened fruits found in the mansions of the rich and the noble. He has looked at the working of the system in humble life, in the streets and lanes of the great metropolis, and in the glimpse which he has caught of it by a brief visit to the country, where there are fewer cases of casual suffering, and where the effects of the order of society in its settled arrangements may better be seen; and while he is charmed with the culture and refinement of which you speak, he is most painfully impressed with the terrible cost to the lower orders, by which it is brought about and sustained. To use his own expression: 'It reminds one of the sparkling wine pressed out of grapes whose vines are nourished by human blood.' All the splendor of the social system can not compensate for the destitution which it engenders; and he adds: 'Any people who can glory in wealth and splendor, produced by a system which drains the lower classes of even the common necessaries of life, are in great danger, as Herod, who, clad in garments glistening like silver, was smitten and eaten up of worms, because he dared to assume what it belonged not to man to appropriate.' So that he is filled with admiration of the power and glory of England, but he is utterly opposed to a system which confides the legislation of the empire to the control of the very class who are to profit by giving it a direction which shall work to their exclusive advantage."

"He would carry out, then, in the British empire," said Mr. Springfield, "those free-trade ideas which he insists will alone develop the power and glory of this country."

"Just so," said Waring. "He does not oppose a social aristocracy, which holds its supremacy by its own inherent power to regulate the order of things about it, and which maintains its ascendency by its wealth, its culture, and its proscriptive rights; but he thinks that the laws of a country should leave open to every one the paths to success; that they should be equal; and that they should not put it in the power of one class, holding the soil in undisputed possession, to legislate for their own advantage, and to shut out supplies for human comfort, and even human life, while they revel in luxuries."

"And he is right!" exclaimed Miss Godolphin with energy.

"So every one must say, I should think," said Mr. Springfield. "The British government is a wise one, and it is developing the national power and glory to a wonderful extent; but there must be some concessions made to the working classes by the land-holders, or there will follow in its train social evils so great as to darken the brightest pages of her history."

"My own sentiments," said Waring, "are settled. I am not in any respect an admirer of aristocracy. I believe in man, as man, and all the conventionalism under heaven can never impart any elevation to a soul that does not derive its nobleness from something within. Nor would I exclude from any position, political or social, a man who was worthy to fill it, because of his humble birth. I, from my heart, yes, from its very depth, feel with the Ayrshire plowman-poet:

'A prince can mak a belted knight,
  A marquis, duke, and a' that;
But an honest man's aboon his might—
  Guid faith he manna fa' that!
For a' that, and a' that,
  Their dignities, and a' that;
The pith o' sense, and pride o' worth,
  Are higher ranks than a' that.' "

He uttered the lines with extraordinary power. Their beauty and elevation were never before so appreciated by those who heard them; and as he ceased to speak, Miss Godolphin's eyes were fixed on him, while her whole face expressed the highest admiration. Her lips parted, as if she were about to speak, but she remained silent.

"Oh! how fully I agree with you, Mr. Waring!" said Esther. "What are we, to set hedges about us, to keep away from us the poor? It is our privilege to associate with us the good, the true, the refined, the really noble of all classes, and we may limit our social life to such; but surely it is our duty to endeavor to enlighten and elevate even the lowliest."

"Just as our Lord," said Waring, "was welcomed to a home with Martha and Mary and Lazarus, where he found purity and goodness and refinement, after walking through the day with the poor and the outcast, seeking to do them good."

"I mean to say," said Esther, "that our friends and associates we are at liberty to choose by our tastes and our sympathies, but we must not disdain those who are beneath us because we do not make companions of them."

"That is just the thought," said Waring. "How many there are that fail to see it! The truth is, we, as Methodists, are sometimes contemned, because we embrace in our Church so many of the poor and ignorant; just as if our Lord had not, with special earnestness, directed the Gospel to be preached to the poor."

"May it ever be our reproach and our glory!" said Esther. "Is the light sullied because it streams into a hovel, and lights up an abode of wretchedness? Surely the sunbeam that cheers the sick pauper on his pallet of straw, is as pure as that which falls upon the marble corridors of a palace."

Her face, as she uttered these words, glowed with unusual ardor, and the beauty which swept her perfect features was as pure as if illumined by celestial light. Tears trembled on the eyelids of Miss Godolphin, who sat opposite to her; and in her own generous soul she felt, at that moment, how transcendently superior Esther was to all the mere artificial beings which the whole circle of society could produce, if it searched through all its saloons, either in this country, where a self-constituted aristocratic class claimed superiority, or in England, where the ancestral pride of generations sought to perpetuate distinctions by the laws of the realm. She knew that such women were not limited to any class; that in the aristocratic circles of England, where she had observed society, and in the corresponding circles of this country, true, noble, whole-souled women were to be found; women to be valued for their own inherent qualities, and not for the accidental advantages of rank and wealth; and she knew, too, that such women were not produced by those circles alone, but that they existed in many families which made no aristocratic pretensions—households in the midst of which all the pure, gentle, grand, and really elevated virtues flourished, as plants of richest verdure and fairest flowers in their natal soil.

The months flew by. October, with its glories, was making the woods even more beautiful than when they awoke to new life under the breath of spring. The varying hues of the leaves—the bright-red dogwood, the crimson sweet-green, the yellow poplar, the rich evergreens, the clinging vines, running to the very top of the tallest trees—made a picture of rare beauty. The sunsets were glorious; the western sky sometimes flamed with the strong beams as they streamed over the hills, behind which the glowing axle of the sun was already hid; and at other times, the clouds which hung about the king of day, mantling his departing moments with their trails of splendor, were more gorgeous than imagination could conceive. The town, with its trees planted thickly, not only on the sides of the streets, but down the centre of each, except those in which business claimed their entire breadth, was exhibiting its autumnal beauty. The public garden and Leasowes were both giving signs of the decline of summer, and Mr. Swan and Jacob were busy with the falling leaves, which the freshening breeze of the cool mornings would scatter over beds and walks in their respective domains.

Waring had again resumed his labors at the College, after his summer vacation, and was deep in his studies.

Esther, too, was busy at Leasowes, her number of little girls being as full as ever. She was in perfect health, and her form was developing into that matchless combination of robustness with grace so rarely seen in this country.

Mrs. Habersham and Miss Godolphin were yet at Clearbrook, lingering there to enjoy its autumnal beauties; and it had been arranged that on Saturday morning Esther was to make them a visit, attended by Waring. Letters were looked for from De Vane. When he last wrote, he was in Paris; but he was on the eve of starting for Italy. By this time he must have reached Rome, and his friends were eager to know how the objects which would appeal to him there might affect him. Still no letters came; and when Waring called for Esther on Saturday, he was compelled to say that nothing had been heard of De Vane.

The visit to Clearbrook was a pleasant one. There was every thing to make it attractive which wealth and taste could bestow.

Mr. and Mrs. Springfield had been invited to come to dine, and they reached there not long after the arrival of Waring and Esther. Mr. Springfield was a great favorite with Miss Godolphin. She admired him for his intellect, his learning, his religion, and his accomplishments. And she often declared that it was no easy task to decide which was the more attractive of the two, Mr. Clarendon or Mr. Springfield. She never lost the opportunity of hearing him preach, and she expressed her unbounded gratification at the privilege of listening to one whose eloquence in the pulpit rivaled that of Mr. Clarendon in the forum.

The day was delightful. And in the evening Mrs. Habersham and Miss Godolphin returned with their guests to the town. Their establishment was already prepared to receive them, and they had desired to have their friends with them the very last day that they passed at Clearbrook.

Several weeks passed by, and yet no letters came from De Vane. All felt anxious about him.

One morning, Mr. Clarendon met Esther at the bookstore, and said to her: "What on earth has befallen De Vane, Miss Wordsworth? Do any of his friends hear from him?"

"I can not say, Mr. Clarendon," she replied. "I have not heard of late of letters being received from him."

"Confound the fellow!" said Mr. Clarendon. "I suspect he is engaged in some conspiracy for liberating Italy, and they have thrown him into one of their airy dungeons. That fellow at Naples is just the man to do it."

Esther laughed, and said: "I certainly trust that no such ill-fortune has befallen him."

"Or can it be," said Mr. Clarendon, "that the Pope has got hold of him, and is trying to make a Christian of him by confining him in some convenient cell, where he can read him a lecture occasionally upon the absurdity and wickedness of his German transcendentalism? Depend upon it, the fellow has fallen into some such scrape, or he would have written to his friends. He wrote to me from Paris, but I had that letter two months ago."

While Mr. Clarendon was speaking, Mr. Le Grande walked into the store, and came immediately to where Esther was standing. Bowing very low and lifting his hat, he said:

"I am very happy to meet you, Miss Wordsworth."

Esther thanked him, and inquired when he had arrived.

"But yesterday," he said. "I could not be here on Monday, as I should have been, to witness the opening of our session, being kept at home by engagements which I could not put aside."

"I observed that you were not in your seat," said Esther.

"Thank you for taking the trouble to look," replied Mr. Le Grande.

"Why, Le Grande," said Mr. Clarendon, "that we all did. Could you imagine that your vacant seat would be unobserved? Was not the statue of Brutus demanded in the presence of all the thronged procession?"

"You are very good," said Mr. Le Grande. "I was to ask after Mr. De Vane. Has he been heard from lately?"

"We were just speaking of him," said Mr. Clarendon. "My last letter from him was received some two months since, and I do not know what to say about his silence."

"He perhaps finds so much to engross him in observing the objects of the old world, that he can not find leisure to put his sensations into words just yet," said Mr. Le Grande.

"When you and I were there, Le Grande," said Mr. Clarendon, "we were not very good letter-writers, I believe. We dwelt in the presence of objects which filled the imagination, and we could not quit them for the task of coldly recording our sensations."

"Yes," said Mr. Le Grande; "and comprehending Mr. De Vane, as I do, I can very well conceive his emotions in visiting Rome, a spot where there is more to awaken thought as to the comparative claims of the old world—I mean the ancient, the classical world—and those of the modern, than in any other place on earth. He is intensely republican, and as intensely modern, much as he loves the classics; and as he stands in view of the monuments of a past civilization, confronting the objects of the present age, as they are seen there, he will be more than ever disposed to regard America as the field where the ideal and the actual, combining their forces, will produce a higher and nobler civilization than the race has ever yet attained."

"Yes," said Mr. Clarendon; "there is nothing of the actual in Rome. The Eternal City stands upon the ashes of its former glory, and the structures which the Church has reared there seem like solemn temples erected to celebrate the memory of its past, with pompous and imposing ceremonials. One monument yet stands, a fit memorial of its ancient magnificence and colossal power — the Coliseum. What a conception it gives us of the grandeur of the people who once dwelt there!"

"Every thing that one meets there," said Mr. Le Grande, "is so suggestive, that we want leisure to compose our thoughts. We must study our own ideas before we are able to make them intelligible to others. It is impossible to stand in the presence of the shattered civilization of an empire, and observe its seats of power, without feeling disposed to observe more closely and to study more profoundly the institutions about us. There can be no better training for a statesman than to give him the opportunity of observing the working of the political systems of modern Europe, and then place him in Rome, where he may study the history of a colossal empire lying all about him in ruins. He will comprehend what Bolingbroke means when he says 'that history is philosophy teaching by example.'"

"After all," said Mr. Clarendon, "we are working out a grand problem in this country; but it is a problem not yet solved."

Mr. Le Grande shrugged his shoulders, but made no reply. He said to Esther, however:

"And what do you say to that, Miss Wordsworth?"

"Oh!" she said, "I think that the affairs of nations are ordered by One who will conduct them in the right way, if the people acknowledge his right to rule. You know it is written: 'Blessed is that people whose God is the Lord.'"

Both the gentlemen bowed.

Mr. Le Grande took up a number of a Review which had just been published, and asked Esther if she had yet read it.

"Yes," she said; "and I think it promises to be preeminently successful. I have met with no Review which, I think, approaches it in excellence. The State may well be proud of it."

Mr. Le Grande was much gratified; for it was understood that he had contributed largely to its pages. After some further conversation about books, Esther bowed to the gentlemen, and was about to leave the store, when Mr. Clarendon said:

"Miss Wordsworth, suffer me to attend you. You are walking, are you not?"

Esther replied that she should be happy to be so attended; and Mr. Clarendon saw her home, taking the opportunity of saying, on the way, that he was confident De Vane was only waiting to put his ideas of Italy into a satisfactory form before he wrote, and that there was not the slightest occasion for uneasiness.

After he took leave, Esther felt grateful for his considerate kindness, and for the delicacy with which it was expressed; and she was cheered by the words of one who felt, as she well knew, so true an interest both in De Vane and herself.

## CHAPTER XVII.

"AND hopes, and fears that kindle hope,
An undistinguishable throng,
And gentle wishes long subdued—
Subdued and cherished long!"
SAMUEL TAYLOR COLERIDGE.

THE winter, which had been an unusually brilliant one, was drawing toward its close. Miss Godolphin had given to the social entertainments of the season a great charm. The shadow which had somewhat obscured her brightness had passed away, and her fascination was everywhere felt. Tributes to her charms had been offered by more than one gentleman, which might have flattered the pride of many who moved in the circle which she adorned; but she heeded them not. Like some brilliant child of song at whose feet bouquets are showered, but who disdains to stoop to gather them, she passed on, as if unconscious of attracting the admiration so lavishly bestowed.

Speculations were hazarded as to the cause of her indifference to the homage that was tendered her. As to Esther, she had so distinctly repelled all attentions which transcended the formal lines of mere politeness, the impression made very generally was, that she must be engaged to De Vane, and that the high principle which was known to govern her conduct in all things, made her discourage every thing which could lead any one to suppose that she would receive any tribute tinged with sentiment. But in the case of Miss Godolphin, it was believed that no such motive existed. She was frank, perfectly easy, gay, but, it seemed, impressionless. Some pronounced her cold, but yet every feature, every motion seemed informed with soul.

Waring visited her frequently, but he had never even hinted love. Every thing else was freely discussed by them—literature, the arts, religion, society; but of love they never spoke. In many benevolent enterprises they assisted each other, and they often met at Mr. Springfield's, where in delightful conversation their views were interchanged.

Returning on a very fine morning from the College, Waring walked into the public garden to observe some plants of rare beauty which were beginning already to feel the breath of the coming spring. An unusual number of visitors had been attracted by the genial warmth of the day, and as he stood observing the groups scattered over the grounds, he saw Miss Godolphin in a walk not far from him, stooping to speak to a child who was attended by a maid-servant. He walked over to join her, and as he approached, he heard the conversation between Miss Godolphin and the child—a little girl of extraordinary beauty, and dressed with exquisite taste. The fair hair and blue eyes of the child were such as the old painters loved to transfer to their canvas, and her intelligence was wonderful. Only some six years of age, she conversed with grace and propriety. Her language was beautiful, and her manner imparted a womanly dignity to all that she uttered.

"My dear Marie," said Miss Godolphin, "are you about to return home? It is very early yet. Stay and enjoy the flowers a little while longer, will you not?"

"Oh! thank you, Miss Godolphin," replied little Marie, "mamma said I must not stay long out, and I ought to go now."

"But would mamma object to your staying a little longer with me? I will take you home."

The child looked as if she very much wished to stay, but her face was troubled. She wore a pretty apron, and as Miss Godolphin stooped to speak to Marie, she saw a very small stain on it, as if a flower had been crushed against it. The child's eyes, too, were fixed on it, and she said, after a moment's pause:

"I think, Miss Godolphin, I had better go now. I was so unfortunate as to bruise a hyacinth upon my apron, and mamma told me I must not get a speck on it."

The child was very unhappy. She evidently dreaded to meet her mother. The whole splendor of the day was eclipsed for her young soul by that one spot on her apron. Yet with perfect delicacy she said not a word as to what would follow the discovery of the stain upon her return home.

Miss Godolphin's eyes filled with tears as she looked down upon the bright little creature, wretched because of a trifle, which would be magnified into a serious offense by the cruelty of a mother who could punish as a crime a casualty so trivial. At that moment Waring came up, and Miss Godolphin lifting her face to him, he saw her moist eyes. She extended her hand, smiling but silent.

"Ah!" said Waring, "this is my little friend Marie."

The child's face brightened as if a sunbeam had passed over it, and she exclaimed:

"O Mr. Waring! I'm so glad to see you."

He stooped and kissed the child.

"Well, my little Marie," said he, "are you really about to go? I heard you say to Miss Godolphin that you must return home."

"Yes, sir," she said, "it is better that I should go. I'm so sorry that I bruised that flower upon my apron; I ought to have been more careful."

Waring's heart was touched. He thought of the little girl returning home to meet a mother so artificial as to think dress a more serious thing than the happiness of her child, a mother so cruel as to punish as a grave offense a little flower-stain, which a heedless step of little feet had produced; and he resolved that she should not go unattended, that he would go and plead for Marie.

Miss Godolphin looked on. She comprehended how the great, manly nature of Waring was wrought on, as he turned to her, and said: "I will walk home with Marie."

"Thank you, Mr. Waring," she said; "do walk home with her, or rather, as she has perhaps staid a little over the time, take my carriage, which is at the gate, and I will await its return."

He thanked her with one of his brightest smiles, and taking Marie and her servant with him, he drove to Mrs. De La Roche's residence.

As he handed Marie up to the door, she said:

"Will you not come in and see mamma, Mr. Waring?"

"Yes, my dear Marie, that I will," he said; adding in a low tone: "I think lions at the threshold could not turn me back."

Mrs. De La Roche welcomed Waring warmly. She was a young person, of some twenty-seven years, very animated, and not naturally deficient in heart; but she had for some years led a life so artificial as to dull her better nature, and she had fallen into the error of restraining her daughter—an only child—from the sportive exercise so essential to health and physical development. She admired and respected Waring, and she was much flattered by his attending the little girl. Of course, her better nature was awake.

"I am happy to see you, Professor Waring," she said. "I owe the honor of this visit to Marie, I'm sure."

"Yes," said Waring, "I should not have called at this

time, but for the pleasure of escorting my dear little friend. I found her in the public garden, and she was upon the point of starting for home. I prevailed on her to come with me in the carriage."

"I'm very greatly obliged to you," said Mrs. De La Roche, "for I began to fear she would stay longer than I intended she should."

"She was resolute in coming," said Waring. "Both Miss Godolphin and myself urged her to stay longer, but she said her mamma would expect her, and I could not deny myself the pleasure of coming with her. I found her somewhat distressed too about a trifle, and I could not bear to see her unhappy when I knew she was not in fault."

Marie, who was present, began to look conscious, and presently walking directly to her mother, she showed her the stain on the apron. For a moment Mrs. De La Roche's face flushed; she then smiled, and said:

"Oh! that is not a great matter, Marie; but you must be more careful next time."

A glow of happiness suffused Marie's face, and returning to Waring's chair, she looked up into his face with unutterable thanks shining through her blue eyes, and then disappeared.

Waring then proceeded to describe the unhappiness which the little girl had suffered on account of a matter so trivial, and ventured to express his views as to the freedom and unrestraint which children should enjoy, saying something too of the distinction between the demerit of casualties and of crimes; so that before he took leave of Mrs. De La Roche, he had really made her conscious of the errors and mischiefs of the system into which she had drifted. She thanked him warmly for his interest in her child—for Waring had spoken of her in glowing terms after Marie had gone out of the room—and invited him to call often and visit them. Waring's brief visit had accomplished much for the happiness of Marie De La Roche. He left sunshine in a dwelling where too often clouds had surrounded a little form fair as an angel's. Entering the carriage, he returned to the public garden, and found Miss Godolphin seated near the green-house, while Mr. Swan was expatiating upon the glories of some new flowers which he had succeeded in rearing for the first time. He had presented to Miss Godolphin a bouquet of great beauty, and as Waring approached, she rose to meet him, saying:

"See how generous Mr. Swan has been. Are not these beautiful?"

"Very," said Waring. "You must be almost as great a favorite as De Vane."

She laughed, and said: "I really believe that I am indebted for the flowers to the interest which I displayed, while Mr. Swan spoke of him. He has been the subject of discourse since you left me here. But how was Marie received?"

"Graciously," replied Waring.

He then gave an account of his interview with Mrs. De La Roche. Miss Godolphin was deeply interested, and she thanked Waring with warmth for his interposition in behalf of the little girl. She had never admired him so much as at this moment, and her soul shone in her face as she spoke. Waring, too, as he saw the noble nature of the woman, so roused by sympathy with a child's sorrow, comprehended more clearly than ever before her transcendent superiority over the whole tribe of artificial beings who compose the gay world, and who would despise as a weakness the sensibility which could be touched by such a cause.

They were passing down the broad walk leading to the principal gate, and as they approached it, lesser walks, diverging on either side, conducted to the more sheltered parts of the garden.

"Miss Godolphin," said Waring, "are you eager to return to the town? Or will you take a turn with me through the garden?"

She looked up into his face quickly, for there was something in his tone which startled her. There was the indefinable voice of the soul, which her own soul heard; and she read in his face that upon that hour trembled the fate of both.

"I will walk with you," she said, in low tones.

They turned into the right walk, bordered by evergreens; and for some minutes not a word was uttered by either. At length Waring spoke.

"Miss Godolphin, I do not know what fate awaits me. For many months I have observed you; pardon me for saying it, I have studied you, but I have been unable to comprehend you. Some men would risk nothing under such circumstances—they would seek to know, by some token, what was before them. I am incapable of trifling; and, without in the least knowing what may be the result of my frankness, I can no longer restrain the energy of a passion which sways my whole nature. I love you!"

Instantly Miss Godolphin stood still. She turned her soul-lit face full upon Waring. Her lustrous eyes sought his eyes. Steadily for a moment she fixed her earnest gaze upon him; then solemnly she laid her ungloved right hand in his, and burst into tears.

"Forever mine!" said Waring passionately, "forever mine!" and lifting her hand to his lips, he impressed on it a fervent kiss.

After a moment, she raised her bowed head. Her face was radiant, and smiling through her tears, she said: "Let us go."

All about them, plants in tropical splendor bloomed.

They were shut in from all the world. None but these mute witnesses of their vows were present. They walked, as did our first parents, amid the glories of nature; and as they turned their steps once more toward the gate, Waring said:

"My beloved, we quit this garden not with tears, and sorrow, and regret, but with a blessing; and looking upward, we may feel that Providence is our guide."

How brightly she smiled on him, as he handed her to her carriage! The spirited horses dashed away, and as the flying vehicle passed out of sight, Waring looking up to Heaven, uttered thanks, and implored a blessing: thanks for the bliss which was his, and an earnest prayer for the blessing which enricheth everlastingly.

## CHAPTER XVIII.

"But where they are, and why they came not back,
Is now the labor of my thoughts. 'Tis likeliest
They had engaged their wandering steps too far."
MILTON'S *Comus.*

DE VANE was in Rome. Letters came, full of enthusiasm. The ruins, the fallen columns, the shattered arches, the broken monuments of a dead empire, filled his imagination. The modern world, too, interested him profoundly. The arts, painting and statuary, woke his soul to new ardor. He had lingered at Florence longer than he intended; but how could he tear himself away from its galleries, filled with the triumphs of ancient and modern art? How should he quit the banks of the Arno, upon which Milton had lingered? How could he withdraw his gaze from the paintings of Raphael, or cease to look upon the works of Michael Angelo? How leave the garden of Lorenzo de Medici, or the spot where Galileo stood to watch the stars in their wide circuits through the pellucid heavens?

But he was in Rome, treading upon an empire's dust. The past and the present met before him. The pomp of triumph had ascended the steps of the capital, in full view of the spot where he stood; but the very capital was leveled, and the men who thronged its approaches were gone. Saint Peter's rose before him; its matchless dome, its illumined cross—the whole structure a monument of modern civilization, attesting the triumph of Christianity.

De Vane, standing in the midst of such impressive objects, found his soul roused. He re-visited the past, traveled over its track, guided by the lights of history; and he saw at his feet the ruin of the proudest structure man had ever reared—the Roman Empire! What had survived of it? Where were its temples? Where its gods? Where its priests? Where was its religion? The Niobe of nations was voiceless!

How was it that a faith, springing up in a province of that empire, had outlived all its power and glory, and while the palaces of the Cæsars had passed away, reared its own temples upon the hills where they once stood? How was it that while the fierce legions which, returning from the conquest of distant nations, had thundered through the streets of the imperial city, were all gone, the disciples of Him who, upon the slopes of the Mount of Olives, had inaugurated a kingdom, still trod these streets which had been the scene of so much pomp and splendor?

Along the banks of the Tiber, Cicero had walked, uttering his lamentations for a daughter torn from his arms by death—a stricken, hopeless father, seeking to perpetuate the memory of a beloved object, by erecting a temple on the spot where his eyes rested with a fond and yet sad association. But father, daughter, temple, all were gone; while a triumphant faith, making its way only by preaching its doctrines with a simplicity that did not aspire to rival his eloquence, to-day threw its illuminating splendors over a realm wider than the empire in its proudest days, and uttered, in almost every language under heaven, its consolations over the graves of the loved and the departed.

One night, De Vane had walked out. He was alone. The moon was flooding the heavens with its silvery splendor; the distant hills stood looking down upon the Eternal

City. He saw the Coliseum standing out grandly against the sky, and he recalled the fierce sports of the people who once filled its ample amphitheatre. The past rolled before him with all its deeds; the civilization of that age he saw for the first time in all its revolting barbarism—splendid, but hard, barren, and material; and he asked himself if the world had reached its highest triumphs under such a tutelage?

What were the proudest achievements of the mighty men who had bowed at the shrine of the imperial city, compared with the career of a single apostle of Christianity, Saint Paul, whose very presence there had thrown a noonday splendor over the whole empire?

Christianity rose before him in the sublimest proportions. He surveyed its progress; he saw its trophies gathered out of every nation which it had visited—splendid, glorious, and not stained with blood. He saw its silken banners everywhere spread in all climes to cheer and to bless, uttering its invitations to the nations to cease from war, and seeking to gather the whole race of men into one brotherhood. He retraced his steps. He saw the dome of Saint Peter's, and upon the cross the pure light lay. It was the symbol of a faith that upheld the very badge of its humiliation above the proudest monuments of worldly power and glory: the only symbol which it emblazoned on its conquering banners. The clear heavens were spread out upon him. There were the stars that had looked down upon all the eventful history of the imperial city which lay at his feet, brilliant chroniclers of the steady progress of that faith which, without arms, had extended its dominion over the proudest seats of empire that the world acknowledged. The by-gone centuries swept into view; and there, with the past and the present meeting upon the site of the world's capital, shattered monuments of human glory and towering Christian temple, he exclaimed: "CHRISTIANITY IS TRUE!"

From that hour, with the directness and frankness of his nature, he submitted himself to the teachings of the Christian system; and it might be said of him as of Saul of Tarsus, after he had seen the overpowering display of supernal glory which burst upon his vision on the road to Damascus: "Behold he prayeth!"

All this progress in the spiritual development of De Vane had been observed both by Waring and Esther, who, as they read his letters from time to time, expressing his convictions, emotions, and views, comprehended his state; and when they saw at last that the morning-star for which they had so long watched, had risen upon the soul of the wanderer, they rejoiced with exceeding great joy.

The spring came; and nature was once more robed in beauty. The woods were vocal with the songs of birds; the China-trees, with which the town abounded, were covered with their delicate purple blooms; the gardens were brilliant.

Miss Godolphin and Esther saw each other daily, and Waring was often with them. They were in sympathy with each other, and De Vane's letters to Waring were seen by the others, and were, of course, eagerly read by Mr. and Mrs. Springfield. For some weeks none had been received from him. The advancing season was deepening into summer, and the time for De Vane's return-voyage was not distant.

One evening Waring hurried to Mr. Springfield's. He was just in time for tea. Miss Godolphin was there; and entering the library almost without knocking, he found the party rising to pass into the room where the table was spread. All greeted him warmly, and Mrs. Springfield said:

"Ah! Professor, you are very welcome, and I am glad

to have you with us, to partake of the finest strawberries we have had this season."

"Strawberries!" said Waring, "so late as this?"

"Yes," replied Mrs. Springfield, "and the very finest we have had. They are just now in perfection."

"Thank you," said Waring. "I will most gladly join you." And giving his arm to Mrs. Springfield, they all entered the supper-room.

Mr. Springfield said: "Well, Professor Waring, what of Mr. De Vane? Any late tidings of him?"

Waring smiled and said: "How is it that you anticipate me?"

All looked eagerly at him; and taking a letter from his pocket, he handed it to Esther. Perfect as her self-control usually was, she rose to receive it, and, unable to conceal her emotion, she hurried from the room.

"It was my intention to withhold Miss Wordsworth's letter," said Waring, "until after the strawberries were discussed; but there was no resisting such an appeal as her face made to me, after your question."

"It was a little unlucky," said Mr. Springfield; "but I trust that you have good accounts from him."

"Very good," said Waring. "He writes me at some length, and gives a very interesting account of a discovery which he has just made. Miss Godolphin, the mystery which has hitherto hung about your picture—the Daughter of Herodias—is explained."

"Indeed!" she exclaimed. "And how?"

"Do you not remember that De Vane has more than once written about an artist for whom he felt a great liking, from his first visit to his studio?" said Waring.

"Yes; a painter, a native of this country, whom he describes as full of genius and all fine qualities. But I do not know that he has ever given his name," said Miss Godolphin.

"He has never done so till now," said Waring. "He has until recently resided at Naples, but he is now in Rome."

"Can it be Mr. Lawrence," exclaimed Miss Godolphin, "the artist who painted the picture which Esther so strongly resembles?"

"The same," said Waring. "He has explained every thing to De Vane. Do you remember, Mrs. Springfield, to have known some years since, a painter of that name?"

"Perfectly well," she replied. "But I have heard nothing of him for years. I knew that he had gone abroad, but for a long, long while, I have lost all trace of him."

"I do not remember to have known him," said Mr. Springfield.

"I do not know that you ever met him," said Mrs. Springfield. "I saw him when I was very young."

"And how is the mystery explained?" asked Miss Godolphin.

"It seems," said Waring, "that De Vane became intimate with the artist whom he so much admired, and visited his studio habitually. Calling one morning, he found Mr. Lawrence not at home; but still, without hesitation, he entered the rooms of the artist, and seated himself to await his coming. The room where Mr. Lawrence slept opened into his studio, and as De Vane sat awaiting him, he saw what he had never observed before. The door of the artist's bed-chamber was open; it had hitherto been kept as scrupulously concealed from the view of visitors as the interior of a Turkish mosque from Christians. In full view of where De Vane was seated, stood the light, graceful bed of the artist, and over it hung, in an elaborate oval frame, a painting in the highest style of art. It was the bust of a girl of some seventeen years, the face slightly averted but the large, blue eyes visible, and the profuse golden hair falling about the perfect neck. It was a portrait so perfect in its resemblance to Miss Wordsworth, that De Vane started."

"A portrait of Esther?" exclaimed Mrs. Springfield, with astonishment.

"So perfect," said Waring, "that De Vane sprang from his chair, and was standing transfixed with astonishment when Mr. Lawrence entered. Observing De Vane's excitement, he was himself at a loss to account for it; and an explanation followed, which is given at length in the letter which I received this evening. It seems that early in life Mr. Lawrence had known Miss Wordsworth's mother, and had been employed to paint her portrait."

"It hangs now in Esther's room," said Mrs. Springfield, "and answers perfectly the description which Mr. De Vane gives of the picture in Mr. Lawrence's possession."

"The young painter loved the beautiful being whose picture he had been engaged to paint, and meeting no encouragement, did not venture to breathe a passion which he felt was hopeless. He copied the picture which he had painted, and it had, from that hour, been the sole solace of his lonely hours. He has never married; the one fatal, hopeless passion of his youth has continued to flame up in a heart which would be desolate but for its fires. He has never reproduced the form and features so precious to him but in one instance; wishing to paint a picture of the very highest style of art, he represented the daughter of Herodias, with that ineffaceable image enshrined in his heart—the picture, Miss Godolphin, which you possess. De Vane then explained to the artist his own interest in the picture. You may imagine how it deepened the friendship which had already grown into strength between De Vane and a man whom he so much admired, and with whom he now so profoundly sympathizes."

"It is very wonderful!" exclaimed Mrs. Springfield. "I well remember young Lawrence. His genius and his ardor interested us, and my brother contributed every thing within his power to his advancement."

"That accounts for his wish, that the picture which he so much prized should be seen here," said Miss Godolphin; "for he must have heard of Esther, and of her residing here."

"Yes. So De Vane states. Mr. Lawrence has never lost sight of the family of one that so deeply interested him, though he has had no direct communication with them," replied Waring.

"Does he not intend to re-visit this country?" asked Mr. Springfield.

"He has resided abroad so long," replied Waring, "that he has now no attachments to bind him here; and his tastes and habits would unfit him for society, as it exists with us."

"I should be very happy to meet him," said Mr. Springfield.

"He is one of the most agreeable persons I have ever met," said Miss Godolphin. "His library is immense, and his collection of works of art would enrich a king. His conversation of itself would attract you; and if there were neither pictures, nor statues, nor books in his house, it would be still filled with the first people of all countries, who travel for sight-seeing, and who know how to prize genius. At Naples his villa was the most attractive place in the kingdom."

"De Vane writes me," said Waring, "that it is the intention of Mr. Lawrence to reside permanently in Rome. He is arranging a residence at this time. He is a man of very considerable wealth. His pictures have brought him a great deal of money. Several of them are in royal galleries. Two of his finest are in the palace of the Duke D'Arenberg at Brussels, and the King of Bavaria has just engaged him to paint an historical piece, which will require two years for its completion."

"I greatly admired the pictures which I saw at Mrs. Habersham's," said Mr. Springfield. "But I shall study them now with increased interest."

"I was never before able to account for the extraordinary resemblance between Esther and the picture of the Daughter of Herodias," said Mr. Springfield. "It has often perplexed me. She is the very image of her mother, at her age. I have never seen a likeness so perfect, and the fact that Mr. Lawrence has in his possession a portrait of the mother, enabled him to paint from it a picture which could not resemble Esther more perfectly, if she had stood before the artist in person."

They rose from the table, and passed into the library.

Esther was seated, still reading the letter which Waring had handed her. It was very long; and after reading it, page after page, she had again read it, and was dwelling upon some of its passages when she was interrupted by the party coming from the supper-room into the library.

It gave even a fuller explanation of the picture of her mother—its possession by the artist, and his enduring loyalty to his first love—than that contained in the letter to Waring; and it described vividly De Vane's own emotions upon seeing it. It was to her a precious letter, full of passionate tenderness and glowing hope. As the party entered the room, Esther raised her radiant face, and looking at Waring, she exclaimed:

"Is it not wonderful?"

"We have all been saying so," he replied; "for, in your absence, I gave to our friends an account of the discovery made by De Vane, which he has, I suppose, communicated to you."

"And did you know Mr. Lawrence, aunt?" asked Esther.

"Yes; and I well remember him. Full of ardor and genius, your father, both before and after his marriage, gave to the young artist such assistance as enabled him to pursue his career."

Mrs. Springfield then gave a full account of the early life of Mr. Lawrence, which interested all, and made them feel as if a new friend had been added to their circle.

De Vane had written that he was about to make a brief visit to Greece, in company with Mr. Lawrence, and that, upon their return to Rome, he should pass rapidly through Germany and Belgium into England, to take passage in an American vessel at Liverpool for New-York.

Weeks fled by, but no letters were received from De Vane. A vague sense of uneasiness began to steal over the minds of his friends. It took no defined shape; but the heart grew sick under the very uncertainty which hung about his fate. To those who love, absence is an ordeal of suffering; but if we are utterly ignorant of the very place where the loved and absent are, of all the perils to which they are exposed, when wide seas roll their fathomless waters between us, the uncertainty which overspreads every thing connected with them, chills hope with its mists, if it can not cool the ardor of a sentiment too strong to be quenched by all the waves and the billows which roll over us.

## CHAPTER XIX.

"WHAT is this old history, but a lesson given,
How true love still conquers by the deep strength of truth—
How all the impulses whose native home is heaven,
Sanctify the visions of hope, and faith, and youth?
'Tis for such they waken!"
*The Awakening of Endymion.*

SUMMER came with its splendors, but no tidings had yet been received from De Vane. Waring and Miss Godolphin were more than ever with Esther, and cheered her with their hopeful view of the causes which had hindered the arrival of letters. The beautiful lines of her own character were now distinctly visible. Never for a moment did doubt cloud the heaven of her soul. She was unhappy, but it was from apprehension that the treacherous sea might have engulfed the object of her solicitude. Her own loyalty was unswerving; and she did not suffer the faintest shadow of distrust of his to steal upon her heart. Prayer was her resource when alone; and often she outwatched the stars. Like Tennyson's Mariana, she would throw open the lattice-blind, and lean upon the balcony:

"There all in spaces rosy-bright,
Large Hesper glittered on her tears,
And deepening through the silent spheres,
Heaven over heaven rose the night."

But hope shed its lustre over her troubled spirit, and she would retire comforted by her trust in Him whose sleepless care is over all his works, and whose power is as great in the wide sea as upon the high places of the earth.

She was at Leasowes, engaged in some of the little tasks which called her there at times on Saturday. Three or four of the larger girls were seated near her; one of them, Mary Sinclair, who was busy with a piece of embroidery. Esther sat with her face drooping over a sketch which she was making, as a guide for one of the little girls, who had exhibited both taste and genius in drawing.

"There is Mr. Waring coming, Miss Esther," said Mary Sinclair. Esther started, sprang to her feet, and ran to the door, borne by an impulse which she could not control. Waring was rapidly approaching the house. His face was resplendent; his great soul beamed through his eyes, and he exclamed: "All's well!"

Esther could not restrain herself. She sank upon a seat, and passionate tears rained from her eyes. It was a summer shower; for, presently recovering her self-possession, she looked up to Waring, as he stood, in mute respect awaiting the subsiding of her emotion, and a smile like sunlight illumined her features.

"O Mr. Waring!" she exclaimed, "you must pardon my weakness."

"You ladies," said Waring, smiling brightly, "are extraordinary beings. If one brings you a piece of good news, you are sure to greet him with tears. But I ought not to reproach you; for, upon calling at the office this morning, when letters from De Vane were handed me, I found the lines which I was reading wet with my own tears; but they were tears of joy. The fellow has been wandering through Greece with Mr. Lawrence; and like a couple of enthusiasts, they were six weeks longer than they had intended, exploring out-of-the-way places and searching ruins, and so neglected to write. De Vane now writes from Dresden, where Mr. Lawrence has accompanied him; for that gentleman seems to have taken a prodigious fancy to our friend, just as if he deserved it. They are now exploring the galleries of art; and De Vane is to be in Paris by the latter part of this month. He has decided to sail from Havre, and he will not re-visit England; so that, if prosperous, he may reach New-York by the middle of September.

He handed Esther a package of letters. She looked her thanks.

"Will you be at home this evening?" asked Waring.

"Yes; and we shall be happy to see you," she replied. "Will you come?"

"With the greatest pleasure," he replied.

"And would you offer any objection," said Esther archly, "if I should propose to invite Miss Godolphin to join us, and hear the tidings from our absent friend?"

"Oh! none whatever," said Waring, laughing, and actually blushing. "And now I leave you to your letters. Good-morning."

"*Au revoir!*" said Esther, not entering the house, but snatching her parasol and hastening to the fountain. There was no spot on earth where she could read De Vane's letters with so much pleasure; and as she opened the package which she had just received, she felt that she possessed a treasure of priceless value. There were several letters, and they were very long. She read and reread them; and the tears of joy which fell upon her soul-lit face, were as bright as the waters of the little fountain which sparkled in the sunbeams, glancing upon them through the surrounding shrubbery.

In the evening, when Waring arrived at Mr. Springfield's, he found Miss Godolphin already there. She had learned from Esther the good tidings respecting De Vane, and a glow of happiness overspread the party assembled in the library.

"So Mr. De Vane is really on his way to this country, it may fairly be concluded, from what he reports of himself," said Mr. Springfield. "I suppose he may have sailed by this time."

"Yes," said Waring, "he may be on the ocean at this moment, and I shall soon look for his arrival in New-York."

"Of course he will make some stay in Virginia," said Mr. Springfield.

"Oh! yes," said Waring; "and yet I shall look for him here early in October. I called at his place to-day, to give some instructions to his servant, who was almost frantic with joy upon hearing that his master was so soon to be here."

"He has inquired of me, I think, at least three times a week for the last three months," said Mr. Springfield, "to know if I had heard any thing from Mr. De Vane; and the fellow seemed to think that I ought to set out to look for him, if he did not return pretty soon."

"He is a faithful fellow," said Waring, "and has his master's horses in perfect condition."

"My friend Hobbs is about as impatient as Cæsar. He has actually called on me every Sunday morning for a month past, to know if I have had any accounts from his friend De Vane; and the last time he called, he began to swear that he thought some of the people across the water had shown him foul play, and was especially hard on the British."

"Oh!" said Miss Godolphin, laughing, "that must be a prejudice of his, derived from reading the Life of Marion lately, which you gave me some account of, Mr. Waring."

"Quite likely," said Waring; "but I shall be able to relieve his mind in the morning, for he will certainly call."

At this moment Mr. Clarendon entered the room, and all rose to welcome him.

"Mrs. Springfield," he said, "these young people do not treat me well, and I have come to you to complain of them."

"Is it possible?" she replied. "We must inquire into that. How have they offended?"

"Why, madam," said Mr. Clarendon, taking a hand of each of the young ladies, "they do not permit me to share their confidence. They receive letters from persons at home and abroad, and never inform me of their contents; and I appeal to you to say if this conduct is not wholly inconsistent with their professions of regard for me."

"I do think," replied Mrs. Springfield, "that they deserve some mark of your displeasure, if they have committed so grave an offense; but I can scarcely believe that it was designed, for they both speak of you in terms so glowing, that I am sure they are delighted to have the opportunity of speaking to you about any thing that concerns them."

"We shall see about that," said Mr. Clarendon. "Here is that fellow De Vane, for whom I had some regard, takes himself off—at the instance, I suspect, of one or the other of these ladies; he wanders in Europe, does not give me a single line for months together, writes to these ladies, one or both, and they say not one word to me on the subject. Now I insist, that after taking that young gentleman from under my control, and then banishing him from the country, they should at least keep me informed of his movements, that I might do something for his relief, if he should require it."

Mr. Clarendon looked very much like an injured person, and still stood retaining the hands of Miss Godolphin and of Esther.

"I assure you, Mr. Clarendon," said Miss Godolphin, 'that we are delighted to see you. We were burning with impatience to talk with you about Mr. De Vane, and your coming is most fortunate."

"We are indeed delighted to see you," said Esther. "Your coming has completed our happiness."

"Then, Mrs. Springfield," said he, "I must pardon the seeming slight, and restore them to favor." And kissing the hand of each, he released them.

"Well, Professor Waring," he continued, "what is this about De Vane? Is he really intending to come back to us? I met his servant riding one of his horses to-day, and he told me that you had letters from his master; so calling at Mrs. Bowen's to inquire after our friend, I was informed that I should find you here, and pursued you."

"I am very glad that you did so," replied Waring. "We have the best accounts from De Vane. He was at Dresden, *en route* for Paris; and expected to sail from Havre, with as little delay as possible."

"Indeed!" said Mr. Clarendon. "Then we shall have him with us presently. What has detained him?"

"A visit to Greece with an American artist of celebrity, Mr. Lawrence, who has for some years resided at Naples, but is now establishing himself in Rome."

"Lawrence!" exclaimed Mr. Clarendon. "I very well remember him. I met him in Paris, and was proud of him as an artist from my own country. Le Grande and I both predicted his great eminence."

"The pictures which you have observed at my aunt's are by him, Mr. Clarendon," said Miss Godolphin.

"You amaze me," said he. "I remember that you said they were by an American artist, but it did not occur to me to ask his name. They are pictures of extraordinary merit. Do you not think them such, Mr. Springfield?"

"I quite agree with you," replied Mr. Springfield. "I have admired them greatly. Do you know that one of his early pieces is in this house?"

"In this house? How does that happen?" asked Mr. Clarendon. "Has De Vane sent it over?"

"Oh! no," replied Mr. Springfield. "It was painted long before Mr. De Vane knew the artist. Esther, may we have the picture brought down, that Mr. Clarendon may see it?"

She instantly rose, and, quitting the room, soon after returned, a servant bearing the picture. It was a portrait in the highest style of art; and the resemblance to Esther was so perfect that Mr. Clarendon exclaimed: "What mystery is this? I do not comprehend it."

Esther smiled, and replied: "That, Mr. Clarendon, is a portrait of my mother, painted by Mr. Lawrence, before he left this country."

"My dear young friend," he replied, "it is absolutely wonderful. I could fancy that it was yourself, looking out of that oval frame as a lady looks from her lattice. There is the great charm of Lawrence's pictures. Their naturalness is perfect, and the coloring has all the transparency that distinguishes the works of the old masters."

"The picture, when painted, was thought to be perfect," said Mrs. Springfield. "Esther's resemblance to her mother is really wonderful."

"I thank you, Miss Wordsworth, with all my heart, for permitting me to see this. I can imagine how you must prize it," said Mr. Clarendon.

The picture was restored to Esther's chamber.

"I shall be delighted to see De Vane," said Mr. Clarendon. "He has not written to me of late, and I was not in any way informed as to his recent plans of travel."

"In his letter to me, received to-day," said Waring, "he wishes me to assure you of his warmest regards, and says that his friend, Mr. Lawrence, the artist, has asked after you with the greatest interest, recalling vividly your visits to his studio."

"Indeed!" said Mr. Clarendon. "I wonder that he has not forgotten me long since."

"That would argue himself unknown," said Miss Godolphin.

"Thank you," said Mr. Clarendon; "that is so flattering to my *amour propre* that I must pardon your late neglect."

It was late before Mr. Clarendon took leave. Miss Godolphin took her departure soon after, and Waring accompanied her.

It was distinctly understood that they were to be married at some time, but no day had been agreed on. With perfect independence she conducted herself, and took no pains to conceal her engagement to Waring. Such was her respect for him, that she disdained the affectation of indifference; and without avowing to others her regard for him, she left it to be inferred from her deportment.

Mrs. Habersham had long known and appreciated Waring, and she did not conceal her gratification at his preference for her niece. She said to Mrs. Springfield: "Some persons might suppose that I would regard Professor Waring an unequal match for my niece. He has no fortune, and he avows his purpose to adhere to the Methodist ministry; but I really rejoice at the inequality of their circumstances, for it affords us the opportunity of showing our appreciation of a true man. My niece has an ample fortune, quite sufficient for them both; and if it were not, I would make up the deficiency. I should be delighted to enrich such a man as Mr. Waring."

Waring intended to await the arrival of De Vane before asking Miss Godolphin to appoint a day for their marriage; and she comprehended and approved the feeling which restrained him.

The weeks flew swiftly. The approach of autumn was visible. Already some of the students were returning to the College, making their arrangements for the approaching session; and the town gave signs of cheerful activity. The streets were filled with young, bright, happy groups, meeting again after a separation of months; and the place wore that air of animation which so preëminently distinguished it—the animation not of trade, but of society, in its activity and refinement, exhibiting itself in the many forms of life.

Letters came from De Vane. He had reached New-York, and it was his purpose to pass some days there. Then he was to visit Virginia, and he proposed to reach "home," as he wrote to Waring, by the middle of October. His letter to Esther breathed unchanging love. He was eager to return to her, that he might assure her of his loyalty, and claim her with the sanction even of his father—a sanction which he was confident would not be reluctantly given, now that he had borne the ordeal of TIME and ABSENCE.

His love had conquered by the deep strength of truth. Even when broad seas had roared between them; when he trod the streets of gay cities, and moved in the brilliant circles of the capitals of Europe; or when dwelling in the midst of the soul-awakening scenes of those climes where glory still lingers at its ancient shrines, never had his love known languor nor decline; but, glowing, strong, and full of hope, it reigned supreme.

The visions of hope, and faith, and youth were now to be realized.

The exile was ended. LOVE and TRUTH had triumphed.

## CHAPTER XX.

"Ask me no more: thy fate and mine are sealed."
TENNYSON.

A MILD October evening had succeeded a brilliant day. The lingering rays of the sun fell upon Leasowes, and touched its foliage with golden tints. Esther, after a day of unusual exertion—for some two or three little girls had just been admitted for the first time into her establishment—sat at the fountain, her favorite resort for repose and meditation. The place had grown into perfect beauty. The rarest flowers bloomed around it, and the roses, yet as fresh as if spring still breathed upon them, bent over the clear water, and mingled their perfume with the spray which fell in the marble basin. Esther was dreaming. She recalled the events of the two past years. On such an evening as this she had met De Vane for the first time. Since then, how had he influenced her very being! How blended was his image with every vision of the future! She might exclaim, in the language of Tennyson's lines:

"I strove against the stream, and all in vain;
Let the great river take me to the main."

She was alone. The thick shrubbery shut out the view of the house and the grounds, and yet the solitude was radiant with the light of love and hope.

She was startled by the sound of footsteps very near her, and turning, she saw De Vane. Instantly she started to her feet, and with an impulse too strong to be resisted, she threw herself into De Vane's arms. He pressed her to his heart, and for the first time imprinted upon her glowing lips a long, lingering kiss of love. Her eyes rained tears, and yet the face was bright with unutterable joy.

"And are you mine now, Esther?" he asked.

"Oh! yes," she exclaimed, "forever."

Again he kissed her rapturously, and looking down into her true, fathomless eyes, he said:

"Yes, my own Esther, you will walk like an angel by my side through all the future. Do you remember when I first spoke my love to you here? Then you were too true to deceive me. You would not consent to be mine. Now every lingering obstacle has been removed. My father is ready to receive you as a daughter, and my aunt is eager to embrace you. We have triumphed, my Esther, and we shall now live for each other."

Her soul beamed in her face. Her large, deep blue eyes, her golden hair, her perfect features, made her beauty dazzling; and as De Vane looked down upon her, he felt that in all his wanderings he had not beheld such matchless charms. Neither in the aristocratic circles of Europe, nor in the day-dreams of the old masters still glowing in the galleries of art, had he found any form that could rival hers.

They turned their steps toward the house, for Esther had said that she must call for a moment, to give some parting instructions to Mrs. Green. De Vane had called on entering the grounds, and had received a warm welcome from Mrs. Green, who, in answer to his inquiries, had told him that she believed Esther had gone to walk in the direction of the fountain. He therefore walked now to the gate to await her, that she might be unembarrassed in making her arrangements. She soon joined him, and they proceeded to Mr. Springfield's. De Vane had already called there to ask for Esther, but none of the family were at home. He now entered the house with Esther, who, conducting him to the library, went to seek her aunt. At that moment Mr. and Mrs. Springfield drove up, having just returned from an evening's drive, and entering the library, they welcomed De Vane as they would have received a long-absent son.

"I need not say that we are delighted to see you, Mr. De Vane," said Mr. Springfield. "We have long since given you a place in our hearts."

"I am very grateful," said De Vane. "If you could only know how I have longed to enter this house once more, you would comprehend how delightful this welcome is to me. In all my wanderings, my heart has been here every evening; and but for the intervening space, I should have entered this circle every day at this hour."

"You should have been most welcome," said Mrs. Springfield. "You have never been out of our thoughts, and we are delighted to see you here once more. When did you arrive?"

"Some two hours since," said De Vane. "I found Waring upon the point of starting for the College, and I told him that I should pass the evening here, so that you may expect him very soon."

A moment after, he entered the room, and exclaimed: "So you are really here. Well, I am delighted to see you in this library once more."

"And I am most happy to be here," said De Vane.

"I hope that we shall now resume our old habits," said Mr. Springfield; "we must have our evenings here as formerly."

"Let us begin at once," said Mrs. Springfield. "Esther, will you send for Miss Godolphin?"

"With the greatest pleasure," she said. "Is the carriage at the door?"

It was driven round in a moment, and Mr. Springfield rising, said: "I claim the privilege of escorting Miss Godolphin this evening. She is too great a favorite of mine to be confided to any one else under these circumstances."

He entered the carriage and drove off.

"I believe," said Mrs. Springfield, laughing, "that no one loves Miss Godolphin better than Mr. Springfield does. If she were a daughter, she could not be dearer to him."

"She is a very lovable person I suspect. Waring, is she not?" asked De Vane.

"I believe, De Vane, that you always admitted her to be such," said Waring, "and I do not wonder that Mr. Springfield is attached to her, for she loves him dearly."

"Yes," said Esther, "she loves and venerates him beyond expression. Their views of literature, of religion, and of society harmonize perfectly. And if they were members of the Roman Catholic Church, I think that Miss Godolphin would hardly wait for his death to have him canonized."

"Mr. Springfield's esteem for Miss Godolphin is such," said Mrs. Springfield, "that he actually converses with her upon the gravest theological questions, and he says that he often find his own views much enlightened by her opinions."

"I have always thought her a superior person," said De Vane, "and I have learned to appreciate her more than ever since my visit to her relatives in England. I did not know before what she had endured. Her own account of it softened its severity."

"And what has become of Hubert Godolphin?" asked Esther.

"You will be surprised to learn," said De Vane, "that he is to marry my friend Clara Guilford."

"Is it possible?" exclaimed Esther. "I am really delighted."

"Yes," said De Vane; "they will suit each other perfectly. Clara's ideas of life will now be fully met—wealth, splendor, and a rigid aristocratic circle, where her beauty will make her an object of constant admiration."

Wheels were heard approaching the house, and Esther, springing up, ran to receive her friend. Miss Godolphin entered the room, and De Vane, hastening to where she stood, took her hand in both his, and said:

"I am indeed happy, Miss Godolphin, to meet you once more."

"And I am delighted to see you here, Mr. De Vane," she said. "You must never wander again."

"Never until we can all go together," said De Vane.

"I consent to that," said Waring.

Esther said nothing, but smiled brightly as De Vane turned his glance upon her.

The evening passed with charmed hours. A supper, after the old fashion, at Mr. Springfield's, was enjoyed by them all, De Vane declaring that he had found nothing to equal it in all his travels. He had grown somewhat more robust since his departure. He was now in high health, and as he sat by the side of Esther, his dark hair and bronzed face afforded a striking contrast to her golden curls and perfect complexion. Waring observed them with silent pleasure, in his generous and noble nature forgetting for a time his own happiness.

In the library, De Vane asked Esther for a song; and seating herself at her harp—a splendid instrument, which De Vane had sent to her from Paris—she sang those beautiful lines of Moore, beginning:

> "'Tis believed that this harp which I wake now for thee,
> Was a siren of old who sang under the sea."

Her voice, unrivaled in depth and tenderness, was full of true passion, and gave to the closing sentiment an eloquent power which was felt by De Vane to transcend any music he had ever heard. The perfect grace, too, of the tribute to his presence which the selection of the song conveyed, was deeply felt by him; and as the music ceased, he said to Esther, in tones of subdued tenderness, simply: "I thank you."

She rose from the instrument. Miss Godolphin was invited to sing, but she declined. She felt that the beautiful appropriateness of the song which had just been heard should not be disturbed.

It was late when the little circle of friends was broken by Miss Godolphin's rising to take leave. Waring accompanied her, and soon after De Vane said: "Good-night!"

On the way to Mrs. Habersham's, Waring pressed Miss Godolphin to name the day for their marriage, urging that as De Vane had now returned, there could no longer be any reason for delay. It was agreed that it should take place on Christmas morning, and that they should make a brief visit to Waring's friends in Georgia, at that time.

As but two months intervened, no time was to be lost in making preparations for the event, and Mrs. Habersham's residence was the scene of the greatest activity for several weeks; Mrs. Springfield and Esther aiding with their labors to prepare for the important coming event. Every thing was arranged with perfect taste.

Winter wore its brightest robe. Snow had fallen the night before, and the sun that ushered in Christmas morning saw his splendors reflected back by every object upon which they fell. The bridal party consisted of Waring and Miss Godolphin, attended by De Vane and Esther, Mr. and Mrs. Springfield, Mrs. Habersham, Mr. and Mrs. Clarendon, and a few other friends. The marriage took place in the Methodist church at nine o'clock in the morning, and the service was performed by Mr. Springfield.

Immediately after the ceremony, Waring and his bride

entered a handsome traveling-carriage, and drove to Mrs. Habersham's, where the whole party assembled, and sat down to a Christmas breakfast.

When it was ended, Waring and his bride, taking leave of their friends, entered their carriage, upon which their trunks were strapped, and drove away.

They were absent but a fortnight, and upon their return Mrs. Habersham insisted so earnestly that they should reside with her, that they consented to do so. Happy months followed. One evening in every week, the friends now so endeared to each other, met at Mrs. Habersham's; and every Thursday evening found them assembled in Mrs. Springfield's library.

It was arranged that De Vane and Esther should be married on the first day of the following May. She would not consent to an earlier day. She was very young, and she for some time insisted that the marriage should be deferred for twelve months; but she yielded to De Vane's earnest wish. Immediately upon his arrival, he had made arrangements for a handsome residence, to be built upon his place, and it afforded him great gratification to observe its progress. He consulted Esther from time to time as to changes in his plans, and her taste suggested several improvements which he at once adopted. The shrubbery was already beautiful; it had grown under Mr. Swan's fostering hand, and it rivaled the public garden in its attractions.

Spring came at length, and the town was once more robed in beauty. Never had a lovelier season opened upon the earth. Leasowes was in its glory, and it was there that the marriage was to take place. Esther preferred it, and so did De Vane. It was endeared to them both by the most precious associations. The first of May was cloudless. The morning was balmy, and Leasowes welcomed it with foliage and flowers of the rarest beauty.

It was arranged that the ceremony should be performed at six o'clock in the evening; that a few friends only should be present; and that after it was over, the party should drive to De Vane's residence, which was to be opened for the first time that evening.

Never had Esther appeared so beautiful. She wore white, always becoming to her; and the flush upon her face heightened her charms. There were no attendants, but the little girls, all dressed in white, stood near her, objects of her generous solicitude and witnesses of her happiness.

Mr. Springfield performed the ceremony, and the blessing which he uttered sounded in the ears of De Vane and Esther as if an angel with outspread wings had hovered over them, to seal it with the impress of Heaven. Mr. Clarendon came forward, his face lit with the ardor of his great soul, and taking a hand of each, he said:

"De Vane, if I had been a younger man and an unmarried one, you should not have borne away this prize without breaking a lance with me; but I feel bound to say that I doubt if, in all the world, Miss Wordsworth could have given herself to a young fellow who deserved her better."

Both thanked him warmly. There, too, was Waring and his wife, splendidly beautiful, both full of joy. Mrs. Bowen and Mrs. Green, and Mr. Swan and Mrs. Gildersleeve, and some other friends, partook of the overflowing happiness; while Jacob and Cæsar were as jubilant as was consistent with their importance on the occasion.

Refreshments abounded; and after passing an hour at Leasowes, the party repaired to De Vane's residence, where the amplest arrangements were made for the reception of a large company. Mrs. Springfield received the guests, and presided throughout the evening. The entertainment was very brilliant, and all who saw De Vane, with his young bride by his side, felt that two beings better suited to tread the ways of life together had never plighted their faith since that happy hour when our first parents stood in Eden, hand in hand, and looked up through the stars to praise their Maker.

Music, conversation, and refreshments were enjoyed by all who were present, and the evening was long recalled as one of the brightest ever known in a place remarkable for the elegance and grace of its entertainments.

The guests had departed, and De Vane was left alone with Esther. She was now his own.

She stood before him his wife, and taking her in his arms, he said: "I feel, my own Esther, that we shall live for each other always. Our blended being is an immortal union. From henceforth 'thy people shall be my people, and thy God my God.'"

www.ingramcontent.com/pod-product-compliance
Lightning Source LLC
LaVergne TN
LVHW021242110826
845150LV00002B/386

* 9 7 8 1 4 2 5 5 6 1 1 9 2 *